She stared at the orange-lit sky with its faint sprinkling of stars and a slice of lemon moon on the wane. She was in love with Reggie Ormerod and all she wanted to do was sit alone in the dark and savour the feeling of bewilderment 'Bewitched, bothered and bewildered' was how the song went.

It was a feeling that she'd never had before and certainly not for William with whom she'd thought she was in love. There was another song she remembered: 'This can't be love because I feel so well . . .' She felt marvellous! As if she were walking on air.

She had no idea if Reggie felt the same, though she hoped so, naturally, and one of these days it would be important to find out.

'Don't worry about it, Vanessa,' she told herself. 'If it's going to happen, it'll happen. Go with the flow, as they say.'

She stared at the sky for another few minutes, then went inside.

Have you read them all?
Curl up with a

Maureen Lee

STEPPING STONES

Lizzie O'Brien escapes her dark Liverpool childhood when she runs away to London – towards freedom and a new life. But the past is catching up with her, threatening to destroy her dreams . . .

LIGHTS OUT LIVERPOOL

There's a party on Pearl Street, but a shadow hangs over the festivities: Britain is on the brink of war. The community must face hardship and heartbreak with courage and humour.

PUT OUT THE FIRES

1940 – the cruellest year of war for Britain's civilians. In Pearl Street, near Liverpool's docks, families struggle to cope the best they can.

THROUGH THE STORM

War has taken a terrible toll on Pearl Street, and changed the lives of all who live there. The German bombers have left rubble in their wake and everyone pulls together to come to terms with the loss of loved ones.

LIVERPOOL ANNIE

Just as Annie Harrison settles down to marriage and motherhood, fate deals an unexpected blow. As she struggles to cope, a chance meeting leads to events she has no control over. Could this be Annie's shot at happiness?

DANCING IN THE DARK

When Millie Cameron is asked to sort through her late aunt's possessions, she finds buried among the photographs, letters and newspaper clippings, a shocking secret . . .

THE GIRL FROM BAREFOOT HOUSE

War tears Josie Flynn from all she knows. Life takes her to Barefoot House as the companion of an elderly woman, and to New York with a new love. But she's soon back in Liverpool, and embarks upon an unlikely career . . .

LACEYS OF LIVERPOOL

Sisters-in-law Alice and Cora Lacey both give birth to boys on one chaotic night in 1940. But Cora's jealousy and resentment prompt her to commit a terrible act with devastating consequences . . .

THE HOUSE BY PRINCES PARK

Ruby O'Hagan's life is transformed when she's asked to look after a large house. It becomes a refuge – not just for Ruby and her family, but for many others, as loves, triumphs, sorrows and friendships are played out.

LIME STREET BLUES

1960s' Liverpool, and three families are linked by music. The girls form a successful group, only to split up soon after: Rita to find success as a singer; Marcia to become a mother; and Jeannie to deceive her husband, with far-reaching consequences . . .

QUEEN OF THE MERSEY

Queenie Todd is evacuated to a small town on the Welsh coast with two others when the war begins. At first, the girls have a wonderful time until something happens, so terrifying, that it will haunt them for the rest of their lives . . .

THE OLD HOUSE ON THE CORNER

Victoria lives in the old house on the corner. When the land is sold, she finds herself surrounded by new properties. Soon Victoria is drawn into the lives of her neighbours – their loves, lies and secrets.

THE SEPTEMBER GIRLS

Cara and Sybil are both born in the same house on one rainy September night. Years later, at the outbreak of war, they are thrown together when they enlist and are stationed in Malta. It's a time of live-changing repercussions for them both . . .

KITTY AND HER SISTERS

Kitty McCarthy wants a life less ordinary – she doesn't want to get married and raise children in Liverpool like her sisters. An impetuous decision and a chance meeting twenty years later are to have momentous repercussions that will stay with her for ever . . .

THE LEAVING OF LIVERPOOL

Escaping their abusive home in Ireland, sisters Mollie and Annemarie head to Liverpool – and a ship bound for New York. But fate deals a cruel blow and they are separated. Soon, World War II looms – with surprising consequences for the sisters.

MOTHER OF PEARL

Amy Curran was sent to prison for killing her husband. Twenty years later, she's released and reunited with her daughter, Pearl. But Amy is hiding a terrible secret – a tragedy that could tear the family apart . . .

Nothing Lasts Forever

Maureen Lee

An Orion paperback

First published in Great Britain in 2008
by Orion
This paperback edition published in 2009
by Orion Books Ltd,
Orion House, 5 Upper St Martin's Lane,
London WC2H 9EA

An Hachette UK company

5 7 9 10 8 6

A CIP catalogue record for this book is available
from the British Library.

ISBN 978-1-4091-0210-6

Typeset at The Spartan Press Limited
Lymington, Hants
Printed and bound in Great Britain by
Clays Ltd, St Ives plc

The Orion Publishing Group's policy is to use papers that
are natural, renewable and recyclable products and
made from wood grown in sustainable forests. The logging
and manufacturing processes are expected to conform to
the environmental regulations of the country of origin.

www.orionbooks.co.uk

For Fenella and Dusty Miller.

Prologue

Diana

September 1999

'So, you see, Di, luv,' Michelle O'Sullivan said plaintively, 'it really is time I had a break. I was only twenty when I had you. Then our Damian came along, then Jason, then Garth. And it wasn't long after Garth was born when your dad did a runner.'

This was doing Diana's dad a grave injustice. Publicly, he had divorced his wife on account of their marriage having irretrievably broken down. There was no mention in the divorce papers that the breakdown was due to her adultery with four different men and that it had come to the point when he wasn't sure which of the children, Diana apart, were his. Jim O'Sullivan had then disappeared into thin air.

'Now you're eighteen, it wouldn't hurt for you to take on a bit of responsibility, so your poor mam can have a rest, like,' Michelle continued, her voice wobbling. 'Warren's a really nice chap, but he's a bit younger than me and it's not fair to ask him to move in and support another man's kids.'

Diana wouldn't have dreamed of saying it took Warren all his time to support himself – he was more often out of work than in.

Pausing for breath, Michelle took a long puff on her

3

ciggie and looked appealingly at her daughter, her big blue eyes moist with tears. In her black jeans and red top decorated with a sequinned heart, she could have passed for a woman considerably younger than thirty-eight. She wore sandals with four-inch heels – the red nail polish had worn off the little toes on both feet.

'So, luv,' she went on with a theatrical sigh, 'I thought it'd be nice if I moved out for a while so me and Warren could have some time together, just the two of us, while you looked after your brothers. Him and me could get a little place of our own. In fact, Warren already knows of somewhere in Melling Village no distance from Liverpool; a little cottage with just one bedroom. Oh, but, Di, it's got a dead pretty tree in the garden: Warren said it's cherry.' She threw the half-smoked cigarette on to the hearth and glanced with disgust through the window at the minuscule back yard, the walls of which had needed painting for as long as Diana could remember. The row of houses behind was no more than a few metres away. At the front, the property ended at the door through which you stepped right on to the pavement. 'A tree, Di! Can you imagine – looking out at a tree?'

Diana smiled sympathetically. Her mother had never expressed a desire to see fields, trees, baby lambs, flowers or anything else to do with nature, but her own nature was so sweet and trusting that it didn't cross her mind she might not be telling the truth. 'When will you be leaving, Mam?' she asked.

'I thought I'd go this 'avvy,' her mother said casually, as if abandoning four children at a few hours' notice on a Saturday afternoon wasn't at all unreasonable. 'I'll make a stew before I go so there'll be something to eat for the lads when they get back from the footy. You might need to buy stuff from the supermarket tomorrow. Once me and Warren are settled, I'll make sure you get the Child Benefit for the lads.' All three boys were still at school. She reached for her bag. 'I'll leave you a few bob to be getting on with, shall I?'

'There's no need, Mam. I've got enough money of me own.'

For a moment, Michelle's eyes filled with real tears, knowing she was taking advantage of Diana's soft heart. Not many girls of eighteen would so willingly have agreed to look after three rowdy lads for an unspecified length of time, but her daughter hadn't hesitated. It wasn't the first time, either. Diana had played mother on and off since she was about twelve.

For the umpteenth time, for Di's sake, Michelle wished her daughter hadn't taken after her dad. Jim had been such a clumsy bugger, always tripping over things and bumping into doors. Di was just the same – tall and gangly with giant feet and long white hands. She'd been born the day of Charles and Diana's wedding, hence the name. Thinking about it now, her Diana bore more than a passing resemblance to the late Princess of Wales, God bless her. They even had the same soft heart.

Brodie

October 2004

'Just think,' Colin said, getting into bed, 'there'll be no more need for us to lie awake till all hours waiting to hear her key in the front door. Tomorrow, we can sleep in late and go to midday Mass.'

Brodie didn't say anything, but thought that *she* would probably lie awake for the entire night wondering if Maisie, their daughter, was fast asleep in her bed at the university campus where her parents had left her earlier that very day.

Colin tucked his arm around her waist and pulled her against him. 'When we make love, you can be as noisy as you like,' he said.

'Noisy?'

He kissed her shoulder. 'Before we had the kids, you used to scream your head off when we had sex.'

'I did no such thing,' Brodie said indignantly.

'You did, darling.' He pulled her even closer. 'It's a good job this is a detached house, otherwise the neighbours would have complained.'

'You're exaggerating.' Thinking about it, she realized she had missed letting rip when she came to a climax. 'You don't seem a bit upset that we've lost Maisie,' she told him.

'I'm devastated,' he said simply. 'I'll miss her like mad, but let's look on the bright side: we haven't *lost* her any more than we've lost Josh. I'm proud our two kids are at university. Now we can begin to live like we're just a couple again, as if we'd just got married, starting with you making one helluva row when we make love. The next few weeks are going to be like a second honeymoon.'

'Oh, shut up!' She wriggled and he held her tighter.

'You'll never get away,' he whispered. He kissed her neck, then her shoulder and his hand moved up to her breasts. 'Why are you wearing a nightie? Is it in case one of the children might cry during the night and you'll have to get up? If I remember rightly, that was the reason you gave when you stopped coming to bed with nothing on.'

He had managed the seemingly impossible: making her angry at the same time as turning her on. She wasn't sure which emotion to give way to. On reflection, the second would have a much more enjoyable outcome than the first. She pushed the duvet away and began to remove her nightdress.

She woke up at precisely quarter past seven when a long strip of daylight was just beginning to show through the gap in the curtains. Her nightdress was on the floor where it had been thrown the night before.

Brodie got up, put the nightdress on, and sat on the edge of the bed watching Colin, who was lying on his side, snoring softly. He was forty-four, but looked younger than his age, even more so while relaxed in sleep. His brown, dead straight hair, slightly mussed, showed no sign of thinning and there wasn't a grey strand to be seen, unlike Brodie who had scores. Same with wrinkles. Despite being three years younger, she had acquired a few around her eyes, but Colin's boyish face was quite smooth. Awake, he frowned a lot, as if the world and everyone in it was the cause of perpetual surprise. Asleep, the frown had disappeared and his brow was smooth.

She felt tempted to rouse him with a kiss, but was too tired for what would inevitably follow – wonderful though it had been last night. Yesterday had been exhausting, driving to London, with the boot full of Maisie's stuff and the back seat taken up with Maisie herself and even more stuff. Brodie had ended up with the hi-fi on her knees. It had been a most uncomfortable journey.

They'd stayed with Maisie until four o'clock, Brodie making the bed in the tiny room where her daughter would now live, putting her clothes away in the minute built-in wardrobe and drawers. The toiletries she arranged on the windowsill, which seemed to be the only place for them, and the towels she hung under the sink.

While she did all this, Maisie was in the crowded corridor making friends, something she was very good at. Her voice, with its Liverpool accent, was distinguishable amidst a jumble of others.

'There's boys out there as well,' Brodie remarked. 'Will both sexes be living on the same corridor? I'd've thought they'd be kept separate.'

Colin had plugged in the hi-fi and was arranging the speakers. 'They were when I went to university, but things have changed since then.'

'I think they're arranging to go to a club in the West End tonight.' Brodie stopped unpacking and stood behind the open door where she could hear better.

'Don't eavesdrop!' He turned on the radio and New Orleans jazz filled the tiny room. 'Now, that's something worth listening to, not teenagers arranging their illicit affairs.'

Had Maisie gone to a London club? Brodie wondered now. She felt tempted to ring her mobile and find out, but common sense told her it would be a daft thing to do. Sad though it was – heartbreaking, in fact – she had to let her daughter get on with her own life.

She left Colin to sleep, put on her slippers, grabbed a dressing gown and went downstairs. The sky was a watery grey and it was impossible to tell what sort of day it would be – they'd missed the weather forecast the day before. She made tea, put everything on a tray, and took it into the front room where she switched on a lamp and settled herself in a corner of the settee.

The sideboard on the opposite wall held an assortment of photographs: Brodie and Colin's wedding, other weddings, the children at various stages of their lives, from birth till now. Maisie was making a funny face in her photos – either that or grinning madly from ear to ear – while Josh, their son, looked as serious as a baby as he did at twenty. He'd never been all that liberal with his smiles. When he'd left for university in Norwich, Brodie had been upset, naturally, but not worried. Josh was too sensible to get into trouble and had immediately got a job in a supermarket. Now in his final year, he had never asked his parents for money. Brodie imagined Maisie asking regularly.

The sun came out and her eyes were drawn towards

the garden where a scattering of leaves had fallen on the neat lawn. As soon as Colin saw them, he would sweep them up. The garden was his pride and joy, but then so was the house, as were his wife and children. He loved his job as Head of English in a city centre school and appeared to be contented with his lot. She couldn't ever recall him wishing for something that was beyond his reach. He'd recently bought a 1974 Triumph Spitfire that he was looking forward to restoring to its original condition.

Should I look for a job? she asked herself. Until now, she'd been perfectly happy being a full-time wife and mother. Something interesting and part-time. She was fully computer-literate.

There were footsteps on the stairs and Colin came in wearing jeans and a T-shirt. His feet were bare. He looked so young and handsome that it took her breath away. 'Ah, there you are!' he said jovially. 'Is there any tea in that pot?'

Brodie gave the pot a shake. 'Plenty, but you need to fetch a mug.'

'I was thinking about getting a job,' she said when he came back. 'A part-time one.'

'Have a rest first, darling,' he advised, as if she'd been toiling away in a wash-house or down a mine for the last twenty years. 'Take it easy, do some shopping, go to lunch with your mum. Use some of the money from the house.' Years ago, when Brodie's mother had moved into a flat, she had given her daughter – her only child – the family home in Blundellsands: Chestnuts. It had been let ever since.

'Tell you what.' Colin clapped his hands. 'Let's go to that café on the way to Southport where they serve slap-up breakfasts. We can leave Mass till afterwards. Oh, and I'd like to drop in on my folks this afternoon, see if Mum is still sane after having had Dad home for a whole fortnight.' Colin's obnoxious father had recently retired and his wife, Eileen, had been dreading it. 'Before anything,' Colin concluded, 'I'll just go and sweep those leaves off the lawn.'

Later, Brodie watched him tidy the garden. He was singing, but she couldn't make out the tune. She quite fancied the idea of a second honeymoon. Once she got used to the house without Maisie, life would be perfect. Well, almost perfect. Perfection was perhaps too much to expect.

Vanessa

Easter Saturday 2005

Vanessa sat on the settee in her mother's house making a list.

'What are you doing?' Amanda, her sister, asked with a frown.

'Something to do with work,' Vanessa mumbled.

'For Pete's sake, Vannie, it's your wedding day. Nobody *works* on their wedding day.'

'*I* do.' Vanessa turned over a page and continued to write. 'These are the people who will be interviewed tomorrow and Easter Monday.' She worked for Siren Radio, setting up interviews with local dignitaries and any celebrities who might be in Liverpool. It was a job she loved quite passionately.

'But you'll be on your honeymoon from tonight,' Amanda protested. 'Why should you care?'

'This is for Clare Johnson; she'll be at the wedding.' Vanessa finished writing and signed it with a flourish. 'She's taking over my job while I'm away – and I want it done properly.'

Amanda shuddered. 'I'd hate to work for you, sis.'

Vanessa said with mock severity, 'If a job's worth doing, it's worth doing well.'

Their mother came in wearing a smart blue silk suit,

the effect entirely ruined by a pair of massive fur slippers with tiger faces. 'You used to say that when you were a child,' she commented. 'I longed to slap your little priggish face, though I never did.' She exchanged smiles with both her daughters.

'I bet you're taking your laptop on your honeymoon,' Amanda said.

'It so happens that I am.' Vanessa couldn't see anything wrong with it. She and William had been living together for three years. Making love wouldn't exactly be a new experience. 'I'm taking the laptop in case I get any ideas and can make a note of them.'

Amanda guffawed. 'I bet William won't want *his* ideas put on a computer.'

Their mother sat down and kicked off the tiger slippers. 'Would someone please help me on with these shoes? They cost seventy-five quid, but they'll probably never be on me feet again after today.'

Vanessa knelt in front of her mother and picked up a blue shoe with an incredibly high heel, the upper part consisting of a few narrow straps. 'You should have bought something more practical, Mum. These are all for show.'

'I liked the look of them,' her mother said stubbornly. 'Even if I never wear them again, at some time in the future, if I'm ever stuck in a wheelchair, I can look at your wedding photos with a magnifying glass and marvel that I'd once been able to wear dead gorgeous shoes like these – I'll ask your dad to take a photo of just me legs. It'll buck me up no end.' The shoes on, she stuck out her feet. 'Don't they look the gear?'

'Great, Mum,' her daughters agreed.

Vanessa wouldn't have dreamed of buying clothes for just one occasion. For her wedding, she wore a simple white crêpe frock with shoestring straps and a matching bolero. Unlike a proper wedding dress, it could be worn afterwards for all sorts of occasions, even work. Instead of a hat — she hated hats — the hairdresser had coiled her long blonde hair into a chignon that was sprinkled with tiny white rosebuds. Even Amanda, who had argued she should buy a proper wedding dress, had said she looked absolutely fantastic.

'Every inch the bride,' she conceded.

Vanessa folded the list and asked Amanda to keep it in her handbag to give to Clare Johnson at the reception.

'I'll make sure you don't forget, sis,' Amanda promised.

'I'm not likely to forget something as important as *that*.'

Amanda laughed. 'I just thought, you know, with you just having got *married*, you'd have more interesting things on your mind than work.' She looked curiously at her sister. 'Doesn't today have at least a little bit of magic for you?'

'Of course it does,' Vanessa said irritably. 'But in a way, the wedding is a bit of an anti-climax.'

Amanda mouthed, 'An anti-climax' at her mother, and both women rolled their eyes at each other.

Vanessa's mobile rang and William's name showed on the screen. 'Hello, William,' she said in a crisp tone. 'You should have left for the church by now.' He was coming from their flat in Hunt's Cross where he and the best man had spent the night. And why did they

14

have the television on? It was sport of some sort; she could hear the raucous cheering. If he was late for the wedding . . .

'I can't find my cufflinks,' he groaned.

'They're on the bedside cabinet on your side of the bed,' Vanessa snapped. 'I showed you where they were before I left last night.'

'I know you did, but they're not there now.' The sound of the television faded as he walked around the flat. 'Oh! Here they are, where you said. But they're not in the box,' he said accusingly. 'I was looking for the little red box.'

'You're an idiot, William,' she exclaimed. 'Is that all you've got to worry about?'

'Yes, darling.'

'Then I'll see you in church.' Without saying good-bye, she turned the phone off, annoyed. Honestly, sometimes it was like looking after a child. She found most men much the same.

Her mother had got to her feet, wobbling slightly on the too-high heels. 'Poor William,' she said softly.

'What d'you mean, Mum?'

'I don't know.' She shrugged. Vanessa was a lovely girl, but she was too sure of herself by a mile. That was no way to speak to anyone, let alone the man who was about to become your husband. One of these days her daughter would come down to earth with a bump. She just hoped it wouldn't hurt too much.

Rachel

Christmas 2005

Rachel and Tyler stared down at the baby they had made, hardly able to believe she was real. There was a Christmas tree in the corner of the ward and tinsel pinned around the door. Five other women were there, all with new babies and all fast asleep.

'She's awesome,' Tyler whispered. 'What shall we call her?' He was tall and skinny and wore large horn-rimmed spectacles that made him look incredibly studious, which indeed he was.

'Poppy,' Rachel replied. 'It's me favourite name.' She was almost as studious, but her studies had been interrupted of late, mainly by arguments with her mother over the expected baby's future.

'Cool,' said Tyler. 'Poppy's cool.'

Poppy, not yet an hour old, waved her arms and blew her first raspberry.

'I think she likes us.' Rachel, nursing her daughter in her arms, gingerly touched her chin as if worried she might break.

Tyler sighed. 'I wish I'd got here earlier.' He'd not long arrived at the hospital.

Rachel looked grim. 'So do I! It didn't half hurt. You could have held me hand or something. Did you manage to get out the house without anyone noticing?'

'Yeah, I kept the mobile under my pillow. When you called, I phoned for a cab, then snuck outside to wait for it.' He wanted to pick up Rachel and their baby and fly them away to an uninhabited island with golden sands and trees full of exotic fruit. They would live happily ever after in a grass hut by the sea. 'What about you?'

'I did the same,' Rachel told him in her little pale voice. 'It was nearly midnight when I had the first contraction. Me mam was asleep by then. I told the taxi driver number twenty instead of number ten, so he didn't stop outside our house.'

'You should have called me then, honey,' Tyler said.

'Yes, but it might've taken hours and hours for the baby to come and you've got school in the morning.' He was taking his GCSEs in the summer.

'Jeez!' Tyler sighed again. 'It's the last day of term.' He wouldn't tell anyone that he'd become a father overnight, even though he felt inordinately proud. If the news got through to Pop, he'd insist Tyler went back to New York to live with his mother and there'd be one helluva row because Tyler would refuse to go. It was his intention to stay with Rachel and their baby for the rest of his life.

A nurse arrived. 'I think it's about time you two went to sleep,' she said, nodding at the new mother and her child. She half-smiled, half-frowned at Tyler. 'As for you, young man, you'd better get yourself home.' She clearly had no idea what to make of them. The girl claimed to be sixteen, but didn't look it, and at first she'd thought the young man was her brother, but the way he acted with the girl wasn't brotherly in the least.

They'd met, Rachel and Tyler, in Virgin Records in Liverpool, reaching for an Amy Winehouse CD at exactly the same time. Rachel's CD had nearly landed on the floor, but Tyler had managed to catch it just in time.

'My grandpa used to collect old-fashioned records,' he said as he handed her the CD. 'If you dropped one, it'd break into a million pieces.' His voice had started to break and the words were a mixture of high and low notes, which all sounded a bit rusty.

'Honest?' She waved the CD. 'Thanks, anyroad,' she said, 'for catching it.'

They stared at each other for a very long time. She was barely fourteen and he was almost exactly one year older. Rachel couldn't understand the feelings she was having at that particular moment, but suspected they'd come unnaturally early, that they were the sort of feelings people had when they were eighteen or even older. Some people might never have them in their entire lives.

'Would you like a Coke?' Tyler had asked.

'I wouldn't say no.' She couldn't have said 'no' to save her life.

She'd hardly started her periods when they'd stopped and she realized she was pregnant. She told her mother, who danced around the room in her glitzy lime-green shellsuit, screaming and yelling at her to have an abortion.

Rachel refused.

'In that case,' her mother said in her hard-as-nails voice, 'you can have the bloody thing adopted. Don't think you can just go back to school and leave it with me.'

'I've no intention of leaving me baby with you, Mam,' Rachel said haughtily. 'And I'm not going back to school, either. Me and Tyler are getting married as soon as I'm sixteen.'

'Tyler?' her mother spat. 'Is he that bloody Yank you brought round once?'

'That's right.' She'd never brought him again, ashamed of her mother's crude ways and foul mouth.

'It was a Yank who was the undoing of me Auntie Thelma during the war,' her mother snarled. 'As for you, my girl, I've got to sign something, giving you permission like, before you can get married at sixteen.'

'If you won't, then we'll just have to wait till I'm eighteen. Or I could ask me dad to sign whatever-it-is.'

'If you could get a hold of him when he isn't pissed rotten; most of the time he can hardly remember his name.' She sniffed disdainfully, but there was something incredibly sad about it. 'And if you think that chap of yours is going to hang around for another three years, you've got another think coming.' She burst into tears. They were genuine, Rachel could tell, but she couldn't find it in herself to feel sympathetic. Meeting Tyler and having his baby were the best things that had happened in all her life.

'You're the only kid I've had that I've felt proud of,' her mother wailed. 'You were doing so well at school, you said you wanted to be a teacher.' Rachel's two brothers had been in prison for thieving, and her sister was being investigated for benefit fraud.

'I still want to be a teacher,' she insisted. 'Having a baby won't stop me. Five years and him or her will be at school themselves. You still can be proud of me, Mam,' she said awkwardly, but her mother just shrugged, as if she didn't believe it for a minute.

And now Poppy had been born. Rachel glanced longingly at the door through which the nurse had taken her baby daughter. She wanted her back. She wanted to hold the tiny body against her own and never let go. Very soon, she'd have to return home, where Mam was dead set against her keeping the baby. She'd threatened to fetch social workers who would take her away. Rachel knew it happened. She'd read about in the papers and seen it on telly, the way a person in authority could just pluck a baby out of its mother's arms and give it to someone else.

She dreaded the future. Just thinking about it made her feel physically sick. Even though Tyler had plenty of money, they wouldn't be allowed to set up house together. Rachel slid under the bedclothes and began to cry.

March–April 2006

Chapter 1

Diana stood with her back against the door, arms outspread, as if she were glued to it, worried that if she took another step it would be a sign of her commitment to live there. The room was big and square with tall, floor-length windows. Outside, the sun shone so brightly that everywhere was drenched in a bright golden light, revealing the high ornamental ceiling to be badly in need of a good clean, as well as a coat of emulsion. The furniture was covered with fine dust.

There was an old-fashioned wardrobe and chest of drawers to match, a single bed, a piano, a table and two chairs, and two mainly beige tapestry armchairs. The carpet was pale brown with a border of over-blown roses. It was a pleasant, comfortable room. If one of her brothers had chosen to live there – Jason often spoke about getting his own place – she would have thoroughly approved.

But did she want it for herself?

Over the years, Diana had envisaged all sorts of terrible things happening in the world that would destroy life as she knew it; bird flu, terrorism, weapons of mass destruction, global warming, the central heating boiler exploding, killing them all, that's if escaping gas hadn't done it first. It wasn't for herself that she was worried, but for her brothers.

Since the day her mother had left seven years ago to live with Warren, Diana had devoted herself completely to the care of Damian, Jason and Garth. People told her that she was silly, that it was time she had a life of her own, found a boyfriend, thought about marriage.

Diana ignored them. All she wanted was to look after the lads until they were old enough to look after themselves. One of these days they would leave home, get married, start families, and she would be left alone in the little terraced house in Coral Street, Bootle, where the four O'Sullivan children had been born. It was only then, with her brothers gone and hopefully happy, that she would start to think about herself, about getting married to someone really nice and having three boys of her own.

This vision of the future suited her perfectly. Apart from the ever-present worry over bird flu and terrorism and other horrors, Diana had been extremely happy with her life.

There was one horror, though, that had never remotely crossed her mind – and that was of becoming homeless, of having to leave the house in Coral Street because *she wasn't needed any more*. Since last Christmas, when Emma had moved in, Diana had become surplus to requirements.

She took a tentative step into the room. She tried to imagine sleeping there rather than in the box room into which she'd felt obliged to move so that Damian and Emma could have the middle bedroom with the double bed. There was nowhere in the box room to keep her clothes, and she had to remember to get next day's outfit out of the wardrobe in what was now Damian and Emma's room before she went to bed. Nor was there space for the portable television that she'd watched when she woke up early, unless she wanted to put it on the floor or perch it on her feet.

There was plenty of space in this room for one of those giant plasma screens – not that she wanted one – as well as all her clothes and other possessions, but she wouldn't be able to hear Garth giving a commentary on a football match in his sleep while Jason turned restlessly in his. Could she bear it? On the other hand, she wouldn't hear what Damian and Emma got up to in Mam's old bed, the bed that had been Diana's for the last seven years. It wasn't that she disapproved, but she found it a bit distracting.

She took another step into the room. The cream curtains could do with a good wash – a ladder would be necessary to get them down. She'd need bedding and towels. How would she get everything, a duvet included, out of Coral Street without anyone noticing? She didn't want them to know she was going until she'd gone in case they tried to talk her into staying. If they succeeded things would only continue in the same unsatisfactory way.

She sat on the bed. It had an old-fashioned spring that creaked a bit, but was very comfortable. Next, she tried one of the tapestry armchairs. The arms were wide and well padded, ideal for draping her legs over while she read or watched television.

A movement in the garden caught her eye and she gasped at the sight of a squirrel racing along the branches of a tree. She watched entranced as another squirrel sat on the grass and chewed something held in its paws. The scene was like an illustration out of a children's book.

The house was the last at the end of a short cul-de-sac not far from Blundellsands Station – the railway track was hidden behind a grassy bank about thirty metres away. At that very minute, a train passed along the lines and the house vibrated slightly until it had gone.

The squirrels had gone, too, disappearing into the leaves or the long untidy grass. The house had been built well back from the road and was hidden behind a row of old trees – she could tell they were old because of the size of the trunks. At first, she'd thought it was someone's garden and the man in the paint shop had made a mistake when he'd told her where the place was. It wasn't until she glimpsed the windows glinting through the branches, the creamy bricks, and the faded lilac front door with the name 'Chestnuts' in dull brass letters, that she realized there was a house. It was charming and slightly mysterious, she thought as she'd opened the gate and walked down the brick path, as if it belonged in another place, or another time, even another country, like the American deep South. It would be an unusual spot in which to live. She could lie in bed, watch the squirrels and see the trees change colour as the months passed by.

Oh, but she didn't want to live here! She rested her forehead on the cool window and closed her eyes. She'd sooner stay in Coral Street any day where squirrels were unknown and she couldn't recall the whereabouts of the nearest tree. She remembered

Mam had shown an unexpected fondness for trees when she'd gone to live in Melling Village with Warren; perhaps it ran in the family.

What was she going to *do*? She was trying to unravel her tangled thoughts when the front door opened and someone came in.

Diana went into the square hallway, which was about as big as the main room of the house in Coral Street. The patterns on the stained-glass windows on each side of the door were smudgily reflected on the black-and-white tiled floor. A woman of about forty had entered. She had neat brown hair and a kind face. She jumped when she saw Diana. 'I didn't know anyone was here,' she gasped.

'The man in the paint shop gave me the key and said I was the first person to see the house,' Diana explained. 'He had a card in the window and he said I could pick any room I liked.'

'The man in the paint shop?' The woman looked puzzled. Then her expression cleared. 'Oh, you mean Leonard; he sells artists' materials. He wasn't supposed to put a card in his window yet. I'm having a new kitchen installed and the plumbing needs a good seeing-to. Everywhere wants a thorough clean before it can be let. Didn't he tell you that?'

'No.' This rather disappointing news only made Diana change her mind; she *did* want to live in Chestnuts. She might well be unhappy there, but she couldn't possibly be unhappier than she'd been over the last few months. 'When will it be ready?'

'In about a fortnight or so.' She looked anxiously at Diana. 'I hope you're not desperate. Have you got somewhere to live in the meantime?'

'Oh, yes.' Diana sighed. 'Will you be living here, too?' The woman seemed exceptionally nice and her presence would make the move from the only home she'd ever known more bearable.

'I'm not sure.' The woman went into the room that Diana had just vacated. 'I'd forgotten how high the ceilings were.'

Diana followed. 'Have you been here before?'

'It's my house,' the woman said surprisingly. 'My mother gave it to me.' She tugged at a cream curtain and it gave off a cloud of dust. 'These need sending to the cleaners,' she muttered. She turned to Diana. 'My name is Brodie Logan, by the way.'

'I'm Diana O'Sullivan. Your mother gave you a *house*?'

'Ages and ages ago, yes. It was let fully furnished on a twenty-five-year lease to the Slattery sisters. There were four of them, all in their fifties. The lease ran out last month. By then, three of the sisters had died and the one who was left went in a home. Saturday was the first time I've been here since I got married and, do you know, hardly a thing has changed.' She touched the lid of the piano. 'I wonder if this needs tuning? My mother let me have it so I would avoid Inheritance Tax when she died – the house that is. The Slatterys left the piano behind.'

'Really.' Diana had never heard of Inheritance Tax. There was no one in the world likely to leave her a rabbit hutch, let alone a lovely big house. Before he went away, her dad had bought the house in Coral Street, but there was still a mortgage to be paid.

'I was born in this house and lived here until I got married.'

'Why didn't you stay here?' Diana asked.

'Because my husband and I already had another house, and Mum had bought herself a flat down by the river. She's a widow; my father died not long after I was born.' Brodie opened one of the windows and stepped outside, Diana trailing behind. Everywhere smelled earthy and fresh, as if they were in the depths of the countryside. 'I used to play out here when I was little,' Brodie went on. 'I loved it. The trains didn't bother me and I used to chase the squirrels, hoping I would catch one. I imagined dressing it up in dolls' clothes and taking it to bed with me.' She smiled and dimples appeared in both cheeks. Close up, she was very pretty with a little turned-up nose and full lips. She wore a dark green corduroy suit with a flowered blouse underneath.

'I saw two squirrels earlier,' Diana informed her.

'Mum used to buy them nuts and seed for the birds, then sit just inside the window and watch.' Diana resolved to do the same as soon as she could. 'Would you like a drink?' Brodie asked. 'I've just been to Sainsbury's for the groceries so there's milk, coffee and tea in the car.'

'I'd love a cup of tea, ta.'

'Let's hope we can find mugs and a kettle in the kitchen.' They went back into the house. Brodie told Diana where the kitchen was, and went to collect her shopping from the car.

The kitchen was surprisingly small. It was ridiculous, Diana thought, for such an important room to be a quarter of the size of the hall. It was also very old-fashioned, with a chipped enamel sink, a series of run-down cupboards, an ancient fridge, and what looked

29

like the first microwave ever made. The marble-patterned linoleum had been completely worn away in places to reveal a crumbling concrete floor. There was no sign of a washing machine or tumble dryer.

She thought of the kitchen in Coral Street. It was actually bigger than this, though not by much. Since her mother left, Diana had gradually modernized it, buying appliances on hire purchase, having units fitted and some very superior linoleum laid, painting the walls rose-pink – she'd done them herself – while the lads had helped with the tiling. Her heart lifted with pleasure every time she went in and saw everything glittering and gleaming, particularly when she switched on the light.

But now the kitchen was out of bounds, taken over by Emma, making Diana feel as if she were no use at all.

The thought of being reduced to using this stone age kitchen after the lovely one she'd created for herself, the sheer misery of life since Christmas, made worse by the fact she'd lost her job on top of everything else, was enough to make her burst into tears, which she promptly did. Tears that had been threatening to fall on numerous occasions, but had remained unshed, gushed forth, streaming down Diana's pale cheeks and landing in miniature puddles on her boots and on the floor.

'Oh, my dear girl! What on earth's the matter?' Brodie cried when she came in with the groceries.

'Everything's the matter,' Diana sobbed. '*Everything.*'

'Let's sit down and you can tell me all about it.' Although they'd only just met, Brodie could see that

Diana O'Sullivan was a very unhappy young woman. It was obvious from the eyes that never lit up, the turned-down mouth, and the fact that she seemed to have lost the knack of smiling. She wondered if her own eyes and face sent out a similar message to the world.

'It's Emma,' Diana said in a cracked voice when they were seated on the tapestry armchairs. 'She's our Damian's girlfriend; she's expecting a baby in August. They're not getting married until afterwards so she can wear a dead glamorous wedding dress. She moved in at Christmas and she doesn't go to work, so she does all the things I used to do: the cooking, the washing and ironing, the cleaning. The only thing she doesn't do is darn socks; instead, she just throws them away and buys new ones. I used to love darning socks, but nowadays I can't find any.'

'I don't understand, dear,' Brodie said gently. 'Who is Damian?'

'Me brother,' Diana wept. 'He's twenty-three and the oldest. Jason's twenty, and our Garth is seventeen and still at school.' Now the tears were dripping on her knees rather than her feet. She produced a hand-kerchief from her sleeve and began to mop her eyes. 'When Mam left, she asked me to look after them. And I did. But now when I get home from work, instead of me making the tea, Emma's already made it. She insists on washing and drying the dishes an' all, so there's absolutely nothing for me to do. She even does my washing as well as the lads', though I've asked her not to.' The tears were replaced with indignation. 'And she irons *everything*: tea towels, pillow cases, hankies, even underpants. Me, I didn't have the time.'

'Of course you didn't, dear.' Brodie had loads of time, but wouldn't have dreamed of ironing underpants.

'She won't let me do *anything*,' Diana wailed. 'If I get up to go into the kitchen, she gets there before me and wants to know what I want. But it's *my* kitchen.' She wrung her hands and looked at Brodie with bloodshot eyes. 'And I don't know where to *sit*. The downstairs rooms have been knocked into one, so if Jason and Garth go out, I feel in the way. But I can't go upstairs because I sleep in the box room where it's as miserable as sin and there's no room for a telly or even a chair. Where can I go?' she asked tragically.

'Out?' Brodie suggested. 'Couldn't you go out? Haven't you got friends?'

'All the friends I had at school are married. Anyroad, I was too busy with the lads and the house to make friends; there was always something to do.'

Brodie gathered together her nicest smile. 'Have you tried having a word with Emma?'

'I've tried, but she won't listen. The thing is . . .'

'What?' Brodie prompted when there was a long pause.

'She's *lovely*,' Diana said despairingly. 'She only wants to help. She thinks I like being waited on hand and foot. "Sit down, Di, and take the weight off your feet," she'll say the minute I come in. She even does the shopping.' She got up and began to wander around the room. 'That's why, when I saw the card in that shop window, I thought I'd come and have a look. The rent is awful cheap.'

'That's because I'm not interested in making a profit. I thought I'd let the rooms for a year or so while I decide what to do with the place; keep it as an investment, or sell it and put the money in the bank.'

'Really?' Diana seemed bemused. Brodie reckoned property and investments were way beyond the world as she knew it.

Her outburst appeared to be over. Brodie patted her hand. 'You sit there, dear, while I make some tea.'

'Thank you, Brodie . . . isn't Brodie a man's name?'

'It's Irish and can be a man or a woman's. Do you take milk and sugar?'

'Just milk, thank you. I was called after Princess Diana. She married Prince Charles on the day I was born.'

'Diana is a lovely name – it suits you.' Brodie left for the kitchen. She let the water run for a while before filling the kettle. She found two mugs in the cupboard under the sink, washed them and put a teabag in each. Diana, poor girl, was out of her depth. She wondered if Emma was really as harmless as she made out, or a very clever young woman who was intent on appropriating the house for herself? Maybe she was surreptitiously trying to edge Diana out – successfully, it would seem.

The kettle boiled, she made the tea, and took it into the room that her mother had called 'the parlour'. Brodie had always thought the light shone through the windows with a slightly greenish tinge as a result of the sun being filtered through the leaves. Diana was sitting staring into space. 'Here you are, dear.'

'Ta.' The girl came to with a jolt and leaned forward to take the cup in her long white fingers. She wore an outfit that Brodie guessed came from a charity shop; a badly knitted orange sweater, a grey pencil skirt, and black ankle boots with wedge heels. On Diana, they acquired a sort of elegance. Although the girl's movements were jerky, they had a youthful grace. Everything about her was long and thin; her face, body, arms and legs. Her blue eyes were the most innocent and trusting that she'd ever seen on anyone apart from a child – they were the colour of bluebells. She might well look and act like a teenager, but must be older if she'd been taking care of her brothers for such a long time. Was the mother still around? she wondered. She felt angry, not only with the mother, but with Emma, too, for treating this incredibly nice young woman so uncaringly.

'Where do you work?' she asked.

'In a call centre till last week, when it closed down and moved to India,' Diana said disapprovingly. 'They pay the staff much less over there. That's the reason why I'm not at work on a Monday. I'm starting another job next week in a refugee centre off Cazneau Street. I'm really looking forward to it.'

Brodie carried her mug to the window and looked out on the garden where she'd played as a child. 'Do you think you'd like living here, Diana?' she asked.

The girl sighed. 'I couldn't dislike it more than where I am now. That sounds awful because I love me brothers more than anything in the world, but it's not the same any more.' She came and stood next to the older woman, almost half a head taller. 'It's so pretty here. In Coral Street, the window in the box room where I sleep looks out on to the box room next door.' For the first time, she smiled, though rather sadly. 'At least I'll be at peace. Oh, that makes me sound as if I want to die!' She ran her fingers through the thick brown hair that flew all over the place. 'It's just that at home I feel in turmoil, as if there's a war raging in me stomach.'

'I always loved it here,' Brodie told her.

'It's very nice. Trouble is, I keep changing me mind. Right now, it seems a really good idea to move; five minutes ago, I hated the thought. It was the kitchen that put me off,' she said, adding tactlessly, 'It's really horrible.'

'As I told you, there's going to be a new kitchen. The builders are starting on it tomorrow.'

Diana looked doubtful. 'There isn't room for a washing machine or a tumble-dryer.'

'They're at the back. Look, shall I show you around?' Brodie offered. 'The room next to this is exactly the same and there are two identical rooms directly above. They're the only ones I shall let. There are some much smaller rooms that can be used for storage and a bathroom big enough to hold a dance in. There's a lavatory downstairs as well as up. Come on, I'll show you the laundry room. It's a bit depressing out there, but I'm having it decorated – nearly everywhere is getting a fresh coat of paint.'

The laundry room was fitted with a washing machine and a tumble-dryer, both relatively modern, an ironing board and a clothes maiden on which hung three stockings, none of which matched. The walls were the colour of mud and at least half the paint was flaking off.

Next to it was a conservatory with a glass roof and windows on three sides, mostly covered with untidy tendrils of ivy. It contained an old cane three-piece, with faded flowered cushions, and a small round table.

35

Brodie said it was where her father had smoked his pipe. 'In summer, it gets unbearably hot, but it's as cold as a fridge in winter. My dad actually sat on that very same settee, on the very same cushions.' She touched the cushions and looked at Diana, wide-eyed. 'Gosh, that feels awfully strange. I can't remember anything about him.'

Diana touched the cushions and said it felt strange to her, too. 'What's that?' She pointed to an orange splodge on top of the glass roof.

Brodie laughed. 'That's a ginger cat. I reckon he's a male because he's so huge. I don't know what his name is or which house he belongs to. He was there when I came on Saturday.'

They went upstairs. Brodie asked Diana if she would prefer to live in one of the first-floor rooms, but she said she'd already got used to the downstairs one. 'And I like the idea of having a piano.'

'Can you play?' She had long hands, perfect for a pianist.

'No, but I can read music a bit – they taught us at school – and I wouldn't mind trying to play with one finger. Will you let me know when the decorators are finished so I can move in? I wish it could have been today,' she said wistfully. 'I don't know what to do with meself at home with Emma there. That's why I was wandering around Waterloo. I'd walked all the way from Bootle.'

'We'll make it today if you like.' It was odd, she'd only known the girl five minutes, but Brodie already felt quite fond of her. Since her own children had left home, she'd missed having young people in her life. Josh, twenty-two, had finished university with an average degree and had moved to London. He now lived in a squat off the Holloway Road. She'd sooner not think about Maisie just now. 'If you don't mind the mess,' she said to Diana, 'you can stay in one of the other rooms while yours is being done up – I'll ask the builders to start on it first. Mind you, there might not always be electricity and there'll be quite a lot of noise, so you're not likely to get much peace.'

'Move in today!' Diana looked quite thrilled at the idea and smiled properly for the first time. 'I'd love to move in today.'

'Will you be bringing your things in a car? There's plenty of room in the road to park.'

When the girl said she didn't have a car and couldn't drive anyway, Brodie offered to collect her and her possessions there and then and bring them to the house. 'We'll go now, if you like.'

'Now would be the gear. Afternoons, Emma usually goes to see her sister in Walton Vale and she's out until about three o'clock. I don't want anyone to know I'm leaving, but I'll write a note telling them where I am.'

It took hardly any time for Diana to throw her clothes into a few plastic bags and stuff the bedding in another. Her few bits of jewellery and make-up had of late been downgraded from the top of her mother's dressing table to a drawer in the sideboard. She emptied everything into a smaller bag. She decided to leave her books behind – she could always borrow some from the library – but she'd take her CDs and the CD player, plus the portable television and the DVD player that were now in Damian and Emma's bedroom. They

37

never watched either, having more important things to do in bed.

She didn't feel as sad as she'd expected as she went round the house a final time, though when she went into the big bedroom where Jason and Garth slept, she tenderly stroked their pillows and hoped they wouldn't miss her too much. She said as much in the note she wrote and tucked behind the clock. She put that she didn't want anyone to think she was going away because she was unhappy, but perhaps her presence was no longer necessary now that Emma was there to look after them. She finished: 'My address is Chestnuts, Elm Road, Blundellsands. Come and see me whenever you want. Di.'

On the way back, Brodie asked for her mobile number. 'I'll give you mine in case we need to contact each other for some reason.'

'I haven't got a mobile,' Diana told her. 'I kept meaning to buy one, but never seemed to get round to it.'

'I see you haven't brought a computer with you.'

'We only had the one and the lads would be gutted if I'd taken it. Anyroad, all I did was play card games. I never learned to use it properly.'

'Well, there's a phone in Chestnuts; it's in the hall and it's still connected. I can ring there if necessary.'

'That's fine,' Diana said sunnily. She seemed different now, much happier. 'Have you got children, Brodie?'

'Two, Joseph – he's called Josh – and Maisie. They're both grown up and live in London.'

Well, Maisie was still in London the last time they'd

heard from her, but Brodie had no idea where she might be now.

What a refreshing young woman; she belonged not just in the last century, but the one before, Brodie thought as she drove to Crosby after helping Diana unload her belongings in Chestnuts.

She drove rather faster than she should, having forgotten about the groceries in the boot. By now the frozen stuff would be frozen no more.

Before they'd parted, Diana had asked if it really was her intention to move in. 'Earlier, when I asked, you said you weren't sure.'

'I'm still not sure. I'm like you; things are happening at home that are beyond my control. I'm very unhappy a lot of the time.'

'I'm sorry,' Diana said sincerely. 'I hope you don't think I'm awful for wanting you to come, but I can't help it. It would be the gear if you were living in the room next to mine.'

I'll see what happens over the next few days, Brodie decided as she carried bags of food into the house. She knew you weren't supposed to put food that had melted back in the freezer, but she put it there all the same; it was unlikely to kill anyone.

Emma had been back in the house in Coral Street for more than an hour before she noticed the note behind the clock. When she read it, she couldn't resist a little smile of triumph.

Since before she'd even moved into the house, Damian had been quite firm about her stay being temporary. 'Our Di won't mind you being there, but it can only be until the baby's born and then we'll have to look for a place of our own.'

That had seemed a bit unfair, Emma thought. Di was a single woman, while she was almost married and expecting a baby. If anyone should look for a place of their own, it should be Diana. She hadn't told Damian how she felt; he and his brothers thought the world of their sister and wouldn't hear a word said against her.

So Emma began a campaign to make herself indispensable. She kept the house spotless, did the laundry every day, and made large, nourishing meals – she'd been good at Cookery at school, though it had seemed a waste of time when it was so much easier to open a tin or a packet. Garth had slightly broken ranks and said he didn't know what they'd do without her when she and Damian left. 'Our Di never made such nice food – and she didn't always make the beds, either,' he said.

At this, Damian had nearly bitten his head off. 'Di was out at work all day, that's why,' he snapped. 'And she only didn't always make the beds because some of us were still in them when she left for work. She looked after us when we were all at school,' he told Emma.

At this, Garth had blushed and said he was sorry. Emma realized she would have to tread carefully if she wanted to get rid of Di.

She could tell from the hurt in Di's big blue eyes that she missed taking care of her brothers, so did her utmost to make her feel worse. It was a really horrible thing to do, because she liked Di very much, but the world was a horrible place and you had to put yourself first. If nice people like Di got trampled on in the process, then it was just too bad. A different woman would have told Emma to eff off, but Di was too soft and gentle.

Emma took the note from behind the clock and screwed it into a ball. The longer their sister was away, the more the lads would realize it was possible to live without her. Otherwise, once they knew where she'd gone, they'd be round to this Blundellsands place pleading with her to come back.

But she was bound to turn up one day and swear she'd left a note behind the clock and Emma would be suspected of having removed it. Best keep it and put it in a place like . . . like . . . underneath the fridge! If it ever came to light, everyone would assume it had fallen there accidentally. She smoothed the paper out, took it into the kitchen, and slid it into its hiding place.

She stood in the middle of the room and thought how much she admired it. She loved the way the lights went on underneath the wall cupboards, the frilly lace blind on the window, and the little corner shelves that each held a red wine glass. Damian said Di had got them from Argos and they were called goblets: 'At Christmas, she puts them on the table with nightlights in. They look dead pretty.'

Emma's sister, Sophie, had two kids and lived in a crappy flat in Walton Vale. The cooker in the shared kitchen looked as if it came out of the ark and the washing machine only worked when it felt like it. It was useless trying to get the landlord to do anything about it. Sophie was in and out of the laundrette like a yo-yo – and it cost the earth.

Damian would never let Emma and his own kid live in such a dump, but whatever sort of place he found it wouldn't have a kitchen like this. She ran her hand along the mottled cream top. Most women would die for such a kitchen.

'Our Di's late,' Jason remarked that night when they sat down to eat.

'Perhaps she's stayed behind at work for something,' Emma suggested.

'She never has before.' Damian didn't look too concerned, but by the time the meal was over and Di still hadn't appeared he was obviously worried. 'She would have rung if she'd been held up for some reason.'

An hour later, there was still no sign. Jason went upstairs to play on the computer and came down almost straight away his face as white as a sheet. 'The door to the box room's open and the things have gone off our Di's bed.'

'What?' Damian went upstairs to check for himself. He returned saying he'd looked in the wardrobe and Di's clothes had disappeared, too. 'What's the number of that place where she works?'

'It's seven o'clock, it'll be closed,' Garth said.

'It's a call centre, idiot. It's open till midnight.' Damian picked up the telephone book that Di had filled in with her incredibly neat writing and dialled the number. It was answered immediately. 'I see . . . yeah . . . OK, mate, ta.' He rang off and looked seriously at his brothers. 'That was a guy from British Telecom. The call centre closed last week and they're taking out the lines. Why didn't our Di tell us she was leaving?' he demanded angrily.

'She did,' Jason said. He was the shyest and quietest

of the lads. 'But no one took any notice, only me. She got another job somewhere in town.'

'Somewhere in town!' Damian sneered. 'That's a great help.'

Jason shrugged. 'You didn't even know that much. Anyroad, our Di wouldn't go anywhere without leaving a note. When she's had to leave a note before, she always puts it behind the clock on the mantelpiece.'

A hunt began for Di's note. It was clearly not behind the clock, so Jason started to look under the furniture, 'Just in case it got carried there in a draught.' The other lads went upstairs to look. Emma got a really horrible sickly feeling in her stomach and her heart began to thump unnaturally fast. What if Jason looked under the fridge? It was a daft place to have put the stupid note. She would have gone into the kitchen and eaten it if Damian hadn't come charging downstairs and got there before her.

'I thought she might have stuck something on the fridge with a magnet,' he said, but fortunately he didn't look underneath.

In Coral Street, you never felt on your own. The lads might be out, but next door's kids would be playing in the yard, televisions blaring in the houses either side, the man behind using his electric saw, cars and motorbikes revving, voices raised. There was noise everywhere.

In Chestnuts it was as silent as the grave, yet Diana didn't mind. It was the first time in her life that she'd been completely by herself, without another human being close at hand and a sound of some sort or another in the background. Inside the house, the trains could be more felt than heard – a slight vibration underneath her feet. As Elm Road was a cul-de-sac trains were the only passing traffic. She wandered from room to room, hoping the decorators wouldn't paint over the faded wallpaper that had a lovely satin finish, that they'd just clean, not replace, the even more faded carpets, and that none of the old-fashioned furniture would be taken away.

She really admired the tall lamps with fringed shades, the big, dark wardrobes and chests of drawers as high as herself. The piano was mottled grey and black and the keys deep cream, Diana played a few notes and the sound echoed through the old house.

Kitchens apart, Diana liked old things; not just houses, but films, music, books. She'd lost count of the times she'd watched *It's a Wonderful Life* and *This Happy Breed* on DVD. The Kaiser Chiefs and Arctic Monkeys' CDs rubbed shoulders with those of Al Bowlly and Rudy Vallee, and the novels of Jane Austen mingled with Maeve Binchy's on the bookshelf in the lounge in Coral Street.

She loved this house with its 1930s aura of tea parties and sing-songs around the piano. In the summer, the windows would have been left open for people to wander in and out. Children, who would now be much older than Brodie was now, would have played underneath the trees.

Diana had no illusions that she would have been one of these people. Until recently, what was left of Mam's family had lived for at least a century in the area of Coral Street in Bootle, and her dad was working-class Irish. Had she had any connection with Chestnuts, it would have been as a servant. She would have been

44

slaving away in that disgusting kitchen, not wandering in and out of windows.

It gave her a sense of satisfaction that *her* kitchen was superior to the kitchen here. It just showed how much the world had changed for the better over the last hundred years, forgetting about weapons of mass destruction and other such stuff, that is.

At around sixish, she heated up the Marks & Spencer's cottage pie that Brodie had given her on discovering she'd forgotten to bring food, ate the trifle from the same source, and made a cup of coffee. She ate in the room next to the one that she intended to occupy once it was decorated, plugged in the television and watched the news followed by a holiday programme, followed by *EastEnders*.

Not long afterwards, feeling sleepy, she ventured out to get washed, but decided to leave it until morning because everywhere was a bit scary in the fading light. There were disquieting creaking noises coming from places unseen, and dark shadows flitted across the top of the stairs. It was possible that three of the Slattery sisters had died on the premises, as well as other people whose names she didn't know.

She used the downstairs toilet, then bolted the door of her room and splashed her face in the little corner sink. She went to bed and fell asleep almost straight away. It did cross her mind that her brothers hadn't been to see her, but no doubt they'd come tomorrow.

Chapter 2

'Coo-ee! Diana, are you up, darlin'? It's only me, Megan. I'm just about to put the kettle on.'

It didn't take long for Diana to remember where she was, but she couldn't for the life of her imagine why a woman called Megan who spoke with a half-Liverpool and half-Irish accent was calling to her from the other side of the door. She supposed she'd better get up and find out. 'I'm getting dressed,' she shouted as she struggled into the clothes she'd had on the day before.

'Do you take sugar, darlin'?' the mysterious Megan wanted to know.

'No, ta.' Diana pulled back the heavy curtains and daylight seemed to tumble into the room. Only a patch of the garden was in sunlight. Birds were perched in an orderly row on the roof of an old shed that she hadn't noticed yesterday.

'That's good, because there isn't any.'

Megan had sounded like a young woman, but turned out to be an old one, Diana found when she went into the kitchen where the kettle had just begun to boil.

'Do you think there's ever been a more convenient invention than teabags – in the line of food, that is?'

the woman asked. She looked slim and fit and full of energy. Her short, cropped hair was the most beautiful silver, and eyes the same blue as Brodie's twinkled in her heavily creased face. Of course, this must be Brodie's mother, the one who'd given her the house. She must have had her late in life because she looked almost old enough to be her grandma. She was dressed smartly in a long red skirt with a fluted hem and a black sweater with red piping and, like Brodie, was much shorter than Diana.

'Loads of things, I expect,' Diana replied. 'Sliced bread?' Was she supposed to address the woman as 'Megan'?

'Yes, you're right, of course. Then there's frozen chips and you can buy pastry already made. I always loathed making pastry, the way it got stuck under my fingernails. Have I asked if you take sugar?'

'Yes, and I said I didn't, and then you said that was good because you didn't have any.'

'Did you? Did I? My memory's like a sieve,' she said, rolling her eyes. 'Please, God, don't let me get Alzheimer's.' She picked up the mugs of tea. 'Shall we drink these in the garden? It's quite summery out there considering we're still in March. Later, perhaps you can help me take everything out of the kitchen before the builders smash the place to pieces.'

Diana promised that she would. She followed the woman through the conservatory into a sunlit part of the garden. An iron table with four matching chairs and a sturdy wooden bench had been placed beneath a huge spreading tree with leaves like plates. Dew dripped from the trees and sparkled like little diamonds on the grass. Diana shivered. It might look summery, but it felt quite chilly, and she could feel the dampness of the bench through her skirt. 'What time is it?' she asked.

'Quarter to eight, darlin'. I can never stay in bed once the sun's out.'

'Do you live far?'

'Burbo Bank Road.' Diana had never heard of it and was no wiser. 'It's no distance away. I have a flat with a view over the river. Oh, and call me Megan.' She squeezed Diana's knee with a thin, bony hand. 'Megan Sylvester.'

'Megan,' Diana said experimentally. It was a name she'd never used before. She'd never sat in a garden that was like a little wood before, either. Although she felt cold, she didn't mind. There was something very new about it, almost daring. Even the tea tasted different. She wriggled her shoulders happily. A giant cat, half-ginger, half-white, strolled into the garden looking as if it owned the place. It completely ignored them and stretched out on the grass in front of the shed and began to thoughtfully study the birds. Diana remembered the orange splodge on the conservatory roof. The cat obviously liked it here.

'The workmen will be here at eight to start on the house,' Megan informed her. 'Brodie can't make up her mind what colour to have the kitchen done. She's having new units fitted, light oak, but she hasn't ordered the tiles yet or paint for the walls.'

'Will there be a new fridge?' Diana asked.

'Oh, definitely. She's got one on order. It's half-fridge, half-freezer. And there'll be a new cooker, too, one with a ceramic hob. It looks very easy to keep clean.'

48

Diana nodded her approval. She knew all about cookers with ceramic hobs, having bought one for the kitchen in Coral Street.

There was a rustling sound above them. When Diana looked, two squirrels were racing along one of the branches. They dropped to the ground, paused for a moment, as if to establish their whereabouts, then, quick as a flash, shot up another tree and disappeared into the leaves.

'Oh!' Diana breathed, enthralled. 'Aren't they lovely?'

'They look nice, but they're greedy little buggers,' Megan said disdainfully. 'Mind you, I used to feed them daily when I lived here. You know, darlin',' she gave Diana's knee another squeeze, 'our Brodie called last night and told me all about you. We both wondered what had happened to your mother?'

'She lives in Nottingham with her second husband, Warren. We don't see them all that often. They've got two little boys.' Diana had sometimes imagined she'd end up looking after them, too. She wouldn't have minded.

Brodie was wondering whether to put on jeans and a sweatshirt or something pretty. She intended driving over to Chestnuts soon and everywhere would be in a state if the workmen had arrived, but it was they, not her, who'd be doing the cleaning and decorating. She would keep well out of the way.

Good! She'd never liked jeans. She reached in the wardrobe for a black-and-white check frock with buttons down the front and laid it carefully on the bed, took clean underwear and tights out of the drawer, chose which earrings to wear, then went into the shower.

As usual, Colin had thrown the towel in the bath after his own shower and it lay in a damp heap. Brodie retrieved it, put it in the laundry basket, and took another out of the airing cupboard.

She thought about Colin while she stood under the warm spray and wondered if their marriage would ever return to its former happy state. She remembered the passion at the start, the wonder and excitement when the children were born, the mutual content-ment of the years in between then and now; they'd been harmonious years.

Climbing out of the shower, she dried herself roughly, rubbing the skin until it hurt. It was unlikely to recover, the marriage. They differed so widely over one, crucially important thing – the first real crisis in their lives. From now on, no matter what might happen, no matter how bad it might be, she couldn't rely on Colin to feel the same as she did about any-thing. In his misery, he'd turned his back on her. He preferred to be with his odious father, who told silly jokes and treated him like a teenager.

She was about to hang the towel behind the bath-room door when the telephone rang. She draped the towel modestly around her small, shapely body, even though she was alone in the house, and hurried into the bedroom where she picked up the extension. Her heart had begun to beat slightly faster.

'Hello, Mum. How's things?'

'The same as ever, love.' She sank on to the bed and put her hand over her heart, as if trying to make it slow down. She was bitterly disappointed it was Josh, though she loved her son with all her heart. The trouble was she was always expecting a call from someone else.

'Is it OK if I come home this weekend with this guy, Murdoch? His dad's crazy about old cars and Murd would like to take some photos of the Triumph to send him.'

'Of course it's OK.' She longed to see him. 'Will you be staying overnight?'

'Over two nights, if you don't mind, Mum.'

'This is still your home, Josh,' she told him warmly, 'and you know you can always bring your friends.' She would enjoy buying groceries for them both. 'Is Murdoch his first name or his surname?'

'Dunno,' Josh said vaguely. 'He's a Scot,' he added, as if this explained everything.

Brodie established that Murdoch wasn't a vegetarian or on a strange diet that required special food and that he wasn't averse to wine. Josh asked after his father. She told him about Chestnuts and Diana: 'I'm going over there shortly to see how she is. The workmen are coming today to start on the kitchen.'

Josh said he'd like to have a look at the house that weekend. Until now he had only seen it from the outside.

'How's the latest business?' Brodie enquired. He must have told her what it was, but she couldn't remember. Josh, a budding and so far unsuccessful entrepreneur, was doing his utmost to make his living without actually going to work in a conventional job. He had started numerous small businesses that had so far failed.

'I've been selling books on ebay,' he told her. 'I'm

not doing so badly, but I don't make nearly enough to live on.'

'You will one day.' Brodie tried to sound encouraging. She just wished her son would get an ordinary job like the sons of all the other women she knew.

'Has there been any news of Maisie?' Josh asked finally. Brodie could tell from the tone of his voice that he'd been saving the question until last because he was afraid of the answer, which could only be bad, as his mother would have told him straight away had it been otherwise.

'There's been no news at all,' she said.

Not long afterwards, Josh rang off.

Still wearing the towel, she went into Maisie's room and stood at the window overlooking the back garden. The house in Crosby had just been built when they'd moved in, the garden merely a patch of red earth. Now it was a sea of green, the small trees and bushes ripe and swollen as if they couldn't wait to burst into bloom. The grass looked ready to be cut for the first time this year.

The children's slide and climbing frame had been given away a long time ago, but the swing was still there. Maisie had insisted they keep it. She liked to sit in the dark, swinging gently, musing about life and things in general, she told Brodie whenever she asked. 'I plan my future there,' she said once.

Brodie gasped. She put her fist to her mouth and bit her knuckles. Maisie couldn't possibly have planned what had actually happened. She threw herself face down on the narrow bed with its buttercup yellow cover and began to cry.

My twenty-year-old daughter is a drug addict. I don't

know where she is. I don't know how she gets the money to buy the drugs.

All she could do was imagine the worst.

And Colin was no help. He'd been upset at first, but had quickly given up. 'It's something Maisie has to sort out for herself,' he said, his expression hard and unyielding. 'There's nothing we can do about it.' He flatly refused to discuss the matter further. Maisie and her troubles could no longer reach him.

At first, Brodie had sent her cheques, but they hadn't been cashed when she examined the bank statements. Then she started to send cash. Colin had told her she was mad. 'She'll only spend it on drugs,' he said coldly.

'I'd sooner she got the money from us – from me,' Brodie argued. She dreaded to think in what way her sweet and pretty daughter would get money if it didn't come from her mother.

Just before Christmas, the latest envelope had been returned from Camden marked 'No longer at this address'. There'd been no more news of her daughter since. Brodie had no idea where she had gone. She'd written to the only person in London, a friend of Maisie's, who might have knowledge of her whereabouts, but Colleen knew nothing. Colleen and Maisie had started university at the same time. 'I've been doing my best to stay in touch,' Colleen wrote, 'but she'd disappeared when I last went round to that dump in Willesden . . .' Brodie hadn't known her daughter was living in Willesden – and in a dump!

Josh had searched for months for his sister, without success.

Downstairs, someone entered the house through the

back door. George, her father-in-law, had arrived to work on his son's car. Colin was renovating the Triumph with a passion that had once been reserved for his wife and children. Nothing was too good for it, no expense spared when having new parts made, and virtually all his free time was spent in the garage where the Triumph was kept. His and Brodie's cars were parked in the drive.

Brodie slipped into her own bedroom and quickly got dressed. She creamed and powdered her face, making sure her eyes didn't look puffy. She didn't want George to know that she'd been crying.

'Morning,' he said brusquely when she went into the kitchen. He was pouring water into a mug that contained a teabag. He was approaching seventy, a good-looking man with iron-grey hair, only slightly thinning on top, and a strong, arrogant face. He'd been foreman in a car manufacturing plant over the water in Birkenhead and was reputed to be a terror to work for.

'Morning,' Brodie replied, gritting her teeth. George never knocked, just came in and out as if the house were his. He didn't ask if it was all right to make tea. She was probably being unreasonable, expecting her father-in-law to behave in a way she herself would have behaved in his house. She couldn't stand him.

She wasn't alone. George's wife, Eileen, had left him after more than forty years of marriage when he retired. She couldn't face being under the same roof as him for twenty-four hours a day. George was a bully who always considered himself right and positively refused to lose an argument no matter how ridiculous his position might be. He insisted on accompanying Eileen when she went to the supermarket, completely

taking over, choosing the cheapest meat and vegetables, refusing to buy anything organic, returning
Eileen's favourite washing power to the shelf in favour
of another he knew nothing about, as if he wanted his
wife to know that from now on things would be done
his way.

'He's never washed or cooked anything in his life,'
Eileen said to Brodie, her daughter-in-law, in a
choked voice – they were the best of friends. 'I've
looked after him and four children for all these years,
yet it counts for nothing as far as George is concerned.
Another thing – he refuses to set foot in the supermarket café when the shopping's done. That was
always one of my favourite treats: a coffee and a
cream cake before going home. There were women
there I used to meet regularly when I went on Friday
mornings.'

Last year, unable to stand life with George any
longer, Eileen had gone to live in London with her
widowed sister, Mary. The pair had spent the winter in
Goa where the weather was fine and the cost of living
a fraction of what it was at home.

'Where's the sugar?' George grunted now.

'Where it always is – in that red jar with "sugar" on
the side.' She wouldn't have been so sarcastic had he
bothered to say 'please'.

He put three large spoonfuls in his mug and plonked
himself on a chair by the kitchen table, rather point-
edly, Brodie thought, as if he knew it would annoy
her.

She'd planned to have a drink herself before she left.
Instead she took a pint of milk out of the fridge and
said goodbye to George more politely than he

deserved. Then she went outside, got in her Yaris, and drove to Blundellsands. Had the relationship between herself and Colin not been so dire, they would have laughed together at his awful father. Instead, it only added to the distance between them.

There was a van outside Chestnuts when she arrived, with 'F. Peterson & Sons, Painting, Decorating, Plumbing and General Building Work' on the side. Leonard Gosling, her mother's friend, had recommended them. They'd decorated his flat beautifully, he reported. As Leonard was incredibly fussy, they must be all right.

Some very destructive noises were coming from inside, as if the place was being attacked with a sledgehammer. Brodie winced.

Her mother and Diana were in the garden seated on a bench, both clutching mugs. They waved when they saw her.

'It sounds as if they've started work with a vengeance,' Brodie remarked. 'Are the water and electricity still turned on? I'm dying for a cuppa. I've brought some milk in case there wasn't any left.'

Mum said she'd filled a clean bucket with water so there'd be plenty enough for the day. She had no idea whether the electricity was on or off.

'I'll go and see,' Brodie said.

Diana jumped to her feet and collected the used mugs. 'You sit down: I'll get the tea for you. Here, Brodie, give us that milk.'

'Isn't she lovely?' Brodie sank on to the bench beside her mother. 'I told you she was nice, didn't I?'

'You did indeed. I like her very much.' Megan

endorsed Diana with an approving wave of her hand. 'Oh, and she's a Catholic so we can all go to Mass together. By the way, it seems the mother has married again and lives in Nottingham. She's had another two boys. And her father sounds a good egg – he bought the house off the landlord before he did a bunk, so there's just a small mortgage payment every month.' Her expression changed, became sad. 'I wish your dad and I had had more children. I would have loved a big family, but three of my babies died before I had you, and then didn't your poor dad go and die before we could try again?' She smiled toughly. Her mother was the strongest and most positive person Brodie had ever known. 'But I'm lucky to have you, darlin', and two gorgeous grandchildren as well. Have you heard from them recently?'

'Josh rang this morning. He's coming for the weekend with a friend. You must come round for a meal, Mum. As for Maisie,' Brodie lied, 'she's got a new young man.' She'd kept the news about Maisie away from her mother, not wanting to upset her – or perhaps because she was deeply ashamed. 'She's probably too wrapped up in him to bother with her family just now.'

'Would you like a cup of tea?' Diana asked the Peterson brothers, Russell and Leo. Their dad was tied up in Everton Valley fixing someone's toilet and would be along later, Leo explained. The kitchen units had been torn away, leaving the walls badly pockmarked and looking like they were suffering from a terrible disease. Only the taps and the sink remained.

Shelves had been removed and everything was piled in the middle of the room, as if ready for a bonfire.

'Wouldn't say no,' Russell said. He was a strapping lad of about twenty with straight, jet-black hair and ferociously bushy eyebrows. He wore a sleeveless vest and had barbed wire tattoos on both arms.

Leo was older, slighter and tattooless. His hair was also jet-black, but very curly, and his eyebrows were tidier than his brother's. Diana liked him the best. He smiled shyly, 'I wouldn't say no, either.'

Diana filled the kettle – the water hadn't been turned off and nor had the electricity. While waiting for the kettle to boil, she fetched five mugs and teabags out of the conservatory where the things had been put. She felt like more tea and she felt sure Megan would too.

Russell said, 'The sink'll be the next to go. I've never seen such an old-fashioned one before. That's a real antique, that is.' The sink was white, deep and square, the sort in which a couple of sheets could be left to soak.

'Do either of you take sugar?'

Russell did and Leo didn't.

Ten minutes later, the women were in the garden and the lads must have finished their tea because the banging in the kitchen had begun again. Megan said it reminded her of the Blitz during the war. 'It's like being in an air raid,' she remarked, 'except there's no danger of being killed.'

At midday, Diana let herself into the house in Coral Street. She shouted, 'Hello, it's only me,' just in case Emma was there but, as expected, there was no response. Emma was paying her daily visit to her sister in Walton Vale.

The note Diana had left the day before had gone from behind the clock, but that was only to be expected, too. She looked around to see if she could find it – it would have been kept, surely, so the lads would know her address. Perhaps one of them had kept it, she thought when she couldn't see it anywhere, probably Damian.

She wasn't sure if it was just her imagination, but the house wasn't quite as tidy as Emma usually kept it, as if, with Diana not there, she was already letting things slide. 'But I've hardly been gone twenty-four hours,' she said to herself. Even so, there were dishes in the sink waiting to be washed and the beds hadn't been made when she went upstairs.

In the living room, there was a strange smell and an ashtray on the hearth containing two unnaturally big dog ends. Diana picked one up and sniffed it.

'Grass!' she said aloud. She felt slightly sick. She'd always been dead set against drugs. Her brothers had been lectured to the point of boredom on how they ruined lives. 'If one of you becomes a drug addict,' she'd told them sternly, 'then it's not just you who'll suffer, but the whole family.' She'd always felt quite pleased that, until now at least, they'd listened.

She took the ashtray into the yard and emptied it in the bin, washed the dishes and made the beds. When Emma came home, she'd realize Diana was still around. As for the drugs, Diana didn't know what to do. Grass wasn't as serious as heroin or cocaine. She wasn't about to move back home and sleep in the box room just so she could keep an eye on her brothers.

Anyroad, she was really hurt they hadn't bothered to come and see her. Perhaps they were only too glad to see the back of their bossy older sister.

It was really ghostly, Emma thought when she got back and found the dishes washed and the beds made. It could only have been Diana, but it still felt weird. That morning, she'd taken it easy for a change, ignoring the housework and smoking a few spliffs while watching telly. Damian would have a fit if he knew what she was smoking when she was expecting his kid. The ashtray had been emptied, but Diana was too bloody stupid to know what a spliff was, so there was no chance of her telling Damian when eventually they met again. Di's note was still under the fridge and, as far as Emma was concerned, it could stay there.

Damian O'Sullivan racked his brains as he tried to think of the names of people his sister had worked with at the call centre, but couldn't remember a single one, although the name 'Murphy' rang a bell, a chap who lived in the next street. Bill Murphy, Phil Murphy, something like that.

He looked up Murphy in the telephone directory and found a G. Murphy in Garnet Street. He dialled the number and a man answered. Damian asked if he had worked at the call centre and, if so, had he known Diana O'Sullivan.

The man agreed on both counts. 'I remember Di, nice kid. Everybody liked her. I've got a feeling she lived in Bootle same as me.'

'Do you know where she's working now?'

'Haven't a clue, mate. Maybe she hasn't got another

job yet, like me. But then, I'm fifty-six, not a youngster like Di. Are you one of her brothers? I know she had three. She was always on about them. Dead proud of them she was.'

'No, I'm just a friend.' Damian was too ashamed admit he was a brother who didn't know the whereabouts of the sister who was so proud of him.

'Well, if you find her, tell her Gil Murphy was asking after her.'

'I'll do that. Oh, by the way, Gordon's, the factory outlet shop on the Dock Road, are looking for more staff: they prefer the over-fifties.'

He rang off before the man could thank him. Damian worked in a Job Centre. He would never have had such an important and responsible job had Di not encouraged him to do his homework so that he left school with eight GCSEs and two A-levels.

He *had* to find her.

When Diana got back to Chestnuts, there was no sign of Megan and Brodie, and the kitchen had been gutted. All that remained were a few pipes and cables sticking out of the wall. The units had been thrown in a heap in the front garden along with the sink and the ancient cooker, the sides of which had been hidden from view for an unknowable number of years and were revealed to be filthy and covered in grease. What remained of the marble-patterned linoleum had been torn to shreds.

Inside, Russell and Leo were plastering a wall each while an older man was on a ladder painting the ceiling.

'Oh, it looks lovely,' Diana marvelled.

'Are you having us on, miss?' the man on the ladder enquired. He must be F. Peterson, the boys' father. 'It's not nearly finished.'

'But it looks much better than before.' The room appeared to be twice as big as well as light and airy.

'You're easily pleased. You won't be able to contain yourself once it's finished,' Mr Peterson said drily.

Diana agreed. 'I probably won't.'

'Do you know what colour missus wants the walls painting?'

'No, but if it was me I'd have them mustard with bright red tiles and a rich brown floor.' She could see it in her mind's eye.

'That's an unusual combination.'

'It sounds the gear to me,' Leo put in. He had a smear of plaster on his nose. Russell was wearing headphones and hadn't noticed Diana was there – or at least he'd given no sign.

The water had been turned off, but Mr Peterson promised it would be on again before they left for the day.

Using Megan's bucket of water, Diana made everyone a cup of tea, then retired to the privacy of her room – or what she really hoped would be Brodie's room one day soon. Poor Brodie looked awful unhappy: there must be something really horrible happening at home. Diana knew the feeling.

The Petersons shouted, 'Tara, luv' and 'Goodnight, Diana' when it was time for them to leave, and silence fell upon the big house. Diana turned on the television and began to eat the sarnies Brodie had brought for her. There was a chippy on College Road, not far away. She might go and buy some chips later. But that would mean coming back to a totally quiet house. And anyroad, she might miss her brothers if they came.

Superficially, they got on well, she and Colin. A teacher, he was already at home when Brodie returned after spending the afternoon with her mother helping to tidy the part of the garden that belonged to her flat. He came out of the garage smiling and kissed her on the cheek. Apart from a few grey hairs, recently arrived, he had lost none of his boyish good looks or the toothy grin he'd had when they first met.

'Hello, love. Had a nice day?'

'Yes, thank you.' They were exquisitely polite to each other, but Brodie only had to mention Maisie or criticize his father and the smile would vanish. He would become brusque and rude. 'How was your day?' she enquired.

He made a face. 'Things got a bit rough at dinner-time. A couple of fourteen-year-old lads came to blows over a girl. One had his nose broken and had to go to hospital.'

'How awful,' Brodie said sympathetically. Teaching was tough these days and she could understand his obsession with the Triumph. It took his mind off things. 'There's quiche and salad for tea. It'll be ready in no time.'

He patted his stomach. 'Good, I'm starving. Oh, and don't forget Dad doesn't like salad. Perhaps you could do him some chips.'

'I didn't realize he was staying to tea.'

A tiny furrow appeared on his brow. 'You know darn well he always stays for his tea these days, Brodie.'

Brodie didn't answer. She went into the house and

Colin followed. When they reached the kitchen, he glowered at her from the door. 'Do you have any objection to my father eating with us?'

'I've been looking forward to it all day.' Why oh why couldn't she keep her mouth shut? Lately, she'd been exhibiting a sarcastic streak she hadn't known she possessed.

'He's a lonely old man. If it wasn't for us, he'd go home to an empty house.'

She wanted to say she didn't care, ask why it was only Colin out of the four Logan children who felt the need to take their father under their wing, that he wouldn't be a lonely old man living in an otherwise empty house if he wasn't so thoroughly objectionable that he'd driven his wife away. She would have also liked to know why he had so much patience with his father when he had none at all with his daughter.

But she didn't ask any of these things. She'd asked before and it was a waste of time, making the atmosphere between them even worse. She took the quiche out of the fridge, started to prepare the salad, and switched on the oven for the chips. Wordlessly, Colin went back to the garage. The evening had already got off to a bad start, but then most evenings did. George might even decide to stay and watch television and then he'd sneer at *EastEnders*, a programme that Brodie really liked. She'd end up watching it upstairs.

It got even worse over the meal. For the umpteenth time, George expressed his approval of the war in Iraq, despite another British soldier having been killed that day. 'And as far as that Saddam Hussein is concerned, it's good riddance to bad rubbish.'

He knew perfectly well that his son and his wife

were opposed to the war. They'd actually been on the famous two-million-strong march through London that took place two years before Maisie went to university and during Josh's second year. Eileen had yet to leave George and, despite the desperate problems in the world, life for Brodie and Colin held only the promise of better things to come. They'd had all sorts of plans as to what they would do in the summer holidays after the children had left home; buy a little property in France, perhaps, or travel to Australia to see Lucy, Brodie's best friend from school who'd gone to live there. They'd discussed working in an orphanage in India.

Life had seemed so good then. Why had everything gone so wrong? As she listened to her father-in-law's rants Brodie was unable to answer her own question.

She thought about Chestnuts, trying to imagine how it would look when it had a new kitchen and the ceilings had been painted, the walls sponged, the curtains washed – she'd already taken the curtains out of Diana's room to the laundry. She thought about living in the house with Diana in the next room and other women living upstairs. (She'd decided that she wouldn't take a male tenant and possibly end up with someone like George, determined to run things.)

The idea was vastly appealing. Things couldn't possibly be worse than they were now. She had an idea that Diana had said something similar.

Years ago, Megan had begun to wonder when she closed her eyes at night, if she would open them again next morning. The notion terrified her, yet it would be a peaceful death and she wouldn't have known anything about it. It was a hundred times better than rotting away, her mind gone, in an old people's home with poor Brodie feeling obliged to visit every Sunday. Knowing Brodie, she'd come every day.

Yes, passing away in your sleep was a blessing. There was much to recommend it. It was a shock for relatives, but preferable to watching a loved one die slowly and painfully.

She snuggled under the clothes. The electric blanket was switched on, despite it being almost April, and she was still using the winter duvet. There were some comforts you never stopped enjoying, no matter what age you reached. When she'd lived in Ireland the children had gone to bed in winter equipped with stone hot water bottles. She'd always hated feeling cold in bed.

She'd had a lovely childhood. Even earlier, when they'd lived in Liverpool, life had been good, though she'd made her mother's life a misery moaning about the uncomfortable bed and other things. She, Mam and Brodie had taken turns to sleep at the bottom, and Megan had made a huge fuss, complaining how much she hated it, as if Mam could produce another bed and another room out of thin air for her to sleep in.

Oh, God! She wished she hadn't thought about Brodie, *that* Brodie, her sister. Now, she'd never go to sleep. Megan felt herself cringe with shame at the memory, sixty years old, of the terrible thing she'd done to her sister. She'd been so much in love and couldn't help it – if it were possible to go back in time she wouldn't have changed a thing. Louis had insisted on calling their daughter Brodie. Perhaps he'd felt guilty, too.

The other Brodie, her daughter, didn't know she had an aunt of the same name who could still be alive, as well as two uncles, Tom and Jim. The other Brodie had always thought her mother was, like her, an only child, yet there was a whole army of relatives over in Ireland.

Every now and then Megan would punish herself in little ways for her sin. Now, she got out of bed and looked through the window at the flat, silvery-black expanse of the River Mersey. It looked desolate, with not a ship in sight and no sign of a light. She stood there, shivering in the cold night air, her feet like blocks of ice. When she felt that she'd been punished enough, she got back into bed, conscious of the bones creaking in her legs and shoulders. It was such a treat to get under the warm duvet that she was glad she'd got out in the first place. It hadn't been a punishment after all.

Ten days later the house was almost finished. Brodie was appalled one day to turn up and find the kitchen decorated in the most ghastly colours, the walls mustard with tomato-red tiles that didn't match, though the brown flooring didn't look too bad.

Diana confessed it was all her fault. 'I said I thought those colours would look nice, but I expected Mr Peterson to ask you first before he did anything.'

Brodie said she couldn't be bothered having the work done again. 'I suppose I'll get used to it eventually. I was going to suggest pink and cream.'

'The kitchen in Coral Street is pink and cream,' Diana said tactlessly.

'Lucky old you.' Brodie laughed, but felt just as

tactless when Diana said she might never see that kitchen again. Her brothers hadn't been to see her and she was deeply upset, though her new job in the refugee centre was really interesting. She loved it there and it took her mind off things.

The walls of the four big rooms that were to be let had been sponged down and the satin wallpaper gleamed. The ceilings were now brilliant white. Elsewhere, the hallway had been painted a deep, buttery cream, all the windows had been cleaned and the garden tidied. The front door had been painted the same shade of lilac as before. Brodie had requested only a little of the ivy covering the conservatory be cut off. 'It's pretty and I don't want it spoilt,' she told Diana. 'Mum said Dad was very fond of that ivy. He'd sit and stare at it while smoking his pipe.'

Leonard Gosling, who owned the art shop, had been asked to put the postcard back in his window. If no one noticed it, Brodie said she'd put an advert in the *Liverpool Echo*, although she wasn't in any hurry.

She had made up her mind to move into the room next to Diana's and had yet to convey this news to Colin.

'*What!*' he gasped the night she told him of her decision. 'You mean you're leaving me?' He looked totally astonished, as well he might.

'Not exactly,' Brodie said. 'I'm leaving you *and* your father.'

It was Sunday morning and George had yet to arrive. They were in the living room that she'd always loved. It was long and wide with windows at each end that caught the sun in the morning and evening.

This was where the drama of their lives had been enacted, where the children had played, where Colin had taught them to read, where they'd done their homework. It was on the cherry-coloured settee that she and Colin had sat companionably holding hands while they watched television before Josh and Maisie were born, and later after the children had gone to bed, sometimes falling asleep if the programme wasn't very gripping. Whoever woke up first would make the cocoa.

Now Colin said dismissively, 'Don't be so bloody stupid, Brodie,' as if he didn't believe a word of it.

'Your mother left, didn't she? Doesn't that make you think?' It probably just reminded him there were two stupidly unreasonable women in the world, not one. 'I'll only be living in Blundellsands,' she reminded him gently, suddenly aware that it was possible she *was* being stupidly unreasonable. 'It's not exactly a million miles away. You can come and see me whenever you like, and I'll still be coming back for clothes and stuff. That's if you'll let me in.' It was a funny way of leaving someone. She grinned, but Colin didn't grin back.

'As if I'd shut you out,' he said stiffly. His voice was always stiff, these days – stiff, or cold or hard. 'You belong here, with me. Dad won't be here for ever. Mum might come back one day.'

'I don't think so, Colin. I reckon your mother's left your father for good. And it's not just because of him that I'm going,' she said in a rush. 'I find it upsetting that I can't talk to you about Maisie. Mum doesn't know and I can't very well ring Josh every day to discuss his sister.'

His boyish face twisted in a scowl. 'Maisie made her bed and now she can lie in it.'

'Now who's being bloody stupid?' she cried. If she weren't careful, she'd burst into tears. 'It's our daughter we're talking about, Colin. Our own little girl, the one you cried over the day she was born.'

'That girl is dead,' he said stubbornly. 'She's become someone else and I don't want to know her.'

'And you thinking like that, Colin, is the real reason I'm leaving.'

Chapter 3

Diana was in the basement where Tinker had sent her to sort out bags of clothes handed in for the refugees. She emptied a large John Lewis bag on to the floor and picked up a black satin strapless ballgown with a heavily boned bodice.

'I can't imagine anyone wanting this,' she said to Tinker, who came in at that very moment.

He regarded the garment, green eyes sparkling. He was only an inch or so taller than she was and reminded her of a mischievous imp with his curly red hair and fantastic smile. He grabbed the dress and held it against his skinny body. 'I wouldn't mind that myself. What do you think?' He began to dance around the room still holding the frock and grabbing Diana on the way so she had no alternative but to dance with him.

She burst out laughing. She wasn't sure if Tinker was gay or just pretending. He was too outrageous to be real. 'It suits you,' she managed to gasp.

'Tinker, you're wanted upstairs, son,' Alan shouted. Alan was a volunteer who came to the centre three afternoons a week. He was a retired boxer, old now, with cauliflower ears.

'Coming, sweetie.' Tinker tap-danced out of the room. Alan hated being called sweetie, dear heart, precious, beloved, or any of the other endearments that Tinker bestowed on just about everybody. It confused the refugees no end.

Left alone, Diana folded the black gown and put it in a bag to go to a charity shop. Someone might buy it and alter it – it would look nice with sequin straps. Or it might be of use to a dramatic society.

She had never dreamed that the call centre's move to India would prove to be as lucky as it had for her. The refugee centre was a really gear place to work. Instead of being harangued all day by extremely irritable people about their incorrect, or so they claimed, gas and electricity bills – Diana was inclined to believe them – here there were only real flesh and blood people. Most couldn't speak English, but she was getting quite good at sign language.

Tinker, who lived on the premises, got up early to make breakfast for the twenty or thirty people likely to turn up. Diana, who came at nine o'clock, would start her day in reception with a cup of tea and a bacon butty. Around ten-ish, breakfast over, she would wash the dishes and get things ready for a light lunch, which was served between twelve and two – only simple things like beans, spaghetti rings or eggs on toast, sarnies or baked potatoes, with an assortment of fillings, and cakes for afters. No more meals were served that day, but tea, coffee and light refreshments were available until the centre closed at seven, by which time Diana had gone home.

She looked at her watch and was surprised to find it

was past four o'clock. Here, time just flew by; in her old job it had crawled.

The centre was run by a charity and supported by Liverpool Corporation with a grant. Tinker held fundraising events once a month that were open to the public. On Saturday, Leo Peterson was bringing his pop group, The Little Dead Riding Hoods, to the centre to give a concert; Diana had arranged it. Leo played the drums. He and Diana had been out together five times since he'd worked on Chestnuts. As he was twenty-two and Diana two and a half years older, she felt a bit uneasy and had so far refused to let him kiss her. She knew she was being ridiculous, but it was a bit like going out with one of her brothers, from whom she still hadn't heard despite it being three weeks since she'd left Coral Street. It was very upsetting, but right now life was too interesting for it to get her down. She hadn't been back to the house again as she didn't want to come face to face with Emma, although it was bound to happen one of these days.

She emptied the last bag of clothes, which were terribly creased, and put them on wire hangers on the racks. There were three racks, one each for men, women and children. Later, if she had time, she'd give everything a quick iron. It was bad enough being a refugee and having to wear other people's cast-offs without the things looking as if they'd been rolled up in a ball for the last ten years.

Diana bought most of her own clothes from charity shops, though it was different for her because she didn't *have* to. She only did it because she didn't like modern fashions and thought old clothes were more interesting. Today, she wore a patchwork skirt that had actually been stitched together by hand, and a shiny wrap-around blouse that looked brown from one angle and green from another.

'Have you finished down there yet, luv?' Alan called.

'Nearly.'

'Rosa's just making us a cuppa.'

'I'll be there in a minute.'

Diana put the shoes in pairs under the appropriate racks and went upstairs. The stout, three-storey building had once been a chapel for some obscure religion. Downstairs had been divided into four separate rooms now used as an office-cum-reception — Diana could hear Tinker inside on the telephone — a lounge with a television, a restaurant and a kitchen. The first floor was just one large room where The Little Dead Riding Hoods would play on Saturday night. There was a dartboard up there and a snooker table. It was where the young men tended to collect and Diana could hear the click of the balls right now. A playgroup was held there in the mornings. Tinker's flat was on the top floor.

Everywhere was very rundown and there was a strange sort of smell that she'd been told was woodworm, but the walls were painted bright colours and the effect was cheerful and inviting. Tinker, who was in charge of everything, did a wonderful job trying to make everyone feel at home.

In the lounge, furnished with a variety of armchairs from the relatively modern to the extremely old, the television was on and an elderly woman in a long black gown, a scarf covering her hair, was watching a programme about buying holiday homes in Spain. A young woman, similarly dressed, was chatting to another who wore jeans and a sweatshirt. Two men slept soundly in chairs turned away from the television. They'd been there every day since Diana had started. She suspected they slept rough and Tinker let them in very early in the morning; he wasn't allowed to let anyone stay overnight. The men came from Zimbabwe where they'd been tortured for demonstrating against the president.

None of the women was a refugee. The older one, Mrs Sharma, was an interpreter; Diana found it amazing how many languages some countries had. Sarita and Wendy helped run the playgroup.

Four men wearing what seemed to be a uniform for the young – jeans and black leather jackets – were sitting on the stairs arguing passionately in a language she didn't recognize.

The restaurant was half full. Alan was seated at a table with a big pot of tea and an assortment of cups and saucers that didn't match. Nothing in the room matched. All the tables were different styles and different sizes, and no two dining chairs were the same. Diana thought the room had a higgledy-piggledy sort of charm. The walls were covered with posters of extremely photogenic dogs and cats. Through the hatch, Rosa Rosetti could be seen in the kitchen. She was Alan's partner and came the same afternoons as he did. Some volunteers merely popped in every other day to do the washing; others came for the whole day or even the whole weekend. Diana and Tinker were the only full-time paid employees. The wages were less than she'd earned in the call centre, but she didn't mind.

Alan patted the chair beside him. He had broad shoulders, a mighty chest and a battered face. His fists were as big as footballs. 'Sit down, luv. Take the weight off your feet, like.' His voice was high-pitched and gentle.

'Thanks.' Diana sat in a chair with a wicker seat that had a frayed hole. There was a radio in the kitchen and Gerry Marsden was singing 'You'll Never Walk Alone'.

Rosa poked her head through the hatch. 'Hi, Di.' She was half-Irish and half-Italian. Her grey ponytail was tied with a frilly red ribbon. Once, she'd told Diana, her hair had been coal-black and people had said she looked like Elizabeth Taylor in *Cleopatra*.

'Hi, Rosa. I'll come and wash the dishes when I finish this.'

'Righteo, luv. I've already cleaned the pans. I'll just see if anyone wants their cups refilling, then I'll come and join you.' She circled the room topping up tea and coffee cups, then came and sat down next to Alan. 'Phew!' She fanned herself with her hand. 'It's been a busy day, but I've enjoyed it. Did you see that young woman with the little boy, Di? Lovely little chap he was, just gone twelve months old. I think they're from Romania.'

Diana confessed she hadn't seen the woman because she'd been in basement for quite a while.

'Her hubby's gone to Norfolk to work on a farm and her bloody landlord only tries to get in her room every night.' She snorted with outrage. 'There's no lock and she has to jam a chair underneath the handle to keep the bugger out. Tinker's going round later to put a bolt on and give the landlord a piece of his mind at the same time; tell him if he doesn't behave himself, he'll call the coppers.'

'Quite right, too,' Diana said indignantly.

'I'd be willing to give him a good going-over,' Alan offered.

Rosa patted his hand. 'I know you would, Al, but you might end up killing the bugger.'

After Diana had finished the dishes, she went into the office and Tinker gave her another lesson on how to use the computer. She was really sorry now that she'd never learned to use the one at home properly.

She sat in front of the monitor and Tinker put his arm along the back of the chair. She could feel his warm breath on her neck. He showed her how to write and send emails – he could type like the wind with two fingers – and how to search the Internet using Google. 'All you have to do is ask a question,' he explained. 'Say if we get someone from Ethiopia, it helps to know a bit about the place, like if there's a war going on, what the political situation is. Me, I'm pretty wired up about most places, but how much do you know about the world outside the British Isles, Di?'

'Not much,' Diana confessed. She'd always been too busy to read the papers, and the lads wouldn't have dreamed of watching the news on telly. But now she could read and watch whatever she liked. She wanted to impress Tinker, with whom she suspected she was a little bit in love, gay or not.

There was a small, purple car parked in the drive when Diana arrived home, and a woman climbed out as she approached. She was extremely overweight and wore a loose black top, black trousers and gold sandals. Her hair was long, blonde and very beautiful. It fell in curls and ringlets halfway down her back. On anyone else the hair would have looked striking, but it only made this woman appear freakish.

'Hello,' Diana smiled.

The woman scowled. 'Brodie Logan told me to come. She said she'd be along later. If you're Diana, you're to show me the upstairs rooms.'

'Of course, luv.' Diana unlocked the front door. The house still smelled of fresh paint. The hall with its black-and-white tiled floor and cream walls looked extremely smart. She felt quite proud of it. 'I'm Diana O'Sullivan,' she said.

'Vanessa Dear,' the woman almost snarled.

'What a lovely name. Would you like a hand upstairs?'

She looked considerably put out. 'I can climb stairs by myself, thanks all the same.'

'I didn't know Brodie had put an advert in the *Echo*,' Diana said chattily. 'She's been meaning to do it for ages.'

Vanessa was making hard work of the stairs. They were only halfway up and she was breathless. Diana slowed down in sympathy.

'It was in last night's paper. I telephoned straight away and she promised to keep a room until I could see it. Apparently there's two. She sounds nice, Mrs Logan,' she said grudgingly.

'Oh, Brodie's lovely,' Diana enthused. 'And Megan's lovely, too. Megan's her mam. My Mam lives in Nottingham and I haven't seen her for ages.'

'Really?' Diana couldn't tell from the tone if Vanessa was bored, being sarcastic, or just plain fed up.

Three days later, Vanessa had more or less settled in her upstairs room. She'd taken the first one she'd gone into, not bothering to look at the other. Something had to be done, she'd decided a couple of weeks ago when she'd got up one morning, stood on the scales, and realized that if her weight increased at its current rate then by this time next week she would be eighteen stone.

It was no good going on another diet. Anyway, she reckoned she must have tried virtually every single one. She'd gone without fat, without carbohydrates, eaten nothing but pineapple, drunk nothing but low calorie milkshakes, tried to exist on a thousand calories a day, considered having her teeth wired together or her stomach stapled, exercised, had hypnotherapy, done yoga, listened to CDs urging her not to eat, and watched DVDs telling her the same.

Nothing worked. While Vanessa did all of these things – some at the same time – she only put on more weight, no doubt due to the tasty little morsels she indulged in between the items on the diet. She'd even joined a group of women determined to celebrate the fact that they were overweight. But that didn't work, either, at least not for Vanessa. She admired them, but didn't share their sentiments.

Twelve months ago, she'd been ten and a half stone and size fourteen. She'd never exactly been sylph-like, but she had no complaints with how she looked. Then *it* had happened, making her so unhappy she'd just let rip, eating everything in sight.

At first, it had made her feel better. Food was compensation for the thing she'd lost. She hadn't taken much notice when her skirts became too tight and she couldn't get her trousers on any more. She'd just moved up a size, then another, until, all of a sudden, she was size twenty. It was then she went on the first diet, during which time she put on a further stone and ended up size twenty-two. She'd put on more weight since and had probably gone up another size.

Her gloomy chain of thought was interrupted by the sound of laughter outside. She went over to the window. It was a pleasant April evening and three women were in the garden seated underneath a tree; Diana, who'd let her in the other day; Brodie Logan, who owned the house, and Megan, Brodie's mother, whom Vanessa hadn't yet spoken to. She could hear music, that 1920s or 1930s sort that she didn't like. A man with a very sad voice was singing, 'Every time it rains, it rains pennies from heaven.' It was terribly depressing.

Megan reminded Vanessa of her grandmother on her father's side. She had two grandmothers and when *it* had happened, they'd vied with each other to be the most scathing.

'That bloody William. I never trusted him as far as I could throw him,' Granny Dear said at the wedding – at the *non*-wedding. Her hat looked as if it could receive Sky television.

'He had a sly face,' Granny Harper said grimly.

'And a mean one.'

'The bugger needs castrating, that's what I say.'

It was her sister, Amanda, who was the first to put Vanessa's dread into words. 'It looks as if William isn't

80

going to turn up, luv.' She'd spoken hesitantly after they'd been waiting at the church for a good twenty minutes, as if she didn't quite believe what she was saying. They were words that she'd never expected to say in her lifetime, particularly to her own sister at her wedding.

By then, guests had started to arrive at the church for the wedding after Vanessa's. She and her sisters were in the porch. Vanessa wished she'd remained in the car, but it was a bit late for that; the car had gone. How on earth was she supposed to know that William wasn't coming to his own wedding? There was no sign of the best man, Wayne Gibbs, but that wasn't surprising, seeing as he and William were supposed to come together.

She hadn't known whether to scream or burst into tears. Most of all, she would have liked to faint and leave her parents and sisters to cope with what was left of the day while she came to a week later to find all the presents had been given back and the fact that Vanessa Dear had been jilted at the altar was no longer a hot topic of conversation in any part of Liverpool, or at Siren Radio where she worked.

But she didn't faint. She didn't scream or burst into tears, either. It would have been undignified. She was hurt, deeply hurt, more hurt than she'd imagined being in her entire life, but she kept her head held high, determined to retain her self-respect when people started coming to the back of the church to see what was wrong. William's mother was absolutely distraught and his father was so angry he could hardly speak. The guests for the next wedding stood outside and regarded the rejected bride with a mixture of curiosity and pity. She looked so beautiful in her simple white outfit, the white roses nestling in her natural blonde hair.

The reception had been held – or at least the food had been eaten. As Mrs Dear said at the time, 'It would be a shame to waste it.' The jazz quartet who'd been hired to play later were paid and told to go home. Vanessa had no idea what happened to the wedding cake. She'd returned home with her sisters, Amanda and Sonia.

At thirty-one, Vanessa was the eldest and the only sister who wasn't married and didn't have children. She had never actually considered herself a feminist, more that she was any man's equal. She would get married when it suited her, have children at her convenience, then go back to work and continue with her career while some other woman looked after them.

But on what should have been the day of her wedding to William James Lunt, Vanessa's confidence turned to dust. She felt old, unattractive, as undesirable as hell. Would she ever hold up her head again? Was she destined to become an old maid? Never have children? Did she care? Could she bring herself to go back to work in two weeks' time after what should have been her and William's honeymoon in the Canaries? (Most of the staff at Siren Radio had been invited to the wedding and had actually witnessed her ordeal.)

Come to that, what was she to do with herself over the next fortnight? Stay at home with her mum and dad? She'd sooner have died than go back to the flat in Hunts Cross that she and William had been buying for the last three years. What if they came face to face?

Fortunately, it was she who had booked the holiday

in the Canaries and had the tickets. She managed to persuade her parents to use them. Just as Vanessa had wanted to faint until the fuss had died down, or at least partially died down, her mother was anxious to avoid, for a little while at least, the disgrace of having one of her daughters so publicly humiliated.

'It would have to be you with your posh job and everything,' she complained bitterly. 'I've been blowing your trumpet so loud for so long that people are sick to death of hearing about you. There's some folk out there who are probably rubbing their hands with glee.'

So her parents went on Vanessa and William's honeymoon while she remained at home. She slept in her old room and ate and ate and ate. She'd always had a healthy appetite, but now it went into overdrive.

There was a knock on the door of her new room and she opened it to Megan, who was as thin as a lath with not a spare ounce of flesh on her. Nowadays, it was people's sizes that she noticed first, not their faces or their clothes.

'Hello, darlin'. Would you like to come and sit with us in the garden? We're only having a cup of tea and a gossip, but we forgot you were upstairs on your own.'

'Actually, I thought I'd go to bed early.' She didn't feel the least bit sociable and had always thought gossiping a waste of time. Where did it get you? People, apart from her immediate family, didn't much interest her. 'And I've still got some unpacking to do.'

'All right then, darlin',' Megan said warmly. 'But if you ever feel like a natter, don't hesitate to come down. Afterwards, we're going to watch a DVD in Diana's room – *Grand Hotel* with Greta Garbo and

John Barrymore.' She chuckled. 'I was only six when it came out. I'll tell her to keep the sound down in case it keeps you awake.'

'I'm sure it won't.' The memory of her failed wedding day still kept her awake most nights anyway.

Megan wished her goodnight and Vanessa closed the door. Then her mobile rang. It was Amanda.

'How are you getting on, sis?' she asked. She sounded worried.

'All right. It's very nice here. The room's lovely.' Much better than Vanessa had expected. She'd imagined house shares to be rather sordid, makeshift places, but her room was gracious and beautifully decorated. 'The bed's really comfortable and there's a brand-new kitchen downstairs,' she said. 'The garden's what estate agents call "mature".'

'You haven't given me your address – and Mum said she hasn't got it, either.'

'I'm not going to, Mandy. I don't want anyone to know where I am.'

'Oh, but, sis!' Amanda wailed.

'I'll be back in touch about this time next year.' By then, she anticipated having reduced her weight to what it used to be.

'Next *year*?'

'I'm going to switch off my mobile for good when I finish this call.' Vanessa felt ruthless and powerful. 'I've got to do this, Mandy,' she went on in a softer voice. 'I need to.'

Amanda sighed. 'I think I understand. I can't even begin to imagine what you've been going through. But, sis,' she said, as if she'd just remembered something, 'we can always get in touch with you at work.'

'I've left,' Vanessa said bluntly. 'I gave my notice in last week.' It should have been a month's notice, but she didn't care – and neither did Siren's manager, Richard Freeman. Vanessa hadn't been the most agreeable of employees over the last year. He was probably pleased to see the back of her.

'But you worked so hard in that job!'

'I know.' Vanessa hadn't told her family that she'd been moved sideways months ago. She'd been hell to work for and the people underneath her had complained. Richard had transferred her to overseas accounts where there was just enough work for one person, but not enough to keep her as busy as she'd been before. She and Richard were old friends and she reckoned if it had been anyone else he would have sacked them.

'Are you going to get another job?' Amanda asked.

'You mean go for interviews looking like I do?' Vanessa snorted. 'No chance.'

'But will you have enough to live on?'

'I've plenty in the bank and William sent back the money I'd paid on the mortgage for the flat.' She'd earned far more than her father and her sisters' husbands. And William.

Amanda groaned. 'But what will you *do* with yourself all day, Vanessa?'

'Exercise and diet.' And try not to think about William – and food.

'Oh, God, sis!' Amanda said, distraught. 'Does it mean when this call is over we'll not speak to each other again for a whole year?'

'I'm afraid it does. Bye, Mandy.' Vanessa turned the mobile off and the screen went blank. It seemed the best way to finish the conversation, not continue while Amanda – and Vanessa – became more and more upset.

She'd had Special K for breakfast, cottage cheese, a tomato and a cream cracker for lunch, and sardines on a wafer-thin piece of toast for tea. She felt very pleased with herself, but after finishing the telephone conversation with her sister, hunger came upon her like a curse and she could have eaten the furniture.

For a good half-hour, she paced the floor, but it only made the hunger worse. She gnawed her knuckles, but it didn't help. In the end, she went out and toured the streets in the car looking for a takeaway, a chip shop, a pizza parlour, anywhere that would sell her something to eat.

In the end, she bought a medium-sized Hawaii pizza and ate it in the car, pushing huge chunks into her mouth, not even chewing it properly. When she had finished, she wiped her hands and started up the engine. Eating had been bliss, but now she felt totally dispirited, like a sack stuffed with sawdust, hating herself for giving in.

Oh, well. At least she'd bought a medium pizza, not a large one.

The thought didn't help much.

In the middle of the night, she woke with indigestion and imagined doughy lumps of pizza lodged in various parts of her body. She burped loudly. It hurt.

The house was completely silent, but outside she could hear the trees rustle in a slight wind. A strip of moonlight showed between the curtains, which she hadn't closed properly.

She sat up, lodged a pillow behind her back, and burped again. Oh, God! She felt so miserable. Achingly, wholeheartedly miserable. How could William, who she had genuinely loved, who she had thought loved her in return, have done this to her? She recalled, word for word, the letter he had sent. It had arrived on the Tuesday after the 'wedding' when she was in the house on her own.

Vanessa,

As you can imagine, I feel terrible about this. [Not nearly as terrible as *I* do, Vanessa had thought when she'd read the letter for the first time.] *On Saturday morning, I felt a strange reluctance to leave for church.* [Oh, really!]

The truth is that you make all the decisions about how our lives are run and I'm not prepared to put up with it any longer. It was you decided when we should buy the flat and when it would be time to buy a house – and where the flat and the house would be. You informed me when you planned to have children and that it was your intention to leave them with a childminder when you do.

I have not been consulted on any these matters. For me, the most important is the last one. <u>I am sorry, but I do not want our children left with strangers</u>. As you earn more than I do, something I am not allowed to forget, then I would be happy to leave work and look after them. However, I can't bring myself to suggest this. You would call me a wimp – you have done before.

On Saturday, it was right after I phoned you — I couldn't find my cufflinks, remember? — that I decided I would sooner not marry a woman who thinks so little of me, who, in fact, regards me with contempt.

I don't quite know how to finish this letter except to say how sorry I am and to wish you luck in the future. I shall arrange for all you have paid into the mortgage to be transferred to your account.

With regards,
William.

'Bastard!' Vanessa whispered hoarsely. 'You *are* a wimp. You're the biggest wimp in the world.' She wondered if he knew how much weight she'd put on. He worked in Manchester and they hadn't had any mutual friends, but Wayne, his best man, had once dated Fiona, Siren's receptionist. That's how she'd met William, when Wayne and Fiona had thrown a party. They no longer dated, but if they still saw each other then William would know his ex-fiancée was almost twice as big as she used to be.

Another three days passed and Vanessa found herself dreaming endlessly about food; soft, crumbly chocolate cake thick with fresh cream, cartons of ginger ice-cream; prawns in curry sauce with rice and sweet chutney; egg and chips sprinkled with vinegar; roast beef and potatoes with crispy Yorkshire pudding; lamb chops and mint sauce; boxes of chocolates, sausage and mash; fresh croissants heaped with butter and strawberry jam; hot dogs with mustard . . . In her sleep, Vanessa would consume entire banquets and not put on an ounce of weight.

These imaginary meals were pleasant, but she needed the food in her stomach, not in her dreams. With not a shred of willpower left, Vanessa would drive somewhere late at night and gorge on fish and chips or pizza.

She felt at the end of her tether. What sort of life was this? She hardly felt like living any more.

Colin was sulking. She was daft, Brodie thought, walking out on her husband then going back to see him two or three times a week. It was a ridiculous situation and she didn't blame Colin for sulking. The poor man didn't know where he was.

She only went in the evenings when George wouldn't be there, first looking to see what was on television to make sure it wasn't a football match, or one of those films in which hordes of people spent two hours massacring each other, which he could well have stayed to watch with his darling son.

When she turned up on Sunday Colin was watching a DVD of Peter Sellers in one of the Pink Panther films and didn't turn the sound down when she went in. 'There's some letters for you,' he snapped.

'Are they real letters or junk mail?' she enquired.

'Don't know, didn't look. You know,' he said nastily, 'you can fill in a form and the Post Office will redirect your post to wherever you happen to be living now.'

'I know.' She thought about the words for a while, feeling desperately sad. Eventually, she said, 'Why has everything turned so sour, Colin? We used to get on really well.'

'Things change, people change, life changes,' he muttered, staring at the screen. 'Nothing lasts for ever.'

'Things haven't changed so much that we have to hate each other.'

'I don't hate you.' He switched the television off and turned to face her. He looked haggard and so unhappy that she wanted to take him in her arms and assure him everything was all right. Except it wasn't. It wasn't even faintly all right. His father was merely a fly in the ointment. It was his attitude to their daughter that Brodie despised, so much so that she couldn't bear to live with him under the same roof. It was strange, but that was what his mother had said about his father, yet the two men were totally different. He sighed. 'Of course I don't hate you, Brodie.'

'I don't hate you, either.' She sat in her old armchair on the right in front of the fireplace. He had the gas fire turned on low. The fire, the kerb and everything else in the room was covered with dust. She didn't want to clean up in front of him, as if she was trying to make some sort of point, but if she came when he was at school, then George would be here. She'd like to bet Colin wasn't washing his shirts and would soon run out of socks even if he had about fifty pairs – it never crossed Josh's mind that his father wouldn't want anything other than socks at Christmas or on birthdays. The collar on his shirt didn't look too clean. It struck her that he must be feeling extraordinarily low to wear a grubby shirt when he was usually so particular about his appearance.

They sat in silence for quite some time, but not the comfortable, laid-back silence they'd once enjoyed. Brodie was trying to think of things to say, and perhaps Colin was doing the same. Or maybe he was wishing she'd go away so he could continue watching the film.

'Do you mind if I take the computer?' she asked. He'd never learned to use it, relying on her to type his notes and look up things on Google. 'I've had broadband installed at Chestnuts. You can always let me know if you want work done. You can bring it round and look at the house, see what it's like now.'

'Take whatever you like.'

'OK.' She nodded sadly.

'What are you living on?' he asked after another long silence. There was something unpleasant about it – not the question, but the sharp way in which he asked it.

'What do you mean?'

'I mean money. How do you support yourself?'

'With money from our joint account, of course,' Brodie explained. 'The tenants each pay two hundred pounds a month rent and I'm expecting a third tenant tomorrow, the last one, but there won't be much over, if anything, once I've paid the bills. The council tax is horrendous on a big house like that, and water, gas and electricity are going up all the time. Now spring's here, the garden's getting very overgrown again and I'll have to get someone in to tidy it.' Until recently, the rent from Chestnuts had gone into the joint account. Now, though, Brodie wasn't contributing a single penny.

'A very large amount has recently been taken out of our joint account, which I assume is what you paid to have the house done up. Do you think it fair,' Colin went on in the same sharp voice, 'that, under the circumstances, I should continue to support you?'

'The circum . . . oh, you mean because I've left you?' Brodie felt herself go cold. Had it really come to this?

'Exactly. You are only a young woman, Brodie, you could easily get a job.' Halfway through the sentence, he wavered a little, as if he was finding it hard to stick to his guns.

'I wanted to get a job when Maisie went to university, but you talked me out of it.' Brodie got to her feet. 'I'll start looking for one tomorrow. You must change the account so that it's in your name only and I'll start one of my own.'

'I didn't mean straight away.' Now he looked regretful, ashamed. Perhaps he hadn't expected her to agree quite so quickly, thought she'd put up some sort of argument. But what was there to argue about?

'I'd better go,' she said with a sigh. 'Where are the letters?'

'In the letter rack on the sideboard.'

They'd bought the wire letter rack on holiday in Greece. They'd hardly been married a year and Brodie hadn't known she was expecting Josh. It held four letters. Two were from charities, and one was from the Labour Party pleading with her to rejoin. 'Did you get one of these?' she asked Colin. He nodded. They'd both resigned from the party after the night they'd watched Baghdad being bombed. It had seemed a strange way of turning Iraq into a democracy.

The fourth letter had a London postmark and her name and address were neatly written with a purple felt-tip pen. She had a premonition it was to do with Maisie. She tore the envelope open. The letter inside was quite short.

Dear Mrs Logan,

I was on the bus on my way to uni the other day and it went down Dodge Street off Holloway Road. There was a traffic hold-up, as usual. I was just looking out the window, when a girl who was the image of your Maisie came out of one of the houses. I took a photo on my mobile and had this picture made. I would have got off the bus and spoken to her, but I was already late.

I hope you are well.

Colleen Short

Colleen, Maisie's friend. Brodie looked in the envelope. She saw the photograph but could hardly bear to touch it. Somewhat gingerly, she took hold of it between her finger and thumb and pulled it out.

'Oh, God!' she groaned.

It wasn't a very good photo, but it was clear enough to see that her beautiful daughter had been reduced to skin and bone, that her eyes had sunk so deeply into the sockets they looked barely human. Oh, and she looked so tired, so weary, as she left the house, her hand on the doorknob to pull it shut. Brodie could just about make out the number three on the door.

Number three Dodge Street, off Holloway Road. She'd go tomorrow.

'What's the matter?' Colin asked tetchily.

'Nothing,' she said abruptly. She wasn't prepared to tell him about the letter, listen to his criticisms. Maisie may well have brought this on herself, but she was their daughter. So far, Brodie's attempts to rescue her had failed, but she was determined to try again.

★

Vanessa was enjoying her early-morning walk on the deserted beach. It gave her a sense of well-being to breathe in the fresh salty air and take long strides on the wet sand – she could feel the moistness through her canvas shoes. A cool breeze penetrated her grey stretchy trousers and matching sweatshirt. She'd only brought two outfits with her to Chestnuts; a black cotton top and trousers; and what she was wearing now, which looked like a babygro and was about as unflattering as a garment could be.

The waters of Liverpool Bay were calm. Overhead, gulls swooped as if they could see a multitude of fish floating on the placid surface. They squawked, possibly in frustration, when they found nothing but bits of seaweed and the flotsam and jetsam of today's world.

She was walking too fast and was beginning to flag. She turned round and retraced her steps. By the time she arrived at Chestnuts she was panting for breath and her sense of well-being had faded, but she was glad she'd gone. It was bound to have done her good, though being overweight put a strain on the heart. She knew that without having to see a doctor. She was dying for her breakfast; half a grapefruit sprinkled with pretend sugar, a Ryvita smeared with low-calorie butter and tea with skimmed milk.

She'd been carrying her shoulder bag across her chest like a soldier and fished inside for her keys; the front door key and her car keys were on the same ring. After a few minutes of fishing, she realized she had forgotten them. In fact, she could see them in her mind's eye on the table where she'd thrown them last night when she'd brought home a double serving of curried prawns and rice.

Vanessa rang the doorbell, which made an old-fashioned buzzing sound. Diana would probably have left for work by now, but Brodie would still be around. But although she rang the bell several more times, the door remained stubbornly closed.

She peered through the letterbox, though it was a silly thing to do. If there was no one in to answer the door, who or what did she expect to see?

What was she supposed to do now? Stand on the doorstep until somebody appeared? Diana wouldn't be home for ages and Brodie could have gone to see her mother and mightn't be home for ages, either.

To her relief, she remembered that Brodie had given her her mobile number and the one for the telephone in the hall. 'You never know, you might need them one of these days,' she'd said.

Vanessa's mobile was in her bag. It had been switched off since her conversation with her sister. She switched it on and found fourteen messages waiting to be read. She ignored them and dialled Brodie's mobile.

It was answered straight away. 'Hello, sorry about the background noise, but I'm on a train,' Brodie said.

Vanessa came straight to the point and explained that she'd locked herself out. 'Will you be long?'

'I'm on my way to London and I won't be home until very late. I might even stay overnight. It depends how things go.' Brodie's voice was very faint. A much louder male voice was announcing that drinks and sandwiches were available in the restaurant car. 'Oh, dear, you can't ask Mum, either, she's gone to North Wales with her friend Gwen.'

'What about Diana? Do you know where she works?'

'Only that it's a refugee centre somewhere in town. Oh, I know. Leonard Gosling has a key. Do you know the artists' materials shop in Crosby Road?'

'No, but I'll find it.' Vanessa was getting impatient even though Brodie was doing her best to help. It wasn't *her* fault that her tenant had left her key on the table upstairs.

'I can't remember the number of the shop, but it's by a school. It doesn't take more than five minutes to get there in a car. Leonard is a friend of my mother's. Tell him that I sent you. He loves helping damsels in distress.' The phone went dead; the train must have gone into a tunnel.

Vanessa set off. The keys to her car were upstairs with the key to the front door, so she'd have to walk. As she came from the south side of Liverpool and this was the north, she had no idea where Crosby Road was and would just have to ask people. Her feet were freezing in the wet shoes. She was dying for a cup of tea. If William James Lunt could have heard the names his ex-fiancée called him as she trudged towards what she hoped was Crosby Road, his ears would have burned right through his head.

Chapter 4

'Oh, my dear young lady. Oh, dear, oh, dear.'

Having collapsed in a chair behind the counter, Vanessa was being vigorously fanned by Leonard Gosling, who was using a large artist's pad. She'd arrived at his shop exhausted, thoroughly out of sorts and, she suspected, just a little bit smelly. She could feel her hair hanging around her shoulders in damp clumps. She wished she were wearing virtually any other garment on earth rather than the stretchy grey babygro.

'How do you feel now?' Leonard enquired solicitously. He was a small, dapper gentleman of around seventy with a full head of wavy brown hair and a pink complexion. She suspected the hair was dyed. He wore pale grey trousers and a lilac shirt with a darker lilac tie. His voice was like that of an actor, loud and very grand without a trace of Liverpool accent.

'Much better,' Vanessa gasped. 'I've nearly got my breath back.'

'Good, good.' He stopped fanning, slightly out of breath himself. 'It's a long way to walk from Elm Road.'

'I walked for miles. I kept turning the wrong way and having to walk back.' Her brain mustn't have been working properly; when she asked people the way their directions didn't make sense. It crossed her mind, much too late, that she could have phoned for a taxi. It was as if some malevolent being had cast a spell on her and she was destined never to be happy again.

'Would you like a glass of water?'

'Please.' Unusually for her, she was enjoying being fussed over.

He went into the back of the shop and returned with a glass of water containing a slice of lemon. 'What did you say your name was?'

'Vanessa Dear.'

'I'm Leonard Gosling,' he said rather shyly, 'but I suppose Megan told you.'

'It was Brodie, actually. I'd locked myself out and she said you'd have a key. Brodie was on a train and Megan's gone to North Wales with a friend.'

'That's right, I'd forgotten. You must call me Leonard and I'll call you Vanessa. Is that all right?'

'Fine.' It was the sort of conversation, going no-where, that normally Vanessa found intensely irritating, but just now didn't mind. In fact, it was quite soothing. No one was trying to get one over on her and she didn't have to appear clever or business-like or even think very hard. 'This is an interesting shop,' she remarked. It was double-fronted, but quite narrow, no more than about four metres wide. On one wall was a large area of pigeonholes containing tubes of paint, pencils, crayons, brushes and artists' pads from the very small to the very large. Other shelves were full of books – how to paint, how to draw, how to do all sorts of crafts – as well as books on famous artists such as Van Gogh, Picasso, Degas, Monet. A full-sized easel stood just inside the door holding a painting that Vanessa could only see the back of. There was a stack of frames in one corner and a stack of canvases in another.

She'd been good at art at school. Since leaving, she'd often had a vague urge to take up painting, but there never seemed to be the time. Well, now she had all the time in the world. Before she left, she'd buy a couple of canvasses and some oil paints, although the one thing she wouldn't do was a self-portrait.

Leonard beamed. 'It *is* interesting, isn't it? I've been running it for nearly ten years – the lease comes up for renewal soon. I don't exactly make a fortune, but I love it.'

'What did you do before?'

He beamed even more. 'I was an actor. I appeared on television quite a few times. I was in *Z Cars* and *Maigret* – I was only a young whippersnapper in those days – and some lesser-known programmes, but I always preferred the stage. When my wife died, I decided to retire and make a permanent home for myself in the city where I was born. I live in the flat upstairs.'

'I'm so sorry – about your wife, that is,' Vanessa said sincerely. 'Whereabouts in Liverpool do you come from?'

'Knotty Ash.' He smiled. 'Where the Diddy Men live.'

If Vanessa didn't have a hot drink soon, she'd collapse. She said, 'Look, I don't like to take up any more of your time. If you could let me have the key to Chestnuts, then I'll go home.'

'My dear,' he said with old-fashioned gallantry, 'as if I minded my time being taken up by such a charming young lady. Have you had breakfast?'

'No.' Her heart began to beat a trifle quicker. Perhaps he had a stove in the back and would offer to rustle up a cup of tea or coffee.

'Then shall we go across the road to that delightful pâtisserie and partake of *petit déjeuner*? They do a delicious hot chocolate heaped with fresh cream, and their croissants . . .' He kissed his fingers and threw the kiss into the air. Vanessa knew exactly what he meant.

'Why not?' It wasn't usually until evening that her diet went for a burton. Today, she must make sure it didn't go for a burton twice. 'What happens if someone comes to the shop?'

'We can sit in the window and I can keep an eye on things. I rarely have customers this early.' He held out his arm. 'Come along, my dear, let's party.'

Brodie walked past number three Dodge Street, eyeing it keenly, trying to see through the windows, which were badly in need of a good polish. It was a dingy terraced house, three storeys high, with a tiny garden containing half a plastic bucket, a collection of empty crisp packets, and hundreds of cigarette butts. It looked as if people regularly emptied their ashtrays there.

It was only a short street with eight identical houses on either side, pubs on two of the corners, and a boarded-up shop and a launderette on the others. Most of the houses were badly rundown and had been turned into flats with numbered buzzers on the walls outside.

Brodie walked up and down the street a few times

before plucking up the courage to approach number three. It had a bell, but she couldn't hear anything when she pressed it, so she used the knocker as well.

She had a strong feeling no one would answer, so was surprised when the door was suddenly opened by a tall black man wearing the bottom half of a scarlet tracksuit and nothing else. 'What you want, man?' he growled. 'I see you walking past and past. Are you the pigs?'

'I'm looking for Maisie Logan, my daughter. I was told she lived here.'

'Then you was told wrong, lady. No Maisie live here. No woman live here, all men.'

'But she's been here,' Brodie argued. She reached into her bag. 'See, I have a photo of her coming out of this very house.'

The man scowled. 'No Maisie here, no woman. Go 'way, lady.' The door was slammed in her face.

Brodie stepped back into the street. She was disappointed, but not all that much. She hadn't really expected Maisie to be there, but there'd always been the chance. It would have gone against the grain not to have followed up on Colleen's letter. Did Maisie live in this area? she wondered. Or had she come to the house on the underground, by bus or even in a car? And what had she been doing there?

She was walking back the way she'd come with the intention of catching the tube to Euston and going home. Josh had gone to Brighton 'on business', so they couldn't meet – anyroad, she had always refused to visit him in his squat. Had the circumstances been different, she would have gone to the West End for lunch, then to the big Marks & Spencer by Marble

Arch to do some shopping. But shopping was out – lunch, too – now that she had to watch the pennies until she got a job. What sort of job? Where? Brodie had no idea.

'Excuse me?'

Brodie broke out of her thoughts. A young woman in a plain black suit, white blouse and sensible shoes had stopped in front of her and was holding up a badge.

'WPC Karen Grant,' the woman announced. 'Can I have a word with you?'

'What about?' Brodie had never committed anything vaguely resembling a crime in her life, but immediately felt guilty.

'I would like to know why you just knocked on number three?' Karen Grant looked almost half Brodie's age, but Brodie envied her air of authority.

'Why?' Her voice wobbled. 'Because I thought someone I know might live there.'

'Can I please have the name of that person?'

Brodie thought before saying abruptly, 'No. No, you can't have her name. Why do you want it, anyroad? What's it got to do with you?' She felt pretty close to tears.

Karen Grant must have noticed. She was rather a nice young woman with pale curly hair and not a trace of make-up on her pleasant, very determined face. She put a firm hand on Brodie's arm. 'Look, there's a café around the corner. I really would like to talk to you. The person you're looking for won't get into trouble. I promise.'

'Oh, all right.' She supposed she had no choice but to talk to a policewoman.

'Am I allowed to know your name?'

'Brodie Logan,' she replied, a touch sullenly.

The café smelt of fried food and made her feel hungry; she'd had nothing to eat so far that day. It was a featureless place with a chalked menu on a blackboard in the window and an old man serving behind the counter. Not a single thing had been done to make it look attractive. The walls were bare and faintly dirty, and the customers, mainly elderly, sat at plain wooden tables, chewing mindlessly, looking lost. No one spoke to each other. The meals came with mountains of chips.

Brodie sat down while Karen Grant went straight to the counter. She returned with a pot of tea and a plate of cheese sandwiches.

'I'm afraid, being lunchtime, there's a minimum charge, so I bought us these. Would you like sauce or pickle?'

'No, thank you.' Lunchtime? Brodie looked at her watch. It was just going on for one o'clock. She'd thought it much earlier. 'Shall I pour the tea?'

'Please,' Karen picked up a sandwich. 'Do you know what number three Dodge Street is?' she asked.

'Only that it's a house.' Brodie shrugged.

'It's a crack house. It's where drug addicts go to buy crack cocaine. I'm from the drugs squad, by the way.'

The teapot nearly fell from Brodie's hand. She quickly put it back on the table, wanting to be sick. Her beautiful, laughing, clever daughter had been to a crack house. How many times? How much did the drugs cost? Where did she get the money from?

'Who is it that you thought might live there?' Karen asked.

'My daughter,' Brodie whispered. 'Maisie. She's only twenty. She was at university in London and then – oh, I don't know what went wrong. She stopped coming to see us, stopped phoning.' A university counsellor had telephoned to ask if Maisie was at home. When an astounded Colin had denied this, he was informed his daughter had disappeared. A few days later, the same counsellor had phoned with the shocking news that Maisie was on drugs. It was at that point that the bottom had dropped out of their world. Maisie had, quite literally, vanished from their lives, but only physically. Brodie thought about her all the time.

'What made you come here, to Dodge Street?'

Brodie gave her the photograph. 'Maisie's friend sent this. She took it on her mobile and told me the name of the street. I only got it yesterday.'

Karen looked at the photograph. 'Maisie Logan,' she said thoughtfully.

'You're not going to arrest her, are you?' Brodie felt alarmed. She didn't like the police knowing her name, knowing Maisie's name, knowing Maisie was a drug addict. She felt exposed and vulnerable, as if she had put her daughter in danger. 'Does it mean that Maisie's taking crack cocaine?' She understood that was the worst drug of all.

'Not necessarily. Crack houses don't just stick to crack; they sell other drugs as well.'

'If you know what that place is, why don't you close it down?' Brodie asked crossly. 'Isn't that what the police are for?'

'Because if we did, another crack house would open somewhere else and it could be a while before we knew where it was,' the young woman explained patiently, as if it was a question she was often called upon to answer. 'At least we can keep an eye on this place. Can I keep the photo?'

'What for?' Brodie asked guardedly. She imagined enlarged versions of Maisie's face pinned to noticeboards in police stations all over the country with 'Wanted' underneath.

'Well, one reason is that if I ever come across your daughter, I could let you know where she is – if you are willing to give me your address and telephone number, that is.' She looked slightly amused. 'Why are you so suspicious of the police, Mrs Logan?'

Brodie denied she was suspicious. 'Not in the least.'

'Getting information from you is like pulling teeth. You were reluctant even to give your name.'

'I suppose I'm terrified of getting Maisie into trouble,' Brodie admitted. 'My husband would have a fit if she ended up in jail. Not that I care about him.' She twisted her lips contemptuously. 'He's disowned Maisie. He doesn't know I'm here.'

'Have you got other children?'

'A son, Josh. He lives not far from here. He's in Brighton on business.' It made Josh sound important – if she didn't mention the squat, or the fact that he had never had a proper job. She remembered something. 'My grandfather was a sergeant in the Liverpool police force. According to my mother, he was killed in the line of duty in nineteen thirty.'

'Really?' Karen Grant's brown eyes widened with interest. 'What happened? Do you know his name?'

'Thomas Ryan. He came across two men robbing a bank at the dead of night and one shot him.'

'I'll see if I can find out about him on the Internet. Oh, good, this tea looks nice and strong. You haven't touched yours yet, and please take a sandwich.' She leaned across the table and squeezed both of Brodie's hands. 'I hope I haven't been too abrupt with you, Mrs Logan. My elder brother died of an overdose when he was only seventeen. I hate drug-dealers. It's why I became a policewoman. If I had my way, every single dealer would be put in prison to rot for the rest of their miserable lives.' Her lips tightened. 'I'm going to find your daughter for you. Now, tell me something about her? Where did she used to live? What was she studying at university? And what's this nonsense about your husband disowning his own flesh and blood?'

Brodie told her. It was cathartic to get every single one of her worries off her chest, things that until now she'd never told a soul.

Afterwards, Karen drove her to Euston and Brodie returned to Liverpool feeling much happier than when she'd come. All right, she hadn't found her daughter, but she felt positive that Karen soon would, and somehow persuade her to come home.

Vanessa had bought two canvases, a box of paints and a packet of assorted brushes. She put everything under the bed and had a short sleep, having found the early morning's events quite exhausting, though the Leonard Gosling part had been relatively pleasant, in particular the breakfast. The hot chocolate with cream and the warm croissant and homemade strawberry jam had been delicious. She licked her lips and could taste them again.

When she woke and opened her eyes, she was

reminded what an attractive room this was, with its old-fashioned, solid furniture and faded brocade curtains. The walls were shell-pink with a slight sheen. Over the fireplace hung a delightful painting of fairies playing in a circle of flowers. By the door there was another painting of the same fairies flying through a wood. She really should be happy in a room like this. Hopefully, she would be – as soon as she started losing weight.

She read the text messages on her mobile and listened to the voicemail. Amanda and Sonia had sent some of both, all saying more or less the same thing. Did she really have to cut herself off from her family? For a whole year? Wasn't she being just a little bit silly? Overly dramatic? 'All you're doing is drawing attention to yourself,' Sonia texted. 'And not for the first time.' She'd never got on as well with Sonia as she had with Amanda.

Vanessa couldn't see how disappearing out of sight for twelve whole months could be taken as drawing attention to herself, more the opposite.

'What on earth am I to *tell* people if they ask how you are?' her mother sobbed. Her father told her cheerfully to look after herself. Someone from Siren informed her an interview had been arranged with Wayne Rooney. Someone else said they were sorry to hear she was leaving. There was a message to say she'd won a holiday in Spain. To her annoyance, there was a voicemail from William. Amanda had told him what she was up to and he warned her not to do anything silly.

Anything silly! What did that mean? Did he

seriously think she was likely to commit suicide because of *him*? Huh!

The house was empty. Diana was still at work, Brodie out somewhere. Vanessa had a lazy bath. When she got back to her room, she weighed herself and the needle swung past eighteen stone.

Suicide didn't seem all that bad an option, she thought wearily.

At around six o'clock, Vanessa heard Diana come home from work. Within minutes, she had put on a CD, one of those stupid Stone Age numbers she was so fond of. 'Are the stars out tonight?' a man with a plaintive voice whimpered. 'I don't know if it's cloudy or bright.'

'Hello, puss.'

Diana had gone into the garden. She spent a lot of time there, even when it was dark and sometimes cold. Vanessa watched the girl from the window. In her weird, old- fashioned clothes and wedge-heeled boots, she looked like a model in a retro photo from a fashion magazine. She was speaking to a ginger cat that had jumped out of a tree. It came and rubbed itself against her legs. She bent down and stroked it. 'What have you been doing with yourself today, puss?'

Vanessa rolled her eyes. She'd always had poor relationships with cats. Did Diana really expect the animal to answer? The girl wasn't exactly the Brain of Britain, but she couldn't be *that* stupid. She turned away from the window in disgust. She couldn't stand Diana. It was nothing to do with the fact that she was envious of her beanpole figure and air of natural elegance, more that she was lacking in basic intelligence.

Half an hour later, the doorbell rang and Diana let someone in. There were footsteps on the stairs. Vanessa tensed, praying that her whereabouts hadn't been discovered and it was someone coming to see her. Another part of her prayed exactly the opposite; that there'd be a knock on her door and she'd open it to a familiar face – any face apart from William's. She was in urgent need of company just then. A comforting hand, a friendly kiss, even a nice smile would do.

But the footsteps went into the room next door. The new – and last – tenant must have arrived.

Diana said, 'Brodie told me to expect you at about six. I'll fetch the rest of your stuff up. Would you like me to make you a cup of tea?'

The person must have accepted the offer, because Diana said, 'I won't be a minute.'

Vanessa hoped that didn't mean it was someone old, because *she* had no intention of making tea and waiting on them. She had enough to do looking after herself.

She lay on the bed, dozed off again, and woke to the sound of a baby crying. It was just her luck, she thought wretchedly, to find she was living in a haunted house.

Brodie knocked on Diana's door as soon as she came in. 'Has Rachel arrived?' she enquired. Rachel was the new tenant. She'd been to the house a few days before and paid a deposit on the room. She looked awfully young, but had assured Brodie that she was sixteen.

'I don't get on with me mam at home,' she'd told her.

'Will you be able to afford the room?' Brodie

enquired. It was a question she didn't like asking. It made her look like a greedy, grasping landlady, but she needed the money. Rachel had assured her she could afford the rent and had paid a month in advance and a month's deposit, there and then, all in cash.

'She seems really nice,' Diana said. She said exactly the same about everybody, even Vanessa, whom Brodie didn't think was very nice at all. She wasn't happy, either – but not unhappy like Diana, or Brodie herself, because of the behaviour of other people. Poor Vanessa was unhappy with herself. 'But I didn't know', Diana went on, 'that Rachel had a baby.'

Neither did Brodie. There'd been no mention of a baby the other day. The girl had taken the room under false pretences. The elation Brodie had felt when leaving London had already dissipated. She'd arrived in Liverpool worried and sick at heart. It was an easy move from this to intense anger at the idea that she'd been fooled. She ran upstairs and knocked sharply on the rear bedroom door. Rachel opened it, a fearful expression on her heavily freckled face. She was tiny, no more than five feet tall, and very slight. Her eyes were almost hidden behind a thick, brown fringe. She reminded Brodie of a doll she'd had as a child.

'You've got a baby!' she said accusingly. As if in confirmation, a little chirrup came from inside the room.

'Yes.' Rachel hung her head and looked ashamed.

All Brodie's anger fled. 'Why didn't you tell me?' she asked limply.

'Because I didn't think you'd let me have the room.'

'I wouldn't have turned you away, not with a baby, but I don't like being misled.'

'I'm sorry.' The girl sniffed pathetically. 'Other people did.'

Brodie remembered that she adored babies and it would be lovely to have one on the premises. 'Is it a boy or a girl?'

'A girl. Her name is Poppy.'

'Can I see her?'

'Of course.' The girl stood aside, a touch reluctantly, Brodie thought.

She crept into the room and across to a large, very expensive three-wheeled pushchair with massive tyres in which lay a pink-clad baby staring into space, her eyelashes twitching ever so slightly now and then.

'She's beautiful,' Brodie breathed. 'How old is she?'

'Three months.'

'If you ever want any help,' Brodie whispered, 'don't hesitate to ask. I have two children, but they're grown up.' It was hard to believe that Josh and Maisie had once been so small and looked so helpless.

'Thank you.'

Brodie sensed Rachel wanted shot of her. She left the room after repeating her offer of assistance should it ever be needed.

She was in the kitchen making her tea when Diana came in. Together, they wondered if the baby's father knew he had a daughter.

'And how old is *he*?' Diana mused. 'Rachel only looks about fourteen.'

'Does she?' Brodie felt concerned. 'She assured me she was sixteen.'

'Are you allowed to leave home when you're under sixteen?' Diana asked. 'I mean, can you be forced to go back to your parents?'

'I hope not.' Brodie shuddered, suddenly worried she'd be prosecuted for harbouring a minor.

That aside, she felt happy with her three tenants. Diana was one of the nicest people she'd ever known. She suspected something horrible had happened to Vanessa and Chestnuts provided sanctuary of a sort while she recovered. As for little Rachel and her daughter, Poppy, they needed looking after, and Brodie would make sure that they were.

Diana mentioned that she'd met a reporter from the *Liverpool Echo* at work that afternoon. 'He's writing an article about the centre. He asked what I did. Oh, and he brought a photographer who took all our photos.'

'When will it be in the *Echo*?' Brodie enquired.

'Tomorrow, I think.'

'I must make sure I buy a copy.'

The next day, Garth O'Sullivan, who was in his last year at Liverpool College and about to take his A-levels, caught the train home from Central Station. He sat next to a woman in a bright red coat who smelled of disinfectant, though it might have been dead expensive scent. She was reading the evening paper. Being a woman, she wasn't reading the sports' pages, but the local news, which Garth knew would be dead boring. He glanced at the open pages and turned away in disgust.

He wished their Di would be there when he got home. He was fed up with Emma's cooking. It was the same old horrible stuff every stupid day: mincemeat fried, mincemeat boiled, mincemeat baked in the oven. He couldn't remember their Di making mincemeat, except when she did it curried with rice and chutney. *That* was one of his favourites.

Emma had stopped making the beds every day an' all – there hadn't been any clean bedding since Di had gone. He and Jason had tried to work out what Emma did with herself all day, but couldn't come up with anything, apart from going to see her sister in Walton Vale.

Or shopping. Jason swore she wore different clothes every single day. 'And earrings,' he added. 'She must have a couple of hundred pairs.'

Both the lads were very anti-Emma these days. They had a feeling that if it hadn't been for her, their Di might not have done a bunk. It was useless trying to complain to Damian about it. Emma was his girlfriend, she was expecting his kid, and it went without saying that he'd stick up for her.

'Make your own flippin' tea,' he'd said, though he hadn't used the word 'flippin' ' but another beginning with 'f'. 'And make your own flippin' bed while you're at it.'

'If that's the flippin' case,' Jason said, 'then I'm holding back me keep. I mean, what am I paying fifty quid a week for if it's not to have a decent flippin' tea made as well as me flippin' bed?'

Garth was convinced that Damian must have seen the logic of this. He didn't argue. In fact, he didn't say another word, but ever since a slightly better meal had been waiting when they arrived home and the beds had been made, if not as neatly as when Diana had done them.

The woman next to him on the train turned to another page of the *Echo*.

113

'Flippin' hell,' Garth gasped.

'Do you mind?' snapped the woman.

'That's me sister there, that is.' Garth pointed excitedly to a picture at the top of the page. 'That's our Di. Where does it say she is, missus?'

The woman looked interested. 'At a refugee centre in Winstanley Place off Cazneau Street. It says here that her name's Diana O'Sullivan and she works there.'

'That's right, that's our Di. I'll get the phone number on me mobile and give her a ring right now.'

'The number's here, lad. It asks for people to ring if they want to make donations or volunteer to work there.' She reeled off the number and Garth dialled it on his mobile.

It was Di who answered. Garth was so happy, so relieved, so flippin' *touched* to hear his sister's voice that he wanted to cry, despite being a tough, cynical seventeen-year old who'd forgotten what tears felt like. The woman with the newspaper was listening quite openly, nodding as if she approved of the conversation.

'Oh, but I left a note,' Di explained when Garth asked why she'd gone without telling them where. 'I put it behind the clock on the mantelpiece. It had me new address on.'

'We couldn't find a note, Di. We looked every flippin' where.'

'Don't swear!' Di said severely. 'I hope you're not all swearing your heads off just because I'm not there.'

'As if we would, Di,' Garth said virtuously.

Di asked after Damian and Jason and finally Emma. Garth assured her everyone was fine and asked when he could come and see her.

114

'Come whenever you like, luv. I'm in most nights.'

'Give us the address, Di, and I'll come tonight. We all will.'

All three lads came, leaving a scared and extremely anxious Emma behind in Coral Street. What if they persuaded Di to come back? This time, Di might not be so willing to be sidelined, not if she found out that Emma had been slacking a bit in the kitchen – well, more than a bit. It was a lovely kitchen to look at, but she wasn't exactly keen on *working* in it. Her sister, Sophie, had been to look at the house a few times and told Emma she was dead lucky – the father of *her* kids had walked out before the second had even been born.

'I wish I had a feller like Damian and a house like this,' she said enviously. 'And he treats you like Lady bloody Muck. When I had our Carly, I was working until two weeks before she was born, but you're not expecting until August and all you do is laze around the house all day smoking spliffs.'

'I come to see you, don't I?' Emma argued. Never the less, she resolved to pull her socks up and start watching cookery programmes on telly. She wasn't married yet. It mightn't be a bad idea to keep up the pretence of being interested in housework until she became Mrs O'Sullivan.

'The lads'll be along later,' Diana had informed Brodie as soon as she got in. 'Our Garth saw me photo in the *Echo* and rang up the centre from the train. The day I left Coral Street, I put a note behind the clock, but Garth said they never got it. It must've blown away or something.'

'I hope this doesn't mean you're going back home,' Brodie said. 'I'd really miss you if you did.'

Diana assured her that she had no intention of leaving Chestnuts. 'I'm glad I came when I did. The lads are old enough to look after themselves. I know that from the centre; there's young people there who've been through some dead horrible stuff back in their own countries – and they haven't got a nice, warm house to live in. Anyroad,' she went on with a confident grin, 'it was about time I struck out on me own. I was dead miserable at first when me brothers didn't get in touch, but after a while I was enjoying meself too much to think about it.'

They were lovely boys, Brodie thought. Handsome and polite, glowing with health, they obviously thought the world of their sister. With a mother who'd walked out on them when they were still at school, brought up by a sister who wasn't much older than themselves, it was amazing that they'd turned out as well as they had. Diana ought to feel very proud.

Having entertained them on the piano with a one-fingered version of 'Yellow Submarine', Diana was now showing them around the garden. The youngest, Garth, had climbed a tree in an endeavour to capture the ginger cat.

'It's the gear here, sis,' he said peering through the leaves.

It made her wonder where she and Colin had gone wrong with their children; one a drug addict, the other wasting his time on failed business ventures. Yet they'd never gone short of money or attention or parental love. Colin had helped with homework; Brodie had kept them clean and warm and well-fed. Had they been given too much love, or not enough? Perhaps it would have done them good if life had been a bit harder.

The sounds of merriment coming from the garden were getting on Vanessa's nerves. She drove to Sainsbury's to buy groceries, hoping the visitors would be gone by the time she got back.

She wandered round the shop, gazing longingly at Battenbergs and chocolate biscuits, the cartons of fresh cream and the meat pies with crispy pastry that would taste delicious warmed up. She stacked up on thin-sliced low-calorie bread, cottage cheese and salad vegetables. It was an unappealing selection for a woman with a voracious appetite.

What she needed was to go on a sensible diet, the sort where you could eat a bit of almost anything, not leaves accompanied by stuff that tasted like cotton wool. The trouble was genuine diets were so *slow*. Vanessa wanted to lose weight quickly, imagining whole rolls of fat disappearing overnight like magic, except the more strictly she dieted, the more likely she was to be overcome with a hunger that she couldn't resist satisfying with something really fattening.

She walked quickly away from the food and looked at the CDs, the DVDs and the books, but nothing caught her fancy, mainly because they weren't edible. With an effort, she pushed the trolley towards the till. The female assistant looked at her sympathetically when she paid for her motley collection of unappetising foodstuffs.

'You'll get there in the end,' she said with a nod of encouragement.

'Get where?' Vanessa snarled. Sympathy was the last thing she wanted.

'You know where.' The woman smiled, not in the least put out.

For five days, Vanessa didn't leave the house except for an early-morning walk along the sands. She spent a lot of time lying on the bed staring at the ceiling and thinking gloomy thoughts, one of which was glum awareness that she had become the hopeless, helpless sort of person she'd used to loathe. Downstairs, the telephone in the kitchen rang frequently but, as it couldn't possibly be for her, she didn't answer. Sometimes, the doorbell went, but she didn't answer that, either.

Neither did Rachel, who was living in the next room with her baby. Vanessa had intended to complain if the baby cried a lot, but when it did she could hardly hear. She wondered why the girl didn't take the child into the garden. Weren't babies supposed to have plenty of fresh air?

It was unnerving to have such a quiet neighbour. She never heard Rachel go down to the kitchen, was only aware of it when she heard the click of the kettle being switched on, or the opening and closing of the fridge. The same with the toilet, which would suddenly flush, making her jump.

She hadn't much minded being the only person in the house once Diana and Brodie had gone, but there was something unnatural about two women living so close together, literally yards from each other, yet having no communication whatsoever. Only once had they come face to face.

Sometimes, late at night, Rachel would sing to her baby, her voice high and sweet. '*Rock-a-bye baby, on the treetop, when the wind blows, the cradle will rock . . .*'

Vanessa would shudder. There was something really creepy about it.

Late on Sunday morning, Vanessa was still asleep when Diana knocked on her door and shouted that she had a visitor.

'Who is it?' she shouted back. If it was one of her sisters, she wasn't sure whether to fling her arms around them or demand they go away. But the visitor was most unexpected.

'It's Mr Gosling from the shop. He said he's been telephoning you all week and he's called at the house twice, but there was no answer. He wants to take you out to lunch.'

Vanessa eased herself out of bed. 'Tell him I'll be down in a minute.'

'There's no need to hurry. I'll make him a cup of tea.'

She took pains with her appearance for the first time in ages, brushing her blonde hair until it shone, then screwing it into a bun at the back of her neck when she looked in the mirror and discovered she resembled a blown-up version of Marilyn Monroe with it loose. She put on her black top and trousers and supposed she didn't look so bad when she was ready.

But, oh, how she wished she were ten and a half stone again and about to go to lunch with William, wearing a smart blouse and the silver silk trouser suit that had cost £350.

The door to Diana's room was wide open. She must be proud of her ability to play tunes with one finger. When Vanessa went in, she was playing 'Night and Day' to Leonard and Brodie. They clapped when she finished and said, in a really friendly way, 'Hello, Vanessa.'

Vanessa's face cracked into a smile. She actually felt quite normal for a change, but knew it wouldn't last for long.

Half an hour later, Leonard was driving Vanessa to Southport in his elderly but beautifully preserved Morris Minor, Diana was on her way to Coral Street to have dinner with Emma and her brothers, and Brodie and her mother had met at Crosby station to catch the train into town to do some shopping. At least, her mother could shop; Brodie couldn't afford to and would just have to watch.

Rachel listened until the house was empty, then pressed the keys on her mobile. 'It's all right to come now,' she said when it was answered.

She lifted Poppy out of the pram and held her very close. The baby's shape seemed to fit snugly against her neck and shoulder like the piece of a jigsaw. 'Daddy's coming, sweetheart,' she whispered. 'He won't be long. We'll look after you; don't worry. We won't let them take you away.'

May–June 2006

Chapter 5

It had been Diana's idea for the centre to have a coffee morning once a week to which everyone, not just refugees, could come. 'Thursday would be a good day,' she said to Tinker. 'It's a way of raising funds. We can put signs at the end of the road, and have a bric-à-brac stall, too. If we don't charge too much for the coffee, it'll be somewhere for old people to come.'

Tinker reminded her that it wasn't in the centre's remit to provide for old people, but never the less agreed that Diana could go ahead. 'I'll leave all the arrangements to you, dear heart,' he said with his infectious grin. 'I like the idea of our clients and the local population getting together.'

So Diana made notices using a black felt-tip pen on white cardboard, and drew flowers in each corner merely because there was the space. She nailed one to each end of Winstanley Grove.

Ten women and two men came to the first event, not all of them old, and more than fifteen pounds was raised. Since then, there'd been another two coffee mornings and each had raised more money than the one before. Today was the fourth and at least twenty-five people had come. The lounge and dining room were crowded with local residents and people from all over the world chatting away to each other, even if some were only using sign language.

There was a lovely atmosphere, warm and friendly. Everyone seemed very much at home. Tinker thought it important that the refugees who used the centre found it a happy place. 'Some have had a horrendous time getting here,' he said. 'It might have cost them all their savings, and they arrive and find themselves with nowhere to live. I want them to realize that life won't always be so black. "Look for the silver lining . . ." ' he sang tunefully.

'I'm doing a roaring trade,' Megan, Brodie's mother, said when Diana passed on her way to the lounge with a tray full of coffees. Megan had felt at a bit of a loss when Brodie started work a few weeks ago, and now came to the centre regularly to give a hand. On Thursdays, she was in charge of the bric-à-brac stall, usually bringing lots of bits and pieces that she'd cadged off friends. There was more stuff that she'd found in the jumble in the basement.

'It's going really well.' Diana surveyed the depleted stall. 'How much have you taken?'

Megan looked pleased. 'I'm not sure, darlin'. Between thirty and forty pounds, I reckon.'

Tinker would be thrilled, Diana thought. 'What's that sequinny thing?' she enquired.

'It's a blouse.' Megan held it up. It was black and truly beautiful, the material as fine as a spider's web, scattered liberally with gold and silver sequins. 'It's size thirty, darlin'. Much too big for you. You can have it for nothing.'

'I'd like it, please.' Diana had no intention of not

paying for the blouse. She was scrupulous about such things and would give Megan the money later. She distributed the coffees and returned to the kitchen for more of the jam sponge cakes that she'd made with Brodie's help the night before. There hadn't been time for baking cakes in Coral Street.

'Diana,' Tinker said a touch distractedly when she went in, 'I'm in a desperate tizzy. Will you please try to get rid of your lot as soon as you can?' Tinker was in a desperate tizzy a lot of the time. He was by the stove stirring a giant pan of beans while slices of faintly brown bread popped out of the toaster. He pushed the bread back in, cursing. It was a hopeless toaster.

'My lot?'

'The coffee morning lot. Any minute, we'll have *our* lot in for lunch and there's nowhere for them to sit because *your* lot are taking up all the seats.' He ran his fingers through his red hair and it stood up on end, reminding Diana of a clown's wig. 'Next week, precious, ban them from the dining room and keep them in the lounge.' He began a vain attempt to tear his hair out by the roots. 'Actually, I'd better run this coffee morning thing by Mrs Banana. She might not like the idea of the centre being overrun with English pensioners when it's supposed to be for refugees.'

Mrs Banana was actually Mrs Bannerman. No one knew exactly what her job was. She seemed to be a sort of co-ordinator between the council, the government and various refugee agencies, and turned up at the centre from time to time to make sure things were running smoothly and that nothing untoward was going on, such as illicit coffee mornings.

Diana promised that next week she'd make sure *her*

crowd left at half past eleven. Tinker kissed her on the cheek and thanked her profusely. 'What have I done to deserve a gorgeous girl like you, Di?'

'I don't know,' Diana said, blushing madly.

She blushed again when she took the sponge cakes into the lounge and saw Ahmed Rusafi. A doctor from Iraq, of philosophy not medicine, he was about forty and drop-dead gorgeous. Women, young, old and in between, were enchanted by his exquisite manners and old-world charm. Megan was one. The other day she claimed he was the spitting image of a film star called Clark Gable.

'I was crazily in love with him when I was a teenager,' she said dreamily. 'My sister was, too. It's almost like meeting him in the flesh after all this time.'

'I thought you didn't have any brothers and sisters,' said Diana. She considered Ahmed better-looking than George Clooney.

'Of course . . . I didn't – haven't. What on earth made me say that?' Megan had got all hot and flustered. As Diana couldn't imagine why anyone would deny they had brothers and sisters when in fact they had, she'd not given the matter another thought. Megan had later said she had the DVD of *Gone With the Wind* starring the one and only Clark Gable along with loads of other old film stars and she'd bring it round one night and they could watch it together, adding, 'Our Brodie might like to see it, too. It's nearly four hours long, so it would be best if we watched it at the weekend and we can stay up as late as we like. I've seen it loads of times, but would love to see it again.'

'We could order a takeaway,' Diana suggested.

'And buy some wine.' Megan rubbed her long, thin, wrinkled hands together.

'And get dressed up, as if we're going to the theatre or something.'

'What a lovely idea, Diana.'

'Can we make it Friday?' She was meeting Leo Peterson on Saturday at his brother's twenty-first birthday party. Each time she saw Leo she told him she didn't want to see him again, but he talked her out of it. He was so nice and she didn't like to hurt his feelings.

'Friday's fine. I'm already looking forward to it.'

Diana was looking forward to it, too. She was enjoying life in a way she had never done before. Until recently, the lads had always come first, but now, although she still worried about them and always would, she was able to think of herself before anyone else. She really enjoyed being able to do whatever she pleased.

Ahmed Rusafi came over, smiled into her eyes, and took a cake. She didn't like saying it was part of the coffee morning and he was supposed to pay for it.

'Have not got nowhere to sleep this night,' he said with a dramatic shrug and a devastating smile.

'Why not?' Diana was shocked. She had a feeling she might be in love with him as well as Tinker.

'Peoples who own house need my room for other peoples.'

'But that's awful! Can't you find a cheap hotel?'

He shrugged again, raising his shoulders and spreading his hands. 'No such thing as cheap when person have no money.'

'I'll lend you some—'

'No, no, no, no.' He shook his head, horrified at the idea. 'I manage somehow: sleep in park maybe, or shop doorway. Never take money off woman.'

'OK.' On reflection, Tinker would be cross if he found out. He had advised her never to get emotionally involved with the refugees. 'It'll tear your heart out, Di,' he'd said. 'Some have suffered really horribly and you don't want to suffer with them. Treat them with love, kindness and generosity, but try to remain detached.'

Tinker was so *wise*!

The coffee morning raised £55.37. Tinker was contemplating buying a six-slice stainless-steel toaster with the proceeds. Diana and Megan felt extremely pleased with themselves when they went home that evening on the same train. They got off at Blundellsands station and Megan went to collect her bike, while Diana commenced the walk home to Elm Road.

All in all, it had been a really satisfactory day.

Vanessa had spent the afternoon watching a horror film on television. It had made her flesh creep. It was still creeping while she contemplated what to have for tea, going through all the choices in her head. That morning, she'd gone mad and eaten the whole day's ration of butter on two poached kippers. The room still stank. How could something that tasted so nice smell so horrible?

Ham salad, cheese salad, sardine salad, omelette with salad . . . An apple for afters. Tea without milk she was slowly getting used to, but she couldn't acquire a taste for black coffee. She wondered if the day would ever come when she would find any of the choices tempting. They were fine for a snack, but a meal?

She sighed. She'd been living in Chestnuts for six weeks and the only weight she'd lost was the amount she'd put on since she'd arrived. A few times a week her willpower would desert her and she would rush out, usually late at night, and indulge in something ultra-fattening. The subsequent enjoyment was better than sex, but afterwards she felt ashamed and depressed.

Omelette and salad, she decided. It would be more filling than sardines, a lump of cheese or a slice of ham.

She opened the door to go down to the kitchen and found Diana outside about to knock.

'Hello, Vanessa,' she said shyly. 'I've brought you something. Today, we had a coffee morning at the centre and I found this on the bric-à-brac stall.' She held up a pretty lacy garment decorated with sequins. 'It's a blouse,' she explained when Vanessa looked nonplussed. 'It's size thirty. Is that big enough for you?'

'Yes,' Vanessa said in a cracked voice. She had a feeling that size thirty was the biggest you could get. Or was it thirty-two? 'Thank you.' She felt like wrapping the blouse around the girl's neck.

'Oh, and another thing: tomorrow night Megan and Brodie and me are going to watch *Gone With the Wind* in my room and I wondered if you'd like to come? We're having wine and a takeaway and we're going to get dressed up as if it was a film premiere or something. You could wear your new blouse.'

'I could, couldn't I?'

'That would be the gear. Do you think Rachel would like to come? We hardly see anything of her.'

'I don't know. You'll just have to ask her.' As the weather became warmer, the girl had begun to appear in the garden with her child in a pram. For some inexplicable reason, the sight of the tiny girl nursing the tiny baby almost brought tears to Vanessa's eyes. There seemed something very wrong about her being on her own. Where were her parents and the baby's father? She told herself it was none of her business. The baby was happy and seemed to be thriving, so there was no need to interfere.

Diana went away and Vanessa went down to the kitchen to make an omelette.

It was a stupid idea, getting dressed up to watch a DVD in your own home, Vanessa thought the next night as she watched the three women in the garden, each with a glass of wine. She'd been alerted by the music. 'Moonlight becomes you, it goes with your hair,' a man was singing in a frightfully posh voice. Perhaps they were waiting for the food to be delivered. She wondered what had been ordered.

Brodie was wearing an ordinary blouse and skirt made to look dressy with the addition of a white lace stole, and Megan a pink linen frock with a cherry-red velvet jacket. Diana actually had on a genuine evening frock, blue taffeta, very old-fashioned, the sort of thing women wore in wartime, with a little white fur cape. She looked utterly ridiculous. All three were giggling as if they'd already had too much wine. Or perhaps not. Vanessa gloomily remembered behaving in exactly the same way when she went out with her friends, laughing hilariously at nothing at all yet being perfectly sober. She couldn't remember the last time she'd gone out with friends, only that it was before William had dumped her at the altar.

She sniffed dejectedly as she pressed her face against the window. The scene outside was like something out of a play: the music, the women with their wine, the darkening trees casting darker shadows underneath as dusk fell, the light from the downstairs' windows shining on the grass. A single bird sang from somewhere inside the trees and the ginger cat was curled up on one of the chairs.

The doorbell went and Diana ran inside, holding her skirt with one hand and the wine glass with the other. She was wearing *diamanté* shoes with high heels, and managed to look graceful and awkward at the same time.

'Shall we go in?' Megan called to Brodie. 'We can't eat out here, the food will get cold.'

Vanessa turned away for a second to blow her nose. When she turned back the garden was empty except for the cat, which jumped off the chair and lazily stretched itself before strolling away into the shadows. The bird continued to sing, but mournfully now, or so Vanessa thought.

Then the light disappeared. Diana must have closed the window and drawn the curtains. Left with nothing but trees that were getting blacker by the minute, Vanessa drew her own curtains and settled down to . . .

What?

Watching television while thinking about food? It was all she had to do. She couldn't have read a book to save her life, having lost all powers of concentration. There'd been a time when she'd read a newspaper every day and knew everything that was going on in the world, but no longer. The television news was horrendous, nothing but people being killed. She'd brought her laptop with her, but what was she supposed to do on it? Play games when it had once been used for extremely important work.

She wondered if there were any messages on her mobile. Seven, she discovered when she checked. She deleted the lot without reading them. Each time she looked there were fewer. The day would come when there'd be none at all and she would feel as if she had died and nobody was thinking about her any more. The thought made her blood run cold. She quite literally felt as if she were freezing. If she got any colder, she really would die.

Vanessa jumped to her feet and began to rub her arms, stamp her feet and shake herself all over in order to bring herself back to life.

This couldn't go on. For Christ's sake, she was only *fat*. And she'd been jilted by the manager of a video rental shop, who had earned less than half as much as she did. It wasn't the end of the world. She didn't have a deadly disease. She had relatives who loved her, a roof over her head, and plenty of money.

Why, then, did she feel more wretched and more lonely than she'd ever felt in her life?

She could hear the women in the kitchen, sorting out the food. She'd been invited to share that food, see the film and drink the wine, but had refused.

No, she hadn't: she'd accepted. She'd agreed to come and wear the second-hand, size thirty blouse that Diana had bought from a bric-à-brac stall in a refugee centre. Looked at in a certain way, it was an extremely thoughtful gesture.

Vanessa put on her black trousers and the sequinned top, which was miles too big – it felt quite heartening to put on something that was too big instead of too small – but looked very glamorous. She felt a tiny bit drunk as she brushed her beautiful blonde hair and left it loose, put on lipstick and a pair of sparkly earrings.

'Hello, darlin',' Megan gushed when Vanessa went into the kitchen where numerous cartons of Indian food were being shared out on plates.

'I'm glad you've come,' Brodie said. 'Pass us another plate and I'll give you a bit of everything. There's loads here; we ordered far too much.'

'That blouse looks really pretty on you,' Diana said admiringly.

The film ended just after midnight. Vanessa was stuffed to the gills with cinnamon fried rice, horse-radish bread, dahi ki dahl, egg curry, prawn curry with coconut, rogan josh, and finally steamed dessert dumplings, washed down with copious amounts of wine. The film had been lovely as well as the wine and the company.

Why, then, did she start to cry? Start to weep so intensely and so terribly that she felt as if her heart would break, literally break, into a dozen pieces, never to be put together again? Every part of her hurt with the sheer effort and energy she was putting into such tremendous weeping.

The women gathered around, patting and stroking her, murmuring words of sympathy and encouragement, telling her everything would be all right in the morning, that she might be just a little bit drunk and would feel better when she was sober.

They took her up to her room, helped take off her clothes, found her nightdress under the pillow and tucked her up in bed.

Vanessa waited until they'd gone. She got out of bed, looked for the scissors and stood in front of the wardrobe mirror. Bit by bit, she hacked off her hair until it was barely an inch long all over. She felt freer, lighter, younger, better.

Then she got back into bed and fell fast asleep.

The next morning, Brodie knocked on Vanessa's door. 'I've brought you some tea,' she shouted. If she didn't answer, she'd drink it herself. Poor Vanessa had been in a terrible state last night. Mind you, *Gone With the Wind* was awfully sad. Brodie could remember crying buckets the first time she saw it.

She was about to take the tea away when there was a croak from inside the room and Vanessa opened the door still in her nightie. 'G'morning,' she said grumpily, rubbing her eyes.

'You've cut your hair!'

Vanessa patted her head. 'It was getting too long. I thought I'd have it short for a change. What does it look like?'

Brodie searched for an appropriate word, one that didn't sound too tactless. 'Remarkable,' she said at last. 'Quite remarkable.'

'Anyway, thanks for the tea,' Vanessa said, almost smiling.

★

Vanessa closed the door, put the tea on the bedside table, and went to look at her hair in the mirror.

'Bloody *hell*!'

She screamed, but caught it just in time, jamming both her hands over her mouth. She looked *ghastly*. What on earth had possessed her to hack off her hair so carelessly, as if she didn't give a damn what it looked like?

Because she didn't give a damn, that's why. Because she didn't care what she looked like. Because life was shit and she wanted no part of it.

'You should see what Vanessa's done to her hair,' Brodie said when she went into the kitchen where Diana was cooking bacon, tomato and eggs. She leaned against the fridge-freezer to watch. 'It looks awful – Vanessa's hair, that is, not the food.'

'She must have done it when she was drunk.' Diana expertly turned over an egg. 'Would you like your egg fried both sides?'

'Yes, please. I hate them watery.'

Diana tipped her head sideways. 'If I'm ever stranded on a desert island, I shall shave me hair off. I'm told that if it's shaved, it can grow back curly when it used to be straight, or even a different colour.'

'That's probably an old wives' tale. If you were stranded on a desert island, you're unlikely to have a razor. Anyroad, our Josh shaved his head once and it grew back exactly the same.' She couldn't understand why Diana wanted different hair when the hair she had now was such a lovely colour, light-brown with streaks of gold, and very thick. Compared with

Diana's, Brodie considered her own hair to be thin and tired-looking.

'Do you mind getting the plates out of the oven?' Diana gave the frying pan a shake. 'Shall we eat this in your room or mine?'

'Mine,' said Brodie. 'Yours is still in a state after last night. I'll help you tidy up when we've eaten this.'

'It's all right, honest,' Diana assured her. 'Just a few glasses and empty wine bottles, that's all. The leftover food's in the fridge. Don't throw any of the meat away, will you? I can give it to Kenneth.'

Brodie laughed. 'Kenneth is an awfully odd name to give a cat, Diana. What's his real name?

'I dunno.' Diana shrugged. 'He doesn't wear a collar. I don't even know where he lives. And don't ask why I call him Kenneth. It just came to me out of the blue. Would you like a piece of fried bread?'

'I would love a piece of fried bread more than anything I can think of,' Brodie said, noisily licking her lips, 'but I'd better not.' She pulled a face. 'It's probably the most fattening food there is.'

'I'm going to have two slices.'

Diana ate like a horse and never put on an ounce of weight. Brodie told her she was a truly horrible person. 'I hope you're not going to eat them in front of me.'

'You'll just have to close your eyes.'

Brodie put the warmed-up plates on top of the draining board. 'You know,' she said with a glance around the room, 'I'm beginning to get used to the colours – red and mustard. It's a strange combination, but very original, sort of oriental.'

'I think it's the gear.' Diana sounded a little defensive. She was probably still feeling guilty about the kitchen, though it had been Mr Peterson's fault, not hers, for going ahead without consulting Brodie.

They ate at the little table in front of the window in Brodie's room. It was a dull, damp May day. Even Diana, who loved the garden and sat under the trees whenever she could, felt disinclined to do so today.

Diana left straight after breakfast. Although she wasn't supposed to work on Saturdays, she often went into the centre to give this amazing Tinker chap a hand with whatever was happening that night: a pop concert perhaps, a social, some sort of party.

Brodie lay on the bed, really glad that it was Saturday and she had the day off. *She* didn't have to go to work today.

When she'd thought about getting a job, office work had seemed the obvious choice. At school, she'd learned to type and do shorthand. When she'd left at sixteen with five O-levels, she'd gone straight into a bank as a junior secretary to one of the senior clerks. It had been extremely boring, but she'd got on with everyone and had made friends that she still occasionally met.

Brodie had never planned on having a career. She was perfectly happy to leave the bank after four years and marry Colin Logan. Since that day she had never worked again, unless she counted the thousands of nappies that she'd washed, the mountains of ironing, the meals she'd made, the dusting, cleaning, shopping, gardening, mending, occasional decorating, and the multitude of other tasks that constituted being a wife and mother of two children. She'd always had a typewriter and later a computer.

So, the other week, when she'd been told, to put it

brutally, it was time she earned her own money, she'd approached an agency and asked for temporary office work. She didn't want to commit herself to a full-time job just yet.

She'd spent the first week at Starks & Putney, solicitors, in Water Street down by the Pier Head, working for Robert Priest whose secretary was on holiday.

He was the most arrogant man she had ever met and she disliked him straight away. It didn't help that she was almost old enough to be his mother. He never thanked her once for the dozens of letters she typed each day, after having make sense of his scribbled, barely legible notes. It was even worse when he dictated whole jumbles of words at a hectic, barely discernible rate.

She and Robert Priest swiftly became mortal enemies. At night, she cried herself to sleep. It was Colin's fault she was in this position because she loved their daughter and he didn't give a damn. She was heartily relieved when the week came to an end and she could leave and transfer to another office.

This time she'd worked with five young women in the claims department of an insurance company over the water in Birkenhead. For five whole days she was barely spoken to. The women weren't being rude, they just weren't interested in a woman at least twenty years older than themselves who wore skirts that covered her knees, hardly any eye make-up, and didn't have a tattoo or a stud anywhere on her body. When the need to speak to the temp became unavoidable, they called her 'Erm'.

It was impossible to hide the fact that she was working from her mother. When Megan heard what

Colin had said, she called him every horrid name she could think of and offered to give Brodie all the money she needed.

'It's only lying in the bank, darlin',' she said forcefully. 'It'll all be yours one day, and I'm not likely to need it, not at my age. You'll not catch me going into a home where they'll stuff me in an armchair and let me dribble meself to death.'

But Brodie flatly refused to accept her mother's money. 'I don't want Colin thinking I can't manage on my own. Anyroad, Mum, it'll do me good to support myself for a change.' She really meant it. So far, she'd led a very easy life, especially when compared to Diana whom she admired so much.

The third week Brodie went to a different agency and enquired about being a cleaner. After all, she'd had more experience of that than office work. Hopefully, she would be left to her own devices. She made up her mind to refuse if she were asked to climb a ladder and clean upstairs windows or shift heavy furniture. She wasn't sure how she felt about cleaning lavatories, particularly if they were dirty.

But Mr Dougal was lovely to work for. He was in his eighties, very chatty, and could only walk a bit. Brodie found herself sitting for hours listening to stories of his time spent in the Navy during the war, then racing around the house to give it a bit of spit and polish when it was time to leave. Sadly it was only for a fortnight while his wife was in California where she'd gone to see her sister.

Home again, Nora Dougal had telephoned to thank Brodie for looking after the house while she was away.

'I didn't look after it all that much,' Brodie

confessed. 'I spent an awful lot of time listening to your husband.'

'I know you did, dear. He drones on and on about things that young people have never heard of. You were very kind and patient with him. Should I ever go away again, is it all right to ask the agency if we could have you?'

'Of course.'

Now, lying on the bed the day after she'd watched *Gone With the Wind*, Brodie wondered what the next week's job would be like. She didn't like the uncertainty. She was neat in her ways and liked life to be the same: tidy and predictable. Next week, she was due to work for a Mrs Cowper in Southport and was looking forward it with a certain amount of dread.

Vanessa heard music in the room below. Diana was home and a woman was singing 'Every time we say goodbye, I cry a little'. She went down and knocked on the door.

'Come in, come in,' Diana cried.

'No, thank you,' Vanessa said stiffly, standing outside. 'It's just that when Leonard comes tomorrow to take me to lunch, will you please tell him I'm not feeling well.'

'Of course I will,' Diana said with a perplexed frown. 'But why don't you phone now and tell him yourself?'

'Because he'll try to talk me into it,' Vanessa said wearily. 'And I don't want to go, I really don't.'

'*Aren't* you well? Or is it because of your hair?' Vanessa winced and didn't say anything. The girl had no tact. 'Brodie said you'd cut it.'

She wondered how Brodie had described the hair to Diana. Right now, her head was covered with a scarf tied in a big bow. She looked a bit like Mammy in *Gone With the Wind*. She shrugged and looked numbly at Diana, not knowing what to say.

'Why don't you go to the hairdresser's on Monday, ask them to tidy it up a bit?' Diana suggested.

'Don't want to,' Vanessa said sulkily. They'd think she was mad. They'd be nudging each other, grinning and whispering, making fun.

'Would you like me to do it?' Diana offered, her blue eyes shining with kindness.

Vanessa winced again. The girl was too bloody nice by a mile. One of these days someone was bound to kill her.

'It doesn't matter.' She wished she didn't sound so sullen.

'Oh, but I'm quite good at cutting hair. I used to cut the lads' hair until I left home. I mean, all I'll do is tidy it. Come on in.' She made an inviting gesture with her head. 'I've got proper scissors. Sometimes I trim my own hair.'

'Oh, all right.' She still sounded sullen.

The blue taffeta dress she'd worn the night before lay on Diana's bed. In an effort to be friendly, Vanessa asked where she'd got it from.

'From the refugee centre. I only borrowed it. I shall take it back on Monday. Tonight I'm going to a twenty-first and I'm wearing it for that.' Diana opened the door of the wardrobe and revealed a mirror on the other side. She placed a chair in front of it.

'It looked very nice on you.'

141

'And that blouse looked very nice on you,' Diana responded.

Vanessa supposed she'd asked for that. She sat on the chair and Diana draped a towel around her shoulders, then prowled around her, studying her hair and opening and closing the scissors with a loud clicking noise that Vanessa found vaguely threatening.

'It's a lovely colour,' Diana remarked. 'Is it natural?'

'Yes.'

'It's said that hair is a woman's crowning glory.'

'I know.' It had been the only bit of glory that she'd had left.

Diana stopped prowling. 'Have you ever had a fringe?' she enquired.

'Not since I was a little girl.'

'Well, I think you should have one now. You'd look better with it combed on to your forehead, it being so short, like.'

'Whatever.' In a way, Vanessa didn't give a damn about her hair, but didn't fancy giving herself a fright every time she looked in the mirror until it grew to a respectable length again, which would take months, years even. William had always loved her hair. He would run his fingers through it, saying it was her best feature.

Diana took ages, cutting off infinitesimal amounts so the hair began to look feathery rather than clumpy. 'We don't want it to look *too* neat,' she said, rumpling it with her fingers.

When she finished, Vanessa was despatched upstairs to wash it. 'Do you have a hairdryer? I left mine at home,' Diana said. 'I keep meaning to go and get it.'

'I've got one – you can borrow it whenever you

142

like.' It was the first kind gesture Vanessa had made since she couldn't remember when.

'Do you still not want to go to lunch with Leonard tomorrow?' Diana asked when Vanessa's hair had been washed and dried and didn't look too bad at all considering the damage she'd inflicted on it. It had the look of a crew cut on top, but the rest appeared neat and casual, much better suited to a woman with a fuller figure than the old style. In retrospect, it had made her appear a bit blousy.

'I'd still like to give lunch a miss this week.' At first, she'd enjoyed the lunches, but last Sunday Leonard had squeezed her knee and she'd had the horrible feeling that he might be making a pass. He was seventy-three and she was thirty-one, yet she'd actually felt a tiny bit flattered. It was essential for the sake of her pride that it never happen again.

It seemed odd to have nothing to do on Saturday. Early in the afternoon, the sun had come out and at tea-time Brodie was lying on the bed again feeling unnaturally idle and thinking about the garden. Very soon, the hydrangeas and rhododendrons would bloom. There was already blossom on the lilac tree and little red buds on the climbing roses. The grass was ankle-high and badly in need of cutting. It was wild grass and grew rapidly.

Mum was going to the theatre with friends. It had been arranged months ago, long before Brodie had left Colin. 'Otherwise we could have gone somewhere together, darlin'.' She'd looked worriedly at her daughter. 'I don't like the thought of you being on your own on a Saturday.'

'Mum,' Brodie had said patiently, 'you don't have to look out for me. I'm forty-three. I can read a book or watch television. It'll be nice to have my own company for a change.' And the evening would be George-free, which was a blessing.

'Even so,' Mum had said, 'it doesn't seem right.'

'It doesn't seem wrong, either.'

Brodie wasn't the only person on her own. Vanessa was, too. She scarcely ever left the house, just once a week to do some shopping and sometimes late at night when she was never out for more than half an hour. Brodie would have loved to know what she was doing in Chestnuts. Last night she'd been so distressed, crying as if the world was about to end.

Rachel and her baby were also upstairs. Surely a health visitor should be visiting Poppy regularly? She hardly ever cried. There were times when Brodie was tempted to report the situation to Social Services, but it might result in the baby being taken away and she would feel like a really horrible snoop. She'd tried to approach the girl a few times, take an interest in the baby, but Rachel just looked at her suspiciously and didn't want to know.

Tonight, Diana was going to Leo Peterson's brother's twenty-first birthday party wearing the blue evening frock and little white fur cape she'd worn last night to see *Gone With the Wind*. It seemed that Leo wanted them to get engaged, but Diana wasn't exactly keen. Brodie hoped she wouldn't let Leo talk her into it. The girl was too concerned with hurting people's feelings.

She got off the bed, wandered across to the window, opened it and went outside. A train passed and she could feel the ground shiver beneath her feet. There was a lovely fresh smell in the air and the birds had come out with the sun and were singing merrily in the trees.

It was very easy to wish that Diana, not Maisie, were her daughter, though Maisie had once been just as sweet and just as nice. Brodie walked through the moist grass, not noticing it was soaking her shoes. She remembered holding Maisie's hand as she skipped along beside her. She closed her eyes and could actually feel the small hand in her own and hear quite clearly the things that Maisie had said: 'Mummy, why doesn't the sun come out every day?' 'Mummy, where is heaven?' 'Do you love me, Mummy?' Brodie had picked her up, hugged her, told her she was the most loved little girl in the whole, wide world. She remembered a much older Maisie sitting on the swing, grinning widely, full of life. 'I plan my future here,' she'd said. Well, she wouldn't have planned on becoming a drug addict.

Karen Grant had telephoned about three weeks ago. She had nothing to report: there'd been no sign of Maisie. 'But I'm still on the case. I'll get back to you as soon as I hear anything,' she'd said.

Brodie sat on a bench, aware but not caring that it was damp. She heard the gate creak and Colin came into the garden. She felt so surprised she thought she was dreaming.

He said, 'I thought you might be out here, that's why I didn't ring the bell.'

'Why have you come?' Brodie asked. She still felt odd and dreamy. She noticed that his brown hair needed cutting and his sweatshirt hadn't been ironed. There were oil stains on his jeans: it being Saturday, he must have been working on the Triumph. He looked very young, hardly old enough to have two grown-up children. She realized that, despite everything, she loved him very much, but there was a barrier between them that neither he nor she could – or would – cross.

'I've come to cut the grass,' he said surprisingly.

'There isn't a proper lawnmower.' There was just a manual one, very elderly. It would take a week to cut the grass with it and she kept meaning to throw it out.

'I've brought the one from home. It's in the boot.' He aimed a kick at the grass. 'It'll go through this in no time.'

'That's very kind of you,' Brodie stood, suddenly aware that her behind was freezing; the moisture on the bench had soaked through her skirt. 'But there's no need.'

'Of course there's a need,' he said huffily. Perhaps he was hurt that she didn't appear grateful. 'It looks as if it hasn't been cut for ages. I'll just go and get the mower.'

Their mower had a petrol engine. Brodie had never been able to start it, but Colin had no difficulty. It sliced through the long grass leaving a bright green flat ribbon behind. Brodie stood and watched for a while, then took a rusty rake from the shed and began to gather the cut grass into heaps.

Eventually, the whole garden was bright green. Brodie fetched plastic bags from the kitchen and held them for Colin to fill with grass, weeds and the few leaves that had fallen. It was the way they'd worked together all the years they'd been married, though the lawn in their old house had never been allowed to grow so long.

When it was finished, she thanked Colin and made him tea and a sandwich. They sat in her room and he started to mumble something about not having meant it when he'd suggested she go to work, but she cut him short.

'You meant it at the time,' she told him.

He went red. 'I'm sorry. It was a mistake. I don't mean it now.'

She didn't say that now was too late. She was determined to work and support herself, if only to prove that she was capable of doing it.

They sat in silence for a while. Someone upstairs, Rachel or Vanessa, had a television on, but the sound was very faint. At one point, Colin said, 'Will we get over this, do you think?'

'I've no idea,' Brodie replied.

They sat in silence again until Colin said he'd better get going. Brodie thanked him for cutting the grass. He nodded briefly and went home.

Russell Peterson's girlfriend wore a black leather dress that was extremely revealing at both ends, exposing most of her rather pimply breasts and only narrowly missing revealing her bottom. Most of the young women there were similarly attired, leaving only a few square inches of their bodily charms to the imagination.

By contrast, Diana's full-length evening frock looked very old-fashioned. She quickly became a favourite with the elderly women present, who could remember wearing similar frocks when they were Diana's age. And it wasn't just the older men who thought there was something awfully appealing and downright sexy about the young woman with the flushed face and radiant smile who was covered from neck to toe in blue taffeta. Leo Peterson was deemed an extremely lucky fellow.

The party was being held in a new hotel by the river. It was nearly over when Leo took Diana's hand and led her into the lounge, where it was much quieter and barely half full.

'Let's sit down a minute, Di,' he said. There was a tremor in his voice and perspiration glistened on his upper lip.

'But I was enjoying the dancing,' she protested.

'We'll go back and dance in a minute.' He swallowed nervously. 'I've got you a present.'

'That's nice.' Diana smiled delightedly. 'What is it?'

'This.' He produced a little black velvet box out of his trouser pocket, opened it, and showed her the contents. 'It's a ring,' he announced. 'An engagement ring.'

Early next morning, Sunday, Diana knocked on Brodie's door.

'Come in,' Brodie shouted. 'I'm nearly ready.'

Both women usually went to Mass together along with Megan, but Diana had come about something else. 'Look!' She held out her left hand. A solitaire diamond ring glittered on the third finger.

Brodie gasped. 'What's that?'

'An engagement ring.' Diana flared her fingers and wiggled them. 'Leo and I are engaged.'

'Really? Congratulations. When are you getting married?'

'I dunno. I said I needed time to think about it.'

Diana looked faintly worried. 'He just bought the ring without telling me. Luckily, it fitted.'

'You didn't have to take it, love.'

'I did, really. I think poor Leo would have cried if I'd refused. He was already hurt because his mam and dad had paid through the nose for some group to play at the party, when they could have had the Little Dead Riding Hoods, Leo's group, for free. I mean, he's got these lovely sad brown eyes and I felt so sorry for him. I couldn't possibly have not taken it.' Diana stared critically at the ring, 'It must have cost the earth. It's a real diamond.'

It was Brodie's turn to be worried. 'If you don't mind my asking, Diana, do you love him?'

'A bit.' To Brodie's relief, Diana burst out laughing, putting her whole heart and soul into it as she always did, making her eyes shine as brightly as the ring. 'The thing is, since I haven't had the lads to think about, I seem to fall a bit in love with every man I meet. I quite fancy Tinker, even though he might be gay, and there's this Iraqi doctor at the centre who's really gorgeous. I love him as well.'

'So, if these men gave you a diamond ring you'd agree to marry them, too?' Brodie began to laugh, too.

'Probably.' Diana collapsed, still laughing, on the bed. 'Leo's mum and dad are dead pleased. Mr Peterson called me a "nice old-fashioned girl".'

'Well, you are!' Brodie said warmly. 'I'd be dead pleased if you were marrying Josh.' The only girlfriend of Josh's that she'd met had chain-smoked foul-smelling black cigarettes. She was glad when they'd split up.

'I really liked Josh, too.' They'd met briefly the first

weekend Brodie had moved into the house when Josh had come to Liverpool with his friend, Murdoch.

'Shall we go to Mass?' Brodie tucked a lace scarf in her handbag. It wasn't necessary to wear a hat in church any more, but old habits died hard and she felt undressed without one.

Diana said, 'On the way back, shall we go to that place opposite Leonard Gosling's shop and have coffee and a cream cake? I can tell him Vanessa doesn't want to go to lunch today – I think she's still a bit upset about her hair.' She grinned. 'Actually, I think I might be a little bit in love with Leonard, too.'

Chapter 6

Brodie and Diana had gone to work when Vanessa returned from her morning walk along the shore and found a rusty Ford Cortina parked outside the house and a strange woman waiting by the front door. The woman was in her forties, with dyed blonde hair and bright orange make-up plastered on her hard face. She wore bright pink combat trousers with a lime-green T-shirt and said that she was Rachel Keen's mother and had been ringing the bell, but there was no answer. Although Vanessa didn't like the look of her, she had little choice but to let her in. Perhaps Rachel was still asleep.

'Rachel's in the upstairs room at the back,' she said. She wasn't thanked when she unlocked the door and stood aside to let the woman in.

She was washing at the sink in her room when an unholy scream rent the air. Grabbing a towel, she rushed on to the landing. There was another scream: it came from Rachel's room where the door was wide open.

'Just give her to me, girl,' a rough female voice was saying, not unkindly. 'Let your mam have her and come on home. You can go back to school again. It'll be the best thing in the long run, Rach, I promise.'

Vanessa paused in the doorway. Rachel, still in her nightdress, was standing in the corner holding Poppy tightly against her breast. Her mother stood threateningly in front of her, arms outstretched towards the baby.

'No,' Rachel screamed. 'I'm keeping her, she's mine, she's my daughter. How did you find out where I was?'

'Our Frances followed Tyler when he came out of school the other day. We had to find out, girl,' the mother said, a faint note of contrition in her voice. 'Women from the Social Services keep coming round asking about you and the baby, where you've gone, like. They're dead worried about you.'

'What's going on here?' Vanessa enquired. Poppy had begun to cry. It was an unpleasant situation and she tried not to sound as nervous as she felt. On reflection, she should have asked Rachel if she wanted to see her mother before letting her in. She might have deliberately not been answering the door.

'It's none of your effing business,' the woman snarled over her shoulder. 'Eff off.'

'I have no intention of effing off,' Vanessa said with as much dignity as she could muster. 'If no one's going to tell me what's going on, then I shall ring the police.'

It was Rachel who answered. 'She wants to take Poppy away and send her to be adopted.' She began to cry. 'But she's my little girl, *mine*, and I want to keep her.'

The mother said, without looking at Vanessa, 'Do

you know how old she is? Hardly fifteen. The father's a year older. They only want to set up home together.'

'What's wrong with that? I'm sure it's been done before.' Vanessa took a step into the room. 'I think it's time you left. Rachel clearly doesn't want you here. If you don't go straight away, then, like I said, I'm calling the police.'

'Rachel shouldn't be here.' This time, the woman turned around. To Vanessa's surprise, she looked more upset than angry. Her mascara had smudged under her left eye. 'She should be at home living with her mam. I told you, she's only fifteen. Kids aren't allowed to leave home until they're sixteen.'

'That's not true.' Vanessa had no idea how she knew: perhaps she'd read it somewhere in the days when she'd read serious newspapers or watched serious programmes on TV. 'Children under sixteen are entitled to leave home if they don't get on with their parents, as long as they move to a safe environment. I keep an eye on the baby,' she lied, 'and a district nurse comes once a week.'

'If she keeps that baby,' Mrs Keen said a touch despairingly, 'it'll ruin her life. The same thing happened to me. And if she thinks the dad'll marry her when the time comes, she's got another think coming. She won't have a childhood, and she won't finish her schooling, either. She's a clever girl, wanted to be a teacher when she grew up.'

'She still can,' Vanessa said smoothly. She felt strongly that Rachel should be allowed to keep Poppy, despite her young age. She tried to lead Rachel's mother towards the door, then towards the stairs, without actually touching her, just standing behind and urging her along with her stomach.

When they reached the front door, the woman seemed to regret she'd given in so easily. 'I'll be back,' she promised, scowling. 'There's thousands of women who can't have kids and will give Poppy a much better life than our Rachel ever could. It's not fair on any child to have a mother who's only a child herself.'

Vanessa opened the door and practically pushed the woman out. 'That's open to question, Mrs Keen.'

The woman's expression changed. She looked pleadingly at Vanessa. 'You'll look out for her, won't you? And the baby?'

'Of course I will. And will you promise not to tell Social Services where Rachel is? I can assure you she's perfectly safe here.'

'I suppose so,' Mrs Keen said grudgingly. She lit a cigarette before getting in the car, and Vanessa closed the door with a sigh of relief. She was shaking, though pleased she'd managed to handle the situation as well as she had. At the same time, she wasn't exactly happy about having committed herself to look out for a teenaged mother and her baby. She couldn't help but wonder what had prompted her to do it.

'She's horrible.' Rachel was standing at the top of the stairs, still holding Poppy. Her face was pale and her eyes enormous. 'I hate her.'

'I think she loves you very much.'

'Well, she's got a funny way of showing it. When I told her I was expecting Poppy, she nearly burst a blood vessel. Then she rang up some place and told them I wanted the baby adopted. Women kept coming round to try and talk me into it. They said I was too young to be a mother.'

'Despite that, I still think that in her own way your mother loves you. I don't think she'll give you away to the authorities, not again, not now she's seen you managing so well.'

Rachel just shrugged. 'Perhaps.'

'Anyway,' Vanessa said as she climbed the stairs towards the girl, 'you are obviously a very good mother, but I do think you should let Poppy be seen regularly by a district nurse or a health visitor.' She knew hardly anything about motherhood. 'My sisters have children and I'm sure that's what happened when they were babies. I think they also went to a clinic and had injections for . . . things. We can soon find out.'

When Rachel pursed her lips and looked stubborn, she went on sternly, 'Look, I told your mother I was keeping an eye on you and Poppy, which isn't true. I also said the district nurse came regularly and that isn't true, either. I would feel very irresponsible if I let things continue the way they are. I think we should have a word with Brodie when she comes home. She's had two children and she'll know what to do.' She desperately wished Brodie were there now. 'By the way, who is Tyler?'

'Poppy's dad.' Her little face began to glow. 'He's American and he goes to school in Waterloo. He comes most afternoons on his way home. We're getting married as soon as I'm sixteen.'

It turned out to be the day that things changed for Vanessa. Later on, after she'd showered and weighed herself, she discovered she'd lost four pounds. Her weight had been going slowly down in dribs and drabs, but this was the first considerable drop.

Then when Rachel announced she was going to sit in the garden with the baby, Vanessa said she'd better go with her. 'I think one of us should be with you all the time from now on when you're outside.' It was a kind gesture, particularly as Vanessa wasn't normally given to kind gestures.

So far, unlike Diana and Brodie, she hadn't felt inclined to sit in the garden despite the spring weather being really lovely – perhaps it was because she preferred to avoid the other women – but she remembered the canvases and paints she'd bought in Leonard Gosling's shop weeks before. They'd been stuck under her bed ever since. She took them out and carried everything outside. It was a warm day, but not as sunny as it had been. The clouds raced by, obscuring the sun for long periods.

Rachel was already there, her head buried in a book. Poppy was fast asleep in her pushchair underneath a big shady tree. Maybe the girl didn't fancy spending the afternoon in the company of a woman of thirty-one. She seemed to switch from behaving like a frightened, vulnerable child to a sensible young mother.

Vanessa wondered what to prop the canvas on. It measured about half a metre square. She needed an easel, but she wasn't in the mood to go out and buy one there and then. In the shed, she found an old wooden ladder that would do for now. She set it up beneath the largest tree and put the open box of paints on a chair – twelve tubes of different colours. The lid was a palette on which the paints were mixed.

What to paint? It was just an ordinary garden, if a bit bigger than most, and extremely untidy. Vanessa chewed her bottom lip and half-closed her eyes as she scrutinized her surroundings: the old trees, the swollen bushes just starting to bloom, the rundown shed with loose planks and a crooked door, the ginger cat sitting on the roof regarding her critically, the tightly grown laurel hedge at the back of the house and the crumbling brick wall between this garden and the one next door. Then there was the house itself, which had perhaps been built over a hundred years ago, with its old grey bricks and floor-length windows through which could be seen faded carpets with dark shadowy patches here and there. Lastly, Rachel in her blue jeans and red top, the invisible baby hiding behind the hood of her pushchair.

Everything! Vanessa wanted to paint every single thing. It *wasn't* just an ordinary garden; it was a thing of incredible beauty. She looked critically at it again and it made her heart lift.

She painted one of the trees as if she were standing inside it, as if she were the tree's heart surrounded by its leaves. Green leaves were boring, she thought after a while, so she made them red and blue, yellow and purple, pink and cream.

It was a wonderful feeling, imagining standing in the middle of the leaves, exciting, satisfying, incomparable to anything she'd known before: better than sex, better than *eating* . . . she didn't feel even faintly hungry.

'What's that supposed to be?'

'A tree,' Vanessa replied.

Rachel had put down her book and was lifting Poppy out of her pram. The baby sat on her arm and wriggled her feet playfully. Rachel poked her in the stomach: her eyes danced and she actually smiled. Vanessa didn't think babies smiled until they were about one. She couldn't help but smile herself at the sight of the baby shuffling about on her mother's knee.

'She looks healthy enough,' she remarked.

'I do all the things it says to do in the baby book. She has the right vitamins and stuff and I give her the right amount of milk, though I couldn't manage to breastfeed. It's time she had her injections, but I was scared to go to a clinic in case they took her off me. But,' she said, jiggling the baby up and down, much to Poppy's delight, 'I don't mind taking her now that you're coming with me.'

Vanessa couldn't remember offering to go with her to the clinic, but supposed she better had.

'Your painting's very nice,' the girl said. 'I must go and make Poppy her bottle.'

'Let me know if you need a hand, won't you?' Vanessa was still engrossed in the painting. She wanted to put dots on it somewhere, white dots.

Twice during the night she woke and could smell oil paint. Each time, she switched on the bedside light and admired the painting that she'd propped on a chair. Brodie had called it 'remarkable,' which she felt sure was the word she'd used to describe her hair after she'd cut it, and Diana said it was 'the gear': she loved the colours. Neither had recognized it as a tree. But Vanessa didn't care. Tomorrow – she remembered it was the early hours of the morning – today, she would go to Leonard Gosling's shop and buy more canvases, more paint, and an easel. From now on, she would paint every day. She would become an artist.

Leonard was genuinely pleased to see her. 'It's ages since we met,' he said joyfully. 'Diana said you've been feeling off colour. Are you all right now?'

'Absolutely fine,' Vanessa sang.

'You're looking extraordinarily well.' He said this with a little bow. 'You suit your hair short, if you don't mind my saying.'

'Thank you,' she said modestly. Diana had tidied her hair again and it looked as good as if she'd been to a top-class hairdresser – or so they told each other.

'Have you lost weight?'

'A tiny bit.' She couldn't recall hearing any words that thrilled her quite so much, not even when William had proposed, though on reflection, she had a feeling that she'd proposed to him. 'Yesterday, I did a painting,' she told Leonard proudly.

'Did you really?' He looked hugely impressed. 'Would you mind if I came to see it sometime?'

'Not in the least. I've called it *Tree*.'

She told him what she'd come for and he advised that she buy canvas boards rather than genuine canvases. 'They're made by Winsor & Newton and only cost a fraction of the price. Would you like a folding easel or the other sort?'

'What are the other sort?'

'The sort that collapse flat as opposed to folding into a smallish square. All the grand masters had the other sort. They are far more regal and suited to a *real* artist. I can't imagine our dear Queen having her portrait painted by an artist using a folding easel,' he said with enormous pomposity.

'In that case, I'll have the regal sort.'

'You have made a wise choice, Vanessa.'

After she'd paid for everything and it had been stowed in the boot of her car, Leonard asked if she would like coffee and a cream cake in the coffee shop across the road.

She accepted, but said all she wanted was black coffee. She thought how wonderful it was to be alive.

Brodie didn't like her latest job, but didn't exactly dislike it, either. It was just a job. She worked in an old people's home in Southport. It was called Five Oaks for the obvious reason. She cleaned in the morning and helped with the laundry in the afternoon. Her favourite piece of equipment was the polisher. She'd never used one before and she always had the urge to waltz down the corridors with it while singing a Chris de Burgh song.

She had asked if she could work through the lunch-hour and go home an hour early. Mrs Cowper, who was in charge of the domestic side of things, had agreed. She didn't mind when the work was done as long as it was done properly.

Had Brodie had a lunch-hour, she might have been tempted to roam around the centre of Southport, a place where, year after year, she and Colin had brought the children in the summer holidays to play football and cricket on the sands, visit the fairground and the pier, and have fish and chips in the cheap little café that also sold mouth-watering Eccles cakes. She usually bought half a dozen to take home. She knew she would cry if she saw that café now.

Those days had been gloriously happy, but she hadn't been conscious of it at the time. If she was ever that happy again, she'd make sure she was aware of it, appreciate it more.

She was on her way back to collect her car from the car park, another day's work thankfully over, when a voice called, 'Brodie! Brodie Logan! Is it really you?'

A woman in a white top, white linen trousers and gold sandals with high heels was coming towards her with a wide smile on her perfectly made-up face. Her smooth black hair was rippling as she moved. When she reached Brodie, she grasped her shoulders and bestowed kisses on both cheeks. She smelled of very expensive perfume. Brodie smelled of Persil and fabric conditioner.

'How lovely to see you,' she cooed. Her lips twitched. 'You don't remember me, do you?'

'I'm sorry,' Brodie stammered. She had no idea who the woman was and wished she were wearing something smarter than an oldish cotton frock and even older sandals. She had no make-up on and hadn't combed her hair since she'd got up that morning. Although she'd never been keen on trousers, she was particularly taken with the woman's white ones.

'Polly Baker, as was. We lived next door to each other in Crosby when we were first married. We had two children around the same time, though I had the girl first and the boy second. How are your children getting on? And how is your husband? He was a teacher, wasn't he? Colin! He must surely be a headmaster by now.'

'He's head of English.' Colin had never had any ambition to become a headmaster. He loved teaching English. 'Our son, Josh, has his own business and Maisie's in her second year at university.' She wished she'd left work a few minutes earlier, or a few minutes later, and had missed meeting Polly Baker, who, in the old days, had seemed to live in jeans and her husband's old shirts and had her hair cut like a boy. She wasn't in the mood to reminisce about the past and tell lies about the present, yet wasn't prepared to tell the truth, either. 'And what about your children?' she asked dutifully. 'Your husband's name was Roger, I remember that.'

'Natalie works for a top advertising agency in London,' her ex-neighbour said boastfully. 'And Dylan decided not to go to university. He's a member of a pop group. Their latest single narrowly missed getting in the charts.'

'That's fantastic,' Brodie murmured. 'And Roger?'

'Oh, I got rid of Roger yonks ago.' She waved her long white hands with their long red nails dismissively. 'In fact, I'm Polly Michaels now. Edward owns a factory making pipes: exhaust pipes, drain pipes, stuff like that.'

'What are you doing here?' Brodie asked. She recalled having liked Polly during the years they'd lived next door to each other, but she didn't like her now.

'I come once week to see Roger's old dad,' she replied. 'His new wife's a bit of a cow and poor old Albert is sadly neglected. He's a dear old thing and I'm very fond of him.'

Brodie decided she did like Polly, after all. They

exchanged telephone numbers and promised to meet up for coffee one day. She was glad Polly hadn't asked what *she* was doing there, as she wasn't sure if she was prepared to admit she was a cleaner, despite there being nothing shameful about it.

Driving back to Blundellsands, she wondered if Natalie really did work for a top advertising agency and if Dylan hadn't attended university because he couldn't get into one. She would never know, just as Polly would never know the truth about Brodie's children.

The encounter had shaken her, though. She'd never been one for keeping up with the Jones's. Fifteen years ago the Bakers had moved from the house next door to a much better one and she hadn't felt envious at the time, but now she envied Polly's obvious *cheerfulness*. Brodie couldn't remember when she'd last felt cheerful, apart from brief periods such as when they'd watched *Gone With the Wind* and made a night of it. They'd done the same thing last week with *Now, Voyager* starring Bette Davis and Paul Henreid: 'Why ask for the moon, darling, when we can have the stars?' Diana kept saying in a Bette Davis voice while pretending to smoke a cigarette.

Brodie smiled. Diana made her feel cheerful.

When she arrived home, she found Eileen, her mother-in-law, in the garden nursing Poppy, who was fast asleep in her arms. Brodie hadn't seen her since last October when she was about to leave the country to spend the winter in Goa and had come to Liverpool from London to say goodbye. Now she had come to announce she was back.

'I talked her mum into having a nice, relaxing bath,' she said, kissing Poppy's nose. 'She was very reluctant at first, but I managed to convince her that I was related to you, had four children of my own, no criminal convictions, and was extremely trustworthy. She's a sweet little thing. How old is she?'

'Do you mean Rachel or the baby?'

'Rachel.'

'Fifteen.' Brodie hadn't been all that surprised when Vanessa told her about Rachel's mother's visit to the house. 'You look wonderful, Eileen,' she said. 'Incredibly glamorous and the picture of health.' Her mother-in-law was in her late sixties, but could have easily passed for ten years less, even fifteen. She'd worn size twelve clothes since she was a teenager, something she was extremely proud of, and used just enough cosmetics to enhance her features, without looking like mutton dressed up as lamb. Her thick grey hair was streaked with silver. Like Polly Baker earlier, she wore white trousers, though with white sandals and a pink see-through blouse. Eileen was a lovely down-to-earth person with a colourful use of language. She was rarely seen without a cigarette in her mouth, though she was without one now as she nursed the baby.

'I feel wonderful,' she said in a heartfelt tone, 'particularly when I saw George and realized how fortunate I was to have left the miserable old bugger behind. But what's this about you and our Colin?' She looked genuinely distressed. 'Oh, Brodie, luv, you always seemed such a happy couple. I thought you had a perfect marriage. I can't even begin to imagine what went wrong. What do Josh and Maisie have to say about it – and why didn't anyone let me know?'

'I knew you'd find out about it when you came home,' Brodie said. 'It seemed silly to upset you until then.' Clearly, Colin hadn't thought to write and let his mother know their marriage was on the rocks. Was it on the rocks? Or was the present situation just a hiccup? Brodie had no idea. What did Colin think?

'Am I allowed to know the reason why?' Eileen asked. 'Or is it too personal?' Poppy sighed and Eileen stroked her white cheek. 'Poor baby! She sounds as if she has the weight of the whole world on her shoulders. Perhaps she will one of these days. I'm glad mine aren't young any more.'

'I'm surprised Colin didn't tell you why we've split,' Brodie said.

'I haven't seen Colin yet, only George. He was at your house working on that old car when I went round this avvy expecting to see you. His lordship told me sod all, only that you didn't live there any more.' Eileen snorted. 'He was kind enough to give me your address. I suspect *he* could be the cause of your difficulties. After all, I went halfway around the world to escape the bugger, didn't I, only for him to land himself on you. Is he there all the time, luv?'

'Not *all* the time, but he's there enough,' Brodie admitted. 'There've been occasions when I wished you were still around to keep him at home.'

'No such luck, I'm afraid. It seems I was living it up in Goa, while you suffered at home.' She regarded Brodie worriedly. 'Seriously, is George the reason you broke up with Colin?'

'I'll tell you later.' Soon, Rachel would come to retrieve her baby and Diana would be home. 'Have you met Vanessa?' she asked. 'She paints. Well, she has done for the past few weeks.'

Eileen's lively face brightened. 'Yes, I've met her. She was here when I arrived, and was doing this absolutely fabulous painting. I don't know what it was, but the colours were amazing. She's going to give it me when the paint dries.'

'You *liked* it?'

'I told you, it was fabulous.'

'They all look like a load of rubbish to me. Poppy could do as well if someone gave her a brush.' The ginger cat stalked by, eyeing them arrogantly. 'And Kenneth could do even better.'

'Brodie, luv, you have absolutely no imagination. And who's Kenneth?'

Eileen stayed until after tea. They ate – she, Brodie and Diana – in the old dining room where Brodie had eaten when she was child, but which the Slattery sisters had hardly used, preferring to live in the four big rooms that they'd turned into bedsits.

It was Diana's idea that they have a communal dining room. 'It's friendlier,' she claimed. She thought it unsociable that the four women should make their own meals, then take them to eat in their own rooms. And she thought the room should be called 'the snug'. 'I read a book once about a house having a room called the snug.'

'But we can't make our separate meals all at the same time so we can eat them at the same time,' Brodie pointed out. She thought it a lovely idea – she and Diana often had breakfast together – but a bit impractical.

'Then we can all have the same meal. I mean, take turns to cook for four,' Diana suggested. 'I make lovely scouse – least, the lads used to think so.'

'Yes, but what does Rachel do with Poppy?' Brodie said reasonably. Diana's often expressed desire to turn the house into a commune could be a bit of a pain. 'She'll never leave her upstairs on her own: we'd have to get a high chair. As for Vanessa, she's on a diet. Surely you've noticed the salad stuff in the fridge. She won't like sitting down to a lettuce leaf and a slice of tomato while we tuck into scouse. And she's not exactly a friendly person, is she? She'd probably far sooner eat by herself.'

'Probably.' Diana looked downcast. 'Anyroad,' she perked up a bit, 'everywhere Vanessa goes she smells of paint. It'd spoil the meals for us.'

'Exactly,' Brodie said, relieved that Diana had given in. 'But at least us two can eat in the dining room – I mean, the snug. We'll take turns making dinner and if the others notice and want to join us, then it's up to them.'

At this, Diana had been all smiles.

It was nice, though, eating together. They had a Marks & Spencer's chicken pie that Brodie had bought the previous weekend, accompanied by new potatoes and fresh peas. For pudding, they had stewed apple and custard that Diana had made. Eileen said it was years since she'd last had apple and custard, and that she'd forgotten how nice it was.

'I used brown sugar,' Diana explained earnestly, 'that's why the apple was a bit brown. It's so much better for you than white.'

'So I've heard,' Eileen said.

Afterwards, Brodie and Eileen went back into the garden while Diana took a heap of washing into the laundry room.

'You wanted to know why Colin and I aren't living together,' Brodie began. 'First of all, I must explain about Maisie . . .'

'Holy Mary, Mother of God!' Eileen gasped about ten minutes later when Brodie had finished describing, not just her daughter's plight, but Colin's reaction to it. 'Oh, Brodie, luv, it must have been awful for you. As for our Colin, he wants his arse whacking with a broomstick – I'll be tempted to do it the minute I clap eyes on him. Have you no idea at all where Maisie is?'

'Only that she was in London last time I heard.' She'd had another phone call from Karen, who still had no knowledge of Maisie's whereabouts, but had promised never to give up.

'London's an awful big place,' Eileen murmured. 'If you had a clue where she might be, I could look for her meself.' Very soon, she was going back there to live with her sister, Mary.

The phone rang in the hall and Brodie heard Diana answer it. A few minutes later, she came into the garden and announced that their Damian was coming in his car to collect her and she'd be gone for a while.

Brodie sensed trouble. 'Is everything all right?' she asked.

'Not really.' Diana pulled a face. 'I'll tell you later.'

'I'll wait up for you,' Brodie promised.

'Ta.'

'Have you adopted her?' Eileen asked when Diana had gone.

Brodie said with a wry smile. 'I was in need of a

daughter and she a mother. We've sort of adopted each other.'

'Mum,' Diana said when she went into the house in Coral Street, 'are you all right?'

'Not really, Di,' her mother said tearfully, flinging her arms around her daughter. Damian, Jason and Garth were in various parts of the living room wearing frowns that ranged from the sceptical to the plain fed up. There was little love in their hearts for the mother who had abandoned them seven years before. Of Emma, there was no sign. 'I've left Warren, luv,' her mother sobbed. 'He's got another woman. She's nearly twenty years younger than I am.'

'Where are Shaw and Jude?' Her stepbrothers were only five and three. They were really adorable little boys.

'I've left them with Warren, luv. He loves his lads. He won't harm a hair on their heads.' Michelle nestled her own head against Diana's shoulder. 'Oh, luv, I thought we could sleep together in the double bed. No one told me you'd gone away and this Emma girl had moved in. I've got nowhere to sleep, luv. Damian said you're living in this lovely big house and there might be room enough there for me.'

'I said no such thing, Mam,' Damian snapped. 'I said you could sleep here in the box room like our Di did before she left. There's a single bed in there. I only went and fetched Di because you insisted.'

'I don't know what's going to happen to me,' Michelle wailed loudly. 'I've no longer got a home to go to.'

Diana and Damian exchanged glances: this was quite

obviously true. The Coral Street house had been bought by their father and Diana supposed, in law, it belonged to Mam. On the other hand, Diana and the lads had paid the mortgage for the last seven years. It was all very confusing.

Damian said, 'If Warren's been unfaithful, he should be asked to leave the place in Nottingham and you can live there. I'll go and see him at the weekend if you like, Mam.'

Michelle sniffed disconsolately. 'I don't want to be stuck in Nottingham all on me own.'

'You'd have Shaw and Jude,' Garth pointed out. 'Or are you going to walk out on them like you did with us?'

'I told you, Warren loves his lads.'

'But will his new girlfriend love them?' Garth persisted.

Everybody looked at each other, but it was a question only the new girlfriend could answer.

'I feel so *sorry* for her,' Diana said tragically to Brodie much later that night. Brodie had made her cocoa to calm her nerves. 'I mean, the lads were awful short with her, but she can't help the way she is, can she?' They were talking about her mother, who'd been left to sleep in the box room of the house in Coral Street.

'No, but if you carry that way of thinking to its logical conclusion, then you could say the same about Hitler.' It was the sort of argument that Colin would have enjoyed.

Diana, however, completely ignored it. 'You know what I did? I took me engagement ring off before I went because I didn't want her asking to meet Leo's mam and dad. Isn't that horrible? She looked so sad, poor thing, as if she knew. Would you go back and live at home if you were me?'

'No, I would not,' Brodie said firmly. She didn't want to lose Diana. And she wasn't just being selfish, but thinking of the girl as well. 'Where would you sleep?' she asked, 'with your mother in the box room.'

'That's a point.' Diana spoke as if she hadn't given a thought to the sleeping arrangements. They'd been unsatisfactory when she'd left and would be even worse with another person on the premises. 'She asked if she could come and live here.'

'I hope you told her that she couldn't.' Having her mother on the premises, probably expecting to be looked after, would be disastrous for the girl. 'Really, Diana, your mother's not an old woman. How old is she?'

'Forty-five.'

'She's only two years older than me.' Brodie would have liked to give Diana's mother a piece of her mind. 'She's well old enough to look after herself. And she has a nerve, turning up after all this time and expecting her children to take her in.' Colin would have said exactly the same thing. 'Remember the day we met? You were so unhappy. But since you moved in here, you seem to enjoy having a life of your own.'

'Do I?'

'Yes.' Brodie nodded. 'And now your mother's talking about walking out on two more of her children, even younger than your brothers were when she left. What are their names?'

'Shaw and Jude. Y'know,' Diana said, 'I used to

imagine our lads leaving home and Mam bringing the little ones for me to look after until *they* left.'

'By which time, *you'd* be around forty-five! No, Diana.' Brodie shook her head so hard it gave her an instant headache. 'It's about time you put your foot down and told your mother to grow up.'

'I'm not much good at putting me foot down,' Diana said in a small voice.

'I know you're not, dear, and that's just one of the things I like so much about you. You're too soft-hearted by a mile.'

When Diana arrived home from the centre the next day, she was annoyed to find her mother, dressed like a teenager in a red mini-dress over footless tights, in the garden talking to Brodie's mother.

'I've had a terrible hard life,' she was saying. 'I've suffered more than any woman should.'

'You poor thing,' Megan said sympathetically.

'Six kids I've had – *six!*' Her mother spoke as if six children were a terrible affliction.

At this, Megan looked desperately sad. 'I only had the one, I'd've loved to have had six.'

Diana's mother didn't quite know what to say to this. She changed the subject. 'I must say, our Di's fallen on her feet. This is a lovely house to live in. Does it belong to you?'

'No, it belongs to Brodie, my daughter.'

So far, neither woman had noticed Diana was there. When they did, she sensed that Megan was relieved. She excused herself immediately and said she wanted to start making Brodie's meal. 'She's going to be late today. There's a tea party at the home and they asked her to stay and help.'

She disappeared into the house, leaving Diana and Michelle alone together. 'How did you know where I lived, Mam?' Diana asked. It was a truly horrible thought to have about your own mother, and she felt dead ashamed for having it, but she would sooner she hadn't come to Chestnuts. Her presence took the shine off the place. There wasn't such a pleasant atmosphere.

'I asked that Emma girl.' Her mother looked out-raged. 'I could tell she wanted me out the way. You'd never think it was *my* house. What on earth prompted our Damian to get tied up with her? You won't catch me at the wedding, I'll tell you that much,' she finished spitefully.

'Shall I make us a cup of tea, Mam?' Diana offered. 'Afterwards, we could go back to Coral Street on the train and have something to eat there.'

Her mother sighed heavily. 'I was expecting to be given me tea here.' She sighed again, even more heavily. 'But never mind, eh? I know when I'm not wanted, but I never thought it'd be by me own daughter. It would appear I'm not wanted anywhere.'

Ashamed, Diana quickly made scrambled eggs on toast followed by tinned peaches and a spoonful of Cream of Cornish ice-cream – she and Brodie had bought a carton between them the week before. She and her mother, who had become strangely quiet, sat by the little table in her room to eat.

'I think I'll go back to Nottingham tomorrer,' she said when they'd finished.

Diana gasped. 'But what about Warren and the other woman?'

'I might have got hold of the wrong end of the stick. The woman might've just been giving him a lift home from town. She only lives in the house opposite. Sometimes, her little boy plays with our Jude.'

Diana got the distinct impression that the whole thing had been a lie: that Warren hadn't been out with a much younger woman; that her mother had just felt like a break and the cheapest place to have it was in Coral Street. She wondered how much Warren knew about it. 'What time will you be leaving, Mam?' she enquired.

'Oh, I dunno, luv. I suppose you'll be only too glad to see the back of me,' she said bitterly. All of a sudden, she looked old and tired and desperately forlorn. 'No one wants me.'

'Don't be daft!' Diana put her arm around her mother's shoulders and squeezed them. She wondered what sort of star her mother was chasing and if she would ever catch it and be happy. 'I thought I'd ask my boss if I can take an extra-long lunch-hour,' she said. 'We can meet in town, have something to eat, then I'll come with you to Lime Street station and see you on the train.' She had a wonderful idea. 'Oh, and it's your birthday next month. If we've got the time, I'll buy you a little prezzie. You'll find an Argos catalogue at home in the cupboard under the stairs. Have a look through the jewellery and see if there's anything you like up to about thirty pounds.'

They had a lovely three-course lunch in an Indian restaurant in Bold Street, after which they went to

Argos and Diana bought her mother a pretty mother-of-pearl and marquisite ring.

'I'll treasure it for always,' Michelle said tearfully. 'Oh, Di, I was beginning to think you didn't love me any more.'

'I'll never stop loving you, Mam.' Diana felt just as tearful. She'd learned a hard and painful lesson: that no matter how much you loved someone, it didn't mean you wanted that person to be part of your everyday life.

Brodie had a need to satisfy. On Saturday, she caught the train into town and went to T.J. Hughes's, a well-known Liverpool department store that sold goods at amazingly cheap prices, and bought a pair of white trousers. She'd been thinking about them all week. She also bought gold sandals and a lovely gauzy Indian top. The whole lot cost just under twenty-five pounds.

After paying for the things, she went into a cubicle, got changed and went to meet her mother for a coffee, feeling like a million dollars.

Chapter 7

Sometimes there was violence in the centre and Tinker had to call the police if he wasn't able to control it, or if Alan, with his boxer's fists, wasn't there to control it for him. It was usually a fight, always between men: over money, over women, or if someone was suspected of cheating at one of the games. Sometimes arguments between refugees from different countries, tribes or religions would turn ugly. Knives had been flashed but, so far, no one had been hurt.

In their homeland, some refugees had feared for their lives or been tortured. Women had been raped, their husbands killed and sometimes their children. Even worse, the children had just disappeared and couldn't be found anywhere. These sad women came to Britain for a better life, a peaceful one, a genuine refuge from the life they'd had before.

It was these women that Diana felt the most sorry for. They seemed lost and bewildered, with no one to turn to if their application for asylum was turned down, which often happened, though it seemed monstrously unfair. An expert in asylum law came to the centre one afternoon a week to offer advice.

One morning, a few days after Diana's mother had

returned to Nottingham, four young women ran screaming into the centre, not stopping at reception to register as they were supposed to. (Tinker only asked for a person's name and their country of origin. From then on, they were expected to sign in and out whenever they came again so he would know exactly who was on the premises.)

Diana and Tinker looked at each other. Without a word, they left reception and raced after the women, catching up with them in the virtually empty restaurant, where they stood in the middle of the room not quite knowing what to do.

They were only girls, Diana realized. Two looked no more than thirteen or fourteen and weren't even fully grown. The other two weren't much older. They were pale-skinned with light-brown hair except for the smallest who was blonde.

Alan and Rosa were in charge of the restaurant that morning and Rosa was already trying to calm the girls, who were clearly terrified. 'What's wrong, darlings?' she was saying, patting them tenderly.

'We run away,' one of the girls cried shrilly. She was excessively thin with huge, haunted eyes and hollow cheeks. Some of her teeth were missing. 'Him leave open door so we run away, but him follow. Please hide us.'

Diana approached the girl and took her arm. 'Who are you talking about?'

'Hide us! Hide us, please!' the girl begged. The other three clung to her, as if she were their leader. Or perhaps she was the only one who could speak English. She shrank back, screaming. 'No, no, now is too late.'

Two men had entered the room. The first was huge and menacing with the grimmest face Diana had ever seen. His black hair was short, curly and full of grease and his dark eyes were filled with anger. With a growl, he threw himself at the girls, grasped two by the hair, and began to drag them out of the room. The girls yelled in agony.

Alan threw a punch at the big man's jaw. It had an effect, making him jerk his head sideways, but he didn't release the girls, who continued to yell and thrash about. Alan threw another punch, but he was twice the man's age and no longer had the strength to land a knockout blow on someone so obviously powerful. The only other occupant of the room, an elderly Asian woman, aimed a kick at the man's ankle, but she might well have hit him with a feather for all the notice he took.

Without any idea of what she was doing, Diana picked up a teapot off the table. It was full and felt very hot. The lid fell off and she threw the liquid into the man's face. He howled with a mixture of rage and pain, and released the girls. Rosa shepherded them into the kitchen and locked the door. Tinker had tackled the second, much smaller man, and they were rolling about on the floor. Alan was doing his utmost to fell the big man, who was still howling and holding his giant hands over his face. By now, other people had appeared out of the lounge. For a brief moment there was silence, apart from the sound of children singing in the playgroup upstairs.

'I've phoned the coppers,' someone said.

As if this were a signal, the second man aimed a violent kick at Tinker and managed to scramble to his feet. He dragged his companion out of the room, along the corridor and through the front door. Not a soul felt tempted to stop them. They stood, transfixed and silent again, until the sound of the police siren could be heard and everyone began to talk at once.

By lunchtime, things had calmed down, but those involved still felt shaky. The least little thing made Diana jump, and Tinker, who had a massive bruise on his shoulder, had drunk at least half a dozen cups of strong coffee. Rosa and Alan had gone to the pub for something even stronger and the girls had been transferred to a woman's refuge in Everton Valley where they would be interviewed by women police officers once an interpreter had been located.

'They were here legitimately,' the police sergeant said. 'The country they're from is part of the European Union, but they thought they were going to be models or actresses or something just as daft. Instead they got stuck in a brothel. The place is only just across the road. That's how the girls knew where to come; they could see the centre through the windows.'

'But they were so *young*,' gasped an appalled Diana.

'The youngest is thirteen, the oldest sixteen,' the policeman said. 'They were kept prisoner twenty-four hours a day, weren't given a penny of what they earned, weren't even fed properly, poor kids. I'd've given me eye teeth to get me hands on them two bastards,' he made a gesture with his hands as if he were snapping a neck, 'and the others that were running the bloody place, but the house was empty by the time we got there. From what we could tell, there must have been more girls, but they'd gone, too.'

After the policemen had left, promising to come back in the afternoon to take more statements, Diana went down into the basement and searched through the rack of women's clothes. There were loads of T-shirts and she picked four of the nicest, plus some jeans and summer skirts.

In her lunch-hour, she walked as far as Marks & Spencer where she bought two packs of women's briefs. She'd never minded wearing second-hand clothes, but had always balked at the idea of wearing other women's knickers. The young girls in the refuge deserved no less.

Brodie and Megan were horrified when Diana described the events of the morning.

'It must have been *awful*.' Brodie shuddered. 'And it must have taken some courage to chuck boiling hot tea in the man's face.'

'I just picked up the first thing that came to hand.' She looked troubled. 'I hope I haven't blinded him.'

'Why should you care?' Megan snorted.

'Even though he was really horrible, I'd hate to think it was my fault someone lost their sight.'

Vanessa, smelling of oil paints, came into the kitchen and took a bottle of water out of the fridge. Brodie couldn't resist telling her about Diana's adventures that morning. Vanessa's appalled reaction was only to be expected, as was Rachel's when she came to make the baby's bottle later. Diana smiled half-heartedly. She was glad the men had been stopped from taking the girls, but throwing the teapot was playing on her mind. Vanessa said this was a typical female attitude to violence.

'We can't bring ourselves to hurt people even when they're hurting us. If women were stronger than men, the world would be a much more peaceful place,' she said, somewhat illogically.

It amazed Vanessa that she didn't miss the outside world, not a bit. Yet she'd always been a terrifically busy person. Every minute of every day had been taken up with some activity or other. Her job required non-stop action: she was either on the phone, on the computer, or at a meeting. At lunch she ate at her desk, took a client to a posh restaurant in Liverpool town centre, or was taken to one herself. Even when she was alone in the flat, which happened very rarely, she was making notes about the work she had to do the following day or the following week.

Evenings and weekends, she and William had gone out together, sometimes just the two of them, at other times with friends. Often, they drove down to London to see a show and stay the night in a hotel, spending Sunday wandering around the shops and markets.

But now Vanessa rarely left the house except for her early-morning walk on the shore, the fortnightly visit to the clinic with Rachel and Poppy, and calling at Leonard Gosling's shop for more painting materials. The narrowness of her life didn't bother her. Her horizons had widened just a little in that she no longer spent all the time in her room. If the weather was fine, which it usually was – the lovely warm spring having given way to a brilliant summer – she spent hours in the garden painting. She'd begun eating in the little dining room downstairs. One day, Rachel had found her there and they'd begun to have some of their meals together. A few times, Vanessa had given Poppy her bottle. It was a strange experience holding a tiny human being in her arms. She found it hard to describe: there was something almost mystical about it.

She didn't bother about an awful lot of things that had bothered her before. She no longer read newspapers or watched the news on television, so had little idea what was going on in the world outside Chestnuts, whether another war had broken out somewhere, or peace had broken out somewhere else.

It was a lovely feeling, being ignorant. It left her with absolutely nothing to worry about. She felt sorry for Brodie and Diana who had to leave the house every day. Diana's experience with the men who'd invaded the shelter and their young victims had shocked her to the core.

She was thinking about it the next morning when she stood in the garden in front of the easel. Rachel's window was wide open and she was singing to Poppy. She could hear the squirrels moving through the trees. Occasionally, they would appear and chase each other across the grass. Bees hovered around the flowers that bordered the garden, and she could hear the strange noise that grasshoppers made – Megan said they were scratching their legs together. Every now and then a train would pass on the other side of the grassy bank.

The idea for the painting had come to her when she closed the curtains before getting into bed last night. It was all she could do not to start it there and then.

There'd been a three-quarter moon and the sky was a glorious inky blue splattered with stars no bigger than dust-mites. The slate roof on the house opposite looked silver in the muted light and the trees, silhouetted as they were against the dark, gleaming sky, were smudges of black. The grass was the darkest of greens and the garden furniture hardly visible against it.

Vanessa had gone to bed with the image in her mind and it was still there when she woke the next morning when the sky was pale and milky and everything in the garden was bright and full of colour.

She set up her easel in the usual place amidst the trees and began to paint. She painted swiftly, hardly pausing, wanting to get the scene out of her mind and on to the canvas. For some people, the silver roof might have been a problem, but Vanessa used shiny black paint streaked with brilliant white and was perfectly satisfied with the result.

Excitement began to gather in her breast as she neared the end. She could hardly wait to see what her latest work would look like when every single centimetre of the board was covered with paint.

'Hello, I thought I'd find you here.'

Vanessa looked up. Eileen, Brodie's mother-in-law, had come into the garden. She really admired Eileen, who'd walked out on her monster of a husband after forty years of marriage. It was also flattering to know that Eileen considered Vanessa's paintings absolutely fabulous.

'I won't interrupt,' Eileen said, sitting at the wooden table. 'When you've finished, I'd like to talk to you about something.'

'I'm nearly finished.'

'Then would you like me to make some coffee for when you do?'

'Please. Mine's black, no milk or sugar.' She no

longer bothered to weigh herself, but could tell by her clothes that she was growing thinner.

'OK. I'll do it now, shall I?'

Vanessa didn't answer. She was only half-conscious of Eileen going into the house. When she emerged with two mugs on a tray, the painting was complete and Vanessa was standing thoughtfully in front of the easel, her head on one side, not judging her work, or admiring it, just satisfied that it was finished and she'd got it out of her system.

'Can I see?' Vanessa nodded and Eileen came for a look. 'It's fabulous,' she breathed. She said the same thing every time. 'Absolutely fabulous. I can understand why you made the moon so incredibly big, almost as if it can be touched.' She looked imploringly at Vanessa. 'Can I please have it?'

Vanessa had no idea why she'd painted the moon so large – she hadn't realized she had until Eileen had pointed it out. 'Of course you can have it,' she said. She was generous with her paintings, mainly because she was no longer interested in them once they'd been done.

'I wish you'd let me pay for it,' Eileen said. 'This is the third I've had. You say you won't take money, but I'd love to at least buy you a prezzie before I go back to London at the weekend. Is there anything in particular that you'd like?'

Vanessa concentrated hard, but couldn't think of a single thing; she didn't want jewellery, make-up, perfume or clothes.

'Would you like a book on painting?' Eileen asked.

'I can already paint.' She didn't want to know about

technique or scale or balance or perspective or how to mix paint properly or what to mix it with.

'I didn't mean it like that!' Eileen rolled her eyes with embarrassment. 'Of course you can paint, and you do it beautifully. I meant, would you like a biography of Picasso or Van Gogh or some other painter?'

'It's awfully nice of you to offer, but no. I'm flattered that you like my paintings and you can have as many as you want. I don't want anything for them.'

'Oh, Vanessa!' Eileen said emotionally. 'What a lovely person you are! I'm just so thrilled to have met you.'

'Why, thank you.' It must have been the first time in Vanessa's adult life that she had blushed.

'Anyway,' Eileen lit a cigarette and they both sat down, 'what I wanted to say is that I think you should have an exhibition.'

Vanessa choked on the coffee. 'Don't be daft, Eileen,' she spluttered.

'I'm not being daft. There are people like me who love having original paintings. Not only that, yours are *original* originals. I mean, it wouldn't enter the head of any other artist to paint that one you've just done – at least, not in the way you've done it. It's so . . . so natural and down to earth. Your work shows enormous imagination. And it's got *body*.' She was so wholly sincere, so obviously speaking from the heart, that Vanessa was touched. 'I'm sure your pictures would sell like hot cakes. If you don't want to take money for them, then give it to charity – Diana's refugee centre, for instance.'

'And where would I hold this exhibition?' Vanessa asked. 'The Walker Art Gallery? The Liverpool Tate?'

'Here,' Eileen said, glancing around the lovely garden. 'Let the *Crosby Herald* and the *Liverpool Echo* know about it. They'll turn it into a news item if they know it's for charity. Diana will organize it for you, and Megan and Brodie will help.'

'I'll think about it,' Vanessa promised. 'It would be best to wait until I had more paintings.' She didn't want her name or photograph appearing in the paper for William and her family to see. Once Eileen had gone, Vanessa could quietly forget about an exhibition.

It reminded her that Brodie was throwing a party for Eileen before she went away. She might well stir herself enough to go into town and buy something new to wear.

'What was your father like, Diana?' Brodie asked as they were finishing their dinner in the dining room one night. (She referred to the meal as 'dinner', but Diana had *her* dinner at lunchtime and the evening meal was tea.) The sun was shining blindingly into a corner of the room, separating the light from the dark as if a knife had sliced through it.

'Me dad?' Diana leaned both arms on the table and cupped her face in her long white hands. She'd recently taken to painting her nails strange colours and today they were ice-blue and badly in need of re-touching. 'He was lovely,' she replied dreamily, half closing her eyes.

'How old were you when he left?'

'Nine. He was brown-haired, like me, and quite tall.

His name was James but everyone called him Jim. Sometimes he had a beard and sometimes he didn't, because he never shaved while he was away – he was a merchant seaman. He was lovely,' she repeated. 'Soft and gentle – too soft with me mam, that's for sure.' She paused, as if contemplating whether or not to trust Brodie with a further confidence. 'She used to have other men in when he was gone,' she said, making a face. 'Me, I didn't see anything much wrong with it at the time. I suppose I should have, but when you're only nine you think your mam and dad are perfect.'

'Where is he now?' Brodie laid her hand on Diana's arm. 'Don't answer if you think I'm being nosy, it's just that the four of us have been living together for over three months and we know very little about each other.' Vanessa was the most mysterious of all. Leonard Gosling apart, she'd never had a visitor, and if she had a mobile phone then it had never been heard to ring. Nor had she received a single letter.

Rachel was more forthcoming. She had two brothers and a sister, and Poppy's father was called Tyler and went to school in Waterloo. He called at the house on his way home from school and could occasionally be seen leaving on his bike at around half-past five. He sometimes came on Sundays and stayed upstairs with Rachel and Poppy. No one had ever spoken to him, but Vanessa had said he was American. She and Rachel had formed a friendship of sorts.

'I've no idea where me dad is,' Diana said. 'No one does. He divorced Mam and no one's heard from him since. What about your dad? Do you remember him at all?'

The sun was slowly moving across the room,

leaving only a small slice of brilliant yellow. Very soon, it would disappear altogether and the whole room would be in shadow. For some reason, this made Brodie feel sad.

'He died when I was ten months old,' she said in answer to Diana's question. 'I only know what he looked like from photographs and all mine are at home.' This was her home now, she realized, though it didn't feel permanent.

'What was his name?'

'Louis. Louis Sylvester.' The other girls had been envious of her name at school: Brodie Sylvester. Her best friend, Wendy, said it was a film star's name. 'Me, I'm Wendy Lott,' she'd said disgustedly. 'When I become a film star, I'll have to change it.' Wendy hadn't become a film star. Instead, she'd married a builder called Timothy Houghton and gone to live in Australia.

'My dad was born in Ireland,' Brodie said to Diana. 'He and Mum met on a boat − a liner − sailing from New York to Liverpool. They got married soon afterwards.'

'It sounds dead romantic.' Diana edged her chair into the very last of the sunlight. Her untidy hair turned from brown to a tangle of gold. 'What was your mum doing in New York? I've always wanted to go there.'

'Nearly everyone does. Mum had an aunt over there who was on the stage. Don't ask what her name was because I've no idea: she was only in the chorus.' At junior school, some children had taunted Brodie for not having a father, but she was too sensible to care. It wasn't *her* fault he had died of pneumonia when he was only thirty-nine.

'He had a weak chest,' her mother told her many years later. 'His family back in Ireland were dirt-poor and he hadn't had the proper nourishment when he was a child.' But he'd been brilliant at figures, Brodie's father. He'd actually gone to university and become a forensic accountant, able to charge fantastic fees.

The sun disappeared altogether and it was as if a black cloud had settled on the room. Brodie got to her feet. 'Shall I make a drink and we'll take it into the garden? It's sunny out there.'

Diana stretched her arms tiredly and nodded.

'Tea or coffee?' Brodie asked.

'Whatever you're having.'

'Then it's coffee.'

When Brodie said she was throwing a party for Eileen before she returned to London, Diana asked Tinker if he would like to come. Leo wasn't very pleased. 'But I'm your boyfriend,' he protested. 'Your *fiancé*. You shouldn't be asking other men out.'

Diana laughed. 'Don't be silly. Tinker's just a friend. I'm not asking him *out*, just to the party.' If the truth were known, she sometimes forgot she and Leo were engaged, which wasn't exactly fair. He was awfully nice and would make some girl a wonderful husband.

'Mum and Dad are taking us to Ormskirk at the weekend to look at houses,' he announced. 'They're building a new estate there.'

'Really?' She kept hoping he would go off her, but he showed no sign of it.

Brodie said she was silly to let the engagement

continue. 'The longer it goes on, the more difficult it will be to extricate yourself and the more poor Leo will be hurt. Before you know it, you'll be walking down the aisle, and when the priest asks if anyone knows any reason why the two of you shouldn't be joined together in Holy Matrimony, I'm going to shout, "*She doesn't love him, Father.*"'

Diana giggled. 'Oh, you wouldn't, would you?'

'I would,' Brodie said sternly. 'I just hope you see sense before it gets that far. And I'm not being funny, young lady, but deadly serious.'

It wasn't the least bit funny, Diana thought now. Leo's parents had offered to put the deposit down on a house for their wedding present and now Leo was inviting her to *view one!*

How was she going to get out of it?

Brodie switched on the computer every morning to see if there was an email from Karen Young. She would check again each evening when she got home from work and again before she went to bed, though she knew, if it was really important, Karen would telephone. There'd been a time when she'd used the computer every day, mainly to search Google for information that Colin wanted or send emails of her own. Now she only turned it on hoping for news of her daughter.

'What a coincidence!' she murmured the night after her talk with Diana about fathers, to find an email from Karen, not about Maisie as she'd hoped, but concerning Brodie's grandfather, Thomas Ryan.

'I kept forgetting to look him up on Google,' Karen wrote, 'but when I eventually did it was very interesting. There's loads of Thomas Ryans, but your one is called Thomas Edward Ryan and there's actually a photo of him. There's still no news of Maisie, I'm afraid, but I feel confident that I'll find her soon.'

Brodie sighed. The day couldn't come soon enough. She brought up Google, typed 'Thomas Edward Ryan' and, within seconds, a sepia photograph, faded at the edges, appeared on the screen. It must have been taken at a passing-out parade or something similar. It showed Thomas Ryan from the waist up wearing an old-fashioned policeman's uniform with a high collar and loads of brass buttons, his domed helmet held stiffly underneath his arm, his hair cut unnaturally short. She found herself smiling at the young, extremely handsome face. He looked terribly serious, but there was something about his eyes and the way his lips curved slightly that indicated he was extremely pleased with himself.

'Hello, Granddad,' she whispered, tears coming to her eyes. Why hadn't she done this before? She'd never dreamt she'd find her own grandfather on the internet.

Growing up, she'd never known another relative: no grandparents, aunts or uncles, no cousins, just Brodie and her mother.

She began to read the text accompanying the photograph. She knew her grandfather had been killed in 1930, that he'd disturbed two men who'd broken into a bank and one had shot him.

But as she read on, Brodie's jaw dropped further and further and her eyes grew rounder and rounder. 'I've been lied to all these years,' she said to the photo. 'Why?'

As Brodie had expected, Diana threw herself whole-heartedly into the preparations for Eileen's party, which was to be held in the garden if the weather was good or in the house if it wasn't. It turned out to be a perfect late-June evening with the setting sun a blazing ball of yellow in the sapphire-blue sky. An air of expectancy hung in the air, as if the garden itself was looking forward to the party.

Diana had been hard at work. Dozens of white balloons had been tied to the trees, and candles were burning on the iron table, on the headless statue where the head should have been, and in other places where it was deemed safe to put them. Earlier, she'd been in the middle of drawing up a list of games to play when Brodie assured her there was no need.

'It's not a children's party. Adults only want to stand around and talk.'

'Won't they want something to eat and drink?'

'And that as well. Everyone's been asked to bring wine, and Mum and I are doing the food. You can help if you like.' Colin would be there, as well as his two sisters and his brother and their partners, plus their grown-up children if they could find babysitters for *their* children – Eileen had three great-grandchildren. Brodie wasn't sure if George was coming: she hoped not.

'Can I be in charge of the music?' Diana asked eagerly.

'Of course you can.' Brodie was awed by her enthusiasm.

At seven o'clock, she stood in the kitchen waiting for the guests to arrive. She was wearing her new white trousers and gauzy top. Diana was re-arranging the little three-cornered sandwiches into a cone-shaped mountain. She had borrowed a long black skirt from the clothes donated to the refugee centre and a dark-green silk blouse that had a cape reaching as far as her elbows.

'You look like a character out of a Jane Austen novel,' Leonard Gosling said. He was the first to arrive.

Vanessa had gone all the way into town to buy something befitting a 'late-night garden party', as she called it, returning to say the sales had started and showing Brodie the floaty cream dress she'd bought. 'I'm down to a size twenty,' she said with a pleasurable sigh.

Rachel appeared in the jeans she seemed to live in, but Poppy, who was growing rapidly, wore a poppy-coloured frock that was all frills. 'Her daddy bought it for her,' Rachel said. Tyler arrived soon afterwards, a tall, beanpole of a young man with matchstick-thin limbs and a slightly withdrawn manner. Brodie reckoned he was shy.

'How do you do, Mrs Logan?' he said when they were introduced, but she insisted he call her Brodie.

'This is a lovely set-up you've got here,' Eileen said at some time during the evening. Ella Fitzgerald had just started to sing 'Every Time We Say Goodbye'. 'I cry a little,' Eileen sang.

Brodie raised her eyebrows. 'Set-up?'

'This lovely house and lovely garden.' Eileen waved her glass at both. 'Diana, Vanessa, Rachel with her pretty little baby. I'm almost reluctant to leave. But our Colin's terribly unhappy.' Her eyes turned to her son, who was standing moodily on his own clutching a bottle of beer. 'Have you spoken to him yet?'

'I did when he first came, but only for a minute.'

'He loves you, you know,' Eileen said soberly despite appearing to be just a little bit drunk, as were most of the people there, Brodie included.

'I love him,' she said, 'but I can't *live* with him while he thinks the way he does about Maisie.'

'I understand. I'd probably feel the same.' She half smiled. 'Did you know he smoked cannabis at university?' Brodie shook her head. 'I told him the other day he was a hypocrite. Mind you, a lot of the students used to do it and there's a big difference between that and cocaine or heroin.' Suddenly, for no apparent reason, tears began to trickle down her cheeks. 'Thank you for my party, Brodie. It's been a fabulous, magical evening.' She turned away, saying she wanted someone to dance with. 'It's a pity George didn't come. That's one good thing I can say about him, he was a fantastic dancer: still might be for all I know. Who's that drop dead gorgeous young man over there? I really like the look of him.'

Brodie watched as she made her way over to Tinker, who was talking to her mother. Mum was taking quite an interest in the centre and now went two or three times a week. Tinker bowed gallantly when Eileen approached. Next minute, they were waltzing on the grass, along with Diana and Leo and Colin's sisters and their husbands.

The night air was becoming dusky, making the candles seem to glitter more brightly. The earthy evening smell was mixed with that of melting wax. Balloons drifted silently to and fro on the trees like ghosts. Kenneth was stretched on a branch, coolly watching the goings on below. Every now and then someone would reach up and feed him a titbit. Ella Fitzgerald sang 'Someone to Watch Over Me'.

Brodie went over and asked Colin if he would like to dance. He didn't say anything, just took her in his arms and rocked her back and forth on the spot.

'Is this dancing?' Brodie asked.

'It's the best I can do under the circumstances.'

'What circumstances?'

'I'm missing you badly, I'm as miserable as sin, I'm not sleeping properly, I'm out of clean shirts, I've had too many beers . . .' He stopped rocking and looked into her eyes. 'Are those circumstances enough?'

'I suppose so,' she conceded. It felt as if they were young again and hadn't long met. There was a slight turbulence in her breast.

'I'm enjoying holding you.' He held her closer and buried his head in her neck. 'When are you coming home, darling?'

The 'darling', and the touch of his lips on her ear, really got to her. She gasped. He was her husband and she loved him. She couldn't bring herself to snap at him, say, 'When you change your attitude to our daughter, that's when.' Instead, she mumbled, 'I don't know.'

He whispered, 'Can I stay tonight?'

And Brodie whispered, 'Yes.'

Poppy was a long time settling down. She wasn't used to being made a fuss of by so many people. Brodie could hear Rachel's light footsteps as she walked to and fro across the floor, probably trying to lull her to sleep before laying her in her cot.

Vanessa had a bath, then came downstairs to make a drink. She was humming softly. She had clearly enjoyed herself tonight. Mind you, Eileen had given her a tremendous build-up when introducing her to her family. 'This is the artist I told you about,' she'd said. 'She's absolutely fabulous. One day she'll be as famous as Picasso.'

In the next room, Diana giggled. Someone was in there with her, a man. It could only be Leo. Brodie wondered if they'd made love. Although she would soon be twenty-five, Diana seemed too young to have sex. I hope she doesn't fall pregnant, Brodie thought, and *have* to marry Leo.

She said to Colin, 'Would you like some tea?' They were lying on the single bed, both stark naked, having just made love themselves. The time before had been months ago and this time they'd been greedy for each other. It had been better than ever, but now she felt embarrassed and was wondering how she could bring herself to cross the room with nothing on to get her dressing gown from behind the door.

Colin sighed. 'I'd like a ciggie.'

'You can't have a ciggie: it's bad for your health.' They'd both smoked when they first met in Waterloo delivering Labour Party leaflets prior to the 1983 election. They'd delivered the rest together, taking them to alternate houses, which was a very inefficient way of doing it.

Then they'd gone to the pub, had a ciggie each and a drink – Brodie a medium sherry and Colin half a pint of best bitter. They'd both known that this was 'it'. A year later they were married. Another year later she was expecting Josh. Maisie had arrived eighteen months afterwards.

'Would you like tea?' she asked again. 'Seeing as you can't have a ciggie.'

'I'd love some.'

She steeled herself, got out of bed and went to get her dressing gown from behind the door, doing her best not to hurry. She tied the belt around her waist. When she turned around, Colin was watching.

'You're very beautiful, Brodie,' he said. His voice was strangely tired.

'You're not so bad yourself.' She tried to sound light-hearted as she went to make the tea.

When she got back with the drink in two mugs, Colin was sitting moodily on the bed fully dressed. He got to his feet. 'I don't think I'll bother with that, thanks. I'm going home.'

'But why? What's wrong? It was all right . . . before, wasn't it?'

'It was more than all right; it was bloody marvellous.' He glowered at her. 'But how long will it be before it happens again?' He ran his fingers distractedly through his hair. 'Come home with me,' he pleaded.

'What about Maisie?' Brodie asked.

'What about Maisie?'

'I can't be bothered explaining,' Brodie said. She felt exhausted. She put the mugs on the table and sat heavily in a chair. 'You know what I mean.'

'I'll never agree with you about Maisie.'

'In that case I shall never come home.'

★

Two of the candles were still burning in the garden. Brodie opened the window and went to blow them out. There was very little rubbish scattered about: people had been very good about leaving the place tidy.

Back in her room, she turned on the computer and pressed the keys until she found her grandfather.

'Hello, Granddad.' The young face regarded her impassively. 'I've been meaning to discuss you with your daughter, Megan,' she told him. Earlier, Mum had demanded to talk to *her*, but she'd been too busy serving food. 'Later, Mum,' she'd said, but her mother had gone home early. Brodie had got the impression she was in a huff.

'But not in as big a huff as *I* am,' she told her granddad.

July–August 2006

Chapter 8

The black van was parked in Cazneau Street, its bonnet jutting forward just enough for the young man behind the wheel to see down Winstanley Grove and the front of the refugee centre where his brother, Rudi, had lost his sight. The young man, Jagar, wore a baseball cap pulled down as far as his eyebrows.

Although no doctor had confirmed it, Jagar was convinced that Rudi would never see again. The trouble was he couldn't be taken to any hospital in the country. Police records would show what had happened that morning almost a month ago and hospitals would be on the alert for a big foreign man who spoke broken English and had had boiling liquid thrown in his face. Since then, all Rudi had done was sit in front of a television that he couldn't see because a bandage covered his eyes. His shoulders were hunched and he rarely spoke. Every now and then Jagar would remove the bandage, but so far all his brother had done was shake his head.

Those four little bitches who'd got away would have provided a good description of Rudi and himself, along with names, places, and other information that was making living in this country a much riskier operation than it had been before.

Jagar didn't know which way to turn. These days, Rudi was helpless, a mere shadow of the powerful, dominating individual that Jagar had always known, that the whole village back home had known.

It had been Rudi's idea to bring the girls and set up business here. The money had come rolling in and they were well on their way to becoming millionaires. The plan was to return home in a few years and build a palace for their mother, though Jagar had other ideas. He wanted to live in London in a luxury apartment and run a couple of girls of his own. He'd wear gold chains around his neck, buy designer clothes and have sex whenever he felt like it. Until now, it was this, the sex, that he'd appreciated most; a selection of young women, every single one at his disposal to do with whatever he chose. Jagar licked his lips at the thought of it.

The two men who'd come with them were fools, incapable of lifting a finger without Rudi's instructions. But now it was up to Jagar and he honestly didn't know what to do. The girls they still had were missing Rudi's iron hand and getting restless. They were different from the four who'd got away. Older and more experienced, they had a used look about them and weren't nearly so appealing to the clientele. Most men preferred young bodies and were willing to pay more.

Jagar worried that everything was falling apart. The new place they'd found was within sight of the Catholic cathedral and it made him feel uneasy that the holy building could be seen from the front windows. He didn't know how to advertise the services they had to offer. In the past, Rudi had cards printed and had taken them round clubs and bars. Jagar had done the same, but in the first bar he'd gone to he'd been told to fuck off so many times he'd given up.

'You're in the wrong place, mate,' one man had said. 'This is a respectable pub. And while we're at it, why don't you go back to your own country?'

Jagar had fled. He'd never be as good a businessman as his brother.

He'd been watching the refugee centre all afternoon, taking in every person who went in and out. It was past five o'clock when *she* appeared and he recognized her straight away.

She walked towards him, accompanied by a much older woman. In some secret part of his brain he recognized that she was very lovely, but his prime thought was how much he hated her for what she'd done to Rudi.

'I get you, lady,' he swore as she walked past, skirt rippling, shoes clicking delicately on the pavement. Her arms were bare and brown and her hair had streaks of gold. She was the reason for his and Rudi's misfortune, his bad luck charm, the reason why their amazing, unbelievable life had come to an end. 'One day I get you for what you do to my brother.' The girl would pay. It was only fair.

Brodie hadn't seen her mother since Eileen's party. She'd rung a few times, but had been fobbed off with various excuses; she was tired, had letters to write, had promised to decorate a cake for a raffle.

'For goodness' sake, Mum,' Brodie had said that afternoon when she'd called her mother at the refugee centre and she'd said she was washing her hair that night, 'leave your hair for now and come to tea.

Anyroad, don't you possess a hairdryer? I've got fresh salmon, your favourite.'

She grudgingly agreed. Brodie hadn't got the salmon, but bought some on her way home from work, along with some cherry tomatoes and other bits and pieces for a salad. Tonight, Diana was going straight to Coral Street for Garth's eighteenth birthday party so she and her mother could have their tea together in the snug and perhaps Mum would divulge exactly why she had such a cob on.

The table was already set when her mother arrived with pursed lips and unsmiling eyes. Brodie wasn't prepared to sit through the meal in stiff silence. 'What's eating you, Mum?' she demanded before they sat down. 'It's ages since we spoke to each other, so what's wrong?'

'You may recall,' her mother said in the icy voice she reserved for occasions when her daughter had annoyed her, 'that I tried to speak to you at the party, but apparently you were too busy.'

'I *was* too busy. I was seeing to the food.' It wasn't like her to be annoyed over something so petty.

'It seems you had plenty of time to speak to other people, though – Eileen, for instance. Why was *she* told that Maisie had become a drug addict, yet you couldn't tell your own mother?'

Was that what it was about? 'Eileen was worried I'd left Colin because George was always in the house,' Brodie said patiently. 'She felt guilty, thinking it was her fault. I felt obliged to tell her the real reason I'd left was because Colin hasn't an ounce of sympathy for Maisie and all we did was row.'

Her mother contemplated this for several seconds. 'I still don't understand why I couldn't be told the truth about Maisie,' she said in an aggrieved tone. 'She's my granddaughter, the only one I'll ever have.'

Brodie reached for her mother's hand and squeezed it. 'I didn't want to upset you, Mum. I didn't want you knowing there was anything wrong with Maisie.'

'Do you think I'm an idiot, Brodie?' The icy voice returned. 'Maisie hasn't been home for six months or more. She used to come at least once a month. I haven't had a single letter or phone call, or even a card at Christmas. Of course I knew there was something wrong. I expected you would tell me when you were ready, but it seems everyone in the world knew except me.'

'Eileen was the only one who knew, Mum.'

'Even so, I'm very hurt.' She pulled out the chair and sat down.

Brodie's heart sank. It looked as if this was going to be one of the rare occasions when forgiveness wasn't easily forthcoming. She would have to wait a few days until her mother decided she'd been punished enough. Then she remembered that *she* had a bone to pick. 'Come in here a minute,' she said. The food could wait; it was only salad.

'Where?'

'My room.'

In the room, Brodie switched on the computer, then waited silently for the machine to start.

'What's this all about, Brodie?' Her mother was sitting on the bed.

'Wait and see.'

The machine was ready to use. Brodie typed in her grandfather's name, Thomas Edward Ryan, and his photograph appeared on the screen.

'Do you recognize him?' she asked.

Her mother put her head on one side and studied the screen from across the room. 'No, but the picture looks very old.'

'It's your father – *my* grandfather.'

'Holy Mary, Mother of God!' Her mother put a hand to her throat and went as white as a ghost. 'Is it really me dad?' she asked in a young voice, like a girl's. She looked quickly at the screen, then away again.

'Yes, Mum.' Brodie knew she was being rather brutal, but it served her mother right for being so unreasonable.

'Is he wearing his police uniform?' she asked.

'Yes.'

'I've never seen that photo before. We lost all our photos, see, when our house off Scotland Road was bombed just before Christmas in nineteen forty. The Christmas presents went at the same time as well as Mam's clothes, the money she'd saved, everything.' Once again she looked at the picture, but this time didn't look away. 'I wonder where this one came from. Perhaps it was on the police files or something.' She got up, crept across the room, sat in front of the computer and closely studied her father's face. She kissed her forefinger and placed it on his firm lips. 'He was a lovely man. I was dead proud of him. I'd forgotten how handsome he was. But Brodie,' she said in the little girl's voice, 'what on earth is me dad's photo doing on a computer?'

'You told me he'd been killed in the line of duty,' Brodie said, 'and when I mentioned this to a police-woman in London, she thought he might be on the Internet.' She waved her hand at the computer. 'And he is.'

'And what does all this writing say? Will you pass me my bag, darlin'; it's got my glasses in.'

Brodie fetched her bag from the dining room. She stood by the window and looked out on the garden. Vanessa was half-hidden behind a tree, wearing a straw hat and that awful stretchy tracksuit, painting one of her weird paintings. How strange that Eileen had liked them so much.

She heard her mother search through the bag for her glasses. There was silence while she read what was on the screen.

'Ah,' she sighed when she'd finished. She was still pale when Brodie turned around. 'There's a saying, isn't there? Your sins will find you out. I suppose the same goes for lies. I never dreamed that one day our family history would be there for the entire world to see.'

'It says Thomas Ryan had *four* children. You claimed you were an only child. Does that mean that somewhere in the world I've got aunts and uncles and cousins that I would love to have known when I was growing up?' She would still like to know them.

There was an air of defeat about the way her mother nodded. 'They're in Ireland. In a little village called Duneathly, but I suppose they could be all over the place by now.'

'How can I find them?' Brodie was bubbling over with questions, but there was only room right now for the really important ones. 'Are the other three children younger than you or older? What sex are they? And Mum,' she added indignantly, 'why have you been telling me all these years you were an only child?'

Her mother retreated to the bed and sat down. 'Could we leave this till another time, Brodie, luv?'

she said shakily. 'I'm not in the mood to explain things just at the moment.'

'Well, I'm not in the mood to wait any longer.' This was something Brodie should have known all her life. It was a while since she'd found her grandfather on the Internet and she'd been trying to think of how she could broach the subject with her mother without upsetting her too much. It was for the same reason that she hadn't told her about Maisie. She was fed up trying to be tactful and understanding. 'I'd like to know why all this,' she waved her hand at the computer, 'was kept from me – and I'd like to know *now*, not one day when you feel in the mood.'

'Can I have a drink?' her mother asked pathetically.

'Would you like tea or wine?'

'Both, please.'

While Brodie waited for the kettle to boil, she uncorked a bottle of *rosé* wine and put it on a tray with two glasses. She fetched the salads out of the dining room and put them in the fridge, by which time the water had boiled and she made the tea. She carried everything into her room where her mother had returned to the computer and was sitting, gazing at her father's face.

'He's awful good-looking, isn't he?' she said softly. 'His hair was always cut very short. What is it people say nowadays? – drop–dead gorgeous. I was only four when he died.'

Brodie put the tray on to the little table in front of the window. 'Which would you like first, the tea or the wine?'

'The wine, please. Oh, it's *rosé*, my favourite.' She picked up the glass and took a hefty mouthful. 'I was the eldest,' she said in a rush, as if the wine had already given her the courage to tell all. 'Brodie came next, then Joe, and finally Tom. He was born after me dad died. You were called after Brodie,' she said when her daughter looked surprised. 'I used to bully her something awful. I won't explain every little detail right now, but I'll tell you why I cut her, Joe and Tom out of my life – and Mam, too.'

Brodie picked up her own wine and prepared to listen.

'I was nineteen when the war finished,' her mother began. 'We lived in Duneathly and I was engaged to this chap called Richard O'Rourke who worked in a bank. We planned to get married on my twenty-first birthday. Anyway, right after the end of the war Annemarie came to see us. She was our auntie and she'd spent the last twenty years in America.'

'I know who Annemarie is,' Brodie said, interrupting. 'It says on Granddad's website that his wife, Mollie – your mother – was the sister of Anne Murray, the famous Broadway star. I looked her up on Google; her real name was Annemarie Kenny. She was incredibly pretty, but you said she was just a chorus girl.'

Her mother flicked away the interruption as if she were swatting a fly and took another long swallow of the wine. 'Anyway, Mam, Brodie and me went to stay with Annemarie in her apartment in New York. We were there for over a month. We'd only been there a few days when Brodie went to St Patrick's Cathedral on Fifth Avenue for some reason – she was always in and out of church, our Brodie; lighting candles, praying for this and that, doing the First Fridays. I used to tell her she should have been a nun. Hours later, she brings a young man back for afternoon tea.' Her voice was soft and husky, her eyes dreamy. Her face, so white before, was now pink. She looked very different from the mother Brodie had always known. 'He was beautiful, truly beautiful; tall, with dark wavy hair and remarkable blue eyes. Very Irish.' Her lips twisted in the briefest of smiles. 'He was, of course, your father, Louis Sylvester, and he and Brodie seemed quite smitten with each other. I was insanely jealous, having fallen head over heels in love with him on the spot.'

Brodie visualized the scene. Mum at nineteen, Brodie, who for some reason had a saintly halo around her head, two years younger, her grandmother, Mollie, who would have been about forty, all at Annemarie's Manhattan apartment, which she imagined being terribly smart, full of fine furniture and carpets you could lose your feet in.

Her mother finished the wine and re-filled her glass. 'I was determined to steal him off her,' she said grimly. 'I did every single thing I could to make him aware of me. Brodie, poor innocent Brodie, didn't notice, but Mam did. She said if I succeeded she'd disown me. I'm not sure if she meant it, but I didn't care if she did. I loved my family, but I loved your father more. I was besotted and determined to have him.'

Brodie was beginning to feel very slightly embarrassed, but she'd asked for an explanation and was getting one. She poured tea for herself – her mother was monopolizing the wine.

'I didn't manage it until we were on the boat back to Liverpool – of course, I didn't meet him on the boat like I've always told you. Anyroad, he'd been staying with an American friend from university. He changed his passage home so he could sail with us. He and Brodie weren't engaged or anything, but it was understood that one day they would get married. I suppose you could say I seduced him,' her mother said thoughtfully. 'I won't go into the intimate details,' her daughter breathed a sigh of relief, 'but by the time the boat reached Liverpool, he realized it was me he was in love with.'

'What happened then?'

'Like craven cowards, the minute it docked we got off and ran away.' A strange look passed over her face, as if she could still feel the guilt and the crazy passion of the time. 'I even left some of me luggage behind on purpose so no one would realize for a while that we'd gone. A week later we got married by special licence. From that day on I didn't look back. I resolved never to contact my family again; I was too ashamed. Your father bought this house and we settled down. I thought that fate was taking revenge when I started losing my babies. When I had you, it was your father who insisted we call you Brodie. But you know, darlin',' she said, smiling radiantly and looking very young again, even it if was only for an instant, 'despite everything, I've never regretted a thing. For some people, love isn't easy. Haven't you and Colin just discovered that for yourselves?'

'The thing is, Colin, *I* regret it, even if Mum doesn't,' she said two hours later after she'd driven her mother home because she was too drunk to ride her bike. She'd desperately wanted to talk to someone and Colin was the only person she could think of. She'd called him and he'd come straight away. 'According to her website, Anne Murray – that's Annemarie – didn't die until nineteen ninety when she was eighty-one. I could have written to her, gone to *see* her in New York. And Mum had a sister called Brodie and two brothers, all younger than her. They're probably still alive. And I might have loads of cousins.'

'Are you going to try to track them down?' Colin asked.

'Oh, I don't know.' She sighed. Her grandfather was watching from the screen, his steady gaze directed on her. 'I was all for it earlier, but it happened sixty years ago.' Her voice trailed away.

'Would your mother mind?'

'She hasn't objected. Anyroad, I'm not sure if I'd care if she did. She had no right to keep my extended family hidden from me.'

'No one would bear a grudge against your mum after all this time, surely. They might be really thrilled to see her again – and to meet you,' Colin said encouragingly. He was being so nice and helpful that she wondered why she was living in one house and he in another miles away. She supposed she'd only have to mention Maisie and she would find out. 'Would you like me to do it for you?' he offered.

'How? You haven't got a computer.'

'I've bought one. I needed to find out all sorts of things for work and you're no longer there to do it for me. It seemed time I learned to do it myself.'

Unreasonably, Brodie felt a bit put out. She preferred to think of him being unable to cope without her. 'How are you getting on?'

'Quite well, actually. It's easier than I thought. There's a new teacher at school who lives quite close.

She's coming round tomorrow night to show me how to set up an email address.'

She? Brodie felt even more put out.

'Hello.'

Vanessa looked up from the easel, but could see no sign of who had spoken. It had sounded like a child. She willed the voice to go away, but it didn't work.

'Hello,' it said again. 'I'm over here, next door.'

It *was* a child – with short red curly hair, exceptionally rosy cheeks and a good scattering of freckles. Vanessa couldn't tell if it was a girlish boy or a boyish girl. And he or she must be standing on something, or else they were about seven feet tall, as the crumbling brick wall was at least six feet high and he or she was resting his or her freckled arms on it.

'What are you doing?' the child enquired.

'What does it look as if I'm doing?' Vanessa asked testily. 'I'm painting.' She hated being interrupted while she was working. It was the best time of the day, morning, not long after Brodie and Diana had gone to work and before Rachel and Poppy appeared on the scene. There was a slight haze lingering in the trees and the air felt damp, but she could tell it was going to be another lovely day. She was loving this summer with its endless sunny days. She felt lucky that this was the year she'd become an artist. She couldn't remember another summer quite so fine, but then she'd been stuck at work without time even to look out of the window.

'I can see that you're painting,' the child said a trifle haughtily. 'What I meant was, *what* are you painting?'

She felt tempted to tell the little sod to mind his or her own business. She wasn't too sure what she was painting that morning; she'd just felt like daubing colours on a canvas and seeing what she ended up with. 'I'm experimenting,' she snapped, wishing the child would go away.

But it seemed he or she had no intention of doing anything of the sort. 'It looks a very nice experiment,' it remarked. 'I'd like to do one, too.'

'Well, no one's stopping you.' That was a horrible way to speak to a child. 'Shouldn't you be at school?' she asked a bit more pleasantly.

'I'm not well.'

'You look well enough to me.' He or she was the picture of health.

'I've got a tummy ache. It hurts really bad.'

'Then you should go and see a doctor.' The red cheeks might be the sign that the child had a fever.

'Will you take me?'

Vanessa snorted. 'I'll do no such thing!' How on earth did she get landed in this situation? It sounded awful, refusing to take a sick child to a doctor, but she'd never set eyes on the child before and it wasn't exactly her responsibility. 'Where are your mum and dad?' she asked.

'Dad's at work, Mum's in the Army. They're divorced. Mum told him she wasn't cut out to be a wife and mother.'

'And your dad just went to work knowing that you were sick?' She felt outraged. Some people didn't deserve to have children.

'He'd already gone by the time I got up and realized my tummy was aching.'

'Had he now?' What the hell was she supposed to do? As the only adult in the vicinity she supposed she'd better do something. 'Have you had anything to eat this morning?' Should the child eat if it had a tummy ache? God, she was hopeless at this sort of thing.

'I haven't had anything to eat, no.'

'What about a warm drink?'

'I haven't had a drink, either.'

'What are you standing on?'

'I climbed up the wall; it's got bricks missing.'

'If you'd like to climb over, I'll make you some warm milk.' It was the least she could do, though she was as averse to children as she was to cats and dogs.

'Can I bring my paints with me and we can both paint a picture together after I've had the milk?' the child asked eagerly.

'I suppose so,' she replied, teeth gritting, heart sinking, longing to refuse, but it would have made her feel like the Wicked Witch of the West. It looked as if today was going to be ruined. 'What's your name?' At least she'd know if the child was a boy or a girl.

'Charlie. I'll just get my painting set.'

He disappeared and reappeared more quickly than one would have expected from a child with a tummy ache. Back again, he climbed on to the wall with a paint box, a cheap sketchbook, and a rag doll with unnaturally long legs tucked underneath his arm. Vanessa lifted the small, slight figure down, dismayed to see he was wearing a brief denim skirt and red tights.

'What's Charlie short for?' she asked.

'Charlotte.'

'That's a nice name.'

'I hate it. What's your name?'

'Vanessa.'

'I don't like that, either.'

'I'm sorry about that.' As it happened, Vanessa had never cared much for her name.

'I think we should be able to christen ourselves and change our names every five years. I used to want to be Stacey like the girl in *EastEnders*, but now I'd sooner be Angelina.'

'That's not a bad idea, changing your name every five years,' Vanessa agreed. She'd always fancied being something Shakespearean like Olivia or Rosalind. 'How old are you, Charlie?'

'Seven, but I'm old beyond my years – my mummy used to say so.'

The same thing had been said about Vanessa when she was a little girl, though much good it had done her. It hadn't stopped her from being jilted at the altar by William Lunt. 'So, would you like some warm milk?' she enquired.

'Yes, thank you,' Charlie said gravely. 'It will be good for my tummy.' She put her assorted possessions on the metal table and accompanied Vanessa into the house. 'I haven't got a thingy to stand my painting on,' she complained.

'You mean an easel? Well, you're just going to have to do without one, aren't you? I didn't have one straight away.'

'It's nice in here,' she said when they entered the kitchen. 'I like the tiles. Did you paint them?'

'No.' Vanessa filled a mug with milk and put it in the microwave.

'You're a woman of a few words, aren't you?' she said with all seriousness.

'You talk too much,' Vanessa riposted.

'My mummy used to say that, too.'

While the milk was warming, Vanessa made coffee for herself. She stole two chocolate biscuits out of the fridge, having no idea who they belonged to, and gave them to Charlie. 'I hope they don't make your tummy worse.'

'Oh, they won't. Anyroad, it's beginning to feel just a little bit better. Maybe it's the thought of the milk.'

Vanessa was beginning to doubt she'd ever had a bad tummy. She looked too well and acted too chirpy. 'What does your father do?'

'He's a whiz with computers,' Charlie answered proudly. 'He's invented loads of games and has his own business on Kirkby Trading Estate. I can play them all, even though they're much too old for me.'

She was probably one of those nauseating kids who went to university at twelve and emerged a few years later with half a dozen first-class degrees.

Vanessa said, 'Shall we go back into the garden? Here, take these biscuits and I'll carry the milk.' She felt rather pleased with herself, a little bit saintly, as if she were being awfully nice taking this odd, clearly lonely child under her wing. If she ever came across the father, the computer whiz, she'd have a few words with him about leaving his daughter on her own when she was ill.

For the rest of the morning, Charlie lay on her bad tummy on the grass behind Vanessa, copying every stroke of her painting. The doll, whose name was Gwendoline, was draped around her neck. Kenneth, the cat, strolled into the garden. Charlie said she had no idea who it belonged to, but tomorrow she'd like to paint it.

'Shouldn't you go to school tomorrow?' Vanessa reminded her.

'It depends if my tummy ache is *really* better.'

'You must tell your father about your tummy ache tonight so that if you still have it he can take you to the doctor's in the morning.'

'Mmm,' Charlie said vaguely.

Vanessa gave her a sharp look. 'If you don't attend school, your father will get into trouble.'

'It won't bother him.' She shrugged carelessly. 'He's too busy inventing these awesome computer games.'

'He can be sent to *prison*,' Vanessa stressed.

'Honest? Shouldn't it be me who's sent to prison? After all, I'm the one who's not going to school.' She sounded as if she quite fancied a spell behind bars. 'I could write a book about it. I've already written a book; it's called *The Curse of the Crypt*. Would you like to read it?'

'It doesn't exactly sound my cup of tea.' Now she felt churlish again; she just wasn't used to conversing with children. 'Perhaps I could have a little peek at it one day.'

At around midday, Rachel arrived in the garden with Poppy – sometimes, it took all morning for the girl to get herself and her baby ready for the world. Poppy always looked as if she was ready to be entered in a baby show and would have been a credit to any mother. Today she wore a pink embroidered frock, pink socks, and a pink ribbon in her freshly washed fair hair.

Rachel said that at this very moment Tyler was flying to New York to spend a few weeks with his mother, his parents being divorced. 'They're going to some place called The Hamptons where his grandmother lives.

He's dead pleased his stepfather's staying in New York because he doesn't like him very much.'

'He doesn't like his stepmother in England, either,' Vanessa commented. Privately, she wasn't very keen on Tyler, whom she considered an arrogant young man. But there was no denying that he adored Rachel and Poppy and was extremely protective towards them.

'He doesn't dislike his stepmother as much as he does his stepfather,' Rachel explained. 'The truth is, he didn't want his mam and dad to get divorced.' She reminded Vanessa it was clinic day. Vanessa had forgotten all about it, but promised to be ready to leave by two.

Charlie had abandoned her painting to admire Poppy. 'It's an amazing name. I wish my mum and dad had called me that. Gosh, she's pretty. Can she walk and talk yet? Well, what *can* she do?' she asked exasperatedly when Rachel shook her head.

'She's only six months and she can sit up by herself.' Rachel spread a blanket on the grass and laid Poppy on her tummy with her rattle. The baby beat the hell out of the blanket, then rolled on to her back and regarded her mother with a beatific smile.

'She's beautiful,' Charlie breathed. 'I'd like to have a baby like Poppy when I grow up.'

Vanessa wasn't quite sure how it happened, but all of a sudden Rachel and Charlie were playing tick, climbing trees and kicking an old collapsed football they'd found in the bushes to each other. Of course, Rachel was still a child, she remembered. She was incredibly brave; leaving home, insisting on keeping the baby and looking after it all on her own. Vanessa felt a surprising lump come to her throat. She wasn't sure if she would have had the courage to do the same

219

thing at Rachel's age. It would probably do the girl the world of good to let herself go like this.

Poppy fell asleep on the blanket so Vanessa picked her up and nursed her until the girls finished playing and collapsed, giggling excitedly, on to the grass.

When she'd recovered her breath, Charlie announced she was hungry and was going home to see what was in the fridge, but Vanessa told her not to bother. 'I'll see what we've got here. Would you like something?' she asked Rachel.

They ate in the dining room, which Diana called the snug, where the sun had turned the top of the polished dining table into a mirror. She made Welsh Rarebit, which William always made for breakfast on Sundays when they got up late. It had filled a corner until they went out to lunch. Today, they had a carton of fruit yoghurt each for afters. None of the food was hers; after she'd been to the clinic, she'd call in the supermarket and buy replacements.

Of course, Charlie asked if she could come with them to the clinic. 'Aren't you worried someone from school will see you and you'll get into trouble?' Vanessa said.

'I go to this stupid girls' school in Southport so no one's likely to see me, are they?' She looked terrifically annoyed about it. 'That's why I never have anyone to play with; none of the girls live round here. Anyroad, I only didn't go to school because I've got a tummy ache, didn't I?'

'How does it feel, your tummy?'
'Middling.'
'What does that mean?'
'It could be worse and it could be better.'
Vanessa didn't believe her for a minute.

★

Poppy was thriving. The nurse in the clinic was all smiles and couldn't find a single thing wrong. The baby was the right weight and progressing normally. As often happened, she seemed to think Vanessa was Rachel's mother and Vanessa didn't bother to disabuse her. It saved Rachel being questioned about her ability to manage on her own.

'You've got a lovely family,' the woman behind the till in the supermarket said when Vanessa paid for the groceries. Poppy was sitting in the trolley propped up with a pink organdie pillow, queen of all she surveyed, while the girls helped load it. Far too much food had been bought. Vanessa, used to shopping so carefully, always keeping an eye on the calories, had just flung stuff in without a care.

On the way home, she wondered what William, her parents, her sisters, or anyone from Siren Radio would think if they could see her now, steering a pushchair with a baby in it, Rachel and Charlie each side clinging to the handle while sucking strawberry Cornettos. The groceries were piled in a tray underneath. No one would believe it was her; they'd think it was a double.

She paused to cross the road. 'Be careful,' she murmured just in case one of the girls shot into the traffic. There was a strange feeling in her throat or in her chest, possibly in her stomach. She couldn't work out exactly where or what it was.

Happiness, she realized after a while. At that particular moment in time, she felt utterly weary, excessively moidered and, for some strange, unaccountable reason, purely and supremely happy.

Chapter 9

Diana had hardly been at work five minutes when the telephone rang. 'Di? Is that our Di?' an agitated voice demanded.

'Damian!' she cried. 'Yes, it's me, Diana.'

'Can you come to the ozzie straight away, sis. Something's happened.'

'Have you hurt yourself? Oh, Damian, what's wrong?' Diana's heart beat like thunder in her breast.

'It's not me: it's Emma. She's had the baby. It came earlier than expected, at least a month. Oh, Di,' Damian sounded as if any moment something would snap, 'come quick. I think I'm going round the twist here.'

'I'll be there straight away.' Diana turned to tell Owen Hughes, a volunteer who was almost ninety and had been manning the office until she arrived, that there was an emergency and she had to leave. 'When you see Tinker, tell him I'll be back as soon as I can.'

'Be off with you, girlie,' Owen said. 'I couldn't help but overhear. I hope everything's all right. Shall I ring for a taxi?'

'Please.'

Diana had virtually told the taxi driver her entire life story by the time they reached the maternity hospital.

'Well,' he said, when he stopped, 'I hope Emma's baby is all right, kiddo. Give Damian my congratulations. Say they're from Tony.'

'Thanks, Tony. Oh, look! There he is outside.'

Damian, wearing odd trainers, no socks, and tattered jeans, was marching up and down outside the hospital entrance as if he were on guard. He virtually dragged his sister out of the taxi. 'What am I going to do?' he demanded croakily.

'What about? Oh, Damian, please tell me what's the matter?'

'It's the baby,' he paused.

'What's wrong with the baby?' Diana rarely had violent thoughts, but she felt like beating him to death with her handbag. 'Is it a boy or a girl?'

'A boy and there's nothing wrong with him: it's just that . . .' Another pause.

'*What*?' Diana screamed.

'He's not white.'

'Shit,' Tinker said later that morning when Diana arrived back at the centre and told him. 'What's Damian going to do?'

'He doesn't know what to do.' Diana still hadn't got over the shock. 'He doesn't like to chuck Emma out, not with a baby. But he isn't really in love with her and doesn't want her back in Coral Street. They met in the Job Centre when she came looking for a job and he asked her out. Then she came to live with us because she told him she was pregnant and said it was his. They were going to get married one day.' She'd been really proud of her brother for behaving so responsibly, but look where it had got him! She'd like to bet Damian thought he was the first man in Emma's life, but he couldn't have been more wrong.

'Shit,' Tinker said again. 'What does Emma have to say for herself?'

'Nothing. She and Damian haven't talked about it. She was nursing the baby when he was allowed in to see her, but they both ignored the fact that he wasn't white. If Emma does leave,' Diana went on, 'I hope the lads don't expect me to go back and look after them. I really like living at Chestnuts. You liked it, didn't you, when you came to Eileen's party?'

'I adored the place, darling,' Tinker gushed. 'I can't wait to go again. As for the lads, I should imagine they're big and strong enough to look after themselves. Anyway, you and Leo will be getting married soon, won't you?'

Diana ran her fingers through her already untidy hair. 'No . . . yes . . . oh, I don't know,' she stammered.

'I like a girl who knows her own mind.'

In her lunch-hour, Diana bought a mobile phone. Damian had rushed Emma into hospital at around four o'clock that morning. 'If you'd had a . . . a stupid *mobile*,' Diana reckoned he'd really wanted to use a much stronger word than stupid, but knew she'd disapprove, 'then I could have phoned you, but I didn't want to wake up the whole house by calling the one in the hall. I would have liked you with me earlier, Di,' he'd said pathetically.

'I desperately wish I'd been there for you.' Diana squeezed his hand. Emma was a truly loathsome individual for tricking him into believing it was his baby she'd been carrying.

Tinker made her swear she wouldn't sign a contract for the mobile. 'Knowing you, you'll get tied up for some ridiculous monthly amount for the next ten years or something. Just buy a Pay-As-You-Go. They're the best if you're not going to make all that many calls.'

'All right.' Diana had no intention of making many calls once she had a mobile. Sometimes, on the bus or train, people would be on their mobiles for the entire journey, leaving them with no time to think. Diana loved thinking.

After leaving work, she met Damian in a coffee shop by Central Station to work out what he should do next.

'All I can do is dump her,' Damian said gloomily. 'But that seems awful. I mean, where will she and the baby go? Yet there's no way I'm having her back in our house with another bloke's kid. I mean, just imagine what the neighbours would say! I'd look a proper idiot.'

'Maybe she thinks you won't mind – or you haven't noticed.'

'Well, I *do* mind. I mind very much. And I noticed straight away.'

They sat there for a further half-hour, but couldn't think of a way out that didn't hurt the completely defenceless baby. In the end, Damian went to talk to Emma. Before parting from his sister, he said the baby was an amazing little chap, a real charmer. He just wasn't *his*.

As Damian had said last night, it was obvious for the whole world to see that he wasn't the baby's father. He'd suggested quite nicely and rather sadly that Emma make other arrangements.

She couldn't go home – she didn't *want* to go home. Her mother was an out-and-out bitch and her step-father a pig. It was why she'd left the minute she'd finished school at sixteen and got a job. And she couldn't bring herself to live in her sister's shitty flat in Walton Vale. Besides which, there wasn't the room.

But she knew what had to be done and it nearly broke her heart. She loved Damian, and the house in Coral Street, especially the kitchen, and had genuinely thought the baby she was carrying was his.

After two nights in the hospital, Emma was discharged. With the baby – she still hadn't thought of a name for him – in one arm and small rucksack in the other, she caught a taxi outside the hospital and asked the driver to take her to The Shining Light restaurant in St Philomena's Street by the Pier Head.

The place was still closed, but when she looked through the window she could see the staff getting the tables ready for lunch. She banged on the door. Someone shouted at her to go away, 'We're not open yet,' but she banged even harder and eventually an elderly Indian gentleman wearing a turban opened the door.

'Is Ravi here?' she asked, praying that he hadn't gone back to India as he'd often said he might. When the man, who she was pretty certain was one of Ravi's numerous uncles, nodded courteously, she said, 'Tell him Emma's here to see him.'

The post arrived – Vanessa heard the postman open and close the rusty iron gate. She settled in front of the easel. Charlie, lying on the grass behind, waited for her to start painting so she could copy it stroke for stroke. The school in Southport had closed for the summer holidays so she now had a perfectly legitimate excuse for being at home. Vanessa thought it disgraceful that her father didn't appear to care that his young daughter would be alone in the house for the entire seven weeks.

She picked up a tube of white paint and squeezed out a quarter on to the palette, and so did Charlie. She softened the paint with the brush and out of the corner of her eye saw Charlie do the same: it was like having a miniature shadow. She was wondering what colour to use next when a shrill scream rent the air. It came from the open window of Rachel's room.

As one, Vanessa and Charlie made for the back door, which was usually kept open during the day. Rachel's mother must have got in somehow, Vanessa thought, determined to have another go at getting her hands on Poppy.

Charlie reached the top of the stairs first and flung open the door of Rachel's room. When Vanessa arrived, there was no sign of Rachel's mother. Poppy was lying in her cot clutching her feet and giggling, completely oblivious to Rachel's distress, while Rachel was waving a sheet of paper in the air.

'It's from Tyler,' she screamed. 'He's not going to marry me. He said his mother won't let him. And she's not letting him come back to England, either.' She collapsed face down on the bed. 'I'm never going to see him again.'

'Oh, dear,' Vanessa said, somewhat inadequately. Tyler's mother clearly hadn't known about Poppy until he arrived home and told her. She didn't suppose his father did, either.

Charlie burst into tears of sympathy and threw herself on to the bed with Rachel, the baby continued to giggle and Vanessa hadn't a clue what to do. She went downstairs and made a pot of tea, as much for herself as anyone.

When she got back with the tea on a tray, the girls had quietened down somewhat. They were sitting up in bed reading Tyler's letter. Charlie said, 'He's spelt maintenance wrong. He mustn't have a spell check on his computer.'

'What does he have to say about maintenance?' Vanessa asked, sitting on the edge of the bed and handing out the mugs – both girls took loads of sugar.

'That he'll send a cheque every month,' Rachel said thinly.

Vanessa frowned. 'I think we'd better see a solicitor about that, have something drawn up legally.'

'Can I come with you?' Charlie asked eagerly.

'I expect so.' She couldn't imagine going anywhere without Charlie for the foreseeable future. 'Can I read the letter?' Rachel handed it over with a sigh. The letter was typed and, although Vanessa didn't say so, she got the impression that Tyler's mother or another adult had written it, not Tyler. It was full of stiff phrases, such as: 'I am too young to take a decision that will last a lifetime'; 'I will be too busy with further education for many years to properly fulfil my role as a father'; 'I regret having behaved so irresponsibly and hope you will forgive me.'

Crap, crap, crap, she thought. It was all crap. The letter finished by saying a cheque for $200 was enclosed and a similar cheque would be sent monthly from now on. More crap. The letter was signed. 'Yours sincerely, Tyler Carter Booth', and the cheque came from Mrs E. Carrington.

'Two hundred dollars won't go very far,' she told Rachel. 'In fact, it's peanuts – roughly a hundred pounds. It's important we see a solicitor very soon.' She'd find out about one later.

Simon Collier was one of the names Vanessa was given by the Citizens Advice Bureau. He specialized in Child Support and similar matters and agreed to see them that afternoon. He was shocked to learn that Rachel wasn't in receipt of any benefits from the State. 'There's housing benefit, child benefit and other allowances. Would you like me to claim them for you?' he asked kindly. He was a nice young man, anxious to please, who looked much too young to be a solicitor specializing in anything. He had baby-blue eyes, a snub nose, and a crew-cut. He told them to call him Simon.

'Until now I've never needed benefits: Tyler always paid for everything,' Rachel explained. 'He left me plenty of money before he went away. His dad gave him loads of pocket money – Tyler called it an allowance.' She lowered her head and said in a small voice, 'I thought he really, really loved me.'

'Perhaps he does, Rachel.' Simon picked up Tyler's letter between finger and thumb, as if he was worried he'd catch something. He gave it a look of disgust. 'This might have nothing to do with Tyler. I wouldn't be at all surprised if it came from his mother – or *her* solicitor.'

'That's what I thought,' Vanessa put in.

'Ah, great minds think alike.' He smiled. 'What do you think, Poppy?' Poppy, who was sitting on Vanessa's knee, just waved her arms and smiled back. 'At this stage,' Simon went on, 'I think I can treat the case on a Legal Aid basis, so there are some forms for you to fill in, Rachel. If we do them together, then it will be much quicker. Vanessa, would you like tea or coffee while you're waiting?'

'Coffee, please.'

'And what about you, Charlie? There's always fruit juice in the fridge.'

'I'd prefer coffee, please.' She could be exquisitely polite when the situation called for it.

'Like mother, like daughter, eh?'

'Oh, but I'm not . . .' Vanessa began, but before she could finish the sentence, Charlie said loudly, 'We nearly always like the same things.' She beamed at Vanessa, but there was a sadness in her green eyes, a look of longing, as if she desperately wanted to belong to someone. Vanessa felt a lump come to her throat. Lumps were forever coming to her throat these days for all sorts of different reasons, but being taken for Charlie's mother and Charlie wanting her for a mother made the biggest lump yet.

The white paint was like a little hard worm on the palette. It hadn't been touched since Vanessa had squeezed it out yesterday morning. By now, she'd gone off white and reached for a tube of red instead. At that exact moment, the gate creaked and seconds later the front doorbell rang. She put the paint back. She wouldn't open it until she felt sure everything was going to be all right.

Charlie said, 'I'll go and see who it is. Perhaps it's the postman with a parcel.' She came back seconds later saying it was a man to see Rachel. 'She opened the door and let him in as if she was expecting him.'

'What did he look like?'

'He was tall and thin with big spectacles and a funny accent.'

'I wonder if it's Tyler's father?' Vanessa mused.

'I wouldn't be surprised if it was,' Charlie said in her grown-up way.

Once again Vanessa picked up the tube of red paint: once again she paused and stared at the open window of Rachel's room. She could hear a man talking, but couldn't make out his accent. Then, as she'd almost anticipated, there was a scream, followed by, 'Vanessa, *Vanessa*!'

With one accord, Vanessa and Charlie streaked into the house and up the stairs. The door to Rachel's room was open and she was in exactly the same position as she'd been when Vanessa had found her months ago the day her mother had come to take Poppy away: standing in the corner like an animal at bay clutching the baby to her breast.

'It's Tyler's dad and he wants Poppy,' she wailed. 'He thinks he's entitled to her because he's her grandfather.'

'I didn't put it quite so bluntly. I was trying to be reasonable,' Tyler's father said in an unemotional, dry-as-dust voice. He was tall, thin and bespectacled, exactly as Charlie had described, with pale receding hair, pale eyes and a prominent Adam's apple. His clothes were casual – cotton trousers, check shirt, beige linen jacket, cream leather loafers – but Vanessa could tell they'd cost a bundle, as had the wafer-thin gold watch on his knobbly wrist.

'What is there to be reasonable about?' she asked. 'Poppy is Rachel's baby; you can't just come in here and demand she be handed over.'

'Hear, hear,' Charlie said supportively.

'Who are you?' Tyler's father asked, looking at Vanessa and entirely ignoring Charlie.

'Vanessa Dear. I'm Rachel's friend.'

'And I'm Charlie Ormerod.' Again, the little girl might well not have spoken for all the notice the visitor took of her.

'Is this a lesbian household?' he enquired.

Vanessa laughed. '*No!*'

'What's a lesbian?' Charlie enquired.

'You'd better ask your father that,' Vanessa told her.

'I only learned yesterday from my ex-wife that my son had fathered a child.' The man spoke irritably, as if he resented having to explain himself. 'I found this address with a mobile number on his pad at home.'

'He rang this morning and asked if he could come.' Rachel crept out of the corner and sat on the bed. Poppy regarded the newcomer gravely. 'I didn't realize he wanted to take Poppy away.'

'I don't want to take her away.' Any minute now he'll stamp his foot, Vanessa thought. 'As the child's grandfather, I would like access: at weekends, say, or during the holidays. My wife and I plan to visit her relatives in Ireland soon, and she would like to take the baby with us.'

Rachel gave a little scream and Vanessa said, 'In other words, you *do* want to take Poppy away?'

'Only for a few days,' he said.

'Do you honestly think you can come here and expect Rachel to hand over her baby, if not today

232

then tomorrow or next week or something? That's *stupid*.' The man flinched. He clearly didn't like being called stupid. '*Really* stupid,' Vanessa emphasized, rubbing it in. 'I suggest you see a solicitor and find out how the law stands on access. Oh, and talking about the law, it's a crime in this country for a man to have sex with a minor. Rachel was only fourteen when your son made her pregnant. That makes him a criminal, Mr Carter Booth, no matter how old he happened to be at the time.' So put that in your pipe and smoke it, you horrible man, she wanted to add, but didn't. Anway, for all she knew, she might have been talking nonsense.

Tyler's father had gone. Vanessa said she'd take Poppy into the garden while Rachel had a bath to calm her nerves. 'Something horrible seems to happen every day,' she complained.

'Not *every* day,' Charlie argued.

'*Nearly* every day then.'

'Did I run up these stairs earlier?' Vanessa asked when she, Charlie and Poppy were about to go down.

'Yes, and you did yesterday, too, but not as fast as me. Though that's not surprising because I'm only seven and you're much older.'

When she'd first come to the house, she'd lumbered up the stairs, Vanessa recalled. Thinking about it now, she felt much lighter. The new dress she'd bought for Eileen's party was already a bit loose around her hips. 'I might go into town and buy some clothes one day next week,' she said.

'Can I come with you?'

'Naturally. We can have lunch.' She'd see if Megan,

Brodie's mother, could come to the house for a few hours while she was out to ensure Rachel was all right. The girl was badly in need of bodyguards.

Emma telephoned Diana and asked if she'd mind fetching her things from Coral Street. She'd come to the centre and collect them after Diana finished work. 'I don't like asking your Damian or one of the lads,' she said. 'The suitcase I brought with me is under the stairs.'

Diana couldn't bring herself to be cross with the girl she'd expected to be her sister-in-law. She said she'd do it that very night and gave Emma her mobile number, 'Just in case you need to get in touch one day.' She loved her new mobile and had given the number to everyone she knew.

That night, she went to Coral Street and found only Damian in. He was lying on the settee watching an old James Bond DVD and said he was pleased she'd come for Emma's stuff. 'I'd been expecting her to come herself and wouldn't have known what to say. But you'll never guess, sis, I'm missing her a bit,' he said gruffly. 'In a way, I'm missing being a dad, too. I'd been expecting it to happen any day soon.'

'Never mind, luv,' Diana said consolingly. He was a lovely-looking young man and the day would soon come when he'd find another girl, hopefully one much nicer than Emma. She made him a cup of tea and a jam butty. 'It's about time you did some shopping,' she reminded him. 'You're short of virtually everything.'

'Emma always did the shopping. I'll have to start doing it on the way home from work.'

'Make Garth and Jason take their turns, too. If

you like,' she added generously, 'I'll come round on Saturdays and do the shopping for you.'

'You'll do no such thing,' Damian said, shaking his head. 'It's about time us three learned to look after ourselves. You've got a life of your own to live, Di, and so have we.' He said he wouldn't help her with Emma's things, it would only upset him, but she knew where they were. 'And after you've packed them, I'll take you back to Blundellsands in the car.'

When Diana emerged from the centre the following night, Emma got out of the passenger door of a large grey car parked across the road and came to meet her. The driver was a handsome young brown man. There was a middle-aged woman sitting in the back.

'Ta,' Emma said when she took the suitcase.

'Where's the baby?' Diana asked. She longed to see him.

'Ravi's mother's got him in the car. Would you like to see him? We're calling him Umesh.' Emma seemed much happier than Diana had expected. Somehow, in some way, things had turned out well for her.

'Is that Ravi in the front?'

'Yeah. I was going out with him before I met your Damian. I never realized he'd put me in the club.'

An Indian woman in a lovely green sari with a red caste mark between her eyes, beamed and opened the rear car door when she saw Diana approach. 'You want to see my beautiful, beautiful grandson?' She pulled the shawl down from the baby's face. 'This is Umesh.'

'He *is* beautiful,' Diana agreed.

The baby had smooth light-brown skin, long black

lashes, and a head of thick black hair. He was fast asleep, unaware of the turmoil his birth had caused.

The woman closed the car door. Emma walked round to the back and opened the boot. 'I expected Ravi to tell me to get lost,' she whispered. 'But he was dead pleased to find he'd got a son, and his mam and dad were over the moon, though they insist we get married straight away. The thing is, Ravi hasn't got any brothers and both his sisters are married and they've only got girls. Umesh is their first grandson and they said it was the best dowry a girl could have, though I'm not sure what a dowry is. I didn't know Ravi lived in this amazing big house in Princes Park. Even so, Di,' she smiled wistfully, 'I still wish it was your Damian's baby that I'd had.'

Brodie was falling in love with her own grandfather! She kept his picture on the computer screen whenever she was in her room, glancing at it frequently. Every now and then it would disappear and she'd click the mouse to make it come back again.

'Goodnight, Grandad,' she would say when she switched off the computer and went to bed. There was no need to try to imagine what he would have looked like as an old man because he'd never had the chance to grow old. A few years after the photo had been taken he had been killed by a random act of violence. It didn't say on the website what had happened to the man who'd shot him. She hoped he'd been executed, a thought so disturbing that she telephoned Colin to discuss it.

'I've always been opposed to capital punishment,' she said, 'we both have, yet I hope the man who shot granddad was hanged by the neck until he was dead – isn't that what the judge used to say when murderers were sentenced?'

'Something like that.' She imagined him shrugging at the other end of the line. 'It's not sensible to guage something like capital punishment if we're emotionally involved. Every now and then someone in Parliament has tried to bring it back, but it's always been over-whelmingly rejected.'

'I know,' Brodie agreed. 'It's what separates civil-ized countries from the more backward ones. I suppose my head's telling me one thing and my heart's telling me something else.'

'*Because* you're emotionally involved you're as-suming whoever shot your grandfather was a cold-blooded killer. But say if he left his house that night without any intention of killing anyone? Say if the gun was just bravado, that he panicked, that he didn't know it was loaded? And Brodie,' he said gently, 'isn't it just a little bit weird to be getting all worked up about your grandfather when he died seventy-six years ago?'

Brodie thought it was more than weird: it was unhealthy, unnatural. 'The thing is,' she said, 'until we got married and I became your wife, I didn't have a single other relative apart from my mother. There were no photographs, either, only ones of Mum and my father and me when I was a baby. You've no idea what it feels like to see my grandfather's photograph. If he hadn't been murdered he could still be alive.'

Colin guffawed. 'He'd be well over a hundred.'

'Well, it happens,' Brodie protested. 'On the news the other day they said that more and more people are reaching a century.'

'I heard that, too, darling, but I'm afraid you'll just have to get used to the fact that your grandfather was a remarkable man who was destined to die young.' There was a pause and in the background she could hear the introduction music for BBC News 24. 'Have you seen the news? They're still bombing the hell out of Lebanon.'

'I haven't seen the news today.' These days, she avoided watching if she could, though it was often on in the home where she worked. She and Colin had talked about little else but politics in all its various forms, but it had never been a topic of conversation in Chestnuts. There was so much else to talk about: the refugee centre, Diana's brothers, Emma's baby, Rachel's troubles . . . Then there was Charlie, the delightful little girl from next door who had a perfectly awful father according to Vanessa, who kept her own secrets tightly to her chest. And, of course, there was Maisie, of whom there was no news whatsoever. Karen Young still telephoned or emailed from time to time. Last time they spoke, she wondered if Maisie had moved away from London and told Brodie that she'd sent her photograph to other forces throughout the country.

Brodie was upstairs looking through cupboards and drawers in the unused rooms for bits and pieces that could be sold on her mother's stall at the refugee centre. Mum behaved as if the stall was an important career move and was taking it very seriously.

The house was very quiet. There were no sounds at all coming from Rachel's room, and Vanessa's television was on low. Diana was out with Leo, which accounted for the lack of real noise. Brodie missed her.

There were four spare rooms about a quarter of the size of the ones that had been let. They were darker, the windows smaller, the decoration untouched for many years. When Brodie had lived in the house as a child she couldn't remember the rooms having been used for anything except storage of old furniture and cardboard boxes full of mysterious stuff.

There was some sort of unwritten law about the more space you had, the more it would be filled. At their house in Blundellsands, she and Colin were forever having clear-outs. Old bedding would go, along with frayed towels, worn shoes that weren't worth being mended but still had some wear in them, books that had been read, toys that were no longer played with, clothes that were no longer worn or had been grown out of, broken gardening implements, odd dishes. Everything would be piled in the garage waiting to be taken to charity shops or the corporation dump. There wasn't room in their brand-new house to keep anything that wasn't strictly necessary for everyday living. Here, there were even two spare beds and a wardrobe that took up almost an entire wall.

She wondered why her parents had bought such a large house, but remembered mum had wanted a big family. Perhaps her father had, too: she must ask one day. These small rooms might have been destined to become nurseries, painted blue or pink for the babies who would have been her brothers and sisters.

To her relief, apart from the odd glove and occasional coat-hanger, the drawers and cupboards were empty. She hadn't fancied coming across some of the Slattery sisters' old underwear or other personal items.

The boxes were an altogether different matter. The

first she opened was full of ghastly ornaments, such as plaster birds painted hideous colours, brass candlesticks that would make ideal murder weapons, giant ashtrays that looked equally dangerous, and plaques with reassuring messages such as, 'There's no place like home' and 'Home is where the heart is'.

She thought there was a good chance that Mum and Diana would enjoy sorting through the boxes so decided to leave the task to them. She wasn't in the mood.

There was one room that hadn't been investigated. When she opened the door she was greeted with a familiar smell – oil paint. Of course – Vanessa had asked if she could store her paintings there. They were stacked against each other on the floor in three rows. Brodie counted one row and there were twenty, so that meant sixty altogether, and there might be more in Vanessa's room. What did she intend doing with sixty or more hideous paintings? They were being produced at a rapid rate. Some days, she finished one, occasionally two, and would start on another. Others took days and days to complete. Vanessa must have the patience of Job.

Eileen, Brodie recalled, had suggested Vanessa hold an exhibition in the garden.

Diana would enjoy getting involved. She loved organizing things. Brodie would mention it the next time she saw her. If she waited up long enough they could have a cup of cocoa together when Diana came in.

Vanessa was trying on dresses in John Lewis and Charlie was outside the cubicle waiting for her to pull back the curtain and ask her opinion on the latest model.

'What do you think of this?' she asked, showing off

a bright red fitted number with a fluted skirt and flared sleeves.

'I like that one best of all,' Charlie said approvingly. She had dressed for the trip to town in a pink cotton frock, a fluffy pink beret, old-fashioned leather sandals – the sort that Vanessa had worn as a child – and a white plastic handbag trimmed with plastic flowers. 'You suit red.'

Vanessa had always worn what she called 'business colours': greys, browns and blacks, with a pastel blouse when a blouse was called for. 'I think I like this best, too.'

'I liked the green one as well and the white one with cherries on. I think you should buy them all. My mummy used to get me two or three dresses at a time because it meant she wouldn't have to go shopping again for ages. Me, I love shopping,' she added in an aggrieved tone.

'I only want to buy the one. I'm hoping to lose more weight and whatever I get will be too big.'

'I think you're perfect as you are, Vanessa.'

'Why, thank you, Charlie.' She closed the curtain, removed the red frock and put the old cream one back on. Not that it was all that old, only about four or five weeks. She had been in Chestnuts for four months and for a large part of that time had been losing weight at the rate of approximately two or three pounds a week. On the last occasion she'd been down to less than sixteen stone. She was now beginning to look plump rather than fat.

But not *just* plump. Vanessa looked at herself in the mirror, half closing her eyes so that her reflection was slightly misty. Her hair was mussed after trying on the

241

dresses, not that it ever looked tidy these days. She'd been wearing it long her entire adult life and had forgotten how curly it used to be when short. It was time she asked Diana to give her another trim. In the old days, she'd gone to the very best hairdressers to have it highlighted, cut and blow-dried. It had cost the earth, but now Diana did it for nothing and Vanessa blow-dried it herself.

She rubbed her hands over her cheeks. They'd never used to be so rosy – and her face was brown. Her arms and legs, too, due to the outdoor life she led these days, painting in the garden day almost every single day. With her wild hair, fuller figure and red cheeks she looked a little bit . . . *wanton*!

Vanessa felt herself go hot and cold and hot again. She quite liked being this brown-skinned unexpectedly *wanton* person.

'What are you doing?' Charlie shouted.

'I'll be out in a minute.' She slipped her bare *brown* feet into old mules. In bygone days, the only time she hadn't worn tights was in bed. She came out of the cubicle a minute later as promised. 'I'll just pay for this dress,' she said, 'and then we'll have lunch.'

'Where *is* your mummy, Charlie?' she asked while they waited for the meal to arrive. They were in a new, very modern restaurant behind St John's Market. It had white walls, white furniture and a bright red carpet. Carpet apart, it looked extremely hygienic and would make an ideal place to have an appendix out, or a similar operation.

'Iraq. She divorced Daddy because she wanted her independence, but he said that was silly as the last place to find independence was in the Army and she'd be pissed about something awful. He also said that she looked horrible in the uniform, though it went with her eyes.'

'When did this happen?'

'Three years ago when I was four. I cried an awful lot when Mummy went, but I never cry now,' she said stoutly. 'I've got used to the situation, you see. Daddy said you can get used to anything if you try hard enough.' She was extremely practical for such a young child. Her father didn't sound a pleasant character, but Vanessa had thought that right from the start. 'Do you think my burger will be in a bun?' Charlie asked.

'It might be. I didn't notice what it said on the menu.' The waitress had taken the menu away.

'Do I have to eat the bun if it is?'

'Of course not. You shouldn't eat anything that you don't want to. The burger should be nice: it said they're homemade.'

'Then why aren't you having one?'

'I prefer a salad.'

Charlie wrinkled her nose. 'I *hate* salad.'

'Well, I don't, which is why I'm having one and you're having a burger.'

She noticed a couple on the far side of the restaurant were staring at her – a wishy-washy woman accompanied by an even more wishy-washy man. The man stood and came towards her. Vanessa swore underneath her breath. She didn't know him from Adam.

'Vanessa?'

There was something about the way he pronounced her name that was familiar. '*William*!' she gasped unbelievingly.

'You look wonderful.' There was awe in his voice.

'You don't look so bad yourself,' she said, lying through her teeth. Was this really the man she'd cried so many tears over, the man who had caused her to put on so much weight? Had he always been so wishy-washy, his hair the colour of dirty water and his eyes lacklustre, or was she seeing things in a different light? He even looked smaller than she remembered.

'Where are you living nowadays?'

She waved a vague hand. 'Oh, Crosby way.'

'I understand you gave up your job. What are you doing now?'

Vanessa threw back her shoulders and looked squarely at the man who had once been her fiancé. 'I paint,' she announced. 'I'm a professional artist.' Eileen had offered to buy three of her paintings and had suggested she have an exhibition – Brodie had brought up the subject only the other day. Vanessa made up her mind there and then to go ahead.

William – was this *really* William, or merely a pale imitation built by scientists in a laboratory? – looked flabbergasted. 'But you never used to paint!'

'No, I didn't, did I? But I've discovered I have a vocation. Now I paint all the time.'

The waitress arrived with their food. William said goodbye and returned to sit by the pale woman across the room. Was she his girlfriend? Were they getting married? Vanessa silently wished them all the luck in the world. They deserved each other.

Chapter 10

By the time she and Charlie turned into Elm Road, Vanessa was feeling pretty satisfied with herself. She was pleased with her new frock, impressed with her new image and would never forget the look of stunned admiration on William's face when he'd seen her across the restaurant. The improvement in her fortunes had seemed to have happened overnight – no, that afternoon – and was taking some getting used to. But the sight of Brodie's mother, Megan, waiting outside Chestnuts looking terribly worried, slightly lessened her feeling of satisfaction.

'I hope everything's all right,' she murmured, concerned that someone else had turned up wanting to lay claim to Rachel's baby. She waved at Megan and began to hurry. Charlie was holding her hand and skipping along beside her.

As they got nearer, a man emerged from the house adjacent to Chestnuts – Charlie's house. He was tallish, slim, wearing black jeans, a T-shirt and knee-high boots. His thick black hair fell in an untidy fringe on his forehead and the rest was secured in a ponytail at the back of his neck. He scowled and folded his arms –

there was a tattoo of a bird on his right forearm – and watched them approach.

'What the hell do you think you're up to, Charlotte?' he demanded angrily when they got near. He had a broad Lancashire accent. 'I've been out of me mind with worry. Mrs Fuller called me at work. She wanted to know if your grandmother was looking after you for the entire holiday or just part of it? Was she to expect you at any time or not? I had to confess I hadn't a single clue what she was talking about and she said I'd sent her emails about it.'

'What did you tell her, Daddy?' Charlie asked meekly. She hadn't let go of Vanessa's hand. In fact, she was holding on to it more tightly.

His scowl deepened. 'What I *didn't* tell her was that you haven't got a grandmother alive in this world because I didn't want her knowing I had a daughter who's the biggest liar on earth.'

'Not the *biggest*, Daddy.' Charlie attempted a roguish grin.

'Don't be cheeky with me, Charlotte Ormerod,' he thundered. 'I phoned here, but there was no reply. I called your mobile, but there was no reply to that, either. By then, I was in a right old state, I can tell you. I came home straight away, but found the house empty. Luckily, there was a lady next door who told me you had gone off to town with another lady, who has apparently kidnapped you for the entire school holiday.' He turned to Vanessa whom he had so far ignored. 'You are desperately irresponsible, whatever your name is. It's a good job you arrived home when you did: I was about to call the police.'

'Huh!' Vanessa scoffed, equally angry. 'And say

what? That I'd kidnapped your daughter when she's standing right outside your very own house? As for anyone being reported to the police, it should be you for abandoning poor Charlie for weeks on end. You don't give a damn whether or not she's being looked after. One morning, she felt so sick she urgently needed to see a doctor. And where were you?' she asked more shrilly than she had intended. 'At work, that's where. You didn't even know she wasn't at school.'

'Sick?' His jaw dropped and he looked horrified. 'When were you so sick and needed to see a doctor? Charlie, my darlin' girl, come on here.' He held out his arms. Charlie released Vanessa's hand and flew into them.

'I love you, Daddy,' she sobbed into his neck. 'I love you with all my heart.'

'I know you do, sweetheart. And I love you.' He picked her up and carried her tenderly into the house. The door closed and Vanessa felt surprisingly and terribly alone, as if something very important had gone out of her life.

'Come in, Vanessa, dear, and I'll make some tea.'

'Yes, oh, thank you.' She'd forgotten Megan was still there.

'He came round earlier in a terrible state,' she said when they were in the kitchen. 'He thought Charlie was at some holiday club place in Southport, but the little madam had only written to the woman on her daddy's computer to say her gran was staying for the summer and looking after her. Then she was supposed to go to the holiday club with another girl in her mother's car, but she'd written to her, too, and cancelled the arrangement.' She smiled. 'I can't help but admire her nerve. I think I might have done the same thing at her age. And isn't her daddy a sight for sore eyes? He's as dishy as a rock star. Sixty years ago and I'd've been drooling.'

Vanessa hadn't noticed anything faintly attractive about Charlie's father. She took the tea into the garden and listened by the communal wall in case he was beating the living daylights out of his daughter, but couldn't hear a thing.

Diana was in her element organizing Vanessa's art exhibition. Leonard Gosling had designed a large poster to put in his shop window and had another fifty copies made. It was no use having one in Chestnuts; with it being at the end of a *cul-de-sac*, nobody ever walked past. Colin, Brodie's husband, offered to put one in his window, so did Megan, and one went on the noticeboard in the refugee centre and another in the house in Coral Street. All three lads promised to come for their sister's sake, though they were convinced it would be as dull as flippin' ditchwater.

On the Sunday before Diana's twenty-fifth birthday, poor Leo, who had intended taking her across the water for lunch at a posh restaurant, instead found himself driving around all the shops and pubs in the vicinity of Blundellsands and waiting in the car while Diana persuaded people to take a poster. Most did. After all, it was a bit up on the jumble and car boot sales that they were usually asked to advertise.

'All the money is going to charity,' Diana explained, 'every single penny. There'll be refreshments and music and it's on Saturday and Sunday of next week between twelve o'clock and four.' It was Diana who had decided to hold the exhibition on two days because it meant more people would be able to come.

Vanessa had agreed to be interviewed by the *Liverpool Echo*, the *Crosby Herald* and *Bootle Times*. She was unrecognizable in the photo that was taken in which she wore the grey babygro, a giant straw hat and sunglasses. She told the reporters she wished only to be known by her initial, D, and refused to reveal her first name. The *Echo* referred to her as the 'mysterious artist'.

The exhibition was being held in the garden, weather permitting, though it had been a beautiful summer so far and the long-range weather forecast didn't mention rain. The paintings – by now there were seventy-five – were to be hung from the branches of the trees or attached to the trunks. Leonard Gosling had arranged for a friend to look after his shop on Saturday and was put in charge of the exhibition arrangements – which paintings would go where, attaching a tiny label to each indicating the price, and collecting the money when they were sold. The paintings were priced at £25, £35 and £45 depending on their size.

Brodie and Megan were organizing the food. Diana was sorting through her CDs and trying to decide what sort of music was suitable for an art exhibition.

On Saturday morning, Diana woke early. Leaping out of bed, she pulled back the curtains, opened the windows and stepped outside in her bare feet. The very air sparkled and the sky was powdery blue with little white threads of cloud. The garden was at its very best, surrounded by bushes and clumps of glorious flowers of every possible colour. She sniffed deeply: the scent was intoxicating. Brodie's Colin had been the night before to cut the grass on the gently sloping lawn so that it was velvety smooth. She wriggled her feet in it. It was wet and cold, but she loved the feeling.

'Good morning.'

'Oh, good morning.' She hadn't noticed Vanessa half-hidden behind a tree, paintbrush in hand. 'What are you painting?'

'A flower, a big one. I don't know what it's called. It's maybe a hydrangea, a peony or a rhododendron.'

'I don't know, either. I hardly know the names of any flowers, just roses and daffodils. I can't remember what else.'

'Buttercups and daisies, I bet.'

'Yes, buttercups and daisies. I'd forgotten about them. And the ones with faces – pansies. Can I look at what you're doing?'

'Of course.'

'It's a lovely dark pink,' Diana said, studying the painting. She couldn't exactly see where the flower was.

'I visualize myself being inside the flower,' Vanessa explained.

Diana closed her eyes and tried to imagine the same thing. 'I think I understand what you're getting at,' she said triumphantly, and Vanessa looked pleased. Diana said she was badly missing Charlie. 'She's such a lovely little girl. Will she be around today, do you think?'

'I don't know. They've been away, her and her dad. There's been no sign of anyone in the house for a fortnight. I say, Diana, if I were you, I'd change out of that thin nightdress into something a bit less revealing. Leonard Gosling has just arrived and you'll have the poor man all in a flutter.'

Diana went indoors and put on an old pair of jeans and a sweatshirt for now. When she returned, Leonard Gosling, in well-pressed jeans and a pastel flowered shirt, was studying the notes he'd made about where to hang the paintings.

Brodie threw open the windows of her room and came outside to join them. 'I thought I heard voices. Isn't it a lovely morning?'

Everyone agreed that it was outstanding.

'Hello!' Rachel poked her head out of the window and said that she thought Poppy had started teething. 'She cried a lot last night.' Everyone denied having heard a thing, though they all had. They didn't want Rachel to feel uncomfortable about it.

Not long afterwards, Colin arrived and unloaded half a dozen folding garden chairs and a little round table out of his car. For the life of her, Diana couldn't understand why he and Brodie had separated as they got on perfectly well together and were clearly madly in love.

Megan came, and she and Brodie went into the kitchen to make dozens of tiny scones. 'We'll do just a few sandwiches until people start coming, otherwise they might be wasted,' Megan said. 'If the scones aren't used, they can be eaten tomorrow. And if they're not eaten tomorrow, I can take them to the refugee centre on Monday.'

Diana went over to Vanessa, who was deeply involved in painting the pink flower and didn't seem aware of the efforts being made all around her for the exhibition of her work. 'I hope you won't be disappointed if not many people come,' Diana said. Until now, it hadn't entered her head that the day might not turn out to be a great success.

'I won't be disappointed, no. It's nice of everyone to do all this,' she waved her hand around the garden, 'but if no one comes I won't care. You see,' she explained carefully, 'all I want to do is paint. What happens to the paintings afterwards doesn't bother me. Do you understand, Diana?' she asked, smiling sweetly. Vanessa had become much nicer since she'd first moved into the house.

'Yes.' Diana wasn't sure if she did. 'But I worked out that if we sell every single painting, we will have raised over two thousand pounds for the shelter,' she informed her.

'Good,' Vanessa said vaguely, continuing to paint.

Diana went into the kitchen where Megan was rolling out the scone mix on the breadboard and turning it into little frilly circles with a cutter. Brodie was transferring the circles on to a metal tray with a fish slice. The room was warm with heat from the oven.

'Eileen's just been on the phone,' Brodie said. 'She and her sister Mary are driving up from London tomorrow. She wants some of Vanessa's paintings for Christmas presents.' She put her head on one side and said thoughtfully, 'I wonder how I'd feel if I was given one of Vanessa's paintings for Christmas?'

Megan poked her daughter in the ribs. 'You would thank the person politely and pretend to be grateful, darlin'. That's the way I brought you up.'

'You're right, Mum. Of course I would.'

'I'd love a painting for a present,' Diana said.

Brodie looked dismayed. 'Oh, I wish you'd said that before, love. It was your birthday last week and didn't I go and buy you a bottle of perfume?'

Megan wiped her brow with the back of her hand. 'And I got you a box of chocolates.'

'Oh, I'm not complaining,' Diana said hastily. 'It's lovely perfume. I'll be putting some on later – I'm keeping it for best. And the chocolates were lovely, too.' *Too* lovely. She'd eaten the entire box in one go and made herself sick. 'I'll buy a painting for myself.' She'd have the one Vanessa was doing at this very moment of the inside of a hydrangea, a peony or a rhododendron.

Tinker, Alan and Rosa were also coming to the exhibition tomorrow, as well as Leo and his mum and dad, and her brothers, who were going to see a footy match today.

Only thirteen people turned up on the first day. A couple with two children – a boy and a girl of about eight and ten – were the first. As they walked around the garden viewing Vanessa's paintings, the girl kept saying in a loud voice, 'I could do these standing on my head, Mum.'

They left without having a cup of tea or anything to eat, even though the refreshments were free. The man and woman looked rather strained and the children were giggling madly.

After a long gap, an elderly couple arrived. Brodie suggested that she, Diana and her mother go inside leaving only Leonard in the garden, rather than stand around gawping at everyone who came and making them feel uncomfortable. 'Leonard will tell them where the refreshments are if they want any.' Apparently, the elderly couple didn't because when Diana peeped outside they'd disappeared. She changed the music from very new to very old, just in case Jakatta's loud, persistent beat was putting people off. They might prefer something by Cole Porter.

By now, it was almost two o'clock, Vanessa and Rachel had taken Poppy to the shore. Brodie made yet another pot of tea and they ate another sandwich and another buttered scone. They stood in the kitchen, not saying much, until the relative silence was disturbed by the sound of shrieks of laughter.

Diana shot outside to find out why people felt the need to make such a racket at an art exhibition and found four scantily dressed young women walking from painting to painting, pointing at them, gasping in turn, 'Look at *that* one!' 'And look at *THAT* one!' One actually fell down on the grass in a fit of hysterics.

She was amazed that when they finished laughing they bought two of the smaller paintings, handing over a fifty-pound note.

'I hope it's not a forgery,' she said to Leonard when the girls had left. He assured her that it was real.

'Correct me if I'm wrong, Diana,' he said in his courteous way, 'but were those young ladies wearing only their underwear?'

'It looked like underwear, but in actual fact it's the latest fashion.'

'In my young day, those sort of lacy things were called camiknickers.'

'They're called dresses now.' She would never have the courage to wear such a dress herself. Anyroad, at twenty-five she was too old.

Just before four o'clock two women turned up but hardly stayed a minute. Then a man came who said he was an art teacher at a school in Chester. He studied each painting intently, eventually buying one that Vanessa explained was the underside of a mushroom. 'It's got something,' he said. 'I'm in a hurry right now, but I might come back tomorrow and buy more.'

'Well, it wasn't a *complete* failure,' Diana said to Leonard as together they took down the paintings. 'We made seventy-five pounds.'

'Eighty-five pounds. That last painting was thirty-five.'

'I feel awful,' she confessed, 'putting everyone to so much trouble. I know it was Eileen's idea, but it was me who insisted on going ahead with it.'

'You must absolutely not feel awful, Diana.' He patted her bare arm – he had a habit of patting women's bare arms whenever he could. 'It is better to have tried and failed than not to have tried at all – I'm sure someone like Shakespeare must have said something like that. If he didn't, he should have. And it might be quite different tomorrow.'

It was different. If anything, the weather was even better than the day before: the sky bluer, the sun warmer, the air even more dazzling, like bubbles in champagne. Between forty or fifty people came. Diana, wearing an orange jumpsuit decorated with sequins, was the only person who bothered to count and she lost track after a while. At one time, there were at least twenty visitors sitting or standing around with a drink and a plate of refreshments, many of them friends or relatives: Diana's brothers, Brodie's mother-in-law Eileen, who was smoking like a chimney, and her sister Mary, Leo Peterson and his mum and dad, Tinker, Rosa and Alan from the refugee centre. Rosa, who had never had children of her own, was making a big fuss of Poppy.

Inside the house, Brodie and Megan were making sandwiches like nobody's business, and Colin was despatched to buy another three loaves. Soft, romantic music came from the open window of Diana's room, adding to the slightly unreal, almost dreamy quality of the afternoon.

At least half the paintings were sold. If the purchaser didn't want to take their painting straight away, then Leonard self-importantly put a little red sticker in the corner to indicate the picture was no longer for sale. 'It's what they do in *proper* art galleries,' he whispered to Diana.

More than a thousand pounds was raised for the refugee centre. Tinker tried to make up his mind what to spend it on: making the restaurant more attractive, for instance, with chairs and tables that matched; another snooker table; more toys for the playgroup; a carpet in the lounge; a new computer . . .

Neighbours came to see what was going on, astounded to find there was an art exhibition in their very own road. Some stayed and bought paintings.

'Do you actually *live* here?' a woman asked Diana. 'How lucky you are,' she continued when Diana agreed that she did. 'It's a little oasis, so quiet and peaceful, like being in the very heart of the countryside. You can hardly hear the trains at all.'

Vanessa couldn't help experiencing a feeling of elation as she watched people hand over good money for her paintings. She'd told Diana she didn't care what happened to them once they were finished, but she was wrong. She hadn't realized the pleasure it would give knowing that people would hang them on the walls of their homes. Eileen actually bought five, saying, 'I want them for presents, but I reckon I'll end up keeping the lot.'

The art teacher from yesterday returned and bought another two. 'They've *got* something,' he said to Vanessa after asking to meet the artist. 'I don't know what it is, but they've definitely got *something*.'

Could it be that she really had talent? That her desire to get down on paper the corner of a roof, half a window, the inside of flowers and trees, strange patterns, the rusty gate, a patch of sky, Charlie's red hair – just the hair, nothing else – Poppy's little foot or the back of her pushchair actually *meant* something? She must take care in future not to think about people's reactions and the saleability of a painting before she started it.

There was a gentle tug on her skirt and a little voice said, 'Hello, Vanessa.'

She looked down, and had never been so pleased to see anyone before in her whole life. 'Hello, Charlie,' she said, a lump instantly forming in her throat. She suppressed the urge to cry and hug the little girl to death. 'Where have you been?' She guessed the white T-shirt she wore with the letters NY on the front in red and gold provided a clue.

'To California with Daddy,' the little girl replied, starry-eyed. 'There was an exhibition of computer games and his company had a stall. I played loads of games and we've brought even more home with us.

When it was over, we went to Disneyland and then to New York where Daddy has some friends who took us out to dinner every single night.'

Vanessa smiled. 'There's no need to ask if you had a good time.'

She sighed blissfully. 'I had a *marvellous* time, and so did Daddy.' Her hand seemed to creep inside Vanessa's. 'But I kept wishing you were there with us.'

'I wish I had been, too.' She wondered if the father had always intended taking his daughter to America, or if she would have been left with the woman who ran the holiday club in Southport if Vanessa hadn't told him a few home truths. 'Where is your daddy?' she asked.

'He's here somewhere. I think Brodie's making him a cup of tea. He was surprised when he saw what was going on next door and said he was glad we'd got home in time to come.' She rubbed her face against Vanessa's arm. 'And so am I.'

Four o'clock approached and gradually people began to go home, until only close friends and a few relatives were left. Diana's brothers had more important things to do and Tinker, Rosa and Alan were expected at a concert. Leonard took the paintings down, put them in the house, and went home: Sunday was his chess night.

The sun continued to shine as warmly and as brightly as ever. Frank Sinatra sang 'Come Fly With Me' and 'Nancy with the Laughing Face'. Charlie's father and Colin were in deep conversation about cars. It would seem Colin had an old Triumph he was restoring and the other man was anxious to see it. He was dressed as he'd been when Vanessa first saw him, all in black, though this time his dark hair wasn't tied back, but sticking out all over the place as if he'd been dragged through a hedge backwards. She would have expected him to have ginger hair like his daughter, but Charlie must take after her mother.

Leo's mum and dad had gone, but Leo stayed, his eyes following Diana in her orange jumpsuit as she darted like a firefly all over the place, never pausing to rest. He was so much in love with her that it was painful to watch. Vanessa could understand Diana finding such devotion hard to resist.

Rachel and Charlie were playing with Poppy on a blanket under the trees where it was shady. 'I didn't see a single baby in New York,' Charlie was saying.

Brodie revealed that there was wine in the fridge. 'Who'd like a glass?'

'Me!' Eileen put up her hand. 'I'd like two glasses: any colour, dry or sweet.'

'I would, too.' Megan had collapsed in a deckchair. She wasn't a young woman and had had a busy day.

'How about you, Vanessa?'

'Yes, please.' She was sitting on the grass, glad that the afternoon was almost over, only conscious now that it had been a bit of a strain.

Almost immediately, Charlie's father came and sat on the grass beside her. 'I want to thank you for looking after Charlie,' he said. 'And apologize for what I said the other week. I was a pig. I hadn't realized Charlie had been emailing all over the globe cancelling the arrangements I'd made. I hadn't realized she was so unhappy, either, being looked after by all and sundry instead of her dad.' He held out his hand.

'Reggie Ormerod – or Reg, but definitely not Reginald. There's no need to ask who you are: Vanessa Dear, the famous artist.'

'Not exactly famous,' Vanessa said modestly as they shook hands.

'The time will come, I'm sure of it,' he said, smiling brilliantly. He *was* dishy, as Megan had said, and *did* look like a rock star. He also had buckets of Lancashire charm. Normally, Vanessa didn't like men with long hair and tattoos, and couldn't stand the name Reginald in any of its various forms. Perhaps she was going through a personality change because she quite liked Reggie Ormerod, though in an entirely unromantic way. Soon, she thought, there'd be nothing whatsoever left of the woman who'd come to live in this house in March. On second thoughts, she wasn't entirely sure if her liking for him was all that unromantic.

'I want to ask you something,' Reggie said. 'Charlie still has a fortnight to go before she goes back to school. Can I leave her with you? It's what she wants. If it's inconvenient, I can always make other arrangements.' There was something quite touching about this dishy individual being so concerned about his little daughter.

'I love having her,' Vanessa assured him. 'We all do, particularly Rachel and Poppy – that's the young girl with the baby. You can leave her with us whenever you want.'

'Thanks, I really appreciate it.'

It had all gone wonderfully well, Brodie thought as she went round with the wine, far better than expected. It was astounding to think that people were willing to hand over more than a thousand pounds for Vanessa's paintings. How did the old saying go? A fool and his money are soon parted.

Oh, that's most unfair of me, she thought, ashamed. Just because *she* didn't like the paintings, it was silly – no, not just silly, but arrogant and condescending – to expect other people to think the same. The day might come when Vanessa's paintings would be worth ten times, a hundred times as much as they'd gone for today, and Brodie would have to eat her words – thoughts – and wish she'd bought half a dozen as an investment when she'd had the opportunity, just like Eileen.

'I'll buy one later,' she vowed. 'No, I'll get two, one for Diana.' She wondered if her mother would like one.

She returned to the kitchen for a glass of wine for herself and wished she'd thought to buy a few bottles of beer for Colin and Charlie's father, Reggie, who didn't look the sort of person who was into wine. Mum, bless her, fancied the pants off him, and Brodie didn't exactly find him unattractive, either. He and Vanessa had been talking for ages. Wouldn't it be great if they got together? She imagined another day like today with Vanessa and Reggie getting married in the garden.

Colin came in and she remembered what had happened the last time they'd had a party: they'd made love afterwards. Would it happen again tonight? She'd be very easy to persuade once she'd got a few glasses of wine down her.

'Any beer?' he asked.

'Sorry.' She grimaced. 'I didn't think about it until a few minutes ago.'

'It's all right. Reggie's got a six-pack in the fridge. He said he'd go and fetch it if we had none here. Is that your mobile, Brodie?'

'Yes.' One of the Brandenburg concertos was being played at a furious pace in her room.

'I'll get it for you, darling.' He came back a few seconds later. 'I answered it. Someone called Karen wants to speak to you.'

Karen Young, the policewoman she'd met in London. Brodie grabbed the mobile. She listened intently, hardly speaking, just the occasional 'yes'. When she'd finished, she switched the phone off and laid it on the kitchen unit beside the wine. She was shaking.

'Who was it?' Colin asked tensely.

'Karen is the policewoman who's been looking for Maisie.' Brodie didn't know whether to laugh or cry. 'She's been found. She's not very well, though, and Karen is driving her home. She's already come a bit of a way and thinks she'll be about another three hours.'

'She's coming here?'

'Yes, here.' All the antagonism that had built up between them when they'd lived together returned with a vengeance. 'Not the house in Crosby, that's for sure,' she said coldly. 'We both know she's not welcome there.'

He punched the fridge so hard that she wondered if he'd made a dent in it. 'For Christ's sake, Brodie, let her come to her real home, please, and we can both look after her.'

'You don't want to look after her.' Hot tears came to her eyes. 'You've said all along that the drugs are all her own fault, that she doesn't deserve pity – certainly not yours.' She walked into her room and he followed. 'I don't want you near her, Colin,' she shouted over her shoulder. 'I'm not having you accusing her of letting you down and all sorts of other rubbish.'

'As if I'd say that.' He was red with frustration. 'She's my daughter, for Christ's sake.'

'Huh! You've changed your tune, I must say. You didn't think like that before. You virtually disowned her.'

'Then I was wrong, OK?' His hands became fists and he stuffed them into the pockets of his jeans as far as they would go. 'It was the only way I could think of dealing with the situation. You leaving me taught me the error of my ways.' He glared at her belligerently. 'Now I'm sorry and I want to help.'

Brodie tossed her head. 'I can manage on my own, thank you.'

'Where will she sleep?' Colin demanded in a different tone, more practical.

'In here with me.'

'But there isn't the room: it's only a single bed.'

'There are more beds upstairs. I'll put another single in here.' She made to leave through the French window. 'I'll ask Reggie Ormerod to give me a hand.'

He grabbed her arm. 'Don't be so bloody stupid. *I'll* bring one down.'

'You can't do it on your own. It needs two people.' She thought for a moment. 'OK, let's both do it. If I ask Reggie, my mum and yours will want to know why I need another bed downstairs. If they know Maisie's coming home, they'll make a huge fuss, and I'd sooner it was kept between the two of us for now.'

They went upstairs where there were two single beds. Both felt quite comfortable, but the more modern one, which was merely a hollow base with a mattress on top, would be the easiest and lightest to carry.

'This one, I think,' she said. 'The headboard is simple to take off and put back on again.'

Quarter of an hour later, the bed had been erected next to the single bed already in Brodie's room. She looked for bedding in the wardrobe drawer. 'Damn! I've only got one duvet,' she swore. 'I'd forgotten.'

'Shall I go home and fetch one?' Colin asked.

'Thank you. Bring the one from Maisie's bed, and the pillow and the bottom sheet as well.' She pushed the new bed further from her own. Maisie might prefer them not to be too close. Brodie resolved not to smother her with love when she might not be ready for it. She might even prefer to be left alone. If she wanted a room of her own, then she could have this one, and Brodie would sleep in one of the little rooms upstairs.

After Colin had gone, she collected her wine and went into the garden, otherwise someone would be bound to come looking for her. Karen had said she expected to arrive around ten o'clock and it was gone half past seven now.

'Are you all right, darlin'?' her mother enquired.

'I'm tired, Mum, that's all.'

'If that's the case, you'd be better off with tea or coffee, not wine. It'll only make you more tired.'

Brodie merely smiled and tried not to appear irritated. She wasn't in the mood to be told what was best by her mother. And Eileen was getting on her nerves, talking too loudly and drinking and smoking far too much. Her sister Mary, who looked quite sober, seemed to sense Brodie's disapproval and shrugged slightly, as if to say there was nothing she could do.

Reggie Ormerod went home with Charlie, and Rachel took Poppy upstairs, saying she hoped she wouldn't keep anyone awake that night crying. 'I'm sure she's teething,' she said again. 'Her gums look very red.'

'Have you got stuff to rub on them?' Eileen asked.

'Oh, yes.' She was an admirable young girl, Brodie thought. Poppy couldn't have had a more dedicated mother.

Diana and Leo had disappeared into another part of the garden. Vanessa sat in a deckchair close to sleep. It was gone eight o'clock and the sun was setting behind the trees, making long shadows on the grass. Brodie heard Colin return. She went into her room through the window and closed it surreptitiously behind her, hoping no one would notice. Then she opened the front door for Colin.

'I've brought a few other things,' he said, coming in, his arms laden with bedding and a black plastic bag. 'I've got her dressing gown from behind the door, some slippers, and a few clothes out of her wardrobe, including a couple of nightdresses.'

'Thank you.' He was being very thoughtful.

He helped make the bed for their daughter. After they'd finished, he said, 'Surely we should be doing this together, darling? Not just making beds, but looking after her, sharing the responsibility.'

She looked at him impatiently. 'You must have lost your memory. It wasn't long ago that you wouldn't even discuss Maisie. It's the reason I left, because I couldn't stand your indifference.' She was aware she was merely making the same point in another way.

'I've already told you I didn't mean it. I was confused.' He groaned and rubbed his forehead with the back of his hand. 'I don't seem to be able to get through to you.'

She sat on the bed. 'Oh, Colin,' she said, 'I feel terrible.'

He sat beside her and tenderly put his arm around her shoulders. 'In what way, darling? Are you ill?'

'No. But it's been a lovely day. I've really enjoyed myself and hardly thought once about Maisie.' Then it had only been in passing, some swift memory from the past. By now, she'd completely forgotten whatever it was.

'If you let yourself worry about something every minute of every day, you'd very soon go mad,' Colin said soothingly.

She relaxed against him, hating him, yet loving him so much. 'I wish my mother and yours would go home,' she said. 'They make me feel all on edge. I desperately want both of them to be gone by the time Maisie comes.'

'I'll tell mine that our Stephen has a meal ready, shall I?' Stephen was Colin's younger brother, and Eileen and Mary were spending the night in his house. 'I'll offer to take her and Aunt Mary there.'

Brodie gnawed her lip. 'If your mum leaves, mine will only come and see what I'm up to. No, offer *her* a lift home. There's no way she can ride a bike, not in her condition: she's drunk far too much wine. When you come back, you can try to get rid of Eileen.' She was being awful, but could imagine the women following Maisie when she came in, commenting loudly, offering advice, perhaps even shedding a tear or two. Eileen might give her a cigarette, mum would offer to make strong tea with loads of sugar, her remedy for virtually everything.

'I'll see to it,' Colin said. He left and minutes later Brodie could hear him in the garden asking her mother if she'd like to be taken home.

Mum must have agreed. 'I'll go and get my bag,' she said.

The bag was on the table in Brodie's room. 'What on earth is another bed doing in here,' she imagined her mother saying if she came in. She took the bag into the garden and gave it to her mother there. She took ages saying goodnight, what a wonderful day it had been, and fancy raising so much money for the refugee centre. Tinker must be thrilled to bits.

She'd hardly been gone a minute, when Eileen and Mary went through the same routine. Then Vanessa yawned and rubbed her eyes and said she was going straight to bed. Rachel and Poppy had already gone, leaving Diana and Leo the only ones still around, though they were nowhere to be seen.

Brodie breathed a long sigh of relief and returned to her room. All of a sudden, the house and the garden were silent. She wanted to be the only person about when her daughter came home. If Karen wanted a drink, then Brodie would show her the kitchen and suggest she make it herself while she concentrated on Maisie. There were still some sandwiches and scones left over – it felt as if the exhibition had happened a week ago, not that afternoon.

By now, it was quarter to ten and the night was

dark. She made the tea she'd been on the point of making for the last half-hour.

Her mobile went. It was Colin to say her mother had been delivered home safely. He wanted to know if his own mother was still there. If not, did Brodie want him back or was he to take himself home?

Brodie suggested he came tomorrow. He was doing his best to be helpful and it would be silly to keep turning him away.

She sat in her room with the tea. At one point, she got up, turned on the computer, and sent Josh an email telling him his sister was on her way home. Afterwards, she brought up the photograph of her grandfather and sat looking at that until she heard a car stop outside.

'I suppose your legs are stiff,' Karen was saying gently as she helped Brodie's daughter out of the back of her car. 'Here, lean on me.'

'Let me help.' Brodie turned on the porch light and ran down the path. It was hard to believe that this was really happening.

'Here's your mum,' Karen said.

Maisie was having difficulty getting out of the car.

Brodie gasped, 'Maisie, oh, sweetheart.' Karen was holding Maisie's right arm and Brodie took hold of the left. It felt as thin as a stick.

'Hello, Mum,' Maisie mumbled. She stood up at last, clumsily, unsteadily, and took a step forward so that she was fully illuminated by the light from the porch. It was only then that Brodie saw that her daughter was heavily pregnant – at least seven months, perhaps more.

Chapter 11

Brodie's mobile rang. It was Colin. 'I take it Maisie's there by now?' he said quietly.

'She arrived about half an hour ago. But Colin . . .' she began, then paused, finding it hard to continue.

'What?' he asked.

'She's pregnant. Seven, maybe eight months gone.' She also looked awful, like a like a walking corpse, and smelled sour and unwashed.

'Jesus Christ! Did she say who the father is? Does she *know* who he is?'

'We haven't had a chance to talk,' Brodie said tiredly. 'Karen found her in a place in Islington, a rehabilitation centre for drug addicts. She hadn't long been there, only a few days.' She swallowed hard and tried to hold back the tears. 'Karen thinks she's going to be all right.'

'Thank God,' Colin said. 'What's she doing now?'

'She's asleep. When she got home, she just went straight to the toilet, then threw herself on the bed fully dressed. She's very restless. I'm in the garden, actually. I left the window open in case she wakes up and wants something.' She sighed. 'I wish I smoked: it might help me relax.' It seemed to help people like Eileen.

'Why not have a glass of wine?' he suggested.

'I've already had too much. I'm not exactly sober at the moment.' And it hadn't helped. The wine had made her feel nervy and on edge. It was why she'd come into the garden, to walk around, get some fresh air. 'What I need now is a strong cup of tea with loads of sugar — Mum would make it for me if she were here.'

'Would you like me to come over and make it?' He seemed anxious to help and had apparently got over the feeling of antagonism he'd had for their daughter.

'No thanks. I'll do it myself in a minute.'

'But I can come in the morning like you said?'

'Of course, Colin, Any time.'

Despite everything, it was pleasant in the garden. The only illumination came from the window of Diana's room where the curtains hadn't been drawn and the light was spread fan-shaped on the grass. The night-time scent of flowers was much stronger than during the day and the trains sounded louder, making the earth tremble. The trees were black against a sky made dull orange by the lights of the city, as if a giant spotlight had been directed on Liverpool from outer space. There were a few barely visible stars. Shuffling and scrabbling noises came from the bushes, as if little animals were having a party.

Kenneth came and rubbed himself against her legs, tail erect, purring loudly. She bent down, stroked his furry back, and lifted him on to her knee. 'What are you doing out so late?' she asked. 'I hope you're not a stray.' The cat responded by making itself comfortable on her knee and purring even louder.

Diana opened the window and said in a stage whisper, 'Would you like a drink, Brodie?'

'Oh, tea, please, very strong. Thank you.' She'd forgo the sugar. By now, the thought of sweet tea made her feel sick.

'Won't be a mo.' The window closed.

She was a diamond, that girl, Brodie thought. She and Leo had come in from the garden as the same time as Karen Young had arrived with Maisie. Poor Leo had been sent home on the spot and Diana had taken Karen into the snug with a drink and something to eat. While Brodie had been stroking her daughter's head, trying to calm her jerky, troubled sleep, she could hear the subdued, earnest voices of the two women.

Then Karen had knocked softly on Brodie's door to say she was going back to London.

Brodie came into the hall, closing the door behind her. 'Are you sure you wouldn't like to stay the night? My mother has a spare bedroom; she doesn't live far away.'

'If you don't mind, I'd sooner go now while there's hardly any traffic, and sleep tomorrow,' Karen said. Her young face glowed with health and she didn't look even faintly tired after the long journey. 'I've left some leaflets in the kitchen that will help you understand what is happening to Maisie.'

'Would you like to sit down?'

'No, thanks. I'll be sitting down all the way back to London.' She cleared her throat. 'She's only been at this rehab place in Islington a few days. For weeks, she'd been taking smaller and smaller doses of the drug

– it's heroin by the way. She took the last dose the other day and she's been in agony ever since – that's when she went into rehab because she needed some support. Now she's almost over her addiction.'

'That was quick! Is that all that was needed to get over it, a few days?' Why hadn't she done it before? Maisie cried out in her sleep and Diana had turned the television on or was playing a CD. Strains of highly dramatic music were coming from her room.

'Yes, but you have to make the decision to quit,' Karen said earnestly, 'that's the biggest hurdle, then be able to stick to it. The thinking at the centre is that Maisie has given up because of the baby, which is really good. She's shown the most enormous will-power and courage. There'll be another three or four weeks of her feeling pretty rotten: pains in the joints, panic attacks, nightmares, and so on. Try not to let her out on her own, just in case she weakens and goes looking for a hit.'

'We'll be careful,' Brodie promised. 'But what about the baby? I've heard that babies of drug addicts can be born with withdrawal symptoms.'

'That's not likely to be the case with Maisie. She wasn't a heavy user. She never injected, just smoked the stuff. Never the less, make sure she sees a doctor as soon as possible.' She held out her hand. 'I'll be off now, Brodie. I hope everything goes well with Maisie – and with you and your husband.'

Brodie ignored the hand and threw her arms around the girl. 'Thank you so much for finding her and bringing her home.' She would never cease to be grateful. 'I'll keep you informed as to how she's getting on.'

Karen left and Brodie returned to sit by Maisie and try to calm her troubled sleep. Images kept passing through her mind of Maisie as a baby, a toddler, starting playgroup then school, and so on until the day she'd left for university. In all the images, her daughter shone like a light: bright-eyed, glossy-haired, creamy-cheeked.

She thought about Josh and switched on the computer, turning the sound down first. There was an email from him: 'Is Maisie all right? Give her my love and ask when I can come and see her.'

Brodie didn't email back straight away because she didn't know what to say. She'd reply to him tomorrow.

Maisie had settled down, and it was at that point that Brodie went out into the garden and Diana had brought her tea. 'I'm going to bed now,' she whispered. 'I'll see you in the morning.'

'Goodnight, love.' She caught the girl's hand. 'And thank you.' Diana had known Brodie had a daughter – so did Vanessa and Rachel – but they hadn't known that she was a drug addict.

Diana's window closed and the curtains were drawn. Minutes later, the light went out. Now there was no light at all except from the sky. It was only then that Brodie allowed the pent-up tears to stream down her cheeks. She cried quietly, the tears falling on Kenneth's back, thinking about the daughter she'd once had, and the one she had now.

At quarter past four, Maisie woke up and began to moan. 'I'm hurting,' she whined. 'I'm hurting all over.'

Brodie, in her own bed by then, reached out her hand and rested it on Maisie's shoulder. 'What's wrong, sweetheart? Can I get you something?'

'I'm hurting so much. My bones are aching.' She sat up suddenly and Brodie's hand was knocked away. 'Have you got any tablets? Headache tablets? Aspirin?'

'I'll get some.' There was Paracetamol in the cupboard in the kitchen.

'Who are you?' Maisie asked rudely. 'Where am I?'

'It's Mum, sweetheart, and you're at home.' She reached for the bedside lamp and switched it on. 'There,' she said in a bright, unnatural voice. 'Don't you recognize me?'

Maisie stared, stared and stared, until her eyes glazed over and her face looked as if it was about to fall apart. 'Mum,' she said brokenly.

Brodie didn't know whether to hug her or not. She blinked back the tears that threatened to return and said, 'Would you like me to make you a drink, sweetheart? Tea or coffee? Or hot milk? You used to love a mug of hot milk before you went to bed, remember?'

'Milk would be nice. Thanks.' She leaned back against the pillow. 'I feel awful,' she groaned.

'I'll fetch those tablets,' Brodie promised.

They sat up in their beds, mother and daughter, drinking the milk. Brodie couldn't have described how she felt. The situation was so totally unreal. She wasn't prepared for it. Between sips, she made innocuous remarks: what a warm night it was, what a lovely summer it had been, how Josh was still setting up businesses that always failed. Now he'd bought an old van and had started to do removals. 'I expect that will fail like everything else.' She thought about Diana's

274

brothers. Garth, the youngest, had done well in his
A-levels and was going to Manchester University in
October, yet there hadn't been a parent in sight to
offer support. Was it possible, she wondered, to offer
too *much* support? Perhaps that's where she and Colin
had gone wrong.

Maisie started to shiver violently. Brodie had never
heard anybody's teeth rattle before. 'Would you like to
have a bath?' she asked. She'd always considered baths
to be a miracle cure for virtually everything, just as her
mother promoted sweet tea. Colin used to make jokes
about it. 'The water will still be hot.'

'All right,' Maisie said, somewhat surprisingly.

Brodie got out of bed and began to fuss around,
collecting the dressing gown Colin had bought, a
nightdress, slippers. 'Dad brought these earlier,' she
said.

'Dad? Where is he?' Maisie, still shivering, glanced
around the dimly-lit room. 'This isn't Crosby. Why
isn't Dad here?'

'This used to be Gran's house, now it's mine.
You've never been here before. I'm just staying here
for the time being, that's all. Dad's coming tomorrow.'

She was pleased when Maisie didn't question this,
but finished the milk and climbed out of bed. Brodie
was glad she'd agreed to a bath. It would get the smell
off her.

They went upstairs. Brodie ran the water, adding tea
tree bath foam. Maisie just stood by the door, watching. 'Is that enough?' Brodie asked when the water was
six or seven inches deep and covered with a froth of
bubbles.

Maisie sniffed and nodded. Her long brown hair was

hanging partly over her face in greasy clumps. She'd removed her cardigan and the T-shirt underneath was a shade between grey and black. Her jeans looked as if they hadn't been washed in months. In the gap between the T-shirt and the jeans, the skin on her stomach was stretched so tightly it was almost blue.

'There's shampoo here if you're going to wash your hair. Oh, and the pink toothbrush is mine if you want to use it. I'm afraid I haven't got a new one for you. I've hung your dressing gown and nightie behind the door and the clean towels are on the stool. Well,' she said, slightly breathless, 'I'll leave you to get on with it, shall I?' She hadn't been allowed in the bathroom with her daughter since Maisie was ten.

'Please.'

'Don't bolt the door. Oh, and take as long as you like – I'll be right outside if you need me.'

'All right, Mum.'

The 'Mum' held a touch of normality and was rather comforting. As quietly as she could, Brodie fetched a dining chair with a huge padded seat out of one of the small bedrooms and placed it close to the bathroom door. She didn't want to disturb Vanessa or Rachel and Poppy – that's if they hadn't been disturbed already. It had never been the sort of house in which people took baths at half-past four in the morning.

It was a good half an hour before Maisie appeared, looking almost human again, almost like the old Maisie in her lemon towelling dressing gown and white nightie. She'd washed her hair and combed it back off her face. There was a spot, almost a boil, on her right cheek and another on her forehead. 'I fell asleep,' she said.

Brodie had been fighting sleep the whole time, worried she'd fall off the chair. 'I'll dry your hair,' she said, 'and then we'll go back to bed.' She felt as if she could sleep for a week.

Maisie's hair was pitifully thin compared with how it used to be. When it was dry and she'd crawled into bed, she said sleepily, 'I feel better. Don't wake me up if Pete calls.'

'Is Pete likely to call?' Brodie asked. 'You'd better let me have your mobile. Does he know where you are?' If so, he could turn up at any time.

After a pause, Maisie gave a rather rusty laugh. 'I forgot: someone pinched my mobile and even *I'm* not sure where I am.'

'Who is Pete, sweetheart?' Brodie asked.

'My boyfriend.'

At half-past eight the next morning Maisie was dead to the world, there wasn't a sound coming from upstairs and Brodie was in the kitchen waiting for the kettle to boil. She hadn't slept a wink after going back to bed at around five. She'd kept asking herself questions to which she couldn't possibly have known the answers.

She'd heard Diana leave for work. Much too late, it dawned on her that *she* should have left for work by now. It was Monday, the start of a new week. Under the circumstances, she couldn't possibly go. In a minute, she'd telephone Mrs Cowper at Five Oaks and tell her she was leaving – no, had already left. It was an awful thing to do, she was badly letting the woman down, but had no choice.

How quickly life could change, she thought, sometimes for the better, sometimes for the worst. This time yesterday, she'd been in this same kitchen with her mother and Diana. They'd been standing around wondering if the art exhibition would be more successful than it had been the day before. And of course it was.

Now Maisie was home, life had changed for the better. She had her daughter under the same roof and was able to look after her. The trouble was, life felt worse. No, not worse, she reflected, just more troubling, more of a problem, more *real*. She had to worry about Maisie in a different way, no longer from a distance.

The bell on the front door made its strange buzzing sound and she hurried to answer it. The woman outside looked about forty, and was smartly dressed in a business-like black suit and low-heeled shoes. She carried a shorthand notebook in one hand and a pen in the other, and a sensible black handbag over her shoulder. Her black hair was cut in a stern fringe and heavy, horn-rimmed spectacles helped give the impression that in another life she could have been a concentration camp guard. She gave Brodie – in her denim skirt, check blouse and flip-flops – a disparaging look. Brodie noticed and the instinctive dislike she'd felt took a turn for the worse.

'Yes?' she enquired politely.

'I'd like to see Rachel Keen,' the woman demanded in a peremptory tone and without so much as a 'please'.

'She's not here.' Rachel and Poppy were no doubt asleep upstairs, but as far as Brodie was concerned the woman could go and jump in the lake. She didn't feel in the least bit accommodating.

'When will she be here?'

'I've no idea.'

'Does she actually live here?'

'Yes.'

'What sort of house is this?'

'A brick one.' She lost her patience. 'What do you mean, what sort of house is this? It's not a doss house, or a house of ill repute. It's just a house and I'm the owner.'

'I see.' The sarcasm was completely lost on the woman and she wrote something on the pad. 'And what's your name?'

'Hillary Clinton.' Brodie was beginning to enjoy herself.

'Is that Mrs?'

'It is indeed.'

'You must have some idea of when Rachel will be in.'

'I think she might be on holiday.' It was time *she* asked a question. 'What was it you wanted to see Rachel about?'

'We understand,' the woman said grimly, 'that Rachel is an under-aged mother and concern has been expressed that the baby is not being properly cared for.'

Brodie wondered if the person who had expressed concern was Rachel's mother or Tyler's father. Vanessa had reported that the father was a pretty revolting piece of work. She said, 'I know for a fact that Rachel attends the baby clinic every week without fail accompanied by a very concerned adult. She is a far better mother than I ever was and a fine example to mothers of any age. Now, I'm afraid I am very busy. Goodbye.'

She closed the door and stood leaning against it feeling triumphant. She'd certainly won *that* battle. After a while, she began to feel ashamed. The poor woman was only doing her job. She opened the door, but there was no sign of anyone and she could hear a car driving away.

'I'm sorry,' she said to the road in general. 'Really sorry.'

She stepped outside and took a deep breath. It was another lovely day. This was the best summer she could remember. If global warming got no worse than this, then she was all for it.

In the kitchen, she boiled the kettle again, made tea, and took it into the garden. To her surprise, she found Rachel and Charlie squashed together in a deck chair reading a magazine, and Vanessa seated on a bench nursing Poppy, who was chewing madly on a rattle. Kenneth was draped over a branch of a tree like the fur neck thing her mother used to have – she thought it was called a tippet and it had been brown, not ginger.

'What a scene of domestic bliss,' she called as she approached the group. Everyone, including Poppy, looked up and smiled. She decided not to tell Rachel about the visitor. It would only worry the girl and the woman might not come back. She'd have a word with Vanessa next time they were alone together.

'Poppy's got half a tooth,' Vanessa announced.

'Aren't you a clever little girl?' Brodie cried. 'When did that appear?'

'Sometime last night,' Vanessa replied on the baby's

behalf. 'It definitely wasn't there before she went to bed.'

'About last night,' Brodie said, 'my daughter, Maisie, arrived very late and had a bath. I hope she didn't disturb anyone.'

Rachel denied she'd heard a thing.

Vanessa merely said, 'I wondered who it was.'

'Maisie's expecting a baby,' Brodie went on. 'She thought she'd like to have it at home – I don't mean on the premises, but in Liverpool.'

'When's it due?' Rachel enquired.

'She's not absolutely sure. In about six weeks, she thinks.'

Vanessa didn't say anything. Brodie got the impression that she wasn't exactly pleased. Perhaps she'd guessed that Maisie wasn't there because she was pregnant and that there was something else, something that might interfere with the tranquil life she'd led since she'd come to live at Chestnuts. As if to prove this might be the case, a piercing scream came from the house and Brodie rushed inside. So much for a tranquil life!

Maisie was standing in the middle of the room, her arms wrapped across her breasts, looking utterly distraught. The spot on her cheek had bled during the night and the red stain had run as far as her chin.

'There's insects in the bed.' she screeched. 'Spiders! Loads and loads of spiders.'

Brodie pulled back the bedclothes. 'There's nothing there, sweetheart,' she said. 'Look, it's empty.'

'But I could feel them crawling all over me.' She shook herself frantically and rubbed her arms and legs as if she were brushing the insects away.

'Honestly, Maisie, there are no spiders anywhere.' Brodie was just as terrified of spiders as her daughter. Colin had always had to come to the rescue when a spider had been found in the house in Blundellsands.

'Don't kill it,' Brodie would plead. 'It's unlucky.'

'Particularly for the spider,' Colin would say with a grin. The spider rescue kit, as he referred to it, consisted of a sheet of cardboard and a little red plastic bowl. After some complicated manoeuvres, the spider would be caught and transferred to the garden, where, as he pointed out, it was at risk of catching a cold.

Maisie gingerly approached the bed to check that it was completely free from the dreaded creepy crawlies, as she'd used to call them.

'See!' Brodie said with a cheerfulness she definitely didn't feel. 'Now, would you like some breakfast? There's eggs, toast, all sorts of cereals.'

'Is there any ice-cream?'

'Yes, we've definitely got ice-cream.' It was a strange thing to want for breakfast. There was a carton of Cornish in the fridge that belonged to Diana: she wouldn't mind if some was used. 'While I'm gone, perhaps you could get dressed? Dad brought some clothes and they're hanging outside the wardrobe. I'm afraid he didn't think to bring shoes. Oh, and unpack that bag of yours in case there's stuff that needs washing.' The filthy clothes in which she'd arrived were presently in the washing machine.

In the kitchen, she rang Colin in the hope he was still there and she could ask him to bring shoes. To her horror, George, her father-in-law, answered and said he'd left ten minutes before.

'How are you keeping?' Brodie felt obliged to enquire.

'Not so bad. How are you?' It was probably the first time in many years he'd shown interest in her health. He even sounded as if he meant it.

'OK. How's the Triumph coming along?' The Triumph could fall to pieces as far as she was concerned: she didn't give a fig about it. Then she squirmed. What a truly horrible person she was being this morning. The car meant a lot to her husband and his father.

'Very well,' George said. 'Really well.'

'I must come and have a look at it some time.'

'That's a good idea, Brodie. It's almost ready to go on the road.'

Brodie rang off. It would seem she was on far better terms with George than she'd ever imagined. She remembered she'd come for ice-cream and spooned some into a bowl.

'Dad only brought dresses,' Maisie said, allowing herself be guided across the room with the ice-cream to the table in the window. She was wearing a pretty blue flowered thing with frilly sleeves and *broderie anglaise* trim at the hem that was too tight over her tummy. 'It's ages since I last wore a dress. I'd sooner wear jeans.'

'I'm pretty certain you took all your jeans away with you, Maisie,' Brodie said. 'Dad probably just grabbed things out of your wardrobe. You look really nice in that,' she lied, 'even though it's not a maternity dress.' In fact, she looked painfully thin, her knees all knobbly and her anklebones like golf balls. She wasn't in a good state to have a baby.

Maisie wriggled uncomfortably. 'It feels funny.'

'Well, it doesn't look funny. I tell you what, shall we go into town later and buy you some new jeans and tops?'

'All right,' Maisie sighed. A couple of years ago she would have clapped her hands and jumped for joy at the idea and asked if they could have lunch while they were there, but Brodie was glad to have got a positive reaction. She had imagined having to care for someone who was virtually an invalid. That Maisie was willing to go shopping was quite unexpected. Perhaps Colin would come with them, make it a family outing, though without Josh. She recalled she'd vowed to email her son that morning. She'd do it as soon as she had a minute to spare.

The curtains were still closed. Brodie pulled them back. Vanessa and the children were still in the garden. If Maisie noticed, she didn't ask who they were.

There was a knock on the door: it was Colin. He looked tired, too, as if he hadn't slept much. 'Can I see her alone?' he whispered.

'Why?'

He frowned. 'Why not?'

Brodie frowned back. 'You're not going to say anything, are you? Tear her off a strip or something like that?'

'I'm not going to do any such thing.'

'It wasn't long since you were saying things like, "she's made her own bed and she must lie in it," ' she reminded him.

'I know that, but now I've stopped.' He rolled his eyes impatiently. 'I was in a state, not thinking properly.'

'Oh, all right.' She stood aside to let him in, then went into the kitchen, wondering what he had to be in a state about.

'Dad, oh, *Dad!*' she heard Maisie cry, and felt hurt that she hadn't been afforded such a warm welcome.

'Shall we all go out somewhere today?' Vanessa asked. 'To town, say?'

'Go out? But we never go out anywhere except to the clinic and the supermarket,' Rachel said.

'Me and Vanessa went to town the other week to buy her a new dress,' Charlie pointed out a touch smarmily. There was a small amount of rivalry between the girls and Vanessa had to make sure she treated them exactly the same.

'We could go on the train; it's much easier than using the car,' she suggested. She didn't feel herself today. She'd already had a strong suspicion that Brodie's daughter was into drugs – or trying to recover from them – when she'd heard the bath running at about four or five o'clock that morning. There was something about the false way Brodie spoke to the person having the bath – she didn't know then it was her daughter – unnatural, like a grown-up to a child, or a nurse to a patient.

Earlier, when Brodie had come into the garden and said, unconvincingly, her daughter had come home to have a baby, it had only strengthened Vanessa's suspicions, and that awful scream had confirmed them. It rather clouded the house's lovely atmosphere.

The reason she'd been awake so early that morning was nothing to do with someone having a bath, but because she'd felt terribly restless. Something awful had happened: *she no longer wanted to paint*. It was Eileen's fault for suggesting an exhibition, then Diana's for carrying it through.

The exhibition had been like a grand finale, the final overture, the last page of the book. Too much attention had been paid to her; her privacy had been invaded. From now on, people would be *interested*. It was something she preferred to do completely alone.

It was only a few weeks ago that she'd been congratulating herself on the improvement in her fortunes, but now, in the middle of the night, with the trees in the garden swishing in the breeze and the sound of police sirens in the distance, Vanessa's thoughts were distressingly dark. It was nothing to do with William, with being jilted at the altar, putting on weight: it was to do with there being no point to life, not having an aim or something to look forward to. She'd thought painting was all she'd ever want to do, but she'd been wrong.

In the next room, Poppy gave a little cough, and the sound reminded her that people relied on her, at least for the time being. But they wouldn't always. Rachel was convinced Tyler would soon be back from America. Next year, she would be sixteen, there would be no reason for anyone to take Poppy away and she wouldn't need Vanessa's protection any more. As for Charlie, she would be back at school in a week or so.

'I'd love to go to town,' Rachel was saying. 'I'll make Poppy some bottles to take with us and pack some nappies. Oh, and I'll change her nappy before we go.' She scooped Poppy off Vanessa's knee and went into the house.

Charlie said she was going home to get ready. 'But

you look perfectly all right as you are,' Vanessa told her. She wore cotton shorts and a striped T-shirt.

'But I need a hat and a handbag,' Charlie insisted. 'Aren't you going to put your red dress on?'

'Why not?' There was no need to make herself even more miserable by going out looking a sight, wincing every time she glimpsed her reflection in a shop window. 'While you're in there, Charlie,' she shouted as the little girl climbed over the wall into her own garden, 'telephone your father and tell him where you're going, please. I don't want him shouting at me again.' She felt convinced that if anyone so much as raised his or her voice, she'd burst into tears.

They got off the train at Central Station, then caught the bus down to the Pier Head where they watched the ferries sail to and fro across the Mersey. It was a bit of a palaver getting on and off trains and buses with two children – she counted Rachel as a child – a baby and a pushchair, but if other people could do it, then so could she.

She sat on a bench and gave Poppy her bottle while the girls went to buy ice-creams – both appeared to have plenty of money. When the ice-creams were finished, they chased each other around the bench. Anyone watching would never have guessed that one was the mother of the baby, who was clapping her hands and screaming with delight while she sat on the older woman's knee.

They walked slowly back towards town, called in at British Home Stores so Rachel could buy Poppy half a dozen pairs of stretchy leggings, then wandered as far as Clayton Square shopping centre where it was agreed that they stop and have something to drink. They took the lift to the first floor where there was a restaurant within a circle of shops.

'Do you mind if I look in that clothes shop?' Rachel asked after she'd finished her Coke. Poppy had fallen asleep in the pushchair and Vanessa was barely halfway through her coffee.

'Of course not.' She couldn't very well stop Rachel from doing anything.

'Can I go with her?' Charlie finished her drink and jumped to her feet.

Vanessa shook her head. 'I'd sooner you stayed here with me. You're too young to go wandering off on your own.'

Charlie looked outraged. 'But I wouldn't be on my own; I'd be with Rachel.'

'I'll keep hold of her hand, I promise,' Rachel said.

The shop was only about ten feet away. 'Oh, all right, but don't go anywhere else, just that one place. We'll go to St John's Market later where there's loads of shops.'

She watched until they seemed to melt into a crowd of mainly young women shoppers, still holding hands. For some reason that would always remain inexplicable, she began to cry: not noisily, in fact not making any sound at all, just conscious of the tears running heavily down her cheeks, dropping into her coffee, making tiny plopping sounds.

She closed her eyes, first putting her hand firmly on Poppy's tummy in case someone made off with her while she wasn't looking. Everything seemed so bleak. In the not too distant future, the year in Chestnuts would come to an end. What would happen then?

Where would she go? She imagined never seeing Rachel, Poppy or Charlie again. They had their whole lives ahead of them and Vanessa would just be a person they'd once known. They might forget about her completely and she wouldn't even be a memory.

'What's up, Picasso?' a male voice enquired.

Vanessa's eyes snapped open and saw Reggie Ormerod in the seat opposite. His black hair was in its usual state of disarray and his shirt was urgently in need of ironing. He had quite nice eyes, she noticed, very dark grey, and they were watching her with an embarrassing measure of concern. 'Nothing,' she replied. 'Absolutely nothing.'

'Liar,' he scoffed good-naturedly. 'No one cries over nothing.'

'*I* do; it's a habit of mine.' She sniffed and wiped her nose on a paper napkin. 'What are you doing here?'

'Charlie rang earlier and said you were coming into town,' he explained. 'I asked her to phone once you'd got here. I had a meeting with these two American guys this morning in a hotel in Lime Street. I thought that maybe we could catch up with each other.'

Did he mean catch up with Charlie or catch up with her? Vanessa wondered, before deciding she didn't really care, and then deciding that she did, very much so, and she hoped it *was* her. It would do her ego the world of good. 'Charlie's in that shop behind you,' she said.

'I know, I saw her go in.'

That meant he must have been watching her cry for a good five minutes. In similar circumstances, most men would have run a mile. Poppy woke up, grinned at them both, and went back to sleep. At the sight of the grin, Vanessa just couldn't help it: she started crying again. 'I keep thinking the day will come when I won't see Poppy any more: she and Rachel will disappear out of my life, Charlie, too.'

'Charlie and I aren't thinking of moving,' he said gently. He put his hand over hers and a little frisson of something passed between them. Vanessa felt an odd sensation in her breast, as if her heart had skipped a beat.

'But I'll have to move,' she said. 'Brodie will probably sell the house next year. I've no idea where I'll go then.'

'Haven't you got any family?'

'Loads,' she said. 'Loads and loads. But if you're unhappy, you can't always fall back on family. In the end, you have to be able to manage on your own.'

'You don't have to be quite so hard on yourself, Picasso.'

The name reminded her of the main reason she was in such a state. 'I don't want to paint any more,' she said wretchedly. 'I don't know why, but after yesterday I've lost all interest.'

'Don't be daft,' he said flatly. 'In fact, I was going to ask you to do a painting for my office.'

'What sort of painting?' she asked with a tiny pinch of interest.

'Anything you like, as long as it's colourful and at least two metres long. I don't fancy something white with a little dribble of black ink that's supposed to mean something vastly significant. Just throw loads of paint at the canvas and mix it up. That's the sort of painting I like.'

'OK,' she said slowly. Ideas were already racing

through her head. She'd buy some paints while she was in town: no, she wouldn't, she'd buy them from Leonard tomorrow along with a really big canvas.

'Daddy!' Charlie came running up. 'I didn't know you were here. I've bought a new top.' She took a blue frilly T-shirt out of the bag and showed it to him.

'Very nice,' Reggie said approvingly. 'Very nice indeed.'

'And what have you bought, Rachel?' Vanessa asked when the girl arrived, not wanting her to feel left out.

'Just some red jeans and a T-shirt.' She sniffed and made a face. 'Poppy needs a clean nappy. There's a changing room somewhere . . .' She wheeled the pushchair away.

Charlie shot after her. 'I'll come with you.'

'This is great,' Reggie Ormerod said with a happy sigh as he watched them go.

'What is?'

'I don't know, but whatever it is it's great.'

In another part of Liverpool, in another restaurant less than half a mile away, Maisie Logan was clinging to her mother's arm. 'Get me something,' she was saying in a gritty voice. 'Anything, something to chew. Toffees. Get me something *now*.'

'I'll do it.' A panicky Colin jumped to his feet. 'Do they sell sweets downstairs with the food?' They were in Marks & Spencer. Brodie nodded.

'I need a fix,' Maisie said, licking her lips. 'I really need a fucking fix.'

Brodie swallowed hard. 'All right, sweetheart. Dad's gone to get you some toffees. Would you like to drink some of your coffee?'

'*No*. Can you smoke here? Have you got any cigarettes?'

'I'm afraid you can't smoke anywhere in Liverpool these days.' The hand tightened painfully on her arm. 'Anyway, Maisie, you're pregnant. It would be very wrong to smoke when you're expecting a baby.'

'Don't fucking lecture me, Mum.' She gave Brodie a look of what could only be described as hatred.

Two women on the next table glanced at each other. One tut-tutted and shook her head. Brodie tried not to take any notice, but couldn't help but feel ashamed. How would she feel if she were one of those women and heard a young woman swear at her mother like that?

And she'd thought coming shopping would be like old times, a family outing. Instead, it was a nightmare.

'It's all right,' Maisie was saying. Her grip loosened on her mother's arm. She began to breathe deeply, noisily. 'I'm all right now.'

'Of course you are, sweetheart,' Brodie crooned, putting her arms around her daughter. 'Very soon, everything will be all right.' She only wished she could believe that.

September–October 2006

Chapter 12

Tinker told Diana that her happiness showed in her eyes. They were sitting on either side of the desk in the stuffy little office supposedly having a 'staff' meeting, although they were the only official members of staff, the rest being volunteers. The room was lined with battered metal filing cabinets, and an ancient fan whirred away in the corner. It was an exceptionally warm day. Tinker chewed the end of his pen and looked at Diana oddly.

'What's that for?' she asked.

'What's what for?'

'The funny look.'

'It was an admiring look. You're a sight for sore eyes, d'you know that, Di? Where did you get that outfit from?' She wore a flowered corduroy frock with a lace collar, a nipped-in waist, and an ankle-length flared skirt.

'Out of the clothes in the cellar. Rosa said it was called the New Look and came into fashion right after the Second World War. It ponged a bit and I had to wash it twice to get rid of the smell.' She wished she'd worn something lighter as she was sweating cobs. 'I always put money in for the things, Tinker,' she assured him. 'I pay more for them than they'd get if they were sold on the stall.'

'I know you do, Di. I wasn't suggesting you didn't. You look very sweet.' He winked. 'Why exactly are you so happy?'

'I dunno.' She sighed blissfully. 'I expect it's because life's so perfect. I love this job, I love where I live, I love everything.' She waved her arm as if to include the room, or it might have been the city of Liverpool, or possibly the entire world. Upstairs, the click of snooker balls could be heard, the playgroup was on the point of packing up and children were shouting excitedly over something, the telly was on in the lounge, and one of the young men on the stairs was playing a guitar and singing something terribly haunting and beautiful. This cacophony of sounds only served to remind her why she loved the place so much.

'When are you and what's-his-name getting married?'

'Leo. I don't know.' Her face fell. At least once a week poor Leo suggested they set a date for the wedding, but she kept putting him off. She didn't think it was terribly nice always to think of him as 'poor'. Once she'd said jokingly, 'We'll get married on my fiftieth birthday,' and he'd got really, really upset. 'Why did you ask?' she said to Tinker.

'Because if you ever decide to dump the bloke, I'd like to be the first to know.'

'Why?'

'So I can marry you meself before another bloke appears on the scene.'

'Honest?' She felt herself blush.

296

'Honest to God.' He had a smile on his lips. 'Are you surprised?'

'I thought you were gay,' she told him.

The smile turned into a laugh. 'Did you now? Well, I'm not.'

'Do you perm your hair?'

He touched the mass of tiny red ringlets. 'No, it's natural.' He put the pen down, frowned and crossed his eyes at the same time. He wore little gold hoop earrings and a sweater that was purple on one side and green on the other. It made him look like the star of a pantomime. 'So, you thought I was gay with permed hair, eh? I bet you thought it was dyed, too. And here's me thinking you found me desperately attractive.'

'Oh, I do, I do.' She'd been a little bit in love with him since she'd first come to work at the centre. He was a really lovely person with a sunny disposition who really cared for the refugees. Unless you counted the desperate tizzies he was inclined to get into from time to time, he never properly lost his temper. He was also enormous fun. Being married to Tinker would be much more enjoyable than being married to poor Leo, who was so intense about everything. Diana felt as if she had to tread on eggshells all the time in case she hurt his feelings.

'If I give you my card,' he said, 'keep it in your handbag and give us a ring on my moby if you and Leo decide to break up? I doesn't matter if it's in the middle of the night. Any time, and I'll pop the question straight away.' He handed her his business card. It said 'Anthony Taylor', and had the refugee centre address and telephone number and his mobile number underneath. She wondered if he'd been nicknamed Tinker because his surname was Taylor.

'All right,' she promised, keeping a straight face. 'I'll let you know.' She wasn't sure if he was joking or not. She hoped not.

On the train on the way home she showed Megan the christening gown she'd found in the cellar. 'Isn't it lovely? It's pure silk. I know it looks cream, but Rosa thinks it should be white. She's going to find out what to wash it with so it won't get damaged. She thinks it must be at least eighty years old.'

'It's beautiful, Diana. Is it for you?' Megan enquired, fingering the fine lace trimming.

Diana looked at the woman as if she were mad. 'It's a *christening* gown. It'd never fit *me*,' she snorted.

'You silly idiot,' Megan snorted back. 'I meant, is it for you because you're pregnant?'

'No, it's for Maisie. I don't think she's got any baby clothes. D'you think she'll like it?' Diana wondered how she'd feel about being pregnant. It was an impossible state to be in as she was still a virgin.

'She might.' Megan couldn't imagine her granddaughter liking anything much at the moment. She had been at Chestnuts for a week and the only person who could get anywhere with her was her father, which was ironic considering the circumstances. Brodie was being as kind and understanding as it was possible to be, yet Maisie was being perfectly horrible back. Sometimes she used really disgusting four-letter words.

'It's the drugs,' Brodie had said only the other day. 'She doesn't know what she's saying.'

'No, darlin',' Megan had argued. 'It's the *lack* of drugs. She's having withdrawal symptoms. Has she been to see a doctor?'

'She flatly refuses to see a doctor.' Brodie sounded tired to death. 'Anyway, Mum, what do you know about it?'

'I watch television like everyone else. I read the papers. I probably know as much about drugs as you do.' She made Megan feel like a silly old woman. '*My* daughter never went near them, I'm pleased to say.'

Brodie's face crinkled into something that was either a smile or a pained expression, Megan couldn't tell. 'I never led that sort of life. I suppose it's a combination of London and university that did it.'

Since Maisie had come home, Megan felt in the way at Chestnuts. Brodie kept watching whenever she went near the girl, as if she expected her to say something desperately tactless. She was glad there was the refugee centre where she could occupy her time doing things that were worthwhile and interesting. She had friends, but although most were younger than she was, they weren't very active. Their idea of entertainment was to play bridge, preferably in the afternoon, rather than visit the pictures or go shopping. At night Megan felt just a little bit lonely.

'Are you coming with us?' Diana asked when they got off the train and Megan went to collect her bicycle.

'No, dear. I think I'll go straight home tonight.' Megan would have far preferred to go with Diana.

'Ah, come on and have tea with us,' Diana said persuasively. 'I'm going to make sausages and mash with onion gravy. Afterwards, we can watch a DVD. Have you seen *Pride and Prejudice* with

Keira Knightley? I bought it the other day. I love Shakespeare, don't you?'

Megan was about to correct her, tell her that *Pride and Prejudice* had been written by Jane Austen, but held her tongue. She suspected the girl had sensed her loneliness. What did knowledge of English Literature matter when compared to having a really kind heart? 'I love Shakespeare, too,' she said.

Brodie stared at the computer screen and wondered where Maisie was. She'd gone to the lavatory and had been heard coming out. Perhaps she was exploring upstairs or was in the kitchen. She really, really wasn't in the mood to go looking for her. She glanced through the window in case she was in the garden, but there was no sign: just Charlie throwing a ball to Poppy in the hope that she might catch it and Rachel reading a book. Vanessa was painting, a really big canvas for a change.

The computer played a little tune to indicate an email had arrived. It was from Colin and said: 'The other day, I emailed the post office in Duneathly, Ireland, the village where your mother lived as a child, and asked if there were any Kennys or Ryans there. I'm forwarding you an email that came back today from a woman called Roseanna Ryan who claims you are her aunt.' There was a document enclosed and when Brodie brought it to the screen she saw it was a complicated family tree with dozens of names. She didn't want to look at it right now.

The front door opened and Diana came in. She wasn't alone. Brodie winced when she heard her mother's voice. She wished Mum would keep away.

She wasn't doing Maisie any good, kept saying the wrong things.

Diana shouted, 'Hello, everyone,' but Brodie didn't answer.

Seconds later, Diana and Mum appeared in the gardens – followed by Maisie. Brodie stiffened. The window was closed so she couldn't hear what was being said, but there was a great deal of laughter. Diana took something out of a bag – it might have been a blouse – and gave it to Maisie. Rachel and Charlie came over for a look. Then Maisie flung her arms around Diana's neck and the two girls clung together for several seconds before they laughed and broke away.

Brodie sat glued to her seat as she watched this strange drama being acted out. Her mother and daughter, with Diana, returned to the house and went into the kitchen. Maisie sounded quite normal, quite like her old self. 'I've got eight sausages,' Diana was saying, 'so that means we can have two and a bit each. I hope no one minds Smash instead of real potatoes. I'll open a tin of peas.'

'Yummy!' said Maisie.

It was hard to think of a more unhealthy meal: sausages, dried potatoes and tinned peas. Brodie had been feeding her salads and fresh fruit since she'd come home and she was looking the better for it: her skin and eyes were clearer and her hair had acquired a sheen. She even looked as if she'd put on some weight.

Diana asked if they would please keep an eye on the sausages while she got changed. 'The belt on this dress is slowly cutting me in two. I was daft to wear it on a day like this. Oh, by the way, where's Brodie?' she enquired.

'She must be having a little lie-down,' Mum said. 'It's probably best if we don't disturb her.'

Brodie immediately got up and went to lie on the bed, feeling as if she'd been given permission. She wouldn't be missed: no one would expect her to come out. The minute her head touched the pillow she was aware of how tense she was when her neck and shoulders began to throb, as they did so often these days.

The last week had been really unpleasant. Most of the time, she found it hard to relate to her daughter – or perhaps it was the other way round. Brodie thought she was being extremely patient and tolerant, but Maisie seemed to think the opposite.

'Don't bug me, Mum,' she would say, shying away if Brodie so much as touched her or suggested she did something sensible like going to see a doctor.

And what was galling, really galling, was that Maisie and her father got on like a house on fire, yet Maisie was only home because Brodie had gone to London and met Karen Young. It was Colin who'd discovered that Pete, the boyfriend, had been a drug addict, too, that they'd met at university.

'I bet it was him who introduced her to drugs,' Brodie had said bitterly.

'No.' Colin shook his head. 'It was the other way round. She took them first, then he did. But he was sensible enough to recognize what a bad idea it was and gave up. He's been looking after Maisie the best he could ever since, but she kept disappearing.'

'Doesn't it seem strange', Brodie murmured, 'that we're sitting here talking about drugs and our Maisie?'

They'd been in the snug at the time. Maisie was asleep in Brodie's room. Colin got up and began to walk around the table. He looked on the verge of tears. 'She first took the heroin at a party, our little girl. She was just about to sit her first year exams and she says it helped focus her mind: she could see things much more clearly. It also made her feel extraordinarily happy. She liked the feeling so much that she got more. Within a matter of weeks, she was desperate for it, looking for dealers, spending all her money.' He shrugged. 'She was hooked.'

'And what about Pete?'

'He tried to stop her, then he took it just to keep her company, then he got scared and stopped.' He paused by the window. 'Diana's coming. What on earth is she wearing?'

Brodie didn't bother to look. 'I don't know,' she said. The front door opened and Diana came in.

'Whatever it is, she must think life is one long fancy dress party.' He turned back to Brodie. 'They're funny, drugs. Some people can take them or leave them. Others get hooked after a few doses. Is that what you call them, doses? Or is it fixes?'

'I don't know,' Brodie said for the second time. 'I take it Pete is the baby's father?'

'I haven't asked her straight out, but I expect he is. She was lucky to have had him. He's stuck by her as best he could. He must love her very much.'

'I'm home,' Diana shouted.

'We're in here,' Brodie shouted back.

Diana came into the room wearing an extremely

smart dark-green taffeta dress. She beamed. 'Hello, you two.'

'Hello, there.' Brodie smiled, and thought for the umpteenth time how much nicer it was talking to this young woman than it was to her daughter.

'I'm off to make me tea,' Diana said. 'I could eat a horse.' She went singing into the kitchen.

'It's a cocktail dress,' Colin said when the door closed.

'What?'

'What Diana is wearing is a cocktail dress. Until now, I've only seen women wearing them in films.' He sighed. 'At least *she's* happy.'

'She's always happy.' Brodie returned to the topic under discussion before Diana had appeared. 'Does Maisie have any idea where Pete might be? Is he likely to turn up one day?'

'He's either in London or he's staying with his folks. They live in Exeter. In Devon.'

'I know where Exeter is,' Brodie snapped.

'There's no need to bite my head off,' Colin said mildly. 'Anyroad, she's got his mobile number should she want to contact him, which apparently she doesn't right now.'

'I see.' Brodie groaned. 'I can't get through to her. Why is it you can and I can't? Why does she open up to you when she won't to me? Oh!' She dropped her head into her hands. 'It's so *frustrating*.'

'I think you ought to lighten up. Just talk to her normally. Try not to be so gentle and understanding. It makes her feel uncomfortable – guilty.'

'Has she said that to you?'

'No, it's something I worked out for myself. I know

I was being much too tough on her before and it's one of the reasons you left. I'm sorry about that, Brodie. Now you're being too soft.' He stood behind and put his hands on her shoulders. 'I think you should both come home, darling. It's where you belong. Maisie would feel happier sleeping in her old room in her own bed.'

He'd suggested that before and she'd been adamantly opposed to the idea. She still was. 'The holidays are nearly over and you'll be back at school on Monday,' she reminded him. 'It means Maisie and I will be stuck in the house, just the two of us, all day. Here, there's all sorts of people she can talk to – young people. She hasn't asked to go home, has she? She and Diana get on really well and she loves Poppy. Oh, and this is such a lovely garden, Colin, compared to the one at home.' She glanced out of the window, but all that could be seen from the front were the chestnut trees that shielded the house from the road. 'I'll miss this when the time comes for us to leave,' she said.

Now, as she lay exhausted on the bed, shoulders throbbing, feeling as if she was gradually sinking through the mattress, Brodie remembered that Josh was coming on Sunday. He would have come last weekend, but had had too much work on.

Work! She hadn't thought her son would ever mention the word.

On Sunday morning Megan had hardly been home from Mass a minute when there was a knock on the door of her flat in Burbo Bank Road. She opened it to find a woman outside who was somewhat younger than herself. Her hair was light-brown and she wore a white frock with a pattern of green leaves and a green linen jacket. She had pink cheeks, blue eyes, and a face that was only moderately wrinkled.

'Yes?' Megan said after a few seconds, having established in her mind that she'd never seen the woman before in her life.

'Hello, Megan,' the visitor said in a strong Irish accent. 'It's Brodie.'

'*Brodie*!' Megan took a stumbling step backwards and nearly tripped over the doormat. '*Brodie*!'

'Yes. Jaysus, Mary and Joseph, sis, don't go and faint on me.' She came in and grabbed Megan's arm. 'Where's the sitting room, the lounge, the parlour, or whatever it is you call the damn place?'

'The living room. I can get there on me own, thank you.' She pulled her arm away and walked unsteadily into the room. Brodie followed. *BRODIE*! Her sister, *Brodie*. How long was it since they'd seen each other? Sixty years. 'What are you doing here?' she croaked when they were both sitting down. She could easily have had a heart attack.

'The other day, Duneathly Post Office received an email from a gentleman called Colin Logan who said he was your son-in-law and wanted to know if there were any Kennys or Ryans living in the village.' She spoke swiftly and brightly and, from the grin on her face, seemed to find the situation desperately amusing. Her legs were crossed neatly at the ankles and her hands clasped together on her knees. It was a pose that Megan remembered well. She had a feeling she'd used to make fun of it. 'Look at Little Miss Prim and Proper,' she would say, or something like that. 'The email was passed to us and Roseanna sent an answering email: she's our Tom's granddaughter.'

'Our Tom?' Megan whispered. He'd been the image of their dad.

'Our Tom and our Joe both still live in Duneathly. Me an' all. There's a whole tribe of us in the area. Didn't our mam have a sister and three brothers? They're dead now except for Uncle Aidan, but they had twenty-three kids between them and every single one got married and has kids of their own. Anne-marie's side of the family all live in America, but you'll know that, won't you, Megan?' She looked slyly at her sister. 'Weren't we staying in Annemarie's apartment in New York when I met Louis Sylvester in St Patrick's Cathedral? I brought him back and introduced him to you and Mam.'

'I do remember, yes,' Megan agreed. Her throat had gone as dry as a bone. 'Would you like a drink?' she wheezed. 'Tea, coffee . . .?' She was desperate for a glass of water.

'A little drop of the hard stuff wouldn't go amiss, although you look as if you need it more than I do. Have you got any alcohol on the premises?'

'I've got sherry – oh, and there's some brandy left over from Christmas,' Megan recalled. 'I keep it for when I feel a chill coming on.'

'Brandy, then. If I were you, I'd have a double.'

'Well, you're not me, are you?' Megan said crossly. 'I don't need a double. I'm perfectly all right. I admit I was more than a bit knocked back when you showed up on me doorstep, but that's only understandable. I'm not made of stone.'

She took the brandy out of the sideboard. She'd

intended having a mouthful in the kitchen, but Brodie followed and stood in the doorway, watching while the glasses were taken out of the cupboard and the drink poured – exactly the same amount in each glass, plus water for herself.

They carried the drinks back into the living room. 'It's nice here,' Brodie said. 'I love the view of the River Mersey. Is this where you lived with Louis?'

'Of course not,' Megan replied, annoyed that Brodie should think she and Louis had spent their married life in such a poky little flat. 'It's much too small. We had a nice big house not far from here. My daughter's living there just now. Her name's Brodie, too.'

'I know, Roseanne said. It was in the email.' Her blue eyes twinkled with amusement. 'I'm terribly flattered that you called her after me.'

'You don't look flattered,' Megan said sourly. 'You obviously think it's a great big joke.'

'Let's say I suspect you called your girl Brodie because either you or Louis had a fit of conscience. Or perhaps you both did.'

Megan ignored this. 'How did you know where I lived?' she asked. 'Did Colin give you this address?'

Brodie chuckled. 'We've always known where you've lived, Megan. I knew you didn't live here with Louis. I just said that to get up your nose. The nice big house you mentioned is Chestnuts and you hadn't been in Liverpool all that long before you moved in.'

'How on earth do you know that?' Megan gasped.

'You were in the Liverpool telephone directory, darlin'. Remember Nona who worked in the Post Office? She looked you up for us. We knew exactly when Louis died, because the entry changed from his name to yours.' Her voice softened and so did her smile. 'Many's the time I thought about ringing the number, but I wasn't prepared to lower meself. I thought to meself, she's the one who ran off, let her do it first.'

'So, what made you do it now?' Megan wondered if her face was as pale as it felt. Did she look as if someone had just landed an extra-hard blow to her solar plexus?

'Well, sis, you're eighty, I'm seventy-eight, and I reckon one of these days I'd look in the directory and your name wouldn't be there any more. Either that, or I wouldn't be around to look for it. When we heard from your son-in-law, I didn't care about lowering meself: I just hopped on a plane and flew over.'

Megan stared at her knees. 'You're not lowering yourself,' she muttered. 'I'm really glad you came. I've often wondered how you all were: you and Joe and Tom. Did you get married, Brodie?'

'I did indeed,' Brodie said heartily. 'I married a fine gentlemen farmer called Gerry Flaherty. He only died last year. We had three children – two girls and a boy – and they're just as fine. They're all married and we – oh, did you keep saying "we", sis, when your dear husband passed away when you should have been saying "I"? – I have nine grandchildren and six great-grandchildren. Two are twin boys and the liveliest pair of rascals you're ever likely to meet.'

'Three of my babies died,' Megan muttered. 'Brodie was the only one who lived.'

'Ah! Sometimes the Lord can be very cruel. I'm sorry,' Brodie said softly, looking for the first time like the kind, gentle Brodie that Megan remembered from six decades ago. 'That was something your son-in-law didn't tell me. Look, sis, I hope I don't sound rude, but I'm virtually gasping for a cup of tea. I'll make it meself if you're not up to it.'

'Not up to making a cup of tea!' Megan said indignantly. 'Do I look like an invalid or something? I've already admitted that I was more than a bit taken aback when you turned up, but I'll have you know I'd just ridden to and from Mass on me bike. And I work several days a week at a refugee centre in town. I'm as fit as a blooming fiddle.'

'Sorry, sis,' Brodie said meekly. 'In that case, I'll just sit and wait for the tea. By the way, what's that thing on the wall?'

Megan followed her gaze. 'It's a painting, of course.'

'What's it a painting of, if you don't mind my asking?'

'It's the inside of a chimney. See that blue bit in the middle? That's the sky.'

'And did the artist actually lie with his head in the fireplace while he painted it?'

'The artist is a woman and she just used her imagination,' Megan said, adding tartly, 'It's what artists do.' She paused at the door. 'Tell me, do you dye your hair? It's not natural, that brown colour, on such an old woman. And have you had that Botox stuff injected in your wrinkles? There's not as many as there ought to be on someone of your great age.'

Brodie confessed that she had her hair tinted once a month. 'But as for the Botox, I've never touched the stuff. Is it not made out of rat poison or something similar?'

'I do believe it is. Look, after we've had the tea, we'll go round to Chestnuts for our Sunday dinner. My Brodie will be thrilled to bits to meet you.' Megan rubbed her hands together, thrilled at the way things had turned out. It was lovely to be back in touch with her family after all this time. 'Oh, and me grand-daughter will be there, Maisie. She's having a baby, but the father's nowhere to be seen.'

'Well, that's the way of the world nowadays, is it not? Our Tom's youngest lad has been divorced twice and is already on his third wife. Can you imagine in the old days, Megan, a Catholic getting divorced?'

'But you can't get divorced, can you, when you've been married in the eyes of God?'

'Kevin – that's our Tom's lad – managed to avoid that predicament by getting hitched in them heathen register offices, so he was never married in the eyes of God in the first place.'

'It's almost as if he knew he was going to get divorced before he even got married,' Megan said.

'Exactly,' Brodie agreed. 'And then didn't he go and do it twice!'

'I'll make that tea.' Megan disappeared.

Left by herself, Brodie stared at the river, glimmering like molten silver in the late August sunshine. Joe and Tom would be pleased to know that she'd been to see Megan. In fact, she'd give them a call on her mobile later on in the day.

Her mobile! That was just one of the ways in which the world had changed since she'd last seen her sister. Now people carried telephones – rare enough in houses in those days – around in their pockets or their bags. Then there were computers and motor cars all over the place, aeroplanes – people had actually walked on the moon, for God's sake. There was a fellow from Duneathly who'd actually had a heart transplant.

She got up and went to stand at the window, wondering if Megan had enough room for her to stay the night. Tomorrow, early, she'd quite like to go for a walk by that silvery water.

Megan had worn well, she thought: tons of wrinkles, but her back was straight and there wasn't a sign of stiffness about her. She wouldn't tell her sister that there'd been no need for her to go running off with Louis Sylvester the minute the boat had docked in Liverpool in 1946. It hadn't entered Brodie's head that Louis would want to marry her and if he had she'd have turned him down flat. He was a nice enough fellow, but not a bit her type. If Megan had been thinking she'd stolen him away from her sister, then she could go on thinking it.

They caught a taxi to Chestnuts, stopping at a super-market on the way to buy two large roasted chickens, two packets of pre-roasted potatoes and piles of salad stuff.

'It's no wonder young women these days don't spend much time in the kitchen,' Brodie marvelled when they were back in the taxi. 'I mean, spuds already roasted – bought on a Sunday an' all. What do you do with them – heat them up in the oven?'

'I expect so. Me, it's the first time I've ever bought them. And what about disposable nappies?'

'And disposable torches, of all things! They sell them in the supermarket in Duneathly for a euro each.'

'You mean there's actually a supermarket in

Duneathly?' When Megan had lived there there'd been just a few little shops, which didn't only close on Sundays, but on Wednesday afternoons, too. 'And I forgot they don't have pounds any more in Ireland.'

'We joined the euro years ago,' Brodie said somewhat proudly. 'We didn't shilly-shally around like the UK.'

Brodie hadn't even started on the lunch when her mother and her aunt turned up laden with food.

'Aunt Brodie!' she gasped, stunned, hardly able to believe her eyes when they were introduced.

'It's lovely to meet you, Brodie,' her aunt said with a really sweet, rather mischievous smile.

A larger than usual lunch had already been planned: Colin and Maisie were there, and Josh had arrived early that morning, having driven up from London in a large white van. Now there would be two more guests at the table.

Brodie went to see Vanessa, who was painting in the garden, to say she hoped she wouldn't mind if the snug was monopolized at lunchtime. 'I don't normally have people to lunch, but today there's six of us. An aunt has turned up that I never knew I had until quite recently. Her name is Brodie, too.'

'How amazing,' Vanessa commented, adding that she didn't mind at all. 'Rachel, Poppy and I are going next door to have lunch with Charlie and Reggie. He's ordered an Indian takeaway.'

'I hope you enjoy yourselves.' Brodie lightly touched the woman's arm. She had a feeling that she could become great friends with Vanessa in the course of time.

'I hope you do, too.'

'Do you know what Diana is doing?'

'I invited her to come with us, but she's going to Southport with Leo.'

'That's good.' The girl couldn't have been left to have lunch on her own.

In the past, there'd only been her mother, her husband and their two children. But today there was also a pretty, elderly aunt with a soft voice and a lovely accent, who talked about her uncles Joe and Tom and loads of cousins and nieces and nephews with names like Kerianne and Bernadette and Eoin and Finbar.

'You must come and stay with us soon,' the new Brodie said – she preferred that to being called the 'old' Brodie. 'You're all invited. We'll throw a party for you.'

Brodie couldn't wait. 'As soon as Maisie's had the baby,' she promised. If it arrived before half-term, then she and Colin could go together. Mum was returning to Duneathly with her sister for a while.

'I'd love to come,' Josh said.

Colin looked at him in astonishment. 'But I thought you were too busy with your new business, son?'

'I am, but I wouldn't want to miss a party like that. I mean, it would be a once-in-a-lifetime thing, wouldn't it? Even people with their own business have to have holidays,' he said importantly.

Brodie looked proudly at her son. She would sooner he had aspired to be a doctor, say, or an artist of some sort, but Josh had only ever wanted to have his own business and it appeared he was successful at last. Having bought a large van for a few hundred pounds, he was in great demand in London. As he had explained earlier, 'When people move from one flat to another, all they have are tellies, DVD players, computers, books, clothes, and stuff like that. An ordinary car is too small and a furniture van is much too big. My van is just the right size.'

What's more, Josh and his van were available at any time of the night and day. No one was obliged to take a day off work when they wanted to move. He would turn up at the crack of dawn if they wanted, at tea-time, or in the middle of the night.

She hoped he wasn't losing too much sleep. He looked tired, she thought, but happy – and pleased to see his sister looking much better than he'd expected.

In fact, today everybody looked particularly happy, including Colin and Maisie. Her mother, who'd seemed a bit down recently, was smiling fit to bust, as was the new Brodie.

It was during the meal that Brodie decided she would sell Chestnuts when the year it had been let for came to an end. She had no idea what she and the other women in the house would do then. The money from the sale she would divide into three: a third between her and Colin, and a third each for Maisie and Josh. Josh could buy himself a brand-new van and use the rest as a deposit on a property in London – she doubted if he would ever live in Liverpool again, which was sad, but you couldn't expect your children to live close to their parents for the rest of their lives. Maisie could do whatever she liked with her share.

And she was fed up being a housewife. She would train for something – how to use a computer properly, for instance, or study for some A-levels – or try to get a job in a hospital; she'd always fancied working in a hospital.

'A penny for them, Brodie,' Colin said.

She laughed. 'Oh, they're worth much more than that.'

'I hope this lovely weather never ends,' Megan remarked from her chair underneath what Diana called the 'plate' tree, with its big flat leaves. It was late afternoon and the lunch guests had moved into the garden.

'It's global warming, Gran,' Josh reminded her. 'It could be a sign that the world is about to end. Next year, it'll be even hotter and so on and so on until we all frazzle to death.'

'There were nicer summers during the war,' the new Brodie said. 'But some of the winters! You'd think another Ice Age had started.'

'Now the ice caps are melting,' Josh said gloomily.

'Sure, 'tis a terrible thing for young people to look forward to: the end of the world. I'm glad I won't be alive long enough to see it.'

'Me, I never want to die,' declared Megan.

'If the world ends, you'll not have any choice in the matter,' her sister pointed out.

Brodie made tea and Colin opened a bottle of wine. 'Parties in the garden are getting to be a regular event,' he said. 'Let's hope Diana comes back soon and we can have some music.'

Diana turned up just after five o'clock bringing Leo with her. She opened the window of her room and a melancholy voice began to sing 'The Mountains of

Morne'. 'It's a CD of Irish songs,' she told the company, as if they didn't know.

Alerted by the sound of activity in the next door garden, Charlie and Rachel appeared with a sleepy Poppy, followed shortly afterwards by Vanessa and Reggie, who both looked a bit subdued.

'That's Vanessa, the artist who did the painting in me flat,' Megan told her sister. 'There's loads more upstairs if you'd like to buy one. The money goes to the refugee centre where I work.'

'I wouldn't mind one or two to take home with me. I'll have a look at what you've got later. I must say,' the new Brodie remarked, 'there's a remarkably charming crowd of people living in this house. I can't remember when I last enjoyed meself so much. But I still haven't exactly worked out in me mind who exactly lives here and who doesn't.'

'I'll explain later,' Megan promised. 'There are times when I'm not quite sure meself.'

The air felt slightly colder as the night grew darker. Cardigans, shawls and jackets were fetched, and Diana lit candles for the tables and the window sills. Kenneth came and jumped on to Brodie's knee. She'd be sorry to leave him when she left the house. But then she'd be sorry to leave the house too and it would be awful if she never saw any of her tenants again.

She gave the cat a little hug. 'I'll make sure you're not a stray before we leave,' she told him. 'If you are, wherever I go I'll take you with me.'

Her new aunt had really made herself at home. She'd given an exhibition of Irish dancing and had taught Diana how to do a reel. Mum looked happier than she'd done in ages. Brodie had the uncomfortable feeling she'd been sidelining her mother more than a bit, worried she might upset Maisie, whereas it was Brodie herself who seemed to upset Maisie more than anyone. Nothing she could say was right.

She glanced at her daughter, who was nursing her swollen tummy and looking as if she was enjoying herself. She still flatly refused to see a doctor, no matter how hard Brodie pleaded. Colin had joined in with the pleading, but to no avail.

'All I have to do when it starts to arrive is go to hospital,' Maisie insisted. 'They're not going to refuse to deliver it because I haven't registered with a doctor, are they?'

'Well, no, but there might be something wrong,' Brodie would argue – they'd had the conversation more than once. 'The baby might be feet first, or your blood pressure could be too high – or other things,' she finished lamely.

But Maisie said she wasn't in the mood to see a doctor. 'I just know that everything's going to be all right. If I thought it wasn't, then I'd see one straight away.'

And that was the way the matter had been left.

It was gone eleven o'clock and Vanessa was sitting alone in the garden. She didn't think anyone had noticed she hadn't gone indoors when they did. The lights were on in all the rooms except her own. Only Diana hadn't closed the curtains and she could be seen draped over a chair reading a book while the television was on. Vanessa wouldn't be at all surprised if her CD player wasn't on, too. Diana was the sort of person who liked noise coming at her from every direction, as well as being in the company of loads of people. Perhaps it was something to do with growing up in a small house with three brothers: she wasn't used to silence or being alone.

She stared at the orange-lit sky with its faint sprinkling of stars and a slice of lemon moon on the wane. She was in love with Reggie Ormerod and all she wanted to do was sit alone in the dark and savour the feeling of bewilderment 'Bewitched, bothered and bewildered' was how the song went.

It was a feeling that she'd never had before and certainly not for William with whom she'd thought she was in love. There was another song she remembered: 'This can't be love because I feel so well . . .' She felt marvellous! As if she were walking on air.

She had no idea if Reggie felt the same, though she hoped so, naturally, and one of these days it would be important to find out.

'Don't worry about it, Vanessa,' she told herself. 'If it's going to happen, it'll happen. Go with the flow, as they say.'

She stared at the sky for another few minutes, then went inside.

Chapter 13

Someone was pressing the doorbell so persistently it was obvious they weren't prepared to stop until the door was opened.

Vanessa rolled off the bed and crash-landed on the floor. She stared bleary-eyed and slightly stunned at her watch and saw it was only quarter to seven. Downstairs, she heard Brodie shout impatiently, 'I'm coming, I'm coming.'

The door opened, footsteps bounded up the stairs, a fist hammered on Rachel's door and Rachel called, 'Who is it?'

'Tyler,' was the terse reply.

Rachel screamed, 'Tyler! Oh, Tyler! I just knew you'd come.'

Vanessa hauled herself to her feet, struggled into a dressing gown and staggered on to the landing. Rachel's door was open and she peeped inside to see Tyler – tall, deeply tanned and bespectacled – with one arm around Rachel's shoulders and Poppy in the other. He and Rachel were crying, and Poppy was gleefully pulling her father's sun-streaked blond hair for the very first time, but probably not the last.

Vanessa, who'd once considered herself a cynic to

her bones, burst into tears. 'It's so *touching*,' she sobbed when Brodie came upstairs.

Brodie had a peek and began to cry, too. '*Isn't* it?'

Diana came out of the bathroom wrapped only in a towel. 'What's going on?' Her face dropped. 'Something awful's happened, hasn't it?' she croaked when she saw the two women in tears. 'Is it Maisie's baby?'

'No, love,' Brodie assured her. 'It's nothing bad. In fact, it's marvellous news. Tyler's come back to Rachel.'

It turned out that Tyler had never actually left Rachel except to go on holiday. His mother had been scandalized when told about the little family he'd acquired back in England. Rachel's age was questioned, her social position found wanting – she wasn't even remotely related to royalty – and her morals were impugned. Tyler was whisked off to the Carter Booths' isolated summerhouse in Cape Cod to stay with his sick grandmother. His mobile just happened to get lost and he didn't know the number of Rachel's so he couldn't ring. He did, however, write regularly, 'two or three times a week', and left them in the tray by the front door for his mother or one of the servants to post. He had assumed Rachel had received them.

'But I never got a single one,' Rachel told Vanessa and Brodie when they were having breakfast. By then, Diana had gone to work, Maisie was having a lie-in, and Tyler was upstairs getting to know his daughter better. 'His mother didn't post them, apart from the one she wrote herself pretending to be Tyler and saying that he'd dumped me. Even me mam wouldn't be *that* sneaky,' she said, her little face a picture of indignation. 'He was worried *I'd* dumped *him* when he didn't get any letters from me. When he said he wanted to come back to England, he was told his grandmother was likely to die any minute. Oh, and that's why Simon Collier, the solicitor, never got a reply: the family weren't living in their apartment in New York. Is it all right if Tyler stays here sometimes?' she asked Brodie.

'The more the merrier,' Brodie said.

'I hadn't noticed until this morning, but Rachel's grown a few inches since we first met in March,' Vanessa said to Brodie later when they took Poppy in her pram for a walk on the shimmering sands. Although it was gloriously sunny, there was quite a nip in the air, a signal that winter was on its way. Vanessa had offered to take Poppy, assuming that Rachel and Tyler would like to be alone together for a while and preferring not to be in the house, not even in the garden, while they were. Anyway, she was badly missing Charlie, who'd gone back to school on Monday, and was glad to have something to do.

'It must be strange to fall in love and have a baby when you're only fourteen,' Brodie mused. 'I was such a child at that age. I'm pretty certain I still played with dolls.'

'All I cared about was tennis. I had designs on Wimbledon, but I wasn't even good enough to be in the school team.' Vanessa glanced at the sleeping baby and wondered what lay in store for her. Perhaps a life in America beckoned – it would certainly be a life of affluence if Tyler stuck by Rachel. She hoped the boy would be strong enough to defy his mother, who, it would seem, had other plans for him.

'I used to like playing tennis. Perhaps we could have a game one day?'

Vanessa laughed. 'I don't think I can run any more, let alone hit a ball at the same time.'

'Shall we walk as far as Leonard Gosling's shop and have coffee and a cream cake in that little café opposite?' Brodie suggested. 'Leonard can come with us and keep an eye on the shop from over the road.'

'I'd like that.' She'd lost so much weight it wouldn't hurt to have a cream cake for once – a little treat to celebrate Tyler coming home to Rachel.

'You don't seem to be painting as much as you used to, though you still spend a lot of time in the garden.'

'I'm thinking instead,' Vanessa explained. 'I suppose you could say I'm painting in my head.'

Brodie chuckled. 'Well, you won't sell your thoughts for twenty-five pounds each. What happened to that big painting you were doing?'

'It was for Reggie. It's hanging on the wall of his office. He said people keep asking about it. They like it.' She'd divided the canvas into twelve squares and done a little painting in each, all quite different. 'He wants me to do another for the house.'

'Are you going to?'

'I'm only waiting for an idea. That's what I've been thinking about.' And one or two other things concerning Reggie, too.

Leonard Gosling, a picture himself in pale grey and turquoise, was only too pleased to see them. 'I miss your mother,' he said to Brodie. 'I miss popping into her flat for a little gossip now and then. How's she getting on in Ireland? I've had a postcard, but it didn't say much.'

323

'I get the impression she's having a marvellous time,' Brodie said.

Megan had hurriedly packed a bag and flown back to Ireland with her sister. She intended to stay a month and get to know all her relatives. Ever since, she'd been on that thing she'd read about but had never experienced before – an emotional roller-coaster. Sometimes it was going too fast and became much too emotional when she came face to face, first with her brothers, Joe and Tom, who'd been in their teens when she'd last seen them, and the cousins that she'd lived with during the war, and also the ones who hadn't been born when she'd left for New York with her mother and Brodie after the war had ended. There was even an uncle still alive, Aidan, who'd only been four when Megan was born.

The oldest cousin, Patrick, she'd fallen in love with when she was very small. In fact, she remembered telling her mother that she intended marrying him when they grew up. She tried to tell Patrick the story now, but he was a curmudgeonly eighty-one and very deaf. He refused to wear a hearing aid, so the story remained untold. For some reason this really depressed her.

'Old age is a pain,' she said to Brodie after a few days in Ireland.

'It's better than dying young,' Brodie replied.

They were in her sister's neat little bungalow on a modern estate on the edge of Duneathly. The sleepy little village had expanded greatly since she'd left and there were loads of foreigners around, mainly Americans who worked in factories making computers, according to Brodie.

Megan didn't like the bungalow, its unblemished, characterless newness, and loathed the view of similar bungalows across the road, as well as the road itself with its smooth black Tarmac and clean, perfect pavements. The residents all appeared to be elderly – two cousins lived in the same road – though Brodie said it wasn't a retirement area.

'You're right, growing old is better than dying young, Megan agreed, sniffing gloomily. 'I probably think the way I do now because I haven't watched all these people become old. It's as if it has happened behind my back – oh, I know it's me own fault,' she acknowledged when Brodie opened her mouth to argue. 'Even so, it's really depressing and a terrible shock to see everyone so desperately ancient – with walking sticks and hearing aids – when I've always thought of them as sixty years younger.'

In her mind, time had stood still, yet in Ireland it had been marching steadily onwards and the years had taken their toll. Even Brodie's daughter and her sons were well into their fifties with grown-up children who had children of their own. Brodie actually had six great-grandchildren.

'I must admit,' Brodie conceded, 'that when I knocked on your front door I half expected a twenty-year-old Megan to open it. Instead, there you were, all silver-haired and your face as wrinkled as a dried old prune.'

'Do you mind?' Megan said frostily. 'You never used to be so offensive.'

'I was scared of you, that's why. You used to bully me something awful. I'm getting me own back after all this time.'

'In that case I'm dead sorry. I honestly didn't mean to bully you.'

'Apology accepted.' Brodie grinned.

'I don't think our Joe and Tom's wives like me,' Megan said fretfully. 'They look upon me as an intruder.'

'Oh, that pair! They used to hate each other once, but as they've grown older they've formed a witches' coven.'

'I hope they don't put a spell on me.'

'They're probably very inefficient witches and won't know how.'

Megan shuddered. 'I think I'm glad I missed that sort of thing. I mean, having relatives that I didn't get on with and all the backbiting that goes with it.'

'It's all part of being a family, Meg. There's a hundred and sixty-three Kennys around and it'd be a miracle if we all liked one another.'

'A hundred and sixty-three!' It was a terrifying thought having to meet so many people. Uncle Aidan would be eighty-five at the weekend and a party was being held at a grand new hotel on the other side of Duneathly to which every single Kenny had been invited, young and old, including those from the United States and Liverpool. Megan would be the only Liverpool relative to attend as Maisie's baby was expected any minute, and two of the young boys in the States were fighting in the Iraq war. If it hadn't meant hurting Brodie's feelings, Megan would have gone home early in order to avoid Uncle Aidan's party. Fancy having an uncle when you were eighty! But she'd promised to stay a month and a month she would stay.

★

In Liverpool, the weather continued to be fine and warm, but the nights were drawing in, growing dark while the women were still in the garden. Lights were switched on in the house and curtains left undrawn to provide illumination. Diana supplied plentiful scented candles, so that the garden looked like a scene from a fairy tale and smelled delicious. Vanessa felt inspired to paint the way the light made the grass look silver instead of green and the effect it had on the golden leaves that had started to fall from the trees and made crunching noises under foot.

The shops were suddenly full of Christmas decorations. Brodie was disgusted. 'Summer's hardly over,' she complained, but nevertheless started to make lists of presents to buy. 'Will we have our Christmas dinner here or at our respective houses?' she wondered aloud one Saturday morning when they were all having breakfast outside. '*Al fresco*,' Diana said it was called.

'I haven't got a respective house,' Vanessa pointed out. '*This* is my home.'

'Neither have me and Poppy,' said Rachel. Tyler was at school playing rugby. His father wanted the three of them to move in with him and his new wife, but Rachel had refused.

'I'd sooner have Christmas dinner in Chestnuts. I can have me tea in Coral Street with the lads,' Diana said.

'My mother would expect to come, naturally, and Maisie. Would you mind if I invited Colin?' Brodie asked the group. She supposed there was a chance that Josh would be home.

'Not if you don't mind if I invite Reggie and Charlie.'

'Oh, Vanessa, that would be lovely. We can let the

leaves out on the table and there's loads of chairs upstairs. I must start making another list of what to eat: a menu of sorts. I'll get chicken, turkey and pork.'

'Make sure the chicken and the turkey are free range,' Diana reminded her. 'We'll all pay our share towards it.'

Brodie shook her head vigorously. 'You'll do no such thing. It's the only Christmas dinner you'll ever have in this house and it'll be on me. Oh, and I suppose we'd better invite Leonard Gosling. I think that makes eleven.' She rubbed her hands together excitedly. 'I'm really looking forward to it.'

Maisie's baby was likely to be born any minute if her huge size was anything to go by. She had no idea of the date of her last period and still hadn't seen a doctor.

'Don't you think you should at least contact the hospital so they'll know to expect you?' Brodie said late one night when she was tidying the kitchen. She was finding it hard to keep her patience with her daughter, and felt convinced Maisie was refusing to see a doctor out of sheer perversity. Brodie heartily wished she'd go and live with the father she thought so highly of, let *him* have the worry of the baby arriving in the middle of the night and rushing her to hospital.

'Do you seriously think the nurses in a maternity hospital will get in a panic if a woman turns up unexpectedly about to have a baby?' Maisie said with a curl of her lip. She looked infinitely better than when she'd first arrived, almost the old Maisie, except for her figure. 'That's the very reason for their existence, to deliver babies. And it could be any woman from any-where. She might be on holiday in the area or visiting someone and her name is down at another hospital. They're not going to turn her away, are they? They're not going to turn *me* away.'

It wasn't the words that Brodie found were the last straw, but the curl of the lip. She didn't mention, as she had done several times before, anything about blood pressure, which was supposed to be checked throughout the pregnancy as well as the blood itself, which might be lacking iron or something, or that the baby might not be in the right position. Instead she threw the teapot she was holding across the kitchen so it shattered against the wall, landing on the floor in dozens of pieces along with three teabags.

'Sod you, Maisie,' she yelled. 'You're behaving like a total idiot. When the time comes for you to have your baby, then make your own way to the bloody hospital. Don't expect me to drive you there and have to explain why you've never been near the damn place, yet you only live a few miles away. They'll think *I'm* the irresponsible one, not you.'

'And is that all that matters to you?' Maisie said with another curl of the lip. 'People you've never met and are never likely to meet again thinking you're irresponsible?'

Brodie picked up the teabags, contemplated throwing them at her daughter, but put them in the rubbish bin instead. 'No, Maisie,' she said, very coldly and very deliberately, 'that's not what I'm worried about. What I'm worried about is my first grandchild having a difficult birth, perhaps even being permanently damaged for one of the reasons I've already explained. But you, you're so bloody arrogant and full of yourself you don't care.' She took the dustpan and brush out of the sink unit and began to brush the pieces of teapot off the floor. Fortunately, there'd hardly been any tea left so the floor was only slightly wet.

When she looked up, Maisie had disappeared. Brodie put the kettle on. Tea, tea, she badly needed more tea. There was another teapot in the cupboard, a metal one. At least it wouldn't break should she ever feel like throwing it against the wall.

'Oh, all right,' a voice said from the door. 'You can take me to the hospital in the morning.'

'Thank you,' Brodie said tartly. 'Thank you very much.' Until recently, she'd felt nothing but sympathy for her daughter, but now she was fed up with pussy-footing around, being incredibly nice because Maisie was having a baby, when all she did in return was sneer and be outrageously rude. There were some parents who would refuse to have their pregnant, drug-addicted daughters back in the house, but Maisie didn't appear to be the tiniest bit grateful that she'd been allowed to return without a single word of criticism for the disgraceful way that she'd behaved.

'She's made her own bed, so let her lie in it,' Colin used to say. 'She's let us down.' While Brodie didn't exactly feel the same as he once did, she was sorry now that she hadn't given the girl a good telling-off.

'It might have done us both the world of good,' she said to herself. She felt better for having lost her temper, and wondered if Maisie might feel better for having witnessed it.

The tea made, she looked in her room: her daughter was lying on the bed fast asleep or pretending to be. She quietly closed the door. It was too cold to sit into the garden – Vanessa had come in quite a while ago –

so she sat in the snug instead. She was still shaking – it wasn't often she lost her temper – and would have really welcomed someone to talk to. It was a relief when the front door opened and Diana came in.

'Hello,' Brodie called.

'Oh, hello.' Diana poked her head around the door. 'I wondered why the light was on.'

'Where have you been?'

'With Leo to see *The Bourne Conspiracy*. It's very good. I really like Matt Damon.'

'The kettle's not long boiled if you fancy a cuppa,' Brodie said invitingly. 'And there's some nice chocolate bikkies in the fridge.'

'Goody! I won't be a mo. Do you fancy another cup?'

'Thanks, but I've still not finished this one.'

Diana returned with a mug of tea and two biscuits on a plate. She put the things on the table and threw herself into a chair with a sigh. 'On Saturday, I'm going to tell poor Leo I can't see him any more and give him his ring back,' she announced glumly. 'He keeps on at me to get married, but it just wouldn't be fair.'

'On you or him?' Brodie asked. This was just the sort of conversation she needed to take her mind off her own problems.

'Oh, on him, poor thing. I mean, I don't love him, do I?' The girl looked moidered to death. 'If I give him up, he'll get over it, won't he?' she asked anxiously.

'I think you can definitely count on that, love. And don't blame yourself. Leo has been awfully pushy – and his parents put pressure on you, too.' She squeezed Diana's hand. 'You're a catch, that's why.'

'Tinker's asked me to go out with him. I really fancy going.'

'If you do, I hope you won't agree to marry *him* until you're quite sure you're in love.'

Diana nodded solemnly. 'Don't worry, I won't.'

It was ages before Brodie fell asleep. She kept going over the row with Maisie in her head while listening to her daughter's steady breathing. She hoped the baby would arrive during the daytime or, even better, at the weekend when Colin was around.

It felt as if she'd only been asleep a few seconds when Maisie groaned. Brodie was alert straight away, particularly when Maisie sat up and began to scream.

'Oh, Mum, I've got this really terrible pain. Oh, fuck, it's killing me.'

'Where is the pain, sweetheart?' When she thought about it afterwards, this seemed an incredibly stupid question to ask.

'In my stomach. Oh, Jesus, Mum, it's agony.' She screamed again.

'It sounds as if you've got contractions. I think we'd best get you to hospital.' Brodie got out of bed and began to throw on some clothes. 'Where's the suitcase with your things?' She remembered it was on top of the wardrobe and went to fetch it. 'Come on, sweet-heart, put your dressing gown on. I'll ring the hospital and let them know we're on our way. We'd better leave straight away.' Her recent anger was entirely forgotten.

'I can't, I couldn't. I can't walk.' Maisie began to kick the bedclothes away. 'Oh, fuck, Mum, the baby's coming. I can actually feel it move.'

'Jaysus, Mary and Joseph.' Brodie opened the door and screamed, '*IS THERE ANYONE IN THIS HOUSE WHO KNOWS HOW TO DELIVER A BABY?*'

There was silence for what seemed like an extraordinarily long time, then a door opened and Rachel came running down the stairs in her bare feet, her white nightie flowing out behind her.

'I do,' she said. 'The nurse taught us how to do it at school. Have you rung for an ambulance? If you haven't, ring straight away, then fetch some clean towels. I'm going to wash my hands.'

Diana had come out of her room. 'I'll ring for the ambulance, Brodie,' she said. 'You get the towels.'

When Brodie went in with the towels, Rachel was kneeling at the foot of Maisie's bed. 'Are there any problems I should know about?' she was asking Maisie. 'Do you know if the baby is in the breech position?'

'She has no idea,' Brodie said.

'I've got to push,' Maisie screamed.

'Try not to,' Rachel said calmly. 'Pant instead. Like this.' She began to pant like a little engine. Maisie made an attempt to do the same. 'Brodie, put the towels underneath her bum and help me spread her legs. I think I can see the baby's head,' she said a few seconds later.

'Already?' Brodie said frantically. 'Isn't that dangerous? Isn't it too soon?'

Rachel didn't reply. She said to Maisie, 'It's time you pushed.'

'Holy Mary, Mother of God,' Brodie screamed. 'It's coming!'

'Brodie,' Rachel said sternly, 'you aren't helping.

Please go outside, make some tea or something, and ask Vanessa to come in if she's there.'

Holding on to the wall, Brodie limped out of the room. 'She wants you,' she whispered to an anxious Vanessa, who was standing in the hall with an equally anxious Diana. Vanessa went straight into the room and Diana said, 'An ambulance is on its way. It shouldn't be long.'

'Thank the Lord.' Brodie clasped the girl's hand. 'I think I'm going to die.' Together, they walked up and down the hallway, eight steps one way, eight steps the other – Brodie counted them. She felt as if they'd done this for several hours, but was told later it was a mere twenty minutes, when she heard a baby cry, just one little, rather pathetic cry.

Vanessa opened the door looking exuberant. 'It's a boy,' she cried, 'and he's gorgeous. Do you know, I wouldn't have missed that for anything. You can come in now.'

The baby had been wrapped in a towel and was lying on his mother's breast. Maisie was like a wild woman, her hair all over the place, but her face was relaxed and quite beautiful. Her arms were folded over the baby, who had an enormous amount of brown curly hair and looked rather bemused by his recent experience.

'I've got a son, Mum,' Maisie said.

'I know, sweetheart.' Brodie laid her hand on her grandson's back. He felt warm and solid. 'He looks enormous – about nine or ten pounds.'

'I've checked his mouth and nose are clear,' Rachel said, 'but the cord hasn't been cut – they can do that at the hospital – and the placenta hasn't come yet. I'll wash my hands again and go back to bed. If Poppy's woken up she's probably wondering where I've got to.'

'Thank you,' Brodie stammered. 'Oh, Rachel, thank you.'

'I like living here,' Diana said to Vanessa after the ambulance had taken Maisie, the baby and Brodie to hospital. 'It's dead exciting.'

'I like it, too.'

The women smiled at each other and went to bed.

Vanessa couldn't sleep. It was a relief when a glimmer of light appeared around the curtains and she felt justified in getting up. The house was completely silent. When she went downstairs, the door to Brodie's room was wide open, so she went in to see what sort of state Maisie's bed was in and found only the towels were full of blood. She took them into the laundry room and loaded them into the washing machine.

Back in Brodie's room, she made the beds and tidied up. She pulled open the curtains and saw that a fine mist hung over the garden. The sun wasn't visible this early, but she could just tell it was gearing up to be another lovely day, if not as warm as it had been.

She was about to make coffee when she heard a soft knocking on the glass in the front door. Some thoughtful person didn't want to wake the entire house by ringing the intrusive doorbell. She recognized who it was through the stained-glass panels: Reggie Ormerod.

Vanessa was conscious of the fact she didn't look exactly appealing in her old dressing gown, but didn't care. It wasn't the sullen, hopeless not caring that she'd

felt when she first came to live there, but an acknow-
ledgement that this was how she looked when she got
up in the morning and hadn't combed her hair or had a
wash.

'Hi,' Reggie said when they came face to face. He'd
actually made an effort with his own appearance and
his hair was combed for once. He was dressed in his
usual black. There was no doubt about it: Megan was
right to call him dishy, with his tough, yet sensitive
face and dark-grey eyes. 'I was still up when the
ambulance came last night and I wondered if everything was all right.'

'Everything's fine.' Vanessa could actually feel herself glowing. 'It was Maisie having her baby.'

'I thought that might be it. What did she have?' He
looked genuinely interested.

'A boy. Look, come in, if you've got time. I was just
about to make some coffee.'

'I'd love some coffee.'

She stood aside to let him in and he followed her
into the kitchen. 'Did she actually have the baby here?'

'Yes.' She turned to him, wanting to convey how
the birth had affected her. 'I was there, helping, and it
was truly wonderful. I've never known anything like it
before. Maisie was screaming and shouting and all of a
sudden there was silence and this gorgeous little baby
slid into the world.' She felt tears trickle down her
cheeks and rubbed them away with her dressing-gown
sleeve. 'I'm not crying because I'm sad, but because it
was so moving. It was a miracle. Let's have these in
here.' She carried the coffees into the snug and closed
the door. 'I don't want to wake anyone. Oh, and I
haven't told you: Rachel actually delivered the baby.

She was wonderful too, so level-headed. She didn't panic a bit. Poor Brodie was in a terrible state.' She paused, out of breath. He was watching her with a strange expression. 'I'm sorry, I'm going on more than a bit.'

'I don't mind,' he said. 'Go on as much as you like.'

'I can't – you've made me feel embarrassed.'

'I'm sorry.' He picked up her hand and kissed it, picked up her other hand and kissed that, too, and held them both against his cheeks.

Time seemed to stand still. A train passed: it sounded miles away. Birds sang, somewhere a dog barked. Vanessa could have sworn she could hear the leaves outside falling from the trees and the flowers opening up to the sun. Then Reggie Ormerod kissed her again, on the lips this time, and everything seemed to fall into place.

Before, her life had been one long plan of action, but she would never plan anything again. From now on, she would do things first and think about them later, which was why she kissed Reggie Ormerod back.

'We've got a grandson,' Colin chuckled. It was four o'clock in the morning and he was driving Brodie back from Liverpool maternity hospital. Their first grand-child had been washed, weighed, inspected, and was now fast asleep in a crib beside his exhausted mother. 'A big, beautiful, healthy grandson, who looks as if he'll make a first-class rugby player.'

'Thomas!' Brodie breathed. 'Maisie doesn't realize she's called her son after his great-great-grandfather.'

'Will Maisie and Thomas live with you when they

come out of hospital?' he asked tightly after what seemed to Brodie to be a slightly awkward pause. His mood had changed in an instant.

'There isn't room in Chestnuts,' she said. 'The unused rooms are awfully small and they all need decorating.'

'In that case, will they be coming home? I mean *real* home, where you and I used to live together and where our children were raised?' He was doing his best not to sound bitter.

'I don't know. I feel as if I should be with her . . .' She broke off, not knowing how to continue. It was probably silly, but she felt a certain amount of loyalty to what felt like her other family in Chestnuts. She didn't want to leave them in the lurch.

'There's no question that you should be with your daughter,' Colin said so sharply that she felt annoyed. 'It so happens there's a double bed in the house I just mentioned that has room for someone else – a wife, for example. Maisie's bedroom is nicely decorated. And there's room for the cot I bought that's waiting to be put together. By the way, I'm no good at that sort of thing. I need some assistance.'

He'd bought a cot! Brodie couldn't resist it. She said, 'Why don't you ask your father to help?'

'I haven't seen him for a week or two. He's courting.'

'*What*?'

'Her name's Blanche. She's just moved in next door – to him, that is, not us. With Dad out of the way,' he said impatiently, 'perhaps you could review your position about coming home?'

'It wasn't just your father. It was the way you felt about Maisie, the things you used to say.'

'I feel very differently about Maisie now,' he pointed out. 'How many times do I have to tell you?'

'So it would seem, but you were no help when we first discovered she was a drug addict. It was me who went to London and met Karen Young, the police-woman who brought her home.' She turned towards him as they drove through the silent streets. 'Do you mind if we have this argument another time? I feel very tired and I'm not in the mood.' She'd go back to the house in Crosby right now and stay for a few days, help Maisie settle in, but would sleep in Josh's bed, not with Colin. She wasn't in the mood for that, either.

She woke in Josh's room just after half-past eight. It was a beautiful morning and the room was filled with sunshine. Colin had already left for school. Downstairs, she found cornflakes in a cupboard in the kitchen and a fresh carton of milk in the fridge. It felt odd, not quite right, eating in this kitchen and not the one in Chestnuts.

When she finished, she rang Josh on her mobile to tell him he was an uncle, then her mother in Ireland.

'So, I'm a great-grandmother!' Mum sounded thrilled. 'I'll book the earliest flight and be home later today.'

'There's no need for that, Mum,' Brodie protested.

'Oh, darlin', there is,' her mother said in a heartfelt tone. 'Now I've got a marvelous excuse to leave. On Saturday, Uncle Aidan is eighty-five and all the Kennys in the world are expected to be there. I hate the very thought of it. Maisie's baby has arrived at just the right time.'

Brodie dug out the underwear Maisie had left behind when she went to university and a few other items of clothing that might be useful. The cot that Colin had bought would need bedding: she'd go into town that afternoon and buy some. She imagined the pleasure she would get out of choosing a baby blanket – perhaps blue and white stripes. She'd get something nice for Maisie at the same time: perfume, maybe, or some jewellery.

Her car was in Blundellsands. She decided to go on the train, see Maisie now, make sure she was all right, then do some shopping. She would collect the car later.

Maisie already had a visitor, a young man with a lovely, open face and brown curly hair. His eyes were a slightly darker shade of brown and he was nursing Thomas with all the pride and dewy-eyed emotion of a brand-new father. This could only be Pete. She was pleased he looked nice, so wasn't sure why her heart dropped like a stone.

'Mum!' Maisie cried when Brodie approached. She looked radiant. 'This is Pete, Thomas's father. He's just arrived from London. I phoned him from the hospital last night – well, early this morning.'

'How do you do, Mrs Logan?' Pete said shyly, half standing. He had a touch of an accent, Welsh, she thought, and was too scared to let go of the baby to shake hands.

'Call me Brodie, please. What do you think of your new son?'

'He's awesome.' He sat down again. 'This has all turned out much better than I imagined.'

Brodie frowned. 'What do you mean?'

'Well . . .' he began, but Maisie interrupted. 'What he means is I've been behaving like an out and out pig. I left where I was living without telling him, so he's had no idea where I've been for ages. I've put him through hell this last year.' She put her hand on Pete's knee. 'I'm sorry.' She held out her other hand to Brodie. 'And I'm sorry, Mum. I've been a double pig with you. I don't know why, but I wanted to blame people for things that were no one's fault but my own.' She threw back her shoulders and laughed. 'I feel myself again for the first time in ages.'

'I hope you stay that way, sweetheart.' She wanted to ask her daughter what had prompted her to take drugs in the first place, but wondered if there would ever be a right time.

'Are you going home now, Mum?' Maisie enquired.

'After I've done some shopping. Why?'

'I'd like you to bring some of my stuff back here with you: my black coat and boots and I think I had two pairs of decent jeans. The rest can be chucked away – or Diana might like it for that stall of hers in the refugee centre.'

It was then Brodie realized why her heart had sunk like a stone; she must have sensed something like this was about to happen. 'Does that mean you're going away?' she asked, trying to keep her voice steady.

Maisie's eyes shone. 'We're going back to London in the morning in Pete's car. He's got this great bedsit in Muswell Hill and a really good job as a researcher

341

for the Green Party. In a few months, I can leave Thomas with a childminder and get a job myself.'

Brodie's heart began to hammer in her breast. 'Do you think it's all right for two adults and a baby to live in one room?'

'Oh, it's a really big room. Isn't it, Pete?'

'It's massive, Mrs . . . Brodie. Really massive.' Pete assured her. 'There's space for a cot and everything.'

She wondered if they already had a cot. She couldn't bring herself to say that Colin had bought one. He could tell them himself later on.

She was no longer in the mood to go shopping. Anyroad, she didn't know what to buy. Instead, she caught the train home. Despite the tension between them early that morning, she badly wanted to talk to Colin, tell him that Maisie wouldn't be staying in Crosby or Blundellsands. It was the last thing she had expected. She'd been looking forward to their grandson being around for a while at least, not to be whisked away from under her nose when he was scarcely two days old. Was Maisie so insensitive that she didn't give a thought to her mum and dad's feelings? When had she become like that? Or had she always been that way? And, out of interest, who had been supporting Maisie during the time when she and Pete hadn't been in touch? It was something that she, Brodie, would never know.

In Chestnuts, she found Vanessa in the garden staring dreamily into space while holding the handle of Poppy's pushchair, jogging it slightly from time to time.

'She's a bit restless this morning,' she said when

Brodie joined her at the table. 'I think she might be cutting another tooth.'

'Where are Rachel and Tyler?' Brodie asked.

'They've gone to the fairground in Southport. They were going to take Poppy, but I offered to look after her so they can be kids for the day instead of parents.'

Brodie imagined the young couple with ice-cream cornets wandering hand in hand among the rides. She noticed Poppy was wearing a little padded jacket. It depressed her, the fact that summer was so obviously over and everything was about to change.

Vanessa enquired about the new baby. 'Has he got a name yet?'

'It's Thomas and he's fine. He weighed nearly ten pounds.'

'I'm longing to see him.' She looked genuinely excited. 'After all, he's the only baby I'm ever likely to help deliver. Would it be all right if I went tonight? Or will Maisie be coming home soon?'

'I'm afraid Maisie's going back to London tomorrow. I'd go tonight, if I were you: it might be the last opportunity you'll ever have. Diana and Rachel, too.' She prayed Mum would arrive home from Ireland early enough to see Thomas, otherwise she'd be desperately upset.

Diana came home, full of beans. Apparently, she and Megan had been exchanging text messages all day and had planned to get dressed up and watch a film on Friday night.

'*Singin' in the Rain,*' Diana announced. 'It's one of my favourites. I thought we could buy some wine and order a takeaway. I'm going to make a trifle. Have I ever told you I make the most fantastic trifles?'

'No,' Brodie conceded. She was so pleased to see the girl she wanted to cry. Diana would never let anyone down. 'What do you put in your trifles?'

'Everything,' Diana said with her glorious smile. 'The last time I made one we all got drunk.'

Only Diana could have turned watching a more than fifty-year-old film in the house into a grand occasion. Wine was bought, pizzas ordered, the ingredients purchased for the trifle – cider seemed to play an important part. Christmas decorations were already in the shops and Diana came home on Thursday night laden with tinsel.

By then, Maisie, Pete and Thomas had returned to London, but Brodie didn't feel as hurt as she might have done had she not had the film to look forward to. She went shopping, not for baby bedding as originally planned, but for a Per Una skirt and blouse in autumnal colours from Marks & Spencer. Mum had bought a couple of outfits in Ireland and planned on wearing royal purple.

'Oh, it's so lovely to be home,' she said to Brodie on her first night back. 'I feel quite young again. In Ireland, I felt as old as the hills. And thank you for the flowers in my flat. They're beautiful.'

'The flowers were Diana's idea,' Brodie told her.

Friday dawned bright and chilly. Colin rang early before he left for school to ask how she was feeling.

'Not so bad at all,' she assured him. 'How about you?'

'All right, I suppose,' he said gloomily. 'Tomorrow, I'm going to have to take this bloody cot back.'

'I'll come with you,' she offered. 'We could go for a meal.'

'What are you doing tonight?'

She explained about the film and he asked if he could come, but she told him no. 'It's for women only. You can come and sit in the kitchen and we'll feed you scraps. Or you could go next door and have a drink with Reggie Ormerod. Charlie's coming to see the film with us seeing as she hasn't got school tomorrow, though she's not being allowed any trifle.'

He rang off, saying he might well come later.

At five o'clock, Brodie draped the tinsel around Diana's room. Upstairs, Vanessa and Rachel were getting ready. Mum arrived on her bike with a bag full of fairy cakes. The telephone rang in the hall and Brodie answered. It was the worst call she'd ever had. It would be a long time before she was able to answer the phone without a feeling of dread.

'What on earth is the matter?' her mother asked seconds later when Brodie replaced the receiver, having hardly uttered a word. 'You've gone as white as a sheet.'

Vanessa was coming down the stairs followed by Rachel and Poppy. Perhaps there was something in the atmosphere, or perhaps it was Brodie's white face that made them stop and stare.

'What's wrong?' Vanessa whispered.

'That was Tinker,' Brodie said. 'Diana was knocked down outside the centre by a hit and run driver.' She burst into tears. 'I can't believe it. Diana's *dead*.'

345

Chapter 14

There were a good fifty mourners at the church for Diana's requiem Mass. A report of her death had been in the *Liverpool Echo* and the Bootle and Crosby papers along with a photograph, alerting people who otherwise wouldn't have known: neighbours from Coral Street who'd known her all her life, for instance, the call centre where she'd used to work, and girls she'd been at school with. There was a whole crowd from the refugee centre, who found it hard to believe such a thing could happen in a civilized country.

Not everyone came back to the house for refreshments: just Diana's immediate family, Megan, Leonard Gosling, Tinker and Eileen, who'd been dreadfully upset by the news and had insisted on coming all the way from London. She and Brodie's mother couldn't stop crying, and seemed to be vying with each other to see who could drink the most wine. There were also one or two people Brodie had never seen before. Colin had been at the church, having taken a few hours off school. He'd since returned and wouldn't be seen again until later.

Diana's brothers were standing in a circle, arms around each other, heads bent, joined together in their grief. Leo was standing helplessly nearby and the circle was broken to allow him to join.

'Poor Leo,' Brodie whispered, recalling that had Diana lived another day she'd intended telling Leo she didn't want to see him again. At least he'd been spared that.

Why had she been killed? Why had Diana, who wouldn't have hurt a fly, who was one of the sweetest people on earth, been mown down by a stranger in a black van?

'It was intentional,' Tinker said. He'd told that to the police. 'I came out of the centre only minutes behind her and the van quite deliberately mounted the pavement and came straight at her.' He'd managed to make a note of the registration number. The police had a good idea who it was, but weren't prepared to reveal details until they were certain.

It was another beautiful day, the garden a fabulous riot of golden trees and fallen leaves. Brodie wasn't sure if this miracle of nature made the day more, or less sad. She half expected Diana to come bursting out of the house wearing a dramatic hat with a black spotted veil, the star of her own funeral, flinging her arms around everyone in sight.

People had brought their refreshments outside. Michelle, Diana's mother, was absolutely distraught. Her mini-skirt hardly covered her behind and her lacy tights were snagged in numerous places.

'No woman could have wished for a better daughter,' she wept. 'And thank you for paying for the funeral, Brodie; it was lovely. I'd've had to borrow if it had been left to me. I'm not one of those sensible types who takes out insurance and stuff like that.'

'It wasn't me who paid,' Brodie told her. 'It was my mother. She was especially fond of Diana.'

Megan was desperately angry about Diana's death. 'It's not fair,' she raged. 'All those old people back in Ireland with seventy and eighty years on the clock, me included. What are we doing alive when Diana's dead?'

'There's nothing fair about life, Mum. There never has been.' She was glad her mother was home, having missed her far more than expected.

Diana had lain in a white coffin in a white dress, blood-red rosary beads threaded through her long fingers. Brodie and Megan had gone to the funeral parlour every day to say prayers and watch the lovely, untroubled face, eyes closed for the final time. They shed tears until they choked on them.

Vanessa came up. She wore bright green – none of the women were in black, not for Diana's funeral. 'I didn't like her, you know,' she said. 'Not when we first met. I remember she brought me a hideous glittery blouse from that stall in the centre. I felt obliged to wear it. It was the night we watched *Gone With the Wind*.'

'It was also the night you cut all your hair,' Brodie reminded her.

'Diana tidied it up for me. I still didn't like her. She seemed much too bossy, as if she wanted to organize all our lives.'

'She had the biggest heart in the world,' Brodie said soberly. 'All she wanted was to help people, to make them happy.'

'I realized that after a while.' Vanessa nodded. 'The

other day I thought we could all watch *Singin' in the Rain* tonight, but that's a terrible idea, isn't it?'

'Absolutely terrible.' Brodie scrunched up her face. 'We'd cry ourselves to death. In fact, I'll never watch that film again if I live to be a hundred.'

Charlie arrived cuddling Kenneth; the cat was asleep in her arms. 'He's missing Diana,' the little girl announced, 'just like me.' She'd been allowed to come home from school at dinnertime for the wake.

'Do you know that man who's talking to the lads?' Brodie asked Vanessa. Tall and gangly, he was about fifty with fair hair turning grey at the sides. He bore the weather-beaten, slightly weary air of someone who'd travelled a lot and was looking for somewhere to rest. His outfit was informal: jeans, a grey sweatshirt and shabby trainers.

'I've no idea. He's not bad-looking for an older man, is he?' Vanessa said with an approving click of the tongue. 'I expect your mother would call him dishy. Oh, look, he's coming over. I'll see if anyone would like more tea or coffee and leave him to you.' She patted Charlie's head. 'Come along. You and Kenneth can help.'

'Hello.' The man's eyes were a familiar blue and were surrounded by mesh of wrinkles, as if he'd squinted too much at the sun. He held out his hand and Brodie shook it: it felt warm and rough. 'I'm Jim O'Sullivan, Diana's dad. I apologize for the clothes, but I left most of my stuff behind; it wasn't worth fetching home.'

'Di's father!' Brodie was stunned. 'Where have you been all this time?'

'All over the place,' he answered in the sort of voice

that made her think he hadn't exactly enjoyed it all that much. 'I understand your name is Brodie and you're in charge here.'

'I'm Brodie, yes, but I'm not in charge. This just happens to be my house.' They were still holding hands. She squeezed his. 'I'm so sorry about Diana,' she said fervently. 'She was a genuinely nice person. She lived here, you know, with us, and we all loved her. But how awful for you to come back just when she died.'

'I have a mate in Bootle. We write to each other now and again, about once a year. He managed to contact me when he read about Di in the paper.'

'It must have come as a terrible shock.' Imagine getting a message like that when you were in some far-off country.

He sighed. Brodie wondered how many miles he'd come over the last few days because he sounded extremely tired. 'I kept hoping one day I'd come back for her wedding,' he said.

'She was engaged – did you know that? Except she intended breaking it off the day after the accident.'

'I've just been told she was engaged – to that young man with the lads, Leo – but not that she was about to break it off.' He looked surprised and his eyes blinked wearily as if even being surprised was an effort.

'I might have been the only one who knew. Look, when did you arrive in Liverpool? Have you had anything to eat? Anything solid, that is.' He was holding a plate of dinky sarnies.

'The plane from Amsterdam touched down this morning at about ten. I managed to get to the church just before the service finished.'

'That's where you've been working, Amsterdam?'

'No, Ecuador, in a little village about a hundred miles from the nearest airport. Amsterdam was where I changed planes.' He smiled. It was a gentle, sweet smile, just like Diana's, but without the sparkle. 'I'm afraid I'm not much good at sleeping on planes.'

'Would you like to sit somewhere quiet and comfortable for a while?' she asked. 'And I could make you some soup. It might make you feel better.' She put her hand on his elbow, led him inside and sat him down in the empty snug. 'What about the soup?' she asked. 'It'll only be tinned, but a bit more nutritious than what you've got there.'

He perked up. 'Soup sounds great.'

'After you've eaten, you can have a rest in my bedroom. When you come out of this room, it's the second door on the left. I'll look in on you at about four and wake you if you're asleep. You won't miss much. Most people are likely to be here all day.'

'You're being very kind.'

'Well, you're Diana's dad, aren't you? She would have expected me to look after you. In similar circumstances, she would have done the same for me.'

As the afternoon progressed, the atmosphere in the garden lightened, just a little, as wakes often do. The person who had died, no matter how beloved, had gone for ever, and those left behind had to get used to it, as well as feel glad that they were still alive and in a position to enjoy life, even if some didn't have all that many years left.

Brodie noticed that Tinker had been missing for ages. She found him in Diana's room, which was still laced with tinsel, where he was lying face down on her bed, his eyes red from weeping. He wore a hand-knitted cardigan with multi-coloured stripes.

'I loved her, you know, Brodie,' he said brokenly. 'She was a glorious girl. Her brain never stopped working and thinking up new ideas.' He sniffed and, as an afterthought, almost laughed. 'There were times when she drove me crazy.'

'She drove us all crazy. Have you noticed the ghastly walls and tiles in the kitchen? Diana chose the colours.' Mind you, she'd got used to them ages ago and they no longer bothered her.

'I've always really liked your kitchen,' Tinker said wanly.

Tyler and Colin came straight to the house from their various schools. Reggie Ormerod arrived home from work and Brodie saw him pull Vanessa behind a tree. She could only assume they were kissing. She felt enormously pleased and also envious, remembering how thrilling and exciting it had been when she'd first met Colin and they'd begun to fall in love.

Michelle left to go back to Nottingham. Before she went, she asked Brodie if she knew where Jim was so she could say tara. 'He seems to have disappeared.'

'He's in my room, probably asleep.' She'd forgotten to wake him as promised. 'Do you want to tell him that you're going?'

'No, ta, luv. Leave him be for now. Poor chap, he's been travelling for days. He's planning on staying around for a few weeks, so I'm bound to see him again.' She hunched her shoulders and made a face. 'I suppose you think I'm daft, letting a husband like Jim go?'

'Of course I don't. I hardly know him.' Or you, she wanted to say.

'He's a lovely chap, a real diamond.' Brodie vaguely remembered someone using the same word to describe Diana – it might have been herself. 'But I drove him away. I didn't realize which side me bread was buttered. He was a merchant seaman in those days and used to say I needed one of them chastity belt things when he left me behind.'

Brodie could only imagine what she'd got up to. Thinking about it, of the four O'Sullivan children, only Diana bore any resemblance to Jim.

It was nearly midnight. In the snug, Brodie and Colin, Vanessa and Reggie, and Jim O'Sullivan were sitting around the oval table finishing the day with the remainder of the wine. Everyone else who didn't live there had gone home, apart from Charlie, who was fast asleep in Vanessa's room until her father took her home. Rachel and Poppy had gone to bed ages ago. Brodie had no idea if Tyler was with them.

The conversation ranged from greenhouse gases, to the war in Iraq, the rate of inflation, the education system, the health service and, of course, Diana.

'She was nine when I left,' Jim said with the smile that reminded Brodie so much of his daughter. 'I'd swear she had an older head on her shoulders than did me wife. She used to write out the shopping lists and help the lads with their schoolwork.'

'It was a bit irresponsible to walk out on your family, wasn't it?' Colin growled. 'Leaving a wife who couldn't cope and four children under nine.' This wasn't the first critical remark he'd made. It was obvious he didn't like Jim. Nor was he exactly pleased to discover that Brodie had said he could stay in Diana's room while he was in Liverpool. It was also obvious that he wasn't prepared to go home until Jim had gone to bed.

'I didn't say Michelle couldn't cope, but I admit I shouldn't have walked out,' Jim said steadily. 'It's just that things were happening that *I* couldn't cope with. Seven years ago, if I'd known Michelle had left the kids to live on their own, I'd have come back straight away.'

Colin snorted. Brodie wanted to remind him that he hadn't exactly stuck by his own daughter when she needed help, but the atmosphere was already unpleasant enough. In the end, she wished everyone goodnight and went to bed herself. Soon afterwards, she heard Colin drive away and Jim enter his daughter's room.

'Goodnight, Diana, wherever you are,' she whispered as she laid her head on the pillow.

'I'm glad today's over,' Vanessa said when she and Reggie were the only ones left.

'I liked Diana.' Reggie slid his arms around her and kissed her ear, 'Though she had a lousy dress sense.'

'It's the first time in my life that someone of my own age has died – someone I've known, that is.' She was enjoying having her ear kissed, the feel of his arms, and the lemony smell of the aftershave he used.

'Will you come back with me tonight?' he whispered.

'Yes.' She'd slept in the house next door for the last five nights. So far, Brodie hadn't appeared to notice – not that it was any of Brodie's business – but Vanessa felt just a little bit uncomfortable about it. 'Charlie doesn't seem to mind my being there, does she?'

'Charlie's as pleased about it as I am.' He turned her face towards him and kissed her full on the lips.

Vanessa had read of women wanting to swoon in similar situations, but it had seemed a daft idea and she'd never thought it would happen to her. Now it was happening all the time. She gasped when they came up for air. 'Wow!' she said huskily.

'You can say that again.' Reggie tenderly stroked her cheek. 'Is this the right time to ask if you'd consider moving next door permanently?'

'It's the right time and the wrong time,' Vanessa said seriously. 'I will come and live with you, but I can't say when. I promised Brodie I'd be here for a year. I don't want to leave when we've only just lost Diana.' She wanted to spend the rest of her life with Reggie and Charlie Ormerod more than anything she'd ever wanted in the world, but there were other people to consider. 'Do you mind?'

'I mind about as much as it's possible to mind. But I understand,' he said with a grin. 'It's a question of sisterhood.'

'Is it?' She'd never thought of herself as belonging to a sisterhood.

'Isn't it?'

'I suppose it must be.' In a way, she felt closer to the women in Chestnuts than she did to her real sisters.

A train passed, the sound audible in the thick silence that had fallen over the house. Upstairs, Poppy gave a little cry in her sleep. Downstairs, Jim O'Sullivan coughed. Vanessa could hear herself breathe.

'Shall we go?' Reggie asked in a low voice.

Vanessa nodded. 'I need to collect some things from my room.'

'And I need to collect my daughter.'

It was early when Brodie woke. All she could hear was birdsong. She felt as if a great weight was pressing down on her and just knew something bad had happened. Then she remembered: Diana was dead.

She sat up and wished she had one of those machines that made tea at the press of a button. For the first time in months it was cold in bed: she needed a thicker duvet. Maisie's duvet had been put away in the wardrobe drawer and Colin had taken the bed she'd slept in back upstairs. It reminded her that Maisie hadn't sent flowers to the funeral, even though Diana had been incredibly generous and helpful while Maisie had been staying in the house. She'd thought they were friends. On the day Thomas had been born, Diana had gone into town in her lunch-hour and bought half a dozen little white vests as a gift. Brodie wondered what had happened to the lovely christening gown that had come from the refugee center. Had Thomas even been christened yet? Surely Maisie would have invited her parents if he had.

Brodie didn't think she would ever get used to the extent her daughter had changed. It was as if the sweet little girl she'd always known no longer existed. Something had happened, perhaps it was the drug-taking, that had hardened her heart. She'd wanted her mother while Thomas was being born, but maybe that was because Pete hadn't been there. 'You'll just have to get used to it,' she told herself. 'You can't let it get you down for the rest of your life.'

The funny thing was that Josh, who'd hardly known Diana, had sent a beautiful bunch of chrysanthemums tied with a bright green ribbon. 'For the girl with stars in her eyes,' his card had said.

'I know we only met the twice,' he said to Brodie when she'd rung and told him about Diana, 'but to tell the truth, Mum, I really fancied her. I'm sorry now I didn't ask her out, though I suppose it would have been awkward, her being in Liverpool and me in London.'

It had been done before, Brodie thought. Court-ships even happened between couples on opposite sides of the world. For a while, she entertained herself with the lovely idea of Diana being her daughter-in-law, until she could stand the cold no longer. She leaped out of bed, fetched the other duvet and flung it over the bed, then got back in and pulled both duvets up around her shoulders.

'That's better,' she muttered. Very soon, she'd have to collect some warm nightdresses and her fleece dress-ing gown from home. When she was a child and had lived in Chestnuts, she recalled the house had been very chilly in the winter: the central heating was totally inadequate. Since those cold, far-off days, she'd become accustomed to living in a much warmer atmosphere.

Anyway, did she really want to stay there until next March? She had no intention of getting someone else for Diana's room, nor did she intend looking for another job. If necessary, she'd borrow from her mother if she needed money. Eventually, she would go on a course, acquire a skill, start a career, preferably in something medical.

She stiffened when she heard the front door open and footsteps, very faint, go upstairs. The door to Vanessa's room opened and closed. She must have spent the night with Reggie. Brodie sniffed. Lucky thing!

If she didn't have some tea soon she'd die. She got out of bed again, stuffed her feet into sandals, and put a padded jacket on over her thin nightie. In the kitchen, she shivered violently as she ran water into the kettle. The temperature must have dropped about a hundred degrees overnight. The thought of having a shower was unbearable. She tried to remember how the central heating worked, but couldn't. Later, she'd ring her mother who would know.

She was about to go back into her room with the tea when the door to Diana's room opened, giving her such a fright that she narrowly avoided dropping the cup. Jim O'Sullivan appeared, looking much more awake than the day before. She'd entirely forgotten he was staying there.

'Sorry,' he said apologetically. 'I gave you a scare. I was trying to be as quiet as I could. I was hoping you wouldn't mind if I made myself a drink.'

'Of course I don't mind. I'll do it. Would you like coffee or tea?'

'Coffee, please. No milk or sugar.'

'Did you have a decent sleep?'

'Despite everything, I had a great sleep, but the first thing I thought about when I woke up was Diana.' He smiled his sad, sweet smile. She noticed he was in need of a shave: silvery hairs bristled on his chin. His mouth was wide and slightly full, like his daughter's. Brodie thought she must be going mad when she visualized kissing it. Like most women, she had flights of fancy from time to time, but they were usually concentrated on characters who could have been from another planet – George Clooney, for instance, or Antonio Banderas – not real flesh and blood men who were actually within reach.

She gulped. 'As it happens, I thought about Diana as soon as I woke up too.'

The coffee made, she said, 'Would you like to have it in my room? The snug will be rather chilly and the chairs aren't too comfortable.' She didn't like to send him back into the room on his own, though he might have preferred it.

He followed her into the half-dark room and she pulled back the curtains. 'Sit down.' She indicated one of the chairs by the little round table.

'You've got squirrels!' he remarked when the garden was revealed.

'Just the two – at least, I assume it's always the same two. Diana loved them. She used to buy them nuts.' The squirrels were chasing each other up and down the trees. 'Are you warm enough like that?' she asked. He wore jeans and a short-sleeved T-shirt. His sunburned feet were bare.

'I don't feel the cold, or the heat – except when they're extreme. I apologize for my feet. Would you like me to put socks on?'

'Oh, for goodness' sake,' she snorted. 'I've seen a man's bare feet before. I've been married for twenty-three years.'

'To that chap who was here last night – Colin?'

'Yes.' She supposed an explanation was necessary as to why they were on speaking terms, yet not living in the same house. 'We're separated at the moment,' she told him.

'And he's not very pleased about it.'

'What makes you say that?'

He shrugged. 'It was obvious. He couldn't keep his eyes off you, for one thing.'

'Oh, it's a long story,' Brodie sighed.

'When we get to our age,' he said rather bitterly, 'we've nearly all got a long story or two to tell.'

The sun had appeared in the furthest corner of the garden. Kenneth arrived, jumped on the table and began to give himself a thorough wash. Squirrels raced through the branches at the tops of the trees and leaves floated to the ground. There was what looked very much like frost on the grass. The birds continued to sing.

'It's nice and peaceful here,' Jim said.

'Everyone thinks that,' Brodie told him. She sipped her tea. There was something peaceful about him, too, a dignified quietness. She felt totally relaxed in his presence and could have sat there for ever, listening to his quiet voice with just a hint of Liverpool accent. She couldn't imagine him being angry. He might disagree with something, even argue, but wouldn't get worked up about it.

'Would you like some breakfast?' she asked.

'It's great of you to put me up, but you don't have to feed me,' he protested. 'I'll go and buy some bread or something and make toast.'

Brodie hooted, conscious she sounded just like her

mother. 'Oh, don't be ridiculous! As if I'd let you go hungry. You're Diana's dad. We have bread here as well as butter and jam. There's also bacon and eggs in the fridge and loads of cheese and other stuff.'

'A cheese sarnie would go down well. Thank you, Brodie.'

There were sounds upstairs. Someone was having a shower. Brodie was conscious of the air being slightly warmer; the thought of a shower was no longer quite so painful. Someone else came downstairs and went into the kitchen.

She said to Jim, 'Vanessa lives upstairs. She's spent most of the time here painting in the garden. She wasn't very happy when she first came, but now she's become friendly with Reggie, who lives next door, and I'm really pleased about it.' Kenneth stopped washing his face for a moment and hungrily eyed a bird that was perched on a branch directly above him. 'Rachel's in the other upstairs room,' she continued. 'She's only fifteen and has a nine-month-old baby, Poppy. Tyler, Poppy's father, stays with us some of the time. He's still at school.' She stood and reached for his empty cup. 'I thought I'd let you know who your neighbours are while you're here. Here, let's have that cup and I'll make you more coffee while I toast the bread for that sarnie.'

At about nine o'clock, her mother turned up. It seemed she'd promised to take Jim to the refugee centre so he could see where Diana had worked. Later, they were going to lunch in town.

'He's a very nice young man,' Megan opined.

Brodie raised her eyebrows. 'Hardly young!' She resented Jim O'Sullivan being taken away.

'Once you reach eighty, the whole world seems young. Do you intend to go and see your relatives in Ireland?' her mother asked curiously.

'One day, not just now. I've too much on my mind.' Soon, she and Colin would have to go and see their grandchild, even if they weren't invited. She doubted if it would ever cross Maisie's mind to bring him to Liverpool.

'I bet one of the things on your mind is how to keep this place warm in the winter,' her mother said. She touched the radiator in the hall which Brodie knew was stone-cold. 'I noticed how chilly it felt when I woke up this morning and thought about this house. It's a bugger to heat. It probably needs new central heating.'

'It would cost the earth and it hardly seems worth it when I've made up my mind to leave in March then sell the place.'

Her mother gave her an affectionate push. 'I'll pay for it, you know I will, but you're right, it doesn't seem worth it. If it's put on the market, a developer will snap it up, the house will be demolished, and a block of expensive flats go up in its place. This land is worth a small fortune, darlin'.'

Brodie stood at the window watching Vanessa in the garden. Clad in a thick grey cardigan and tweed skirt, she was painting an extra-wide canvas, the one for Reggie's house. It was only a few weeks since she'd told Brodie about it, but since then Diana had died and the world seemed a vastly different place. One day,

Vanessa might move next door permanently – she might even want to do it now, but felt obliged to stay for the whole year.

And hadn't Rachel said that Tyler's father wanted her, Tyler and Poppy to go and live with him and his new wife? When they'd refused – well, Rachel had – he'd offered to buy them a house close by. If things went a certain way, Brodie could be the only person left and the problem of keeping the house warm would be solved. She could go and live in Crosby with Colin, and Chestnuts wouldn't require heating of any sort.

But was living with Colin what she wanted? She remembered meeting Diana and the girl explaining that there was nowhere for her to go, that she wasn't needed any more, that she felt superfluous. Now Brodie felt the same. Her children were managing perfectly well without her and she wasn't sure how she felt about Colin – or how he felt about her.

There was a shuffling noise outside and Rachel shouted, 'Brodie, it's me. Will you open the door, please?'

'Oh, my goodness, she's walking!' Brodie gasped when the door was opened to reveal Rachel holding Poppy's hands and the baby girl standing quite firmly on her white-socked feet. Brodie dropped to her knees and held out her arms. Poppy took a few tentative steps forward, still holding her mother's hands, and fell into the older woman's arms, chuckling loudly.

'You little darling!' Brodie felt the urge to weep until there was no tomorrow, although she had no idea why.

'She did it just now,' Rachel said proudly. 'I was

holding her by the waist and she walked a little bit. I'll just take her out and show Vanessa.'

'You'd better put shoes on her first,' Brodie advised. 'The grass will still be damp.'

'I'll get some from upstairs.'

'I'll mind her while you do.'

She sat on the bed with the little warm body on her knee, stroking the silky hair. Memories poured in of doing the same thing with her own children. Rachel came in with a pair of tiny blue shoes and Poppy regarded her feet with interest when they were put on.

'She's never worn shoes before,' Rachel explained.

There's a first time for everything, Brodie thought. Pretty soon, Poppy would walk unaided. In time, she would learn to ride a bike, start school and so on, until she got married and had children of her own. And how would Rachel feel then?

'Oh, stop it, you stupid woman,' she said out loud. Rachel and Poppy had gone. 'Stop being so maudlin.'

She watched Rachel show off her baby daughter's walking prowess to Vanessa, who scooped the baby up in her arms with a delighted smile.

Right now, what would I like more than anything in the world? Brodie asked herself. It didn't need much thinking about: she wanted Jim O'Sullivan back so they could talk again. She put on her coat, drove to the supermarket and bought the ingredients for a chicken casserole, along with enough apples to make a pie, and a carton of double cream. She'd make him a really nice meal and tonight they could eat it in her room, just the two of them.

She wasn't trying to seduce him or anything: she wasn't that sort of person. At least, she didn't think so.

Her plan went awry when her mother returned with Jim and showed no sign of leaving. Brodie couldn't very well ask her to go home. Then, at about five o'clock, Colin arrived and she couldn't bring herself to ask him to leave, either, though she'd be really cross if he was nasty again.

The four of them ate in the snug and she made a big bowl of rice so the casserole would go further. Colin behaved very well and it turned out to be a very pleasant evening, if not quite what Brodie had in mind, though had she been asked exactly what she'd had in mind, she wouldn't have known.

Her mother had turned on the central heating in the airing cupboard in some mysterious way involving switches and dials that Brodie didn't understand. The antique radiators became barely lukewarm and made strange gulping noises. Jim, who appeared to be a jack of all trades, had a look and said the system was so old-fashioned he doubted if it could be repaired.

'I reckon the parts won't be available any more,' he told her. 'If I were you, I'd get a proper plumber in. See what he has to say.'

The proper plumber said the pipes were probably blocked. 'You need new pipes throughout. As for that boiler, in my view it's highly dangerous. It smells as if there's a slight leak. It's too old to be fixed; you need a brand-new one.'

'How much would new pipes and a new boiler cost?' Brodie enquired.

'For a place this size? I imagine somewhere between eight and ten thousand smackeroos, possibly more. Would you like me to work out a proper estimate?'

'No, thank you,' Brodie said faintly.

On Sunday, four days after Diana's funeral, Jim hired a car and drove to see Michelle in Nottingham. 'I won't be there for long,' he told Brodie. 'We're going out for a meal for old times' sake.'

'That's awfully nice of you,' she said. He'd told her why he and Michelle had got divorced, and that he knew for certain none of the lads were his. 'They've got dark hair and I'm fair,' he'd confided. 'Their eyes are brown and mine are blue, and I'm an inch or two taller than all three of them. The lads aren't stupid and I'm pretty sure they've guessed the truth. But Diana did a real good job with them and I couldn't be prouder than if they really were me own.'

'Michelle couldn't help it,' he said now. 'She wanted more from life than I could give her. Mind you, I still don't think she knows what it is. A good time, I suppose. Maybe all she wants is to be happy, but doesn't know how to go about it.' He grinned. 'Like us all.'

Brodie felt edgy all day without him. She'd got used to him being there. She watched an old film on television and jumped when there was a knock on the door. It was Vanessa asking if they could eat their dinner together.

'Tyler's taken Rachel and Poppy to see his father and stepmother and I'm feeling a bit lonely on my own,' she explained.

'What about Reggie?'

'He's at work – there's a rush job – and Charlie's spending the day with a girl from school whose birthday it is. I've got a steak and onion pie in the oven that's big enough for two and can bake a couple of potatoes in the microwave.'

'That sounds lovely.' Brodie had forgotten all about eating. 'Shall we have it in here, in my room? I'll get the table ready. It's freezing in the snug.' It was freezing everywhere. She'd bought some plug-in radiators for the big rooms, but they hadn't had much of an effect.

'Actually,' Vanessa said when the meal was over and they were finishing a bottle of wine that Brodie had forgotten she had, 'I wanted to discuss something with you.' She cleared her throat. 'I wondered if you'd mind if I went to live next door with Reggie? I wasn't going to mention it until after Christmas – remember we planned to have dinner together on Christmas Day, about a dozen of us? But the other day your mother mentioned you were thinking of getting new heating put in and it was going to cost the earth. I didn't want you to have it done on my account.'

'Well, I *was* thinking about it,' Brodie agreed, 'but that's all. I hadn't made up my mind.'

'Another thing,' Vanessa went on, filling up both their glasses until the bottle was empty, 'Rachel and Tyler have gone to look at a house that Tyler's father wants to buy for them. He doesn't approve of them living here. He's a real nerdy guy. Tyler's a bit like him, but Rachel hasn't noticed. Anyway, there's just a chance they'll want to move out soon.'

367

Brodie sighed. 'Diana's dead, the summer's over and everybody wants to leave.'

'Nothing lasts forever, Brodie,' Vanessa said wryly. 'The house seems darker without Diana and much too quiet. The life's gone out of it. Would you stay living here on your own or get new tenants in?'

'What would you do if you were me?'

'I don't exactly know what you mean by that, whether you're just referring to the house or to your life, but I'll guess.' She put her hand on Brodie's and squeezed it. 'If I were you I'd sell this house or rent it to someone else, then go back to your Colin and live happily ever after.'

Brodie heaved a sigh. 'I see.' She wasn't sure if that was the advice she'd wanted, though the 'happily ever after' bit sounded good. 'Oh, look,' she cried, 'there's Kenneth outside all by himself.' She sprang to her feet and opened the window. 'Here, puss, here.' She rubbed her fingers and Kenneth came prancing across, his tail erect. He walked gingerly into the room and toured the furniture, sniffing, until he jumped lightly on to the bed and fell asleep.

Vanessa said, 'Charlie claims he's missing Diana. I was wondering if he'd come and live next door with us, but the other day I saw him washing himself in the window of the first house in the road. He looked very much at home.'

Leaving Kenneth behind would be a wrench, Brodie thought. He had played a part in the lovely summer that had come to such an abrupt and ugly end. She began to clear the dishes off the table. 'Later, would you like me to help take your stuff next door?'

'I wouldn't dream of going yet!' Vanessa protested.

'I'll stay until you're ready to move, or until the end of the year.'

'That's awfully nice of you, Vanessa.' Brodie was touched. 'But you don't have to.'

'I'd sooner stay,' Vanessa said awkwardly. 'We're friends, aren't we, and that's what friends are for.'

After the dishes had been washed and Vanessa had gone upstairs, Brodie did what she always did when she had something on her mind: she rang Colin.

'I was going to come and see you soon,' he said when he heard her voice.

'For any particular reason?' she asked.

'A perfectly good reason – to see *you*. What can I do for you, darling?'

She explained about the central heating. 'The plumber said that to have a completely new system installed would cost between eight and ten thousand pounds.' Actually, he'd said 'smackeroos', a word she'd never heard before.

Colin gasped. 'Jaysus! But you've got tenants, Brodie, and one is a baby. You can't expect them to live in a freezing cold house. You need to have something done, even it just means radiators in a few rooms.'

'I've bought some radiators that plug in, but they're hopeless. I was wondering what to do next when Vanessa told me she wants to leave and she thinks Rachel will too in the not-too-distant future.'

There was a pause while he took this in. 'I hope you're not thinking of living in that big house on your own,' he said eventually.

'I don't know.' She didn't know anything any more.

There was another pause. 'If you like,' Colin said, 'I mean, if you're really keen on staying, we could sell this house, pay back the mortgage, and get Chestnuts completely modernized with what's over.'

It was then Brodie realized that he truly loved her. To think that he would sell their nice, square house in Crosby with its nice square rooms, the garden that was his pride and joy, and the tidy garage in which he kept the Triumph that he was so lovingly restoring to its former glory. He was willing to give up all these things for Brodie, his wife.

She could go back to the nice, square house and 'live happily ever after' as Vanessa had suggested, but she still wasn't sure if it was what she wanted.

A policeman and policewoman came to see Jim. They were in the snug for almost an hour. Brodie made them tea and apologized for the cold. They thanked her gravely.

'I understand there was an incident at the refugee centre a few months ago,' Jim said after the police had gone. 'Two foreign blokes came chasing after some young girls.'

'That's right.' Brodie remembered it well. 'Diana threw tea in the face of one of the men.'

'The police said the black van that ran her down was the one the blokes escaped in. They expect to make an arrest any minute.' He looked angry and puzzled. 'It would seem our Di was killed just so somebody could get their own back.'

The next morning, Brodie rang an estate agent who offered to come round there and then to provide a valuation when she gave him the address, but she told him she didn't want him until two o'clock, when Vanessa and Rachel took Poppy to the clinic.

In Diana's room, Jim was sorting out his daughter's things. Tinker was having her clothes for the refugee centre and Jim was giving the rest of her possessions to her mother in Nottingham. 'She'd really appreciate that little telly and all the DVDs and CDs,' he said. 'Is there anything you'd like, Brodie, as a memento?'

'I don't need a memento. I'll never forget Diana.' The memory of his shining, gentle daughter would always be like new in her mind.

Not long afterwards, Brodie was in the kitchen giving it a superficial clean, when Jim came in with a plastic carrier bag. 'I found these at the bottom of the wardrobe,' he said. 'They're obviously Christmas presents. There's a little white frock with poppies embroidered round the hem, a knitted patchwork scarf – and this.' He handed her a small cardboard box that contained a brooch made from tiny white and gold enamel flowers forming the letter B. 'It can only be for you, Brodie.'

'Will you be going back to Ecuador?' she asked later when she'd made them both coffee and were drinking it in her room. He was leaving in a week or so.

'I've had enough of South America.' He didn't give the impression he'd given the matter much thought. 'This time I think I'll go to the Middle East. It's been a while since I worked on an oil rig.' He'd worked on a farm in Ecuador, driven a bus in Australia, repaired cars in Canada.

'Oh, but it's dangerous in the Middle East right now!' Brodie gasped, alarmed.

'Not everywhere.' There was a note of hopelessness in his voice.

'Why don't you settle down somewhere in this country?' she suggested gently.

'I'm not ready to settle down just yet.'

'What's to become of you?' She felt achingly sad. 'You should get married and have more children.'

'Should I?' His lips twitched slightly in a smile.

'I can't bear to think of you being unhappy.' She couldn't believe she'd said that. But it was true.

'Thank you, Brodie,' he said gravely. 'I'll always remember that.'

Had he touched her then, she would have willingly responded. She was trembling, her throat thick with excitement and fear at the thought of making love with a man other than her husband.

But Jim merely smiled and went back to Diana's room, saying that he had a letter to write.

Brodie relaxed and studied the garden, empty for a change. Was there really a letter to write, or had he somehow sensed how she felt and had made his escape?

Afterwards, when she was herself again, she was glad he'd gone when he did. She would have hated herself for ever had she been unfaithful to Colin.

Which more or less seemed to settle things. At least now she knew where she stood.

It seemed to happen all of a sudden. A property company offered to buy the house for a sum of money that made Brodie's head spin.

Then Rachel told her that Tyler's father was in the process of buying them a house. 'Tyler's stepmother is really nice, though Tyler claims he doesn't like her. She's only thirty, but can't have children. I'm going back to school after Christmas and she's going to look after Poppy. I'm looking forward to it in a way, school. I always wanted to be a teacher. By the time I'm properly trained Poppy will be at school herself.'

'When are you going?' Brodie asked.

'Well, they're getting a room ready for us in their house because ours will take a few weeks to buy. In a few days, I expect.' She looked uncomfortable. 'I hope you don't mind, but it's been awful cold here lately, even with the radiator turned full on. I've been having Poppy in bed with me to keep her warm.'

'Gosh!' Brodie swallowed hard. She was a hopeless landlady. Perhaps, without realizing it, she was trying to drive everyone away. 'I'll miss you and Poppy terribly.'

'And we'll miss you – and that lovely cool garden.'

With Brodie and Charlie's help, Vanessa had begun gradually to move her stuff into Reggie's house. Colin had now taken it for granted Brodie would move back to Crosby and asked if he should start moving hers.

'Not yet,' Brodie said, though she didn't know why. She felt restless and dissatisfied, though she knew the reason for that.

'You're not going to change your mind, are you? You always said you'd give Josh and Maisie a big chunk of money when Chestnuts was sold. You're not going back on your word?'

'I didn't tell *them* that, did I?' she snapped. 'What

sort of person do you think I am?' There would also be enough money for her to buy a flat of her own and Colin could go and jump in the lake, but was it unreasonable to expect the husband who loved her never to make a stupid remark?

'I'm sorry,' Colin said humbly. 'There are times when I speak before I think. It's just that I'm worried that I'll lose you.'

'You won't lose me,' Brodie said with a sigh.

Rachel and Poppy had gone with the promise they would all meet next door on Christmas Day, Brodie's family, too, when Vanessa would make dinner. 'I'll have to go on a crash cookery course,' she said. 'I've never made Christmas dinner before.'

On a breezy Monday morning, the last in October, Vanessa moved the remainder of her possessions into Reggie's house and put her head around the door of Brodie's room to say goodbye. 'I'm off now,' she announced.

Brodie was sitting on the bed feeling lost and watching the leaves outside swirl around like snow in a paperweight. 'Are you going to look for a job when you've settled in?' she asked.

Vanessa blushed slightly. 'I already have a job. I'm an artist, but I'm going to become a housewife, too, look after Reggie and Charlie, and try very hard to have a baby – several babies.'

'I envy you,' Brodie said thoughtfully. 'Me, I've done the housewife and baby bit; now I want to train for a career.'

'Good luck, then, Brodie.'

'And good luck to you, Vanessa.'

Vanessa had hardly been gone a minute when Jim came back, having been to the shops on Crosby Road. He was travelling to Heathrow that afternoon and catching an overnight flight to Saudi Arabia. Brodie went into the hall to meet him.

'I'm sorry,' he said when he saw her. 'Are you waiting for me to go so you can go yourself?'

'I suppose I must be.' Her heart twisted at the thought that, after today, they might never see each other again.

'I'll just shove these things in me bag. I've just bought meself a new toothbrush and soap and stuff.' He went into Diana's room where his rucksack, already packed, lay on the bed.

In the hall, Brodie rubbed her forehead distractedly. 'I don't want you to go,' she said, but only to herself.

He came out of his daughter's bedroom, the rucksack suspended from his right shoulder, a lonely traveller, wandering the world without wanting anything solid or permanent out of life – certainly not her. He might not have had any of the peculiar and outlandish thoughts she'd been having about him. 'I've promised to stay in touch with the lads,' he said gruffly. 'If you ever need anything, you can contact me through them.'

'All right,' Brodie said. She wondered if she ever would.

He squeezed her shoulders. 'Tara, girl,' he said, grinning now. He shook her hand and kissed her cheek, both at the same time.

'Tara, Jim.'

She looked into his blue eyes for the final time, then turned away until the door had closed. He'd gone.

The sound briefly echoed through the house until everything became quiet and the house seemed to be ticking over like a giant clock. She picked up the bag containing the last of her things and counted up to a hundred so there'd be no sign of Jim when she left.

She opened the door, went outside and stood there blinking, with the feeling that she'd just stepped out of a dream and all the strange emotions she'd been experiencing recently were being blown away. She looked at the intensely blue sky and the fast-moving clouds and laughed for the first time in ages. Her mind was completely clear.

The wind had loosened a piece of ivy and it flapped in front of her face. She was about to tuck it behind the trellis attached to the wall, but paused. Something was shining softly through the dark-green leaves. She moved them carefully to avoid the thorns and found a rose nestling inside. It was a luscious cream, in full bloom and utterly perfect, the smooth petals looking as if they were made of velvet.

'Oh!' she gasped. For some reason she thought of Diana. She felt tempted to pluck the flower, but then it would only live for a few more days. Left to itself, it would die naturally as Diana never had. She touched it with her finger: it felt surprisingly cold.

The last rose of summer.

Brodie threw back her shoulders. She was ready to go home to Colin.

She couldn't wait.

MAUREEN LEE

MAUREEN LEE IS ONE OF THE BEST-LOVED SAGA WRITERS AROUND. All her novels are set in Liverpool and the world she evokes is always peopled with characters you'll never forget. Her familiarity with Liverpool and its people brings the terraced streets and tight-knit communities vividly to life in her books. Maureen is a born story-teller and her many fans love her for her powerful tales of love and life, tragedy and joy in Liverpool.

The Girl from Bootle

Born into a working-class family in Bootle, Liverpool, Maureen Lee spent her early years in a terraced house near the docks – an area that was relentlessly bombed during the Second World War. As a child she was bombed out of the house in Bootle and the family were forced to move.

Maureen left her convent school at 15 and wanted to become an actress. However, her shocked mother, who said that it was 'as bad as selling your body on the streets', put her foot down and Maureen had to give up her dreams and go to secretarial college instead.

As a child, Maureen
was bombed out of
her terraced house
in Bootle

Family Life

A regular theme in her books is the fact that apparently happy homes often conceal pain and resentment and she sometimes draws on her own early life for inspiration. 'My mother always seemed to disapprove of me – she never said "well done" to me. My brother was the favourite,' Maureen says.

> I know she would never have approved of my books

As she and her brother grew up they grew apart. 'We just see things differently in every way,' says Maureen. This, and a falling out during the difficult time when her mother was dying, led to an estrangement that has lasted 24 years. 'Despite the fact that I didn't see eye-to-eye with my mum, I loved her very much. I deserted my family and lived in her flat in Liverpool after she went into hospital for the final time. My brother, who she thought the world of, never went near. Towards the end when she was fading she kept asking where he was. To comfort her, I had to pretend that he'd been to see her the day before, which was awful. I found it hard to get past that.'

Freedom – Moving on to a Family of Her Own

Maureen is well known for writing with realism about subjects like motherhood: 'I had a painful time giving birth to my children – the middle one was born in the back of a two-door car. So I know things don't always go as planned.'

My middle son was born in the back of a car

The twists and turns of Maureen's life have been as interesting as the plots of her books. When she met her husband, Richard, he was getting divorced, and despite falling instantly in love and getting engaged after only two weeks, the pair couldn't marry. Keen that Maureen should escape her strict family home, they moved to London and lived together before marrying. 'Had she known, my mother would never have forgiven me. She never knew that Richard had been married before.' The Lees had to pretend they were married even to their landlord. Of course, they did marry as soon as possible and have had a very happy family life.

Success at Last

Despite leaving school at fifteen, Maureen was determined to succeed as a writer. Like Kitty in *Kitty and Her Sisters* and Millie in *Dancing in the Dark*, she went to night school and ended up getting two A levels. 'I think it's good to "better yourself". It gives you confidence,' she says. After her sons grew up she had the time to pursue her dream, but it took several years and a lot of disappointment before she was successful. 'I was *determined* to succeed. My husband was one hundred per cent supportive. I wrote lots of

> 'I think it's good to "better yourself". It gives you confidence'

articles and short stories. I also started a saga which was eventually called *Stepping Stones*. Then Orion commissioned me to finish it, it was published – and you know the rest.'

What are your memories of your early years in Bootle?

Of being poor, but not poverty-stricken. Of women wearing shawls instead of coats. Of knowing everybody in the street. Of crowds gathering outside houses in the case of a funeral or a wedding, or if an ambulance came to collect a patient, who was carried out in a red blanket. I longed to be such a patient, but when I had diptheria and an ambulance came for me, I was too sick to be aware of the crowds. There were street parties, swings on lamp-posts, hardly any traffic, loads of children playing in the street, dogs without leads. Even though we didn't have much money, Christmas as a child was fun. I'm sure we appreciated our few presents more than children do now.

What was it like being young in Liverpool in the 1950s?

The late fifties were a wonderful time for my friends and me. We had so many places to go: numerous dance halls, The Philharmonic Hall, The Cavern Club, theatres, including The Playhouse where you could buy tickets for ninepence. We were crushed together on benches at the very back. As a teenager I loved the theatre – I was in a dramatic society. I also used to make my own clothes, which meant I could have the latest fashions in just the right sizes, which I loved. Sometimes we'd go on boat trips across the water to New Brighton or on the train to Southport. We'd go for the day and visit the fairground and then go to the dance hall in the evening.

> We clicked instantly and got engaged two weeks later

I met Richard at a dance when he asked my friend Margaret up. When she came back she said 'Oh, he was nice.' And then somebody else asked her to dance – she was very glamorous, with blonde hair – still is, as it happens. So Richard asked me to dance because she had gone! We clicked instantly and got engaged two weeks later. I'm not impulsive generally, but I just knew that he was the one.

Do you consider yourself independent and adventurous like Annemarie in The Leaving of Liverpool *or Kitty in* Kitty and her Sisters?

In some ways. In the late fifties, when I was 16, Margaret and I hitchhiked to the Continent. It was really, really exciting. We got a lift from London to Dover on the back of a lorry. We sat on top of stacks of beer crates – we didn't half get cold! We ended up sleeping on the side of the road in Calais because we hadn't found a hotel. We travelled on to Switzerland and got jobs in the United Nations in Geneva as secretaries. It was a great way to see the world. I've no idea what inspired us to go. I think we just wanted some adventure, like lots of my heroines.

Your books often look at the difficult side of family relationships. What experiences do you draw on when you write about that?

I didn't always find it easy to get on with my mother because she held very rigid views. She was terribly ashamed when I went to Europe. She said 'If you leave this house you're not coming back!' But when we got to Switzerland we got fantastic wages at the United Nations – about four times as much as we got at home. When I wrote and told her she suddenly forgave me and went around telling everybody, 'Our Maureen's working at the United Nations in Geneva.'

'If you leave this house you're not coming back!'

She was very much the kind of woman who worried what the neighbours would think. When we moved to Kirby, our neighbours were a bit posher than us and at first she even hung our curtains round the wrong way, so it was the neighbours who would see the pattern and we just had the inside to look at. It seems unbelievable now, but it wasn't unusual then – my mother-in-law was even worse. When she bought a new three-piece she covered every bit of it with odd bits of curtaining so it wouldn't wear out – it looked horrible.

My mother-in-law was a strange woman. She hated the world and everyone in it. We had a wary sort of relationship. She gave Richard's brother an awful life – she was very controlling and he never left home. She died in the early nineties and for the next few years my kind, gentle brother-in-law had a relation-ship with a wonderful woman who ran an animal sanctuary. People tend to keep their family problems private but you don't have to look further than your immediate neighbours to see how things really are and I try to reflect that in my books.

You don't have to look further than your immediate neighbours to see how things really are

Is there anything you'd change about your life?

I don't feel nostalgic for my youth, but I do feel nostalgic for the years when I was a young mum. I didn't anticipate how I'd feel when the boys left home. I just couldn't believe they'd gone and I still miss them being around although I'm very happy that they're happy.

Are friendships important to you?

Vastly important. I always stay with Margaret when I visit Liverpool and we email each other two or three times a week. Old friends are the best sort as you have shared with them the ups and downs of your life. I have other friends in Liverpool that I have known all my adult life. I have also made many new ones who send me things that they think will be useful when I write my books.

Have you ever shared an experience with one of your characters?

Richard's son from his first marriage recently got in touch with us. It was quite a shock as he's been in Australia for most of his life and we've never known him. He turned out to be a charming person with a lovely family. I've written about long-lost family members returning in *Kitty and Her Sisters* and *The Leaving of Liverpool* so it was strange for me to find my life reflecting the plot of one of my books.

Describe an average writing day for you.

Wake up, Richard brings me tea in bed and I watch breakfast television for a bit. Go downstairs at around 8 a.m. with the intention of doing housework. Sit and argue with Richard about politics until it's midday and time to go to my shed and start writing. Come in from time to time to make drinks and do the crossword. If I'm stuck, we might drive to Sainsbury's for a coffee and read all the newspapers we refuse to have in the house. Back in my shed, I stay till about half seven and return to the house in time to see *EastEnders*.

Don't miss Maureen's bestselling novels: